PRAISE FOR

UP AND DOWN

Finalist, Stephen Leacock Medal for Humour

"Not too many Canucks have ventured to write humorous books. There is Stephen Leacock, of course. And Robertson Davies cranked out a couple . . . Count Terry Fallis among the few to achieve success at the form. . . . Poignant."
— *Ottawa Citizen*

"The wait has been worth it for Terry Fallis fans: his third novel has already earned a well-deserved spot on the shortlist for the 2013 Leacock Medal, Canada's most prominent award for humour writing."
— *Publishers Weekly*

"One of CanLit's crowned king of chuckles, Terry Fallis hits stratospheric heights with [this] well-balanced and unpredictable satire. . . . Fallis is a gifted storyteller."
— *Telegraph-Journal*

"Fallis's hilarious running commentary on the minutiae of modern life recalls the comedy of *Seinfeld*. . . . In *Up and Down*, space is the metaphor for a braver, better world."
— *National Post*

"Gently satirical and intelligently frothy, *Up and Down* achieves a delightful weightlessness as transporting as the space voyage it deals with."   — Andrew Pyper, author of *The Demonologist*

"[A] lighthearted plot involving slamming doors, vaudeville turns, plot twists, and a lot of good-natured badinage. . . . Vivid and dazzling."   — *Globe and Mail*

"Fallis spins a hilarious story. . . . Memorable. . . . Quite enjoyable from start to finish."
— Montreal *Gazette*

"Terry Fallis has done it again. *Up and Down* is another hilarious page-turner that also packs an emotional punch. Only a very talented writer can balance humour and pathos so skillfully. Beautifully written, these characters rocket off the page and straight into your heart. This is satire at its finest."
> – Ali Velshi, former CNN anchor
> and chief business correspondent

"A fascinating story of the divergence of Canadian and American values, the importance of family, unlikely friendship, second chances, ageism, a love of Sherlock Holmes, insight into the awe-inspiring world of space travel, and the importance of using your head but following your heart."
> – *Winnipeg Free Press*

"[*Up and* Down is] the literary equivalent of a roller coaster for kids."
> – NOW magazine

"A rollicking good ride. Funny one moment, serious the next, always compelling: a reminder that we can all dream."
> – Marc Garneau, Member of Parliament
> and Canada's first astronaut

"[Terry Fallis has] done it again. What a great read!"
> – *Waterloo Record*

PRAISE FOR
THE BEST LAID PLANS

Winner, 2011 Canada Reads competition
Winner, Stephen Leacock Medal for Humour

"Amusing, enlightening – and Canadian, it deftly explores the Machiavellian machinations of Ottawa's political culture."
> – *Globe and Mail*

PRAISE FOR
THE HIGH ROAD

Finalist, Stephen Leacock Medal for Humour

"*The High Road* will surely make you laugh. There will be snickers, occasional snorting and hooting, and almost certainly rip-roaring belly laughs."
— Halifax *Chronicle Herald*

"Fallis writes in pictures . . . that the mind's eye can see clearly. . . . An easy-reading page-turner."
— *National Post*

"Terry Fallis scores again with *The High Road*."
— *Guelph Mercury*

"In a perfect world, the federal government would establish a Ministry of Humour and put Terry Fallis in charge of that department. *The High Road* is brilliantly written and hysterically funny. . . . Do yourself a favour and pick up this book, find a quiet place to read it, and enjoy . . . you will laugh out loud on almost every page."
— Ian Ferguson, author of *Village of Small Houses*

"Doing battle with the prigs and prats that rule the halls of power has never been more enjoyable since . . . well, since *The Best Laid Plans*. Thought-provoking and funny."
— Jim Cuddy, singer/songwriter, Blue Rodeo

NO RELATION

Also by Terry Fallis

The Best Laid Plans

The High Road

Up and Down

NO RELATION

A NOVEL

TERRY FALLIS

McClelland & Stewart

McClelland & Stewart is a division of Random House of Canada
Limited, a Penguin Random House Company

Library and Archives Canada Cataloguing in Publication available
upon request.

ISBN 978-0-7710-3616-3

Cover art: Bea Crespo/Imagezoo/Getty Images
Cover design by Terri Nimmo
Typeset in Electra by Erin Cooper

Printed and bound in USA

McClelland & Stewart,
a division of Random House of Canada Limited,
a Penguin Random House Company

www.randomhouse.ca

3   4   5   18   17   16   15   14

For my twin brother, Tim

CHAPTER 1

What's in a name? For many, nothing. For some, not nothing, but not much. For a very few, blessed or cursed, it's everything. I'm one of those few. And if you're wondering, I usually count myself among the cursed.

When I turned forty, I lost the desire, and even the ability, to sleep in. So I was an early riser. Yet, at 7:45, I still wasn't the first into the office that morning. I heard him as I crossed our marble lobby, past the futuristic "reception pod" where Angela and her headset would soon be stationed. He called out to me from down the hall.

"Morning, Hem. Um, you got a minute?"

Bob was standing just outside the corner office, *the* corner office, *his* corner office, at the end of the corridor. This was not good news. Bob was never in before 9:30. And when he eventually did arrive, it was to start a workday that was almost always devoid of any real work. Bob, BOB, **BOB**. I've never really liked the name "Bob." It's just so short. Simple. Primitive. Unrefined. In fact, I have a theory on the name's origin. Six million years ago, when the early hominids first discovered their vocal cords, I think the sound "Bob" may well have been among their first harsh guttural utterings. Shortly after "Grrrrr" and "Aaaah" would have come "Baaaahb." Short, simple, primitive, unrefined. Much like Bob himself.

Conveniently, I disliked Bob as a person as much as I did his name. We'd joined the New York ad agency Macdonald-Clark within weeks of each other nearly fifteen years ago. But we'd been on different trajectories ever since. Over the years, I rose through the ranks as if I were sauntering up a gentle slope, stopping often to lounge at patio rest stations along the way. But soon after we started, Bob seemed to board the space shuttle, docking with the corner office after what seemed to me like a very short ride. How it happened so fast – no, how it happened at all – was more a mystery to me than Bigfoot. I still cannot fathom how Bob parlayed his principal assets of incompetence, paranoia, and mediocrity all the way to the top. But there he was, M-C's general manager, waving me into his palatial enclave, with an expression on his face that suggested his next words just might be "Grrrrr" and "Aaaah."

On the other hand, despite its shortcomings, I'd be thrilled to have a name like "Bob."

"Sure, Bob."

I turned and followed him in.

He led me to the couch and easy chair at one end of the office, far away from his barren desk, where very little work was ever done. I took a spot on the couch, lowering myself into what felt like upholstered quicksand. I sank in so deep that when I stopped, I could almost rest my chin on my knees. I wondered how I was going to get back out. Bob sat in the chair across from me.

"So, Hem, um, how have you been?"

"Just fine, Bob. You?"

"Awesome, thanks."

Cue awkward silence. Bob shifted his position in his chair. I tried to shift my position but the couch simply wouldn't let me.

"Well, um, I guess you've heard the rumours," he continued.

"Actually, Bob, I've been here too long for that. I make it a point never to pay attention to stray rumours or anything else I may encounter in these hallways. If I see a colleague crying in a corridor, or yelling at an intern, or moaning in a bathroom stall, I quickly make a show of checking my watch, turn around fast, and head back the way I came. That's my policy. So, no rumours have reached these tender ears."

"So you really haven't heard anything? No rumblings? Nothing?"

"Not a peep, Bob. Should I have?"

His face clouded.

"Come on, Hem, you're not helping!" he snapped. "We plant those rumours for a reason. They help condition the staff and prepare them for bad news. Strategic rumours are an important part of our internal communications program. You're a senior guy. You've been here a long time. You should know that."

"Well, I'm sorry, Bob. Had you flagged and tagged them as 'strategic rumours from the corner office' I probably would have paid more attention."

"Shit."

"Bob, I'm a copywriter. I sort of work on my own. I just follow the brief and try to think up the right words and how best to arrange them. That's what copywriters do. I don't really hang out much with the account teams. I'm generally oblivious when it comes to office gossip."

"Shit."

"What's this all about?"

Bob sighed, then looked at the ceiling as he spoke.

"You're out, Hem. It's over. We have to let you go. Today. Now. I'm sorry."

I laughed. Well, it was more of a chortle.

"You're kidding, right?" I looked around the office. "Where's the camera? This is for the Christmas party, right?"

I could tell from his face. No, this wasn't for the Christmas party. I just looked at him for a moment as the news settled over me like ash from an angry volcano.

"Bob, I'm shocked. I don't understand this. I'm hurt. You could have at least given me some warning."

"Shit, Hem, I floated the balloon last week. You seem to be the only one in the agency who didn't pick up on it."

Come to think of it, in the last few days folks had been kind of giving me the cocked-head, arched-brow, sad-eyes routine as they hustled by.

"Bob, I've been here fifteen years. I've won awards! You promoted me last year and gave me what I thought at the time was only a modest raise. But still, you did give me an increase!"

"Hem, calm down."

Calm down? That was a surprise. Incarcerated in that couch, how could I look anything but calm? I could move only my upper body. I guess I may have been waving my arms around a bit.

"I am calm. Calm and flabbergasted. Calm and furious. Calm and, um, apoplectic. What possible rationale can you have for firing me?"

"Hem, we're not firing you. We're just letting you go. We're thanking you for your years of service, giving you a generous settlement, and parting ways. That's all. It happens all the time in the agency world."

"Well, it's never happened to me," I said. "And you still haven't explained why."

"Hem, come on. You really don't know? You're a long-form copywriter. You're a relic," Bob said, waving his arms around a bit. "The world has changed. In fact, it changed a decade ago. I'm amazed you hung around this long," he said. "Everything is short and punchy now. We live in the 140-character universe. Ad agencies don't need long-form copywriting any more. We held out as long as we could. I'm sorry."

5

"But I'm good at my job. I'm in on virtually every new biz pitch. My writing has won the agency awards. I'm . . . um, good at my job. I'm great at my job!"

"Come on, Hem, don't fight this. Don't make this difficult," he soothed. He pulled an envelope from his jacket pocket and held it out to me. "Hem, you've got a *huge* package."

"Well, kind of you to say, Bob, but I'm really more interested in the settlement you're offering," I deadpanned.

Perhaps I shouldn't have deadpanned. Bob was befuddled. I opened the envelope. The cheque was for the equivalent of a year's salary. Wow.

"It's well above the legislated requirements. Don't bother trying to negotiate. This is as much as I could get for you. If you choose to push back, the offer will be withdrawn and you will receive the bare legal minimum." Bob said this part like he was reading me my Miranda rights.

I know I should have fired back with both barrels blazing. But I really wasn't good at this. I was out of things to say. I had nothing.

"Hem, think of this as a gift. You've got at least a year to do what you want. You can finally write your novel. Think of this as freedom."

"Freedom?"

"Yes, freedom."

I wanted to say, "Fuck you, Bob," like they do in the movies. But I just couldn't get it out. My civility instinct prevailed.

"Hem, you have to go see Marlene. She has all the paperwork. You need to sign it all if you're going to keep that cheque," he said, almost in a whisper, as if he were talking me off the ledge. "Pop back here before you go."

I nodded and tried to get up.

"Bob, do you mind?' I reached out my hand.

"Sure, Hem." He pulled me up and out of the couch.

It only took a few minutes to deal with Marlene and her stupid paperwork. She was Macdonald-Clark's human resources specialist, or as she was sometimes known among the account teams, Human Overhead. She was nice to me. I signed without even reading the termination agreement. The cheque stayed in my pocket.

It's such a cliché to load your personal effects into a cardboard box before making the long walk to the elevators. So I was relieved when Marlene actually gave me a largish clear plastic bag instead, in return for my key and security card. It didn't quite seem a fair exchange. I emptied my desk drawers and bookshelves of all the personal stuff that just seems to accumulate over a decade and a half spent in the same office. Marlene hovered outside my door as if I might steal a pad of Post-it notes on my way out. I could feel anger building. Finally, I picked up the framed shot of Jenn and me taken at Club Med in Jamaica four years ago, just before we moved in together. We both looked deliriously happy. And I guess we were. I tossed it into my plastic bag where it landed photo side up and stared back at me. The bag was full and heavy. Being able to see my "personal effects" through the clear plastic made the whole scenario seem all the more pathetic. I left the plants where they were. They'd die if they came home with me.

It took some effort, but I thanked Marlene for her assistance, balancing curt and courteous – call it "curteous" – and headed back to Bob's office.

True to form, he was sitting at his utterly empty desk, gazing out the window.

"Settle down, Bob. You have to pace yourself or you'll just burn out," I said.

"I'm sure going to miss your sparkling wit, Hem." Bob sighed as he stood. "Did you sign off with Marlene?"

"I did, but just now, when cleaning out my desk, I had a change of heart. You can tear up the paperwork, I've decided that you can't terminate me because I resign," I said, staring him down.

Bob smiled and held out his hand. It sort of looked like he wanted to shake, so I automatically reached out my hand. He shook his head.

"No, Hem, not your hand – the cheque, please," he clarified. "Since you resigned, you have to give back the cheque. There is no settlement when you resign." His hand stayed there, outstretched.

I thought long and hard, for the next three nanoseconds.

"Whoa! Hang on, I wasn't quite finished," I stammered. "What I was about to say was that I resign, um, myself to the, um, decision and associated settlement that you and I agreed to earlier."

"Sound thinking." Bob smirked as he dropped his hand.

"Well, Bob, it's been a real delight," I said as we shook hands a final time. "Of all the colleagues I've worked with in my fifteen years here, I will always remember you as, um, one of them."

Then, without missing a beat, I spun on my heel and walked out, lugging my plastic bag. Man, I sure told him.

I was in a surly mood by the time I made it into our apartment on Bank Street, almost at Bleecker, in the West Village. It wasn't just losing my job. I'd remembered on the way home that I'd lost my wallet on the subway the day before. Funny how losing your job can make you forget about losing your wallet. It was well and truly gone. Stray wallets don't last long on New York subways, and they never make it to the MTA's Lost and Found.

When the elevator opened, Jenn and her brother, Paul, were standing there in the corridor with a cardboard box and a couple of suitcases.

"Oh hi, Paul," I said. "Are you moving in for a while?"

Jenn had kind of a dazed look on her face.

"Shit," she said.

"Believe it or not, you're the second person to say that to me this morning," I replied.

"Good to see you, Hem," Paul mumbled before turning to his sister. "I'll wait in the car."

Paul took the box and hit the elevator button. When the doors didn't immediately open, he and his box sprinted to the end of the hall and disappeared into the stairwell.

"Very odd," was all I said.

"Hem, what the hell are you doing home at this hour? You're supposed to be at work. Are you sick?"

"I wish I were sick. Instead, I'm unemployed," I reported, trying to hold it together. "I was just laid off. On the upside, I have a big cheque in my pocket that I can deposit just as soon as I can get a new bank card."

"This can't be happening," she said, almost to herself. "Well, that's just great news, Hem. Your timing couldn't be better."

It wasn't the sympathetic response I was looking for. She just stood there with this strange look on her face. Uh-oh.

I figured it out.

"Shit," I said.

"Hem, um, look, here's the thing. I'm really sorry about your job. That just sucks. But, I'm leaving. I didn't want there to be a scene so I was going to call you tonight."

"What? Hang on. For a second there I thought you said you were leaving. I must not have heard you correctly. Just run that by me again." I made a show of leaning in to hear her better as my anger took over.

"I obviously didn't expect you to arrive home in the middle of my . . . um . . ."

"Getaway? Great escape? Betrayal?" I offered. I always try to be helpful when people are searching for le mot juste.

". . . departure," she chose, bobbing her head and scrunching up her nose. From experience, I knew it as the precursor to tears. "Hem, don't make this difficult."

"Believe it or not, you're the second person to say that to me this morning."

"Hem, it's time. You must have seen it coming. We've lived together for four years, but the last two we've really just been roommates. You know that. It all slipped away. You had to have felt it. How could you not?"

"So you were just going to sneak away without saying anything and hope that I wouldn't notice. Were you going to leave me a note?" I said, my voice rising. "Jenn, this isn't public school. We're adults. We talk things through."

"Yeah, right," she countered with an eye roll. "When have we ever 'talked things through'? Whenever I've wanted to talk about it, you've gone to ridiculous lengths to avoid a meaningful discussion. I know how you think, Hem. If we never talk about it, there's no problem. It doesn't exist. Well, I can't do that any more. I'm done with that delusion. There is a problem, and I'm solving it on my own."

I realized we were still standing in the corridor where we could be overheard by curious neighbours with ears pressed to doors.

"Jenn, at least come back in and let's talk about it. I've now got plenty of time on my hands."

"I can't. It's too late for that. We haven't been in a real relationship for a long time. If I don't do something about it, you'll just carry on, stuck in this rut, but unable to take any action to climb out of it. You'll just deny, avoid, distract, and crack jokes. It's what you do. It's what you always do. Well, it's time to be a grown-up, Hem."

She exhaled. It was a sigh of fatigue, not of sorrow, not of regret. I could tell. Again, I had nothing.

"Paul has his van loaded. I'm staying with him for a few weeks until I find a place. I gotta go."

She leaned in and kissed my cheek before bolting for the elevator, dragging her suitcases behind her. Mercifully, the doors opened quickly and she leapt in.

"Think of this as freedom," she said as the doors closed.

"Believe it or not, you're the second person to say that to me this morning," I muttered to myself.

The apartment was pristine. She and Paul had worked hard and fast in the four hours since I'd left that morning. I felt as if I were in some kind of a time warp. The rooms all looked almost exactly as they had before Jenn moved in four years ago. No, they actually looked better. Beyond a couple of framed photos of the two of us, every other vestige of Jenn was gone, as if Orwell's Ministry of Truth had expunged the last four years. It was almost surreal.

I dropped into a chair in the living room. I loved our apartment. Hardwood floors. Big windows. Parking under the building. Blessed air conditioning. A fair chunk of real estate in the West Village for the money. And it seemed I was back to having the space all to myself. I loved my apartment. I may have been in shock right then, but I was thinking about my apartment and not about Jenn bailing out on me, on us.

I took a moment to catalogue the woes I'd collected in the previous twenty-four hours. I had no wallet. I had no job. I had no girlfriend. Losing your wallet is really no big deal. It's a royal pain in the ass, but it's just inconvenient, not a threat to your mental stability. On the other hand, losing your job and your girlfriend in the same day is like getting beaten badly in both ends of a psychological doubleheader. I felt terrible. Miserable. Depressed. But to be completely honest, I probably should have felt worse than I did. Beneath the body blows to my ego that would ache for a long time, I was perched on the precipice of a brand-new start. A rare gift. I like my glass half-full. I had a year's salary, a seriously simplified love life, a lovely apartment that hadn't been this neat and tidy . . . ever, a novel to write, and time on my hands. To coin a phrase, *think of this as freedom.*

I opened my laptop on the kitchen table where I could look out the window and see the trees lining Bank Street below. The canopy of leaves dappled the June sunshine on the pavement. It was time to write. After I had surveyed the scene outside for fifteen minutes or so, I read through the file folder labelled

"Debut Novel." I had no title yet for it. Inside were files with names like "Character back stories," "Settings," "Chronology," and "Basic outline." There was also a subfolder entitled "Manuscript." I opened the "Basic outline" file and shoved it up against the right-hand edge of my screen. Then I clicked on the "Manuscript" subfolder to reveal chapters one through eleven stacked in separate files. My mouse hovered over Chapter 11 and I double-clicked to open it. I spent the next twenty minutes or so rereading the words I had written in my last writing session a week earlier. They weren't bad, I guess. But the prose read as I'd been feeling when I'd written it and the previous few chapters – forced, listless, unfocused, rudderless, and utterly devoid of literary merit. But that was then. Now my world had been stripped of at least two of the principal distractions that have plagued writers since words were first etched on tablets. I had no job and I had no girl-friend. Suddenly taking their place were two commodities writers have always sought but seldom found. Time and money.

If not now, when? So I laced my fingers, turned my linked hands downward, and pushed out, stretching and cracking my knuckles in the clichéd way piano players do before duelling with the keys. I know. It must have looked lame, but it actually felt quite good. I opened a new document in Word and typed "Chapter 12." Then I felt thirsty and got a drink. Okay, Chapter 12. Then I noticed a dustball Jenn had somehow missed in her guilt-encrusted vacuum-ing frenzy. I picked it up and tossed it in the garbage bin under the sink. Now, Chapter 12. I wrote a sentence. It was not a great sentence. It was not "luminous." It was not "elegiac" or "incandescent." But it was a sentence. It was a start. I read it over, again and again. I flipped the front clause to the back and read it again. Then I put it back. Fifteen minutes later, like the Ministry of Truth, I backspaced through the entire sentence, eliminating any signs that it had ever existed. I looked over at my "Basic outline" for guidance, but found nothing of interest.

Okay, Chapter 12. I shook out my arms like an Olympic swimmer just before the gun. Then I took a shower.

Twenty minutes later I was back at my laptop feeling refreshed and enthused. Chapter 12. What's in the fridge? No, that wasn't a new first sentence. That was the question that I simply had to answer before trying to write that first sentence. Writing always makes me hungry. Even trying to write, or avoiding writing, or wanting desperately to write but succumbing to distractions, or falling prey to simple, pure, unadulterated procrastination, all make me hungry. I made a peanut butter and peach jam sandwich. It was very good, with the perfect proportions of peanut butter and jam. It's hard to nail that balance. Writing and eating usually make me tired. Yep. I took a nap.

I awoke two hours later and wondered what I was doing in bed. Then I remembered, and felt discouraged and depressed all over again. When I analyzed my post-nap feelings, I realized I wasn't really grieving Jenn's departure. I wasn't a blubbering mass of emotion, but actually felt okay about it all, and was oddly motivated to get back to my novel. I was supposed to be hurting, but it hadn't hit me yet, and might never. What I did feel seemed more like relief than emotional angst. Strange reaction, I know, but there you have it.

I hauled myself up and was soon back in the kitchen in front of the laptop, staring at a very intimidating screen. By this time, it was three in the afternoon. I decided I simply couldn't put it off any longer. Not Chapter 12, but replacing my driver's licence at the Department of Motor Vehicles. Driving without your licence is generally frowned upon by the NYPD.

I took the subway up to Broadway and 6th and eventually got myself in line at the DMV. I would have arrived sooner, but on the way I was forced to cross the street to avoid two leashed beagles leading their owner up the sidewalk toward me. If I haven't already mentioned it, I don't like dogs. Not at all. Long-haired or short, brown, black, striped, or checked, I just don't like them. More precisely, I'm scared of them. Smaller dogs in particular, for some reason. There was no terrier trauma that I could point to as the root of it all. Dogs just scare me. I'm well aware that my fear is irrational, thanks very much. But that doesn't make a Shih Tzu any less frightening.

The lineup was long. Right out the door, along Broadway, then wrapping around 34th. What a great day. Losing my job, losing my girlfriend, and now lining up at the DMV. The trifecta. At 4:30, I actually inched into the building. By 4:45 I was finally standing at Window 10, in front of a clerk who looked like she worked at the DMV dealing with cranky drivers eight hours a day.

"How can I help you?" she said in tone better suited for "What the hell do you want?"

"Um, I lost my wallet on the subway yesterday and need to get a replacement driver's licence, please."

She had not yet looked up.

"Spell the first name."

I did as I was told.

"Surname, now."

Here we go. I leaned in a little closer and almost whispered the spelling of my last name. Her screen was angled so I could see it, too. She stopped typing at the "w."

"I do not have the time for this. Do you see the lineup behind you, sir? I do not have the patience for this. By 2:30 today I had lost whatever sense of humour I brought in with me this morning. So either you spell your *real* surname, or move along."

This was not the first time this had happened. In fact, I confronted it almost daily in one form or another. I could feel my stomach tightening a little.

"I'm sorry. But I actually did give you my real name. Against all odds, that is actually my name." I said it and spelled it again for her. She wasn't typing. She pushed her glasses up onto her head.

"Let me see some ID, right now!"

"Arghhh." Yes, that's what I said, "Arghhh," while scanning the ceiling for salvation. It seemed an appropriate response at the time. "Look, I'm here because I lost my wallet. So I have no ID. That's where I usually keep my ID. That's why I'm here,"

I pleaded, doing my best to suppress my simmering anger. But my voice was starting to rise a little.

"Look, mister. You expect me to believe that any sane parent would give their son that name. I ain't buying what you're selling. You got no ID. You're getting belligerent. You're practically foaming at the mouth. So back off and go and get your jollies somewhere else. We're busy here. Try the passport office on Hudson. They're loads of fun." She pointed in a vaguely southerly direction as she said it. "Next in line, please!"

I've often heard of people snapping under the cumulative stress of a situation. All of a sudden a bolt pops loose and that nice, gentle man who gives to charity and volunteers at the food bank somehow steps off the deep end and turns into a raving lunatic. Well, it was different for me. You see, I volunteer at the Planned Parenthood Clinic down on Bleecker, not at the food bank. But everything else was just about the same. You know, the deep end, raving lunatic part. So much for my civility instinct.

"Wait just a second," I shouted, yes, shouted. "Wait one second! That is the name I was christened with forty years ago. I am not impersonating anyone. The spelling is not even the same. There's an 'a' in my first name and a double 'm' in the second. See, it's a completely different name. Okay, now try to focus. I've had a very, very bad day and I need a new driver's licence. Your job is to make that happen. Please do it now!"

"Security to 10," was all she said into her headset. She sounded tired.

It felt like an out-of-body experience. I could hear myself yelling, but seemed unable to control it. As an observer, I was impressed with my coherence, despite the higher pitch and volume of my voice.

"Whoa, hang on! I've been waiting nearly two hours. I'm not leaving without my new driver's licence. I've already given you my name. I live at 75 Bank Street in the village. So just process it now and I'll leave quietly!"

I didn't feel the need to utter the "and nobody gets hurt" line. It was implicit.

For the first time, I noticed the crowd behind me backing away, some of them even surrendering their position in the line to get a little farther away from the whack job ranting at Window 10. I felt like I was among them watching this crazy dude melt down.

"Security to 10!"

I was still yelling. At one point I seem to recall banging the glass with my open palms. Excellent idea. I listened to myself shout some more at the woman at Window 10.

"Do you know what it's like to go through life with my name? Do you? It builds a wall around you. It isolates you. It's harder to meet people. Fellow drivers in the DMV think you're crazy. And you know what the worst part is? Are you listening? Do you know what the worst part of the story is? I'm a writer. Yes, that's right. What a hoot! Isn't that a laugh? I am a writer. Say, what's your name? Where's your name tag? Come on, what's your name? I bet it's a normal, average name that has never registered on any radar anywhere in the world. Brenda Cooper, or Linda Baker. Something like that, right? No spikes in notoriety, no front-page stories, no celebrity scandals to make your life difficult. You have no idea how lucky you are, whatever your name is."

The words just flowed out of me. I knew the speech well. I'd been mentally rehearsing various versions of it for many years. I just never thought I'd ever say it out loud. I paused to look carefully at the ceiling again and tried to calm down a bit. That didn't really work. My throat hurt from shouting. I really don't know why I was shouting but it seemed the most natural thing in the world to be doing at that moment.

"You gotta help me! Just make this one little thing go right for me today, because *nothing else has*."

In case shouting wasn't enough to make my point, I also went back to banging on the glass. But for variety, I pounded it in time with my words for added emphasis, as a crazed bongo player might. Yes, my breakdown was syncopated, almost rhythmic.

"You have no idea what I've already been through today! It's been a nightmare and this is not the way I want it to end! This is not the way it's going to end!"

"Code 66! Security to 10! Now would be good!"

"Look, whatever your name is, you are not helping turn my day around. It's your job to help me! And at least you've got a job! I lost mine this morning after fifteen years, and then my girlfriend moved out, *all before noon*! That's gotta be some kind of a record! Just give me this one little victory. Please! Just this one teeny-weeny win. *Give me my driver's licence!*"

Boom, boom, boom, boom, boom went my hands on the glass of Window 10, following the cadence of my words. It just felt so good to get it all out. How do you spell "catharsis"?

I was caught off guard by what happened next. Or perhaps "caught by guards" might be the better way to put it. I felt them before I saw them.

"Hey, wait . . . what gives . . . get your hands off meee . . . I know my righhhhh . . . Heyyyyy . . . arrrrrlllllllchshhhhh . . ."

After that, I was still making sounds with my mouth, but it's hard to be articulate with a nightstick pressed against your trachea. There's not a lot of give in those nightsticks. But I was gurgling as eloquently as I could. It took three of them to carry me, squirming and squealing, to the front door of the DMV. The hordes still waiting in line parted before us, as if I were infected with the Ebola virus.

Now I had always thought that the phrase "They threw him out on his ass" was just a catch-all term to cover any kind of forcible ejection. Well, in my case, it really did mean "They threw him out on his ass." There's not a lot of give in those dirty sidewalks of Broadway either. And there's not a lot of give in my tailbone any more.

I lay back flat on the pavement where I'd landed. The big guard was on me in an instant, her knee pushing down on my sternum, her colleagues towering on either side.

"If you're still lying here in ten minutes, the police will be called. You're lucky they aren't here now," she said, her face pressed quite close to mine.

She spoke to me like I was one small step up from a disobedient dog. "Go home! Do not go back into the DMV! Do you understand? Go home right now!"

I pointed to her knee as politely as I could.

"Need to breathe here . . ." I gasped. She lifted her knee a little and I sucked in all the air around me.

"Do you understand?" she shouted at me again.

"Of course I understand," I replied calmly, lying flat on my back on the sidewalk at Broadway and 6th having been mounted by a burly security guard. "I'm not an idiot."

She just shook her head, stood up, and led her team back into the building. I lay there for a while making sure I had feeling in all my extremities. I can report that I certainly had feeling in my ass.

No one stepped forward to assist the innocent taxpayer unjustly abused by the state. In fact, I'm really not sure any passersby even noticed me. A guy lying on the sidewalk, moaning, is nothing out of the ordinary in Manhattan. From my pavement-level vantage point, I noticed a black miniature poodle closing fast. So I got up, fast.

I turned the key in my apartment door forty minutes later and plopped down on the couch. Then I shot back up again as a tsunami of pain started in my coccyx and then washed over me. My, what a short memory I have. I discovered through trial and error that the least painful position was lying on my stomach. So I did that for a while, after popping twice the recommended dose of Advil.

She was right. Jenn, I mean. Our relationship had been not so much strained, just pallid and pale for the last two years. Whatever spark had kindled the fire early on had become so anemic that the flames petered out before I even noticed. Jenn was right. I probably knew as early as she did, perhaps even earlier. I just couldn't bring myself to deal with it. It was easier not to. Not better, just easier. I see that now. Many relationships limp along because they're convenient. And it's inconvenient to do something about it, and end it. I'm very good at pursuing the path of least resistance. It's what I've always done. But I'm also getting a little better at hindsight. Who knows, perhaps insight might not be far behind.

I managed to get up, put the two pillows from Jenn's side of the bed on a kitchen chair, and with considerable care lowered myself into a pseudo-sitting position. I stared at the screen some more. Chapter 12. I was unable to find any words that worked. I knew where my story was going. I just had to look at my outline. But the words would not come. It felt like they would never come. I Googled "writer's block" and enjoyed twenty minutes of depressing reading as I matched symptoms.

Finally, I surrendered, clicked open one of my existing Word files, and spent some time working on a taxonomy system I've been developing to classify the various kinds of people who, for one reason or another, have famous names even though they are not famous themselves. Like me, for instance. It was my shrink's idea to do the analysis and develop the model. I found it interesting, even fascinating at times. Having thought about this topic for most of my life, I felt as if I'd covered all the bases and had a pretty good handle on the different categories. I just didn't know anyone else with a famous name to test-drive my system. I couldn't sit on my tender tailbone any longer so I stripped down, then went to lie face down on our bed, on my bed. I reached for the phone on my night table, dialled, then I waited for the beep.

"Hi, Dr. Scott, it's Hem. I'm hoping you've got some time tomorrow. That would be Thursday. I'm clear all day. Yep, all day. Look, some stuff has happened and, well, we need to talk. Just let me know when, and I'll be there. Thanks. Bye."

I hung up. It was only 8:30, but I was exhausted after my big and busy day. I was just drifting off when the phone rang. I assumed it was Dr. Scott. But no, my father's name appeared in the little liquid crystal caller ID screen. No, no, no. No thanks. Not now. Absolutely not. I'd rather head back to the DMV, perhaps even with a side trip to the dog pound. Not tonight. Still, it rang. I'd been through enough already. I did not need a conversation with my father to top it all off. I already had a very big pain in my ass, thanks just the same. I just let it ring as I swallowed more Advil. I looked for a while at the empty side of the bed Jenn had occupied for the last four years. I was feeling sorry for myself, but not really for very long. Then I assume I fell asleep, my ass still throbbing.

CHAPTER 2

You've probably figured it out by now. Well done, if you have. And if you haven't, well, as my former ad agency colleagues might say, "Here's the big reveal." My name is Earnest Hemmingway. Yes, it really is. I know, hard to believe, but true. I have absolutely no connection to the famous writer except we happen to have been born in the same city, Chicago. But that's just a freak coincidence. Beyond that fluke of geography, there is no link. None. No relation. In fact, as I tried to explain to my nemesis at Window 10, my name isn't even spelled the same way. I am Earnest Hemmingway. That other writer guy is just plain old Ernest Hemingway. I cling to my extra "a" and "m" to set me apart from the literary titan. Stripped of the extra "a" and "m," his name seems simple and spare to me, like his writing. His name seems almost incomplete, abbreviated, truncated. Conversely, my name is more complex and flowing, like my writing.

It's been hell living with a famous person's name, even one that's spelled differently. It sounds the same, so to the world it is the same. When I say it's been hell, don't misunderstand me. I fully understand that my plight pales when stacked against world hunger, global warming, geopolitical tensions, equality of the sexes, and doping at the Olympics. I like to think I have a sense of perspective, that I can put this into a broader context. Nevertheless, this very personal burden has profoundly affected my life.

My name intrudes daily, with every person I meet. Every one. A laugh. A smirk. A glance tinged with disbelief. A snide remark. Even a well-meaning attempt at humour, without the slightest whiff of malice. It all has weight when it leans on you, day in and day out. There does not exist a line I haven't heard. Some, very lame: "I loved your books, ha ha." Others, more sophisticated: "Sorry about your suitcase." I've heard them all. I cannot recall ever meeting someone when my name did not prompt at least some discernible reaction that would never have occurred had Bob been my handle. To make matters worse, and yes matters can be made worse, I want to be a writer, a novelist, in fact. What a cruel hand to be dealt. Sad, isn't it? Life would be so much easier if my dream were to open a restaurant, or be a dentist, or build my own home by the ocean. I could probably handle that. Instead, because I want to write, I get jokes about shotguns for breakfast.

I truly believe I could handle living with a different famous name that had nothing to do with writing. Basil Rathbone. Richard Nixon. Charles Lindbergh. George Foreman. Bring it on! I'm not saying life would be easy with a different famous name. Far from it. But I ask you, if you wanted to be a writer, is there a worse name to bear than mine? Come on, try.

F. Scott Fitzgerald? Not bad, but nowhere near Hemingway. Charles Dickens perhaps? Impressive, but still not quite there. These literary greats are inextricably linked to their works.

Charles Dickens = *Oliver Twist* / *A Christmas Carol* / *A Tale of Two Cities* / *David Copperfield*
F. Scott Fitzgerald = *Tender Is the Night* / *The Great Gatsby*

But the name Ernest Hemingway conjures up something else, something greater. He transcends his books. Simply put . . .

Ernest Hemingway = Writer
. . . end of story.

I know what you're thinking. Just change it! Change your name! People do it all the time for a host of different reasons.

But it's my name. I've had it all my life. It would be a stretch to say I like my name. In fact, I often loathe it. But it is *my* name.

Then why not use your middle name? you ask.

I don't have one. Nor did any of the other first-born sons in the Hemmingway clan since the early part of the last century. I always thought it showed a distinct lack of creativity on the part of my great-great-grandparents.

But wait, there's more. Here's the kicker. I can't stand Hemingway's writing. I really can't. I hate it. His spare, flat prose never fails to take something inherently interesting, or even exciting – think bull fighting or war – and make it sound, well, spare and flat. To me, the English language is something to celebrate, to explore, to splash around in. My writing, such as it is, is the polar opposite to Hemingway's, which seems to make bearing his name even more of a burden. He haunts me. I feel him looking over my shoulder criticizing my intricate sentences, my lofty vocabulary, my swirling prose. It feels like he's in the room with me, or at least in my head. Or perhaps I'm just obsessed, deluded, and deranged. That's also an option.

I haven't yet explained just how I came to carry my name. I'm no history buff, but you can't grow up in this family and not absorb its story, if only by osmosis. My younger sister is a dedicated student of the family's history. But I know enough to tell the tale.

While it's rarer today, back toward the end of the nineteenth century, Hemmingway was not an uncommon name. My great-great-grandparents, Theodore and Mary Hemmingway, were Christian missionaries in China in the 1890s. What a tough existence that must have been. Every few years they returned to the west to recover, visit family and friends, and report on their success, or lack of it, in converting the rural farming communities of China to Christianity. They often brought with them strange maladies, parasites, and fevers that would lay them low for a month or two before they felt up to heading east again, which they always did, eventually. To the extent that they had a home outside of China, it was in Boston.

In the spring of 1895, Theodore and Mary were in London on their way from China back to the United States. Miraculously, this time around, they were in remarkably good health and could really enjoy a few days in one of the most cosmopolitan cities in the world, before boarding a ship for the harrowing Atlantic crossing to Boston. One night in March, the young couple was given tickets to a relatively new play that had opened the month before to rave reviews. The famous four-balcony St. James's Theatre was located near King Street and Duke Street, a short walk from where the couple was staying. They loved the play. They laughed until they cried. They had never seen such wonderful drama in such an extraordinary theatre. It is fair to say, they were entranced by the experience. Clearly the memorable night did not end when the curtain fell, for nine months later, almost to the day, my great-grandfather was born in Boston.

The proud parents were overjoyed. To commemorate that special night they spent in London, the baby was christened Earnest Hemmingway. No middle name.

Have you figured it out yet?

The play they had so enjoyed that night in London was, of course, one of the first performances of Oscar Wilde's *The Importance of Being Earnest*. If only Wilde had stuck to his original title for the play, *Lady Lancing*, my life, and that of my father, grandfather, and great-grandfather, might have been entirely different. Damn Oscar Wilde.

Theodore and Mary did more than name a son that December morning in 1895. They unwittingly sowed the seeds of an idiotic family tradition that plagues me to this day. Every first-born son in the three generations that followed was also named Earnest Hemmingway. No middle name. Curse Oscar Wilde.

By the way, Ernest Hemingway – you know, the famous writer guy – well, he wasn't even born until 1899.

In our family, the original Earnest Hemmingway, born nine months after a night at the theatre, has always been known as EH1. It follows that my grandfather became known as EH2, my father, EH3, and I, yep, EH4. I know it sounds more like a designation on a laser printer cartridge, but there you have it. It's just so much easier to go with EH4 rather than Earnest Hemmingway the fourth. You understand.

I'm a little hazy on EH1's childhood. I doubt it's particularly relevant to this story anyway. But I do know that as a teenager, he worked in the garment trade in Chicago. He was an enterprising lad with an entrepreneur's creative mind and steely nerves. He came up with an idea to improve a particular garment's strength and quality. Rather than share it with his employer, he kept it to himself and quit the company. Within days, on the outskirts of Chi-Town in 1916, EH1 started his own fledgling operation, still known today, as it was then, as The Hemmingwear Company. The product? Underwear. Yes, underwear for men and boys was the only offering. So what was the idea that gave rise to a four-generation family underwear empire? Well, a bit of background first.

In those days, the "ripper," sometimes called the "yanker," was a standard schoolyard prank. The waistband of the unwitting victim's underwear was grasped at the back and yanked upward quickly and forcefully. Invariably, the waistband ripped apart from the rest of the underwear, hence the aptly coined term "ripper." Across the continent, for many years, the ripper was the tactic of choice for bullies terrorizing their prey. That is, until EH1 changed the game forever.

In his spare time, EH1 developed a new cross-stitching technique that when combined with a wider waistband added considerable strength to the underwear. Throw a stronger but softer fabric into the mix, and EH1 had a winning product on his hands. Men and boys in and around Chicago loved the new product. When the new Hemmingwear underwear caught on, the ripper simply vanished, to be replaced by something arguably just as humiliating and painful, but certainly different. Instead of the waistband pulling apart from the rest of the underwear, EH1's innovative cross-stitching held fast, wedging the garment upward between the buttocks and dangerously compressing the genitals. This usually resulted in ephemeral sopranos and excruciating pain. In EH1's honour, the prank was initially known as the "Hemming." However, much to his relief, a new term eventually supplanted it. It was apparently coined on a military base somewhere in the southern United States when a new recruit was found hanging by his underwear from a fence post demarcating the munitions range. In considerable pain and in a somewhat higher-pitched voice, he declared it a "wedgie." The name stuck.

Yes, it's true. My cross-stitching great-grandfather put the "wedge" in wedgie.

I'm not sure whether the bullies or their victims were pleased with EH1's innovation, but he called it the relentless march of progress.

To be fair, I'm selling old EH1 short. The new and stronger waistband was only a small part of his business savvy. He determined that the other garment companies were struggling and failing by trying to manufacture far too many different products. The manufacturing efficiencies and economies of scale could never be achieved when so many different undergarments were being produced in relatively small quantities. EH1's genius was in sticking to a simple yet powerful business strategy:

1. Focus on one set of customers: men and boys.
2. Make only one product line: underwear.
3. Make it in huge quantities to reduce the per unit price.

And it worked. It worked very well.

Two other factors helped to consolidate the fortunes of The Hemmingwear Company. The first was EH1's version of the more modern business axiom "Location, location, location." In early

1916, at the age of twenty-five, EH1 bought cheap industrial land just outside of Chicago. Over the decades, he and his successors, true to his vision of mass production, expanded the Chicago operation rather than building smaller factories in other parts of the country. One giant factory is more efficient than five smaller operations, provided you can economically deliver your product to those more distant markets. Well, EH1 had thought it all through. Even in the early years of the twentieth century, Chicago was emerging as the largest and most important rail hub in North America. It was no coincidence that the land EH1 bought in 1916, and on which The Hemmingwear Company's massive manufacturing operation still sits, was and remains immediately adjacent to the enormous Chicago rail yards. It was a good idea back then to locate close to the railroad. It's still a good idea today. By building and expanding his manufacturing right next to the Chicago rail hub, EH1 maximized efficiency, minimized product costs, and secured continental distribution in one genius stroke. Smart.

The second and perhaps even more important factor, at least in the beginning, was winning the exclusive contract to supply the U.S. Army with underwear as they were mobilizing to enter the Great War in 1917. In business, as in most things in life, timing is everything. It was a massive contract that played right into EH1's vision of a narrow product line, mass-produced for a specific audience, in this case, some four million soldiers. EH1 used the contract to lever investment in significantly expanding the Hemmingwear manufacturing operations to handle the undertaking. Few companies in the history of business have benefited more from such a timely, lengthy, and sizable military contract. It carried EH1 right through the Depression when all around him factories were closing and workers were losing their jobs. Without the Army contract, who knows what might have happened to Hemmingwear. What I do know is that EH1 never squandered his opportunities. He dedicated his life to making the most of them.

Just after the Second World War, a cursed family tradition began when EH2 returned from Europe and joined EH1 in the family business. When he crossed the threshold at Hemmingwear, the die was cast. It was inevitable. Eventually, EH1 retired and EH2 took the reins. From that moment onward, it simply became accepted and expected that the first-born son, who carried the patriarch's name, would assume the mantle of CEO. Thanks a lot, EH2. This is on your head. Though it's hard to tell if my father, EH3, has ever really been happy, he is doing his duty to the family as CEO. In a very few years, I'll be expected to do mine. The pressure has been building for years. Shit.

There's a line my father likes to cite, too often, when he wants to remind me of the path in life I'm expected to follow. His father, EH2, introduced its overuse in our family but claimed it originally came from the patriarch himself, Earnest Hemmingway I. Quoting those who came before him, my father simply says, "This family tradition is paramount and sacrosanct." Over the years, it's been abbreviated to just "paramount and sacrosanct," and eventually to just two initials. Whenever my father wrote to me when I was away at summer camp, or later at college, he would always add "PS" below his signature. It did not signal that he wanted to add a few more lines. No, his postscript just sat there on the page, a final reminder of my future. No words were needed. His code was well understood. *Paramount and sacrosanct.* Those two heavy adjectives still hang around my neck.

While still honouring EH1's founding business strategy, Hemmingwear remains strong and profitable. It's given me financial security, though I've never touched my so-called trust fund, and it promises a steady job at the helm when EH3 is ready to leave. I won't have to send in my resumé. I won't have to go through a competition or interviews. I won't need references. I just have to move my stuff back to Chicago.

It seems churlish to complain about my lot in life. I know, the world should have my problems, right? But I don't want it, any of it. Yes, I am EH4, but running Hemmingwear will not be my fate. I will not fulfill my birthright. I do not ever want to occupy the corner office at Hemmingwear. I just want to write. Like Ernest Hemingway, no relation, spelled differently. I just want to write. Let someone else make the nation's underwear.

———————

It took me fifteen minutes to slide myself out of bed and assume an upright position. I hadn't slept well at all. My tailbone was still killing me. Imagine a colonoscopy with a red-hot sickle, conducted by a doctor with a severe tremor. Yeah, that's about right. I popped more Advil, but not enough. I stood at the kitchen counter to eat a bowl of multigrain Cheerios. Then I fired up my laptop, carried it to the bookcase in the living room, and placed it on one of the higher shelves. In this way, I could work on it while standing, in the hopes that the red-hot sickle might not be quite so painful. I checked my email with one hand and held a glass of orange juice with the other. My Macdonald-Clark email address had already been disabled, which was fine with me, so I opened my personal Gmail account. I scrolled through the spam until I came upon an email from my younger sister, Sarah, that had arrived moments earlier. All it said in the subject line was "*WTF!*"

I opened the email. The only content was a YouTube link. Without even hesitating to consider the implications, I clicked on it. Next time, I'll hesitate a bit to consider the implications. There was something vaguely familiar about the scene that played out in the little rectangle on my laptop screen. It showed some crazed dude hollering at some kind of customer service rep and banging the glass behind which she was safely ensconced. It looked like the DMV. It *was* the DMV. It slowly came back to me. I'm kidding, I knew immediately what I was looking at. Shit.

Is nothing sacred? Can't a guy have a public meltdown these days without the unholstering of half a dozen video-equipped smartphones? I remained completely calm. I didn't even notice when the glass of orange juice slipped from my hands and headed for the hardwood. Luckily, it didn't shatter when it hit.

The glass wasn't broken, but my big toe might have been. I forgot about my tailbone for the ensuing ten minutes or so and gave thanks for my nearly deaf neighbour.

The YouTube clip had been uploaded the previous evening under the title:

"Famous Writer Flips Out at the DMV"

Very funny. It had been posted just about twelve hours ago so there were only about 309,000 hits so far. I clicked over to the YouTube home page and confirmed my worst fears. The clip was one of YouTube's featured videos. I'd gone viral.

I clicked back and played the four-minute video in its entirety. I was impressed with the cinematography of the shooter. He'd done a very nice job. And the audio was outstanding. You could hear every word I uttered perfectly clearly. As luck would have it, the guy's smartphone was also equipped with a digital zoom and he knew how to use it. So not only was the sound great, but on the tight shots toward the end, at the height of my tirade, you could actually see the spittle flying off my mouth and hitting the glass. Powerful stuff.

Then the scene shifted as I exited, stage left. The shooter stayed abreast of the three security guards who were carrying me out. There was none of the grainy, hand-held, home-movie feel of the Zapruder film in Dealey Plaza. It was as if this guy just happened to be holding a Hollywood high-def Steadicam. Then he perfectly framed my brief flight, my tailbone touchdown, and my final breathless exchange with the security guard. The video then faded to black as I lay on the sidewalk. Very nice.

My mind drifted to what soundtrack music might underlie the sequence – perhaps something from *Les Misérables*, or even *Camelot*. Then I felt sick. So to help ease my pain, I scrolled down to see if any comments had been left. Yes, there were a few. Well, relative to the 309,000 views, 234 comments constitute "a few." The first twenty comments could all be categorized as negative, with subheadings like insulting, hostile, ridiculing, and unstable. But the twenty-first read as follows:

Leave him alone! Do you have any idea what it's like to live with a famous name? Do you? Trust me, it ain't great. So cut the guy some slack.
J. Stalin

J. Stalin? You're kidding. I kept scrolling through another twenty-six negative comments before reaching this one:

Get the fuck off the poor sap's back! Try walking a mile in his shoes, you assholes!
Anne Boleyn

I know a pattern when I see one. I tracked through all of the comments. Of the 234, there were only nine positive ones.

Beyond our friends J. Stalin and good old Anne, supportive messages were also left by an F. Sinatra, Gerald Ford, S. Holmes, D. Beckham, Margaret Thatcher, and two other names that I didn't recognize as famous at all, but I suppose could have been. Interesting.

The ringing phone brought me back.

"Hello."

"Holy shit! What the hell was that? Were you on something?"

"Sarah?"

"No, it's Beyoncé," my sister Sarah replied. "Who did you think it was?"

"Sorry, but I'm more accustomed to the standard telephone opening. You know, the one that goes 'Hi, Hem, it's Sarah.' Something like th – "

"Yeah, yeah, whatever," she cut me off. "Anyway, Hem, you were amazing! It was quite strange and disturbing, but you were still amazing. Oh, and I'm really sorry about your job and about Jenn."

"How did you find out about that? Did she call you?"

"Hello! Is this thing on?" she mocked tapping her phone. "I found out about your job and Jenn the same way 312,000 other people around the world just did. You've gone viral."

"Shit. Right."

"Hem, are you all right? What happened, I mean before the DMV?"

"Yeah, I'm fine. I have a bruised ass and ego, and I may never sit down again, but I'm fine. I just had the day to end all days.

The video sums it up quite nicely. I got laid off and escorted out of the agency I've been with for fifteen years. Then I came home and found Jenn and her suitcases in the hallway, with her brother driving the getaway car. And, oh yeah, I lost my wallet the day before. So to comfort myself, I thought, 'Well, there's always the DMV.' So I went uptown. It was kind of a bad news/good news scenario. I did not get my new driver's licence, but I'm now on the YouTube home page. Other than that, things are great."

"Shit, that is one bad day," she said. "Look, I want to hear everything but have to bail now. I'm coming to New York tomorrow to see you. I should be at your place by eleven."

"Whoa, um, I'm kind of tied up tomorrow, um, like all day. Rain check?"

"Hem, tomorrow is Saturday. You just lost your job. Your girlfriend just bolted. You have no driver's licence. And you can't drive anyway because you broke your ass." Sarah was now using her most patient voice. "You've got all the time in the world. I'm sure you could use the company. And we need to talk. See you tomorrow, and I'm sorry about your day from hell."

Sarah hung up. Shit. At least I didn't need to clean the apartment.

My sister and I don't really get along that well, except Sarah doesn't seem to know that. Thirteen years my junior, she arrived long after my parents decided one son was sufficient. Sarah dubbed herself "the afterthought." I left home for college when she was just turning five, and just turning interesting. Since then, we'd never lived under the same roof, except for a day at Thanksgiving and a couple more over Christmas. To strip it right down to the wood, I really didn't know my sister very well. But she scared me a little.

If my father had noticed, Sarah was actually the first-born son he never really had. She took to business like a morning DJ to coffee. She sailed through a business degree at the University of Chicago before finishing at the top of her MBA class at Northwestern. I was so proud of her. Mom was so proud of her. My father didn't really seem to notice. He went to her convocation a couple years ago but spent most of the time haranguing me about doing an MBA and "taking my place" in the company. If this upset Sarah, she just channelled any frustration into her career.

Even before graduation, she was courted by all the investment houses and management consulting firms in New York. They offered her more to start than I'd ever make in the ad agency world. But she said no. Turned her back on them all to work at, yes, The Hemmingwear Company. The most single-minded, driven, aggressive, diligent, and pugnacious woman I've ever known was trying to climb up the corporate ladder in a men's underwear company. My father did nothing to help her up. In fact, he sometimes seemed to be greasing the rungs. Our mother lived long enough to see Sarah join the family business, before the cancer finally took her. It was a slow and pain-ridden decline that was hard on everyone. Afterwards, our father, or using the more appropriate appellation, EH3, threw himself into the company to the exclusion of all else. But that wasn't really much of a change.

––––––––

I've been seeing Dr. Madelaine Scott for ten years now. Apparently, I have some issues. I like her. She's thoughtful but blunt, and doesn't speak much, even for a psychiatrist. She seems to keep a certain distance from me that I'm always trying to close. I know. She's not supposed to open up. That's my job. I'm the one on the couch. Her office is in a nice brownstone on a leafy crescent on the Upper West Side. She was in her early sixties, but didn't look it. Her short auburn hair made her seem younger. She always dressed casually. I'd never ever seen her in a dress or skirt. Her office was formal but comfortable. Plush beige broadloom cushioned the feet. Lamp light replaced the traditional overhead fluorescent tubes. The art on the walls was nice but not interesting enough to distract you from the task at hand. You know, exposing your innermost thoughts and sifting through your memories, usually just for clues, but sometimes for real answers.

I used to lie on the couch in the sitting area while we spoke. But after I fell asleep for the third time in our first five appointments, we decided I should sit across from her in the same kind of leather armchair that she uses. I don't think she ever fell asleep during our appointments.

"Dr. Scott."

"Hello, Hem. Come in."

"Thanks for squeezing me in."

"No problem. That's what I do," she replied. "The next thirty minutes are yours. How have you been?"

"Well, funny you should ask. But a lot seems to have happened in the last day."

"Yes, I know. Wallet, job, and Jennifer, all gone in twenty-four hours. I'm sorry."

"Wait. I've never mentioned that in my voice mail. How did you know?"

I saw her eyes move to the laptop on her desk.

"You've seen it, haven't you?" I said.

She just nodded.

"You just happened to be trolling through YouTube and stumbled across it?"

"Hem, I, like most psychiatrists, have Google Alerts set up for the names of all my patients. I viewed it shortly after it was posted."

"Were you going to say anything about it to me?"

"I assumed we would come to it, and it seems I was right," she replied.

Mindful of the time, I spent the next ten minutes giving her an abridged version of my big adventure the day before. Throughout, she said nothing, but nodded a few times, brushed some fluff from her pants, and took a couple of notes.

"That must not have been easy for you. Let's start with your job. How are you feeling about being let go?"

"Oh, it's been fantastic! A validation of my contribution to the firm. Recognition of my abilities and achievements as a leading copywriter. And the culmination of a successful and fulfilling career."

"So we're back to your standard 'sarcasm as shield' avoidance stratagem," she observed. "Were you good at your job?"

Easy question. I know this one.

"Yes, Dr. Scott. I truly believe I was good at that job. I helped win new business. I wrote some award-winning campaigns. And at least for those early years, I was busy all the time. I was in demand. But the landscape has changed. Long-form isn't hot now."

"Okay. You were good at your job," she summarized. "Now, tell me honestly, Hem, did you love your job?"

My tender tailbone was throbbing. I shifted very gingerly in my chair. I looked at the ceiling. I gazed out the window. I examined my fingernails. I cleared my throat. And when I could avoid it no longer, I actually thought about her very simple question.

I liked some of my colleagues. I liked some of my clients. I even liked wrestling with some of the creative challenges that were dumped on me over fifteen years. I turned it all over in my mind and really thought about it, perhaps for the first time. In my head and in polite conversation, I've always made a point of ducking that question. I guess I've gotten close to the answer before. But I've always managed to shut down before drawing the harsh conclusion.

"No. I've never really loved my job," I replied. "I've never leapt out of bed on Monday morning so I could get to the office sooner to immerse myself in what I was truly meant to do on this Earth . . . write long-form ad copy. No, I guess I didn't love my job. I'm not even sure I liked it much. The fact of the matter is, I think I can only go as far as 'I didn't mind my job.'"

"Were you aware of this before just now?"

I fidgeted. And look around the office a bit more.

"Maybe. Probably." Silence. More silence. "Okay, yes."

"Hem, just because we're good at something doesn't mean we're meant to spend our lives doing it."

I thought about that for a bit and nodded, not looking at her.

"You told me in our very first session a decade ago that your dream was to become a writer," she continued. "Is that still true? Is that still your dream?"

"Yes."

"Do you need to work right now to earn money to live?"

"No. As my former employer told me, 'I have a huge package.'"

Dr. Scott smiled. I smiled.

"Hem, let's shift to Jennifer," she continued. "Did you love living with her?"

I looked at the clock. We were running out of time so I shed the pretense of deep inner angst and turmoil. I think I knew the answer to this one, finally.

"I loved living with her for the first eight months or so but then I started missing the freedom of my old life. But doing something about it would have been a huge deal. So I did nothing about it. I was paralyzed. Or more accurately, I guess I chose to be paralyzed."

That earned a nod from Dr. Scott.

"Living together just kind of became more of a routine, a habit, and less a real relationship," I admitted.

"Good. It feels like you've thought this through. Okay, Hem, here's a big one. Did you love Jennifer? Did you really love her?"

"No."

"Okay, we're nearly out of time. So let me skip to the end. Hem, on the YouTube video, you seemed like you were very upset and acting out in ways that are not consistent with your personality and beliefs."

I just nodded.

"In light of your candid responses in the last half-hour, is it possible that your little episode at the DMV yesterday was not because you couldn't cope with losing your job and your girl-friend, but rather because you just don't know how to handle the unexpected freedom you suddenly now have?"

———

Five minutes later we both rose from our chairs and I headed for the door.

"Did you notice the comments on the video?" I asked her.

"Well, I scanned a few but didn't really like what I was reading so I stopped. Why?"

"I know there were tons of vitriolic comments, but sprinkled in among them were a handful of supportive ones, most from other people with famous or nearly famous names."

"And . . . ?" she prompted.

"Well, I've never really considered that there are other people out there living with what I'm living with. But of course there would be. I've never in my life encountered anyone who might really understand what it's like. It would be interesting to meet a few, have a beer, and compare notes."

She paused for a moment in thought before responding.

"Well, you never know, New York is a big city. By the way, are you still working on your little famous names classification system? What do you call it again?" she asked.

"I think of it as a taxonomy. Yep, I'm still fiddling with it."

"Good for you. Sounds like an interesting project."

"Thanks for the time, Dr. Scott. Good session."

I always said "Good session" when we finished. It was my standard parting line. But it really had been a good session. A very good session.

———

I was up from the subway on the final stretch along Bank Street to my apartment when my cellphone chirped.

"Hello."

"Hi, Mr. Hemmingway, it's Susan from the U OF C library and archives."

"Hi, Susan. You can call me Hem. Everybody else does. The 'Mr.' always makes me feel a little nervous."

"Sure, Hem. Thank you. I just wanted to follow up on my letter asking about any papers or personal effects you'd like to add to the Hemmingway Archive. It's been a while since we've received any new material from the family. Don't forget, it's a tax-deductible donation."

"Right. I'm sorry, I meant to call you back," I skated. "I've been, um, very busy the last few days. I've got nothing to contribute right now but I'll certainly keep you posted. My sister is really into the family history. I'd give her a call."

"Yes, Sarah is in here quite often looking through the archive. I'll ask her when she's in next," she said. "Oh, and I'm sorry about what you're going through right now. Bye."

Great.

When I got back home, I felt good. I wasn't trying to, I just did. It was strange having your live-in girlfriend bolt and not be broken up about it. But I wasn't. I ordered Chinese and tried for a while to work on the novel. Chapter 12. Nothing. No words. White screen, blinking cursor mocking me, Hemingway's ghost somewhere nearby. Yes, I was quite sure.

On the bright side, the apartment still looked great. Clean apartment = clean slate. In my mind's ear, I could almost hear the cast of *Annie* belting out "Tomorrow." While I brushed my teeth, I had a moment to wonder what it would be like to have pain-free hindquarters again, to be able to sit in a hard chair again, to sidestep a Broadway matinee lineup, accidentally bump my ass on a parking meter, and not yelp and tear up and bite a hole through my tongue. More Advil, then I went to bed, still on my stomach.

It happened about six and a half hours later. I don't know *how* it arrived. I just know *that* it arrived.

CHAPTER 3

It was still dark when I awoke. I wasn't tired in the least, though I should have been. The garish orange digits next to me blared 4:32 a.m. In hindsight, there was no earth-shattering epiphany, no profound revelation. I'm not prone to such dramatic breakthroughs. It was really just a simple, solid, sound idea that seemed to arrive fully formed, along with a sentence I'd heard earlier.

"Well, you never know, New York is a big city."

Yes, it is. Yes, it is.

I turned it over in my mind for about an hour before getting up and wakening my laptop. I mapped out the idea. Fiddled with it. Made it bigger, made it smaller, then made it just right, I hoped. I took about half an hour finding the words for the ad, then copied and pasted them into the little box on the *New York Times* classified ads website. I chose the "New York Region only" option. I could always spread my net wider if this initial approach failed. Now I just needed a date, time, and location to complete the ad.

Where to do it. A local church? No, not the vibe I was going for. A hotel? Kind of expensive, and it may not set the right tone. A bar? Tempting, but too many distractions, like beer, and karaoke . . . and beer. The boardroom at Macdonald-Clark? I could probably arrange it, but unless he was busy, it would probably mean seeing Bob again, and I just wasn't up for that. (Bob busy? Good one.) So no go on the MC boardroom. Public library? Now we're getting warmer, but still a tad restrictive, I thought. Where, where, where . . .

I found myself stalled on location for about an hour as I explored different options. Then it suddenly came to me. The perfect solution. I cannot explain why it took me so long to think of it. I'm a member, after all. I went to the website and confirmed what I suspected. They were open very early in the morning to cater to the before-work crowd. After ransacking the apartment in search of my membership card, I finally dug it out from the drawer in the front hall table. I dusted it off and made the call. I hung up ten minutes later with a meeting room reserved for a couple of hours the following Thursday evening. It didn't cost me a penny. Pays to be a member, even one with a dusty membership card.

I flipped back to the NY *Times* classifieds site and added the final details. I plugged in my Visa card number and hit the big red button to make the buy. I considered a Facebook ad, and even composed a few options, but decided against it in the end. It was a fallback measure I wasn't convinced I'd need. "New York is a big city."

I returned to the YouTube clip to scan the new comments added overnight. The rough one-in-twenty-five pattern that I'd identified the day before persisted. The total comment count had risen to nearly 315. Sprinkled among the 75 or so newly added venomous comments were three positive ones from, I'm not kidding here, Paul Revere, Clark Griswold, and one J. Garland. Very cool.

I admit it. I was kind of excited. I felt like I suddenly had a new mission. Not a lofty, altruistic, philanthropic one. No, not so much. More like a self-interested purpose that might help a few other people similarly afflicted if everything went well. That was good enough for me.

———

"Hey, big bro," she said as she came through the door and gave me a stiff, almost perfunctory hug.

As promised, she'd arrived just about eleven on the dot. She looked great, wearing jeans and what looked like might be a man's button-down collar dress shirt. She'd always looked great, yet never ever gave off the impression that she knew or cared. I'd always liked her short hair, eschewing what *Entertainment Tonight* tells me is the current trend toward longer tresses.

"Hi, Sarah. Safe flight?"

"No, the landing gear jammed so we were forced into a belly-down skid on a runway of foam. There was fire everywhere. Luckily we came to rest near the taxi stand so I just zipped down the inflatable chute into a cab and here I am. That's why I was a few minutes late," she replied.

She looked up and saw my face. I was still stuck on "belly-down skid."

"Hem, the flight was fine," she said. "I always say something like that when people ask me that stupid question. If my flight hadn't been safe, I wouldn't have just walked through your door, now would I?"

"Shit, Sarah, it's just a figure of speech, a friendly, small-talk greeting very commonly directed to people who have just come from the airport. I wouldn't say it's stupid."

She headed for the kitchen and straight for the fridge.

"Whatever. I'm here and I'm safe. Got beer?"

"There's Corona in the door, but it's not even noon," I reminded her.

"Yeah, but I've been up since 5:15, Chicago time, so it feels like happy hour to me."

She popped the cap on a Corona and dropped into a chair. I was still kind of standing there in the centre of my own living room.

"Hem, sit and tell me what the hell happened at the office yesterday. It sounds like you were royally screwed over."

She threw one leg up and over the arm of the chair, making herself very comfortable before taking a long draw on her beer. I tend to follow instructions when they're forcefully delivered, except, apparently, at the DMV, so I sat down.

"Well, it seems I overstayed my welcome at Macdonald-Clark. Idle Bob, the GM, let me go and . . ."

"With cause or without?" she interrupted.

"Without cause."

"What did they offer?"

"I got a year's severance."

"One year. Hmmm. When do you have to sign it back?"

"What do you mean?"

"When do you have to sign back the separation agreement? Please tell me they had paperwork ready," she said sitting forward.

"Oh yes, they had the paperwork ready," I replied. She resumed her relaxed position in the chair. "I signed it all yesterday."

She leapt to her feet and crossed the floor toward me with what looked like fratricide in her eyes. She towered over me and bellowed.

"You what!? You didn't! No you didn't! You did not sign the agreement yesterday! You're messing with me, right? You're just waiting for your lawyer's comments, right?"

She wasn't really tall enough to tower but that's certainly how it felt.

"The paperwork all seemed in order and a year's salary seemed fair to me. In fact, it seemed generous," I replied.

"*Did you even read the agreement?*"

"Well, I read a lot of it, partially."

"*Did it include a section that precludes you from going back for more if you sign and take the money?*"

"Sarah, I'm eighteen inches from you. My deaf neighbour probably thinks you're speaking to her."

"Sorry. Did it have that clause or didn't it?" she asked in a voice that she dropped from earsplitting to loud.

"I don't remember much about the document after, um . . ."

"After what?"

". . . after 'This agreement lays out the terms of separation blah, blah. . .'" I said, looking at the carpet. Sarah exhaled like she might never take another breath.

"Sarah, calm down. Bob said it was much more generous than the statutory requirement and that there was no point in negotiating or I'd only get what the legislation dictates," I explained in my most reasonable voice.

"That's what Bob said, is it?"

I nodded like a five-year-old on the time-out chair.

"Hem, that's what they always say. You'd worked there, what, fifteen years? Any lawyer worth her salt could probably have gotten you more. You should have stood up for yourself more. But it's too late now. Next time, come to me. I can help on these things."

"I didn't really like my job. They did me a favour."

She plopped back into her chair with a heavy sigh that conveyed "You've disappointed me" more effectively than the actual words ever could have.

"Sarah, you know I'm not good at confrontation. You've cornered the family market on that. I get all queasy."

"What do you mean by that?"

"Well, my stomach churns and I feel like I'm . . ."

"Not that part! What do you mean I've cornered the family market on confrontation?" she said in her best confrontational voice.

"I don't know. You're just so good at yelling at people. Shit, you've been hollering at me for a decade. You make me nervous. You intimidate me. I'm not even sure you like me."

"Of course I like you. You're my big brother," she yelled. "I love you the way younger sisters love their older brothers. You just infuriate the crap out of me sometimes, the way older brothers do."

"What have I ever done to infuriate you? Surely not reading my separation agreement and missing out on getting thirteen months' salary rather than twelve isn't infuriating. You can't care that much about it. I certainly don't care that much about it."

Sarah closed her eyes, then pressed and rubbed her face with both hands. She did this for about thirty seconds. That's a long time when it passes in silence. I could hear her breathing.

"You don't get it yet, do you?" she started, this time in a soft voice that made it all the more compelling. I said nothing. "Look, Hem, I truly believe I was born to business. I got all of Dad's business smarts and you got all of Mom's caring, nurturing, artistic genes. All I've ever wanted is to make our company as competitive, profitable, and prosperous as it can possibly be. It's all I want to do. I just want to impress Dad and work my way up to the top. There is so much more the company could be doing to cement our leadership in the market. But we're just sitting back and waiting for shit to happen. In this climate, we need to be bold, and instead, we're hanging on to those archaic founding principles. They're holding us back and may lead us into a decline that could actually take us down if we're not careful."

"So tell Dad. You have to get up in his grill and make your case. You should be great at that."

"Don't you think I've tried that? I've tried to speak to him. When that didn't work, I wrote a strategic plan that I don't think he even read. He's not going to listen to me. He never has. He's not going to start now."

"Sarah, I know he's tough to reach, but he'll listen if you get him in the right setting, at the right moment, with the right message."

"No, Hem. You don't understand. He won't take it from me. He won't," she replied, looking sad and defeated.

"But why won't he?" I asked. She raised her eyes to me. Sad and defeated gave way to something else more akin to fury.

"Christ, Hem, are you that blind? I can't get through to Dad because I don't have a fucking penis and I'm not the fucking first-born son!"

Don't ask a question if you really don't want to hear the answer. We sat there and looked at each other for a time. And then, as if to match her eloquent and powerful declaration, and then raise it, I dug deep into my intellectual and oratorical reserves and countered with carefully chosen words, delivered with passion and gravitas in the awkward air between us.

"Well, that's certainly a charming and elegant synopsis of the situation."

See what I mean? I'm not good at confrontation.

"That's all you've got?" she said, sighing.

"Well, that's all I've got right now. I'm sure I'll have more later."

"Right. And for the record, I stopped worrying about being charming and elegant a long time ago."

"Even if what you say is true, do you have to yell at me all the time?" I asked.

"I'm sorry, it just boils my blood that your destiny is to run the company yet you want no part of it, while I want nothing else but can never have it. It's such a cruel joke. Dad really wants you back to honour his precious family tradition. You won't come back, but I'm right there. I'm just down the hall, his own flesh and blood!"

She paused again, but not for long.

"He barely acknowledges my existence, let alone my work! I get a nod in the corridor if I'm lucky. It's bizarre. So yes, I'm bitter. I'm angry," she said before softening. "That's why I get pissed off with you. You have the opportunity and you have the choice. I have neither. I know it's not your fault. I know you shouldn't have to be someone you aren't, and take on a role you don't want.

No one should have to do that. I also know you're not trying to infuriate me. But in the end, you have something I desperately want. So you get caught in my crossfire. I'm sorry."

"If this is driving you insane, and from my seat it seems to be, why don't you just leave, come to New York, and get a job .here? You could do anything you want in this town."

"But I don't want to leave. I love the company. I love the idea of family tradition. I actually think it's important. I just don't want the tradition to be quite so rigid. I want to change it up a bit."

"Well, I never thought I'd ever say this, but believe me, I truly wish you had been born first and had, you know, a penis," I stammered. "I need a beer." I got up and headed for the kitchen.

Really, this was no revelation, no blinding insight. Deep down, I guess I knew.

This great family conflict had always swirled and flowed just below the surface, only occasionally bubbling up into the open air. As the years passed, I came to believe that we might even escape a cataclysmic eruption. I should have known better. Like the good folks of Pompeii all those years ago, I was surprised when the blowout hit me in my own living room on just another average day. It's not that I hadn't seen it coming. I'd just always chosen to look right through it.

"So what the hell happened with you and Jenn?" she shouted from the living room.

I carried two beers back into the living room and handed one to Sarah.

"In the last twenty-four hours, I've come to think of it as a good thing," I said. "I may not yet have a lot of perspective on it, but it is instructive that I haven't really thought much about her since she left. And I can't say I really miss her that much. It's strange. It seems we'd just been going through the motions for the last couple of years."

Sarah looked perplexed and annoyed at the same time.

"What a colossal waste of time. Why didn't you break it off when it first started to go stale?"

"Sarah, not everyone is born as decisive and direct as you were."

"Hey, I wasn't born this way. This crazy family made me like this," she said and then pointed at me. "You made me like this!"

"You're welcome," I replied. She smiled. "But I think you were born with all the drive, conviction, and tenacity you carry around with you. I think it's been in you from the very beginning."

We sat there in silence for a while. It was overcast, but light still angled in through the window, the shadows of leafy tree limbs floating on the hardwood floor.

"I'll never forget the day you came home from the hospital. I had a hard time wrapping my head around the arrival of a new baby sister. You were tiny in my arms. Even by thirteen, I'd already done a lot of growing. I was a big kid. But my clearest memory was of just how beautiful you were."

"What a shock I must have been to Mom and Dad," she said. "Imagine. You're minding your own business, running a company and running a home, living your life, and suddenly, thirteen years after the family heir is born, I land. The accident. The afterthought."

"Come on. Perhaps you weren't fully planned. But you were loved and supported just as I was."

"You cannot know that for sure. You weren't there for most of it," Sarah said. "One of my earliest memories is of the day you left home for college. It's no wonder I have abandonment issues. I remember Mom holding my hand while Dad stood there in the street watching your car until it turned the corner and was gone. Then he walked right by me and back into the house, as if I wasn't even there. For most of my life, when it came to Dad, I felt like I wasn't really there. I know he loved me, but not like the first-born."

I, too, could recall the day I finally left.

"I was eighteen, so you must have been five," I said. "Sorry about bailing on you just when you were getting old enough to be interesting, but I had to get out of there. Until I escaped, every day was a chance for Dad to drill into me some other insight or bit of advice that would supposedly help me run the company. I was eighteen! I didn't even know how to do my own laundry and he was schooling me on potential manufacturing productivity efficiencies on line number 1. I knew even then I wanted nothing to do with it, but he wasn't listening."

"So you fled," she interjected. "You ran."

"Yeah, I guess I did."

"And you're still running from it more than twenty years later."

"Well, let's not get melodramatic about it," I protested. "Is it such a crime to want to do something else with my life, other than running an underwear empire?"

"No, but ignoring it won't make it disappear," she replied.

We lapsed into silence again for a few moments until Sarah piped back up.

"So what now? What will you do with all the time you suddenly have on your hands?"

"Write."

———————

We went out for a walk through the village. The sun had started to break through the canopy of clouds and it was shirt-sleeves warm. By this time it was early afternoon and I was hungry. So was Sarah.

"Let's try this place," she proposed. "It looks nice."

We had stopped on Bleecker about two blocks from my apartment, near West 11th. I'd walked by the still new bakery/restaurant a few times and had wanted to try it anyway. It was called Let Them Eat Cake! We entered. It was small, clean, brightly lit, and smelled heavenly, as most bakeries do. Even though it was still within what most would consider the lunch hour, it was not crowded. Sarah and I chose a table by the window, giving us a view of the streetscape. Two menus were already on the table. A few minutes later, an attractive woman, I'd guess mid-thirties, who carried herself as if she were completely at ease with everything in her universe, approached us. Her name tag said "Marie."

"Welcome to Let Them Eat Cake!" She greeted us in a strong southern accent, smiling and spreading her arms wide as if to say "Ta-daaa."

"Thanks. You haven't been here that long, have you?" I asked.

"We're in our second month. So far, so good."

"Well, congratulations. This neighbourhood needs a nice restaurant," I said.

"We call it a café-bakery, actually. But thank you. We're very excited about it all."

Her smile was infectious and seemed to warm the air around her.

"What can I get y'all?"

"I'm going to try to your Cobb salad with a Diet Coke, please," Sarah said.

Marie turned to me. I was still looking at Sarah.

"You're in a brand-new café-bakery that smells as good as this one does and you're having a salad?" I asked.

"Look, you order what you want, and I'll order what I want. That's how restaurants work," she replied with a forced smile.

I looked back at Marie and shook my head.

"Well, I've skipped right over the salads, sandwiches, and soups and gone straight for what you call Coronary Chocolate Cake. If that's what's on the counter over there, I want a slice."

"That's the one," she said, pointing to the cake on the counter that I can only describe as magnificent. "Good choice. I made that this morning and I don't think you'll be disappointed if you're a chocoholic like I am," she drawled.

"I am. Oh, and a glass of milk, too. Thanks."

"Done," Marie replied.

"You're not from around here, are you?" I asked.

"Has my liltin' accent betrayed me?"

"Just a hunch on my part," I replied.

"Born and raised in Louisiana, but I'm a Manhattan girl now," Marie said as she turned and headed for the kitchen.

"Okay, so what did you want to talk to me about? Or have we already covered it?" I asked.

"I thought you might have figured it out by now," she replied.

"Sarah, I can do many things, but reading your mind is not one of them. Just put it out there and then I'll let you know if I've figured it out or not."

"All right, all right. Here it is. It's really quite simple. You and I have a shared interest. We have a common vision for the future of Hemmingwear. I just think we should work together so we both get what we want out of it."

"What I want out of it is to *be out of it*. So maybe I haven't yet figured out what you're driving at," I said. "What exactly is our shared interest, our common vision as you put it?"

"Well, you just said it. Neither one of us wants you to run the company," she concluded. "Is that clear enough?"

"Sarah, not wanting to run the company hasn't exactly cooled Dad's jets on the topic. In his mind, it's not whether I'll come home to be CEO, it's when."

"But, by working together, there might be a way to take you

off the hook and put me on it. A win-win. That's a goal we can both get behind, isn't it?"

"Okay, I'm listening."

"Come home and talk to Dad. Make it crystal clear that you don't want, and never will want, to take part in the management of Hemmingwear. Tell him that you think there's another Hemmingway who could honour the family tradition. Tell him I can do it. Tell him I may not be ready quite yet, but I'm on the path and I want to do it. Tell him I'm smart. I'm tough. I have a plan to make the company better. And that he should start letting me get involved in more than just marketing. And tell him that all the parenting books say that fathers should actually talk to their daughters."

"Sarah, doesn't he know all of that? You've been working there for a couple of years now."

"Hem, do you not remember our penis discussion? It was only half an hour ago."

"Keep your voice down!" I hissed. "Do you want Marie to throw us out of her restaurant before the cake comes?"

"Café-bakery, actually, but who's counting?" Sarah said. "Yes, I've worked there for a while now, but I never get any Dad time. He goes out of his way to keep me on the periphery. He avoids me. Keeps his door closed. I'm languishing in marketing and there's so much more I want to get involved in."

"But your MBA was focused in marketing, wasn't it? Didn't he put you there because he thought that's where you wanted to be?"

"Don't get me wrong. I love marketing, and it's important. But it's still one or two rungs removed from where the real action is. I want to do a stint in finance and work on corporate strategy. MaxWorldCorp is coming on strong, and we have no real response. If we're not careful, they're going to blow right by us."

"From what Dad tells me in his interminable phone calls, MaxWorldCorp is in no position to threaten Hemmingwear's market leadership. They just can't touch us."

"Yeah, well, Dad is out of the loop. They've made three new acquisitions in the last three months and have an aggressive expansion plan. MaxWorldCorp is poised to start cutting our grass big-time."

Marie arrived with the salad and my cake. Oh my gosh, the cake. I had to concentrate very hard to keep my mind on Sarah's voice when I was eating that cake. I think it was probably the finest piece of chocolate cake I've ever eaten. It might have been the finest piece of anything I've ever eaten.

"This is unbelievable. This is sublime," I moaned.

"Why don't you and your cake get a room?" Sarah chided. "You're making very strange sounds. Try to focus, Hem."

"Sorry. This cake is from a different astral plane," I explained, my eyes closed in ecstasy. "Okay, I'm back now. So, to summarize, you want me to start working the Sarah angle with Dad in the hope of getting us both what we want."

"Precisely. I think you've got it now."

It really wasn't a bad idea. And what did I have to lose? Well, I guess I had my CEO job to lose, which was exactly what I was looking for. Why didn't I think of this before?

"Okay, I'm in. But I don't think Dad is just going to roll over and hand you the keys to the corner office. This is going to take some time."

"I have faith in your powers of persuasion," Sarah said as she patted my hand. "But when you talk to Dad, this has to be your idea. I don't want him to think I'm a conniving Machiavellian manipulator."

I raised an eyebrow. I must have raised it quite high.

"Okay, I may be a conniving Machiavellian manipulator. I just don't want him to think that, yet," she concluded.

We shook on it.

"So how is Dad these days? I've been avoiding his calls so I haven't actually spoken to him for a while."

"He's getting worse. Ever since Mom died, he's been even more obsessed with the company. It runs his life. It clearly means more to him than, well, than anything else," she said.

"Is he still refusing to believe that the 1960s are actually over?"

"Well, his wardrobe, language, attitudes, and business perspective are certainly stuck in the sixties, if that's what you mean," she explained. "And I don't think it's helping that he's spending such an inordinate amount of time with our jackass of a COO, Henderson Watt."

"Henderson Watt? Isn't that your boyfriend?"

"Bite your tongue," she snapped. "We dated just long enough for me to get him into the company. Then he stopped courting me and started courting Dad. He's ambitious to an entirely unhealthy degree. You think I'm ambitious? This guy is in a league of his own."

"Doesn't Dad see through him?"

"Dad is blinded by this guy's bright light. No one has been promoted faster. He's a charter member of the Executive Sycophants Hall of Fame. It would be embarrassing if it weren't so dangerous."

"Dangerous? What do you mean?" I asked.

"I don't think he has an original, or even an informed, thought in his head, yet he's the only one who's in Dad's head these days."

"Okay, if I'm going to undertake Project Sell Sarah, I need to know who this guy is and where he came from. Just give me the pencil sketch," I asked.

"I met Henderson at Dooley's, where a few of us from marketing go for drinks most Thursday nights. I'd seen him there a few times before. When we finally met, we hit it off. By sheer coincidence, he'd worked overseas for a European skiwear manufacturer but had returned stateside after five years when it looked as if he'd topped out over there. He was looking for work in the rag trade to build on what he'd learned across the pond. I thought his experience in the EU might be useful as I know Dad was contemplating trying to break into the European market. We dated seriously for a few months and all was going well.

Then I finally talked Dad into seeing him. They were locked in his office for three hours. The conversation just kept going. When it ended, Dad hired him on the spot to work in corporate finance."

"Wow. That was fast."

"He ingratiated himself with Dad, buttering him up, and, well . . ."

"Being the first-born son he didn't really have? Is that where you were going?" I filled in the blank.

"Well, yes, as a matter of fact, that is precisely where I was going," she replied. "That was just the start of the courtship. About seven months in, they even went on a weekend fishing trip together. Dad's never even been fishing. Well, when they got back, Henderson was given the COO title. The next day, he dropped me like I had the bubonic plague."

"What did he say when he broke up with you?"

"Not much beyond the need for him to focus exclusively on his new job. There wasn't time or bandwidth for anything else, or anyone else," she said. "I felt angry, betrayed, and more than a little suspicious. The first two don't really matter, but I'm convinced he's up to something. I just don't know what."

"What did Dad say?"

"Sweet diddly. Not a word. I don't think he even knew we were seeing each other. And if he did, he didn't care." She sighed. "He's blinded by the lustre of his golden boy. And I'm to blame for bringing them together."

"He sounds like a real piece of work."

"You'll meet him when you come to see Dad, which you should do sooner rather than later."

She changed the subject after that and forced me to recount, moment by moment, my ill-fated and broken-ass visit to the DMV. So I did. She called the YouTube video up on her iPhone to bring my words to life. Even though she'd already watched my performance several times, my colour commentary seemed to enhance the entertainment value. I don't think I'd ever seen Sarah laugh so hard. She actually squeaks when her laughter crosses a certain threshold. I could hardly blame her. With twenty-four hours' distance, the whole event now seemed almost as funny to me as it must have to the crowd of witnesses.

"Looks like you just lost it in a very big and a very embarrassing way," Sarah concluded.

"Yeah, well, you have no idea what it's like to carry around such a famous name."

"Come on, Hem. Get over it. What's the big deal? So you've got a famous name. So what. Who cares?"

"Spoken like a true 'partial,'" I said.

"What the hell is a 'partial'?" Sarah asked.

"It's someone who only has half a famous name, like you. It's one of the designations in the classification system I've been working on," I replied. "I'm still noodling around with it."

"I bet you are."

———

Sarah caught a late afternoon flight back to O'Hare. She hugged me before she got into the cab. It was not the artificial squeeze I'd gotten when she arrived. There was more behind this one. That was a good sign. It had been a good day. I don't think I'd spent that much concentrated time with Sarah, well, ever. I liked her more than I'd expected. She was growing on me. Bonding was easier when she wasn't yelling at me.

I popped out again later in the afternoon and headed straight for my local florist. I sent a flower arrangement to arrive at Sarah's office on Monday morning. Then I had them wrap up a bouquet of freshly cut flowers to take with me.

I grabbed the subway and was at my destination inside of fifteen minutes. I'd called earlier and lucked out. They were open a handful of Saturdays throughout the year to deal with the heavy demand rolling into the summer. This was one of those open Saturdays. My good fortune continued. She was there. The lineup wasn't too bad for a Saturday afternoon. When it was my turn, I had to let two people behind me go ahead until she was available. There was a flash of recognition in her face when I approached Window 10. I pushed the flowers through the opening in the window and gave her my widest possible smile without looking crazed. I kept my hands high and visible at all times. She didn't touch the flowers but just left them lying there on her side of the glass. She didn't seem thrilled and looked at her phone to confirm it had not moved and was still within reach.

"Hi again," I started. "We got off on the wrong foot yesterday and I wanted to come back to apologize and try again."

She had folded her arms across her chest.

"I don't remember many of my customers, but I sure remember you," she said. "If you're gonna tell me the same story today, well, I don't think we're going to get along any better."

I pushed my passport, my last two tax returns, and four pieces of official mail, all bearing my name and address, partway through the opening in the glass. For good measure, I also shoved through my Macdonald-Clark business card. She didn't need to know that I'd just been turfed. She furrowed her brow but pulled the documents the rest of the way through the slot.

"I know it sounds far-fetched, but my name really is Earnest Hemmingway. I was named for my great-grandfather, who was born four years before the famous writer was," I explained. "We're not related in any way. Our names are even spelled differently." I had one more card to play. "You've heard of The Hemmingwear Company?"

"What, the underwear people?"

"Right. Well, my family owns the company. I'm telling you the truth, I swear."

She stopped looking at me and started examining what I'd passed through to her. Then she punched some buttons on her computer, typed in my name, and up popped my file, just like that.

"Why didn't you bring these docs yesterday? It sure would have saved time and, you know, that little situation we had."

I wanted to ask why she couldn't have just typed in my name the day before, thus saving my tailbone from a very hard landing. I bit my tongue.

"I'm sorry, I didn't think to bring them yesterday. I honestly didn't think I'd need them. I should have brought them. I know that now. It would have avoided so much unpleasantness."

I hung my head in contrition, with my hands still up high where she could see them.

Fifteen minutes later, she'd taken my photo, processed the replacement request, handed back all my documents, and then slid my shiny new driver's licence across the counter to me. She was the picture of public service efficiency.

"Thanks so much, and sorry about yesterday. I'd had a very bad day. I apologize for taking it out on you."

She smiled. Hallelujah, she smiled.

"Can I let you in on a secret?" she asked, leaning closer to the window. "I know Hemmingwear only makes underwear for men, but I got a pair at home that I wear on the weekends, you know, when I do my power-walking. They're a helluva lot more comfy than what I usually have to wear."

"When I see my father next, I'll be sure to mention your choice in unmentionables. Thank you for your help with my licence."

"Thanks for the flowers, and sorry about yesterday. I'd had a bad day, too."

My cellphone chirped as I waited for the elevator in the lobby of my building. The screen on my phone said "Private Caller." I figured it might be Sarah.

"Hello?"

"Son, it's your father. I've been trying to reach you for a few days now. Is everything okay?"

Shit.

"Hi, Dad. You caught me, um, in the middle of something here."

"Perhaps, but the point is, I caught you," he replied. "Tiring of the copywriting game yet?"

"Well, funny you should ask. I'm actually not at Macdonald-Clark any longer. I'm kind of in between gigs right now."

"So you've got nothing on your plate. Why, that's excellent news, son. Exceptional timing, too. Your return to Chicago is long overdue. It's where you belong," he said. "It was my father's calling. It was my calling. Now it's your calling."

"Please don't say it," I pleaded.

"Paramount and sacrosanct."

"You said it." I sighed. "Yes, Dad. I'm quite familiar with the history, the tradition, the heavy expectations, the three-word family motto. I know all of that."

"Then this can all work out very well. Yes, the timing is almost ideal."

"Dad."

"I've got an office waiting for you just next to mine. It'll be easier that way. And there's a lot going on right now."

"Dad."

"Yes, finally, this could work. I want you to meet Henderson Watt."

"*Dad!*"

"Yes, son, what is it?"

"We've been over this before, many times. I'm sorry, but I'm not moving back. New York is my home. I have no plans and even less interest in working in, let alone running, Hemmingwear. It is not who I am."

"Actually, son, it is who you are – just as it is who I am, or was," he said. "So, you're not quite ready. You haven't quite outgrown this writing thing. The sand is running through the family hourglass, but there's still time yet. Take a few more weeks, take a month, and you may feel differently at the end."

"Dad, I know how I'll feel in a couple of weeks. It's not going to happen. We've gone over this many, many times."

"Son, there's no place in business for rash decisions. Continue to deliberate on the matter. You'll come to see it as the right path, I know you will. Oh, and I'm going to send you the Q3 financial statements and draft annual report that Henderson has pulled together. I want you to see what we're doing here so you can be up to speed."

"Dad, you're in denial. But if it helps at all, I am coming to Chicago this coming Friday for a visit. I can't believe I'm saying this, but I'd actually like to talk about this issue and propose a solution that I think you'll agree is in the best interests of all parties concerned."

"Finally, you're coming home."

"Actually, Dad, I'm leaving home, so I can visit Sarah and you in Chicago."

"I'll make sure your office is ready for you."

Shit.

CHAPTER 4

I arrived just after 6:00 p.m., nearly an hour before the meeting was scheduled to start. I was nervous and excited, though I had no idea if anyone would show. The West Side Y on West 63rd, just across from Central Park, seemed like as good a location as any. It was central, easily reached by public transit, and had been a mainstay of the community for nearly a century. One of the Y's community liaison coordinators had asked me to come in early so she could show me around and brief me on all the other activities and resources they offered. I made a mental note to use my membership more often. They even had creative writing classes. And if my writer's block persisted, they had pottery classes, too.

The third floor room I'd reserved was a reasonable size, with two big windows overlooking the street. I could smell the faint scent of chlorine wafting up from the swimming pool in the basement. I spent fifteen minutes arranging the chairs in various configurations until I settled on the simple circle formation.

Someone looking in as they passed by in the hallway might have thought it was an AA meeting waiting to start. I put a sign-in sheet on a small table by the door. Then I sat down in one of the chairs and waited.

By 6:50, I was still alone in the room. Shit. But at 6:55 three people arrived in quick succession. An older white woman walked in first. Short and stout, yes, she was shaped not unlike a teapot. She was followed almost immediately by a young man who looked like he might be Italian, or maybe Spanish. He seemed very anxious and shy, as if a loud noise might induce some kind of a seizure. The third arrival was a tall, big-boned black woman. The three of them stood there and looked around the room.

"Hi, welcome!" I said perhaps a little too enthusiastically as I jumped to my feet. The young shy guy immediately backed away.

"No, no, please come in, you're in the right place if you saw the ad in the *Times*," I went on. "Please write your name and email address on the sign-in sheet, unless of course you're a fugitive and don't wish to be identified."

They looked puzzled.

"Sorry, that was a feeble attempt at humour. Just trying to break the ice. So go ahead and add your name to the list if you don't mind, and take a seat anywhere." I waved my hand around vaguely.

They all signed the sheet and sat down in silence, leaving empty chairs on either side of them. The tall woman was staring at me with an odd look on her face. I nearly forgot about the doughnuts and drinks I'd brought that still sat in my backpack on the floor at my feet. I grabbed them and the plate I'd carried from home, and made a lovely little doughnut arrangement on the table next to me, along with a rather fetching symmetrical array of the dozen or so cans of pop and juice. Finally, I took a moment to fan the napkins beautifully and lay them flat in front of the drinks, which I thought dramatically enhanced the visual appeal of our refreshment table. Martha Stewart would have been proud to host this meeting. Clearly I was quite wrapped up in my food styling, for when I turned back to the group, I was shocked to see another five people had arrived. Eight people had come! Nine counting me. Who knew?

The new arrivals each signed in and made their way to a chair. There was a younger black woman dressed as if she might work in a bank; a great big black guy wearing a Metropolitan Transit Authority uniform; a somewhat scrawny, rough-looking white kid with a buzz cut and plenty of tattoos; a rumpled older man in a corduroy jacket; and a muscular, athletic-looking East Indian fellow who smiled and nodded at everyone in the room. Still, no one was talking to one another. I checked my watch. Five past seven. I walked over to the table and grabbed the sign-in sheet, scanning the names in amazement as I returned to my chair in the circle. Wow.

I'd given some thought to how I'd open the meeting, and now was the time. I stood up holding the clipboard to claim the floor. I could say that the room then fell silent, but it had already been silent for the preceding five minutes or so.

"Good evening. Thank you all for coming. This is very exciting for me, and I hope some of you feel the same way. You've all come tonight because, it seems, for whatever reason, we all share a similar burden. And we've been carrying it for as long as we can all remember. We've been bugged and bullied, and taunted and teased for most of our lives for something over which we have no control. And if your lives have been anything like mine, we endure it pretty much alone. It's hard for anyone else to appreciate the ordeal, except perhaps for those of us in this room tonight."

"Amen, brother," said the MTA guy. Others were nodding now.

Everyone was now looking at me. Several were smiling. The awkward tension that had enveloped the room seemed to dissipate. I could feel it ebb.

"Now let's not be too melodramatic about it. There are many whose lot in life is far worse than ours. What we have won't kill us. But unless we live like hermits, I know that every day we are reminded of the particular cross we all bear, the cross that has brought us here tonight."

"I certainly hope you will not be springing Christianity on us. That is not what I came for!" snapped the suddenly very angry muscle-bound East Indian guy, who had jumped to his feet. Then Mr. Hyde instantly morphed back into Dr. Jekyll. "Oh, I'm so sorry, I did not mean to raise my voice. Please have a butterscotch."

He thrust a foil-wrapped candy toward me and held it there until I finally reached out and took it.

"Again, I'm so sorry about my outburst. I'm working on it."

I slipped the candy into my pocket. He seemed perfectly gentle and happy again, smiling and nodding at the group as he sat down.

"No worries. My reference to the cross was just a metaphor. This is a completely non-religious gathering. Thanks for the candy. Butterscotch is my favourite." I was trying to disguise how shocked I was, fully aware that the awkward tension had flooded back into the room like a tidal wave.

"Okay, I think the first order of business is for us to go around the room and introduce ourselves to one another. And just to add a little twist, why not tell us one dream and one fear you have. I'm happy to start. Believe it or not, my name is Earnest Hemmingway."

That earned a few gasps, even a couple of chuckles.

"Oh, bless you, son. You have got it bad," said the older teapot-shaped woman.

I smiled at her.

"Thank you. Yes, it's quite a handle. I should point out, as I do almost every day, that it's actually spelled differently from the famous writer's name. But it really can't be pronounced any other way, now can it?"

"Wait!" shouted the tall black woman. "I knew I'd seen you before. You were on the front page of YouTube freaking out in the DMV, right?"

"Hey, yeah!" echoed another.

By the intense nodding and looks of dawning recognition on

their faces, it seemed that almost all of them had seen the video, some of them several times. I guess that's why they call it viral.

"It was not one of my prouder moments. I've actually been trying very hard to forget it happened. But some good has come out of it. That little incident is what finally prompted me to try to organize this meeting."

"Well, we're glad you snapped. And look, here we all are," said the older teapot woman, holding both her hands up in the air.

"Right," I said. "Anyway, I also have this belief that our lives are somehow affected in some way or shaped by the famous people whose names we carry. Sometimes it seems almost mystical. Maybe it's just in my head, but there is a connection. For instance, in my case, what makes my situation all the more difficult, and perhaps comical in a way, is that for most of my life, I've dreamed of becoming a writer. Would I have had any interest in becoming a writer if my name were Lee Harvey Oswald? I'm not sure. But what I do know is I've been planning a novel for many years now and I've recently tried to start writing it. But I'm blocked. You know, writer's block. It feels like Ernest Hemingway, the writer, is stuck inside my head, and I can't seem to shake him. But that's a discussion for another day.

"Let me wrap up. I was a copywriter for an ad agency here in New York for many years, but now my time is pretty much my own. Oh, and you can call me Hem. Everyone else does."

I paused for a moment, about to sit down, when I remembered the one-dream, one-fear routine.

"Oh yes, one dream of mine would be that I'll find the will and the wisdom to take charge of my own destiny, rather than letting other people and other forces guide my life. Up till now, I've tended to let things happen rather than make things happen. As for one fear, well, I hope we'll all be open and honest here, because I'm about to be. You see, I have what I know is an irrational fear of small dogs, strangely enough. Yes, I know it's weird, but there you go. Thank you, and thank you for coming tonight."

As I sat down, someone in the group applauded and rest of the room eventually joined in. I turned and looked at the person to my left. The quick-mood-change East Indian guy stood. His English had just the faintest trace of an accent.

"Hello. I'm very happy to be here. Again, my apologies for what happened earlier. You can call me Hat. My full name is . . . wait for it . . . wait for it . . . okay, now, Mahatma Gandhi. No, I'm not jesting. I was born in India forty-five years ago. My parents, in homage to the great pacifist leader who helped liberate India from the colonial yoke, named me for Mahatma Gandhi."

"The skinny guy in the movie? No way. That's terrible! That's just cruel! What morons! What tools!" said the scrawny, rough-looking guy.

"You shut up!" Hat yelled and pointed at the culprit. "My parents were wonderful people who loved me and . . . Oh no, I've done it again, haven't I. I'm fine. I'm sorry. I'm fine. Please have a butterscotch, please take one," Hat implored as he pressed the candy into the skinny guy's hand.

I thought I'd better jump in before the riot police were called.

"Okay, why don't we get back to the story at hand, and let's all be careful in how we react to one another, shall we?" I said, looking first at Hat, hoping not to set him off again, and then at our little group. "Carry on, Hat. The floor is still yours."

"Thank you for your patience with me. I have no ill will toward any of you. I am in a struggle with my own temper, but I will prevail, God and butterscotch permitting," he explained. "So, back to my story. When I was eighteen, I came to America on a scholarship to study electrical engineering at Cornell. Until recently, I worked at the Con Ed cogeneration station on the East River at 14th. I have recently been relieved of my duties, partially due to my own demons, but I will restore my honour and work there again, God willing. I know it. In the meantime, I work the New York Jets home games as an audio technician. I'm the guy on the sidelines aiming that parabolic dish so the TV viewers can all hear the players' profanity and the crunch of the tackles on the field. Even though cricket is really my game – I'm really quite good at it, I assure you – I do love my Jets.

"Really, my only dream is to lead a happy, productive, and normal life. Of course, my fear is that I won't always be able to control my temper and that I might hurt someone I know or love, or even someone I don't know. That fear haunts me even as I get better at self-control. Hmmm, that is quite a downer. My apologies. Okay, enough about me. I'm just so happy to meet all of you, and to know that there are others who face the same challenge as I do. Um, I mean the challenge of our very special names, not my little anger issue. That is mine alone. Thank you. Thank you. I have lots more butterscotch if you wish. They are so good."

"Well, thank you, Hat. Nice to have you and your butterscotch with us," I soothed in my most calming of voices. He bowed and sat back down.

Applause from the circle.

I turned to the teapot woman and she stood, drawing herself up to her full five feet.

"Hello, friends. Isn't this fun?" she began. Hat and several others smiled and nodded. "Drum roll, please. My name is Jacqueline Kennedy. Yes, it is. But my friends call me Jackie. And they were doing that when the more famous Jackie Kennedy was still little Jackie Bouvier. While it's an honour to carry her name – I loved JFK – I still like to say that I was Jackie Kennedy first.

"My husband, Walter, died much too young twenty-four years ago from a heart attack. He was just fifty-two. Fifty-two! He was replacing the linoleum tiles in the kitchen when he just slowly sank to the floor, and that was it. He was gone. I'm seventy-three years old now and I'm still not over him. But I'm trying every day, because that's what you have to do in this life. You have to carry on. We never forget, but we move on.

"I've lived in beautiful Brooklyn all my life. I'm a diehard Dodgers fan, even though they abandoned us for the wrong coast back in '58. But I was there as a kid in the stands in '47 when Jackie Robinson broke the colour barrier. I'll never forget that game or what it meant. I have a daughter who lives in California, but I'll never leave my Brooklyn.

"As for fears, well, I don't much like heights or Republicans. One of my dreams came true in January 2009 when a black man became president. I didn't think I'd ever live to see that day. Now I'm waiting for a woman to take the oath of office. Then I could die happy. Oh also, I'd like to take back, by any means necessary, the words 'Tea Party' from the fascist brigands who stole them."

I scanned the room, worried that Jackie Kennedy's political pronouncements might have put a few ideological noses out of joint. But no one seemed to be offended.

"Right on," said the younger, well-dressed black woman.

"Thank you, Jackie. It's nice to have you here," I said before turning to the big MTA guy. He nodded and stood.

"Hi, everyone. I'm not great at public speaking, so I made me a few notes to help me out," he said. He then put on black horn-rimmed glasses. "I hate these things but I can't read without 'em. But, man, do I hate 'em. Ready? My name is Clark Kent. Yup, you heard me right, Clark Kent. My momma didn't read too good, and we didn't have a TV till I was a teenager. So she never really heard much about Clark Kent. She knew who Superman was, of course, but not so much about Clark. She just liked how the 'Clark' went together with the 'Kent.'

"So I'm thirty-eight years old and I been driving the subway, usually the Lex Ave Express, for more than ten years. I figure I'll be a subway lifer to get me that pension, but I don't much like it underground, if I'm honest.

"Now you should know why I hate wearing these goddamn glasses. I'm always taking 'em off and putting 'em back on 'cause I don't want to leave 'em on. I tell you, the guys at work love to razz me when they see me pulling off my glasses. They're always saying shit like 'Get outta the way, Clark is heading for the phone booth' and stuff like that. They don't mean nothing hurtful by it, but it sure gets on my nerves."

"May I ask why you do not acquire corrective contact lenses? I hear they are quite comfortable," inquired the older man in the corduroy jacket.

"I'd sure like to, but they cost too damn much for my blood. And I really only need 'em for up-close stuff. Anyhoo, I'm married to the best girl in the world and we got ourselves twin five-year-old boys that just take my breath away every time I look at 'em.

"My fear? You mean other than Kryptonite?"

He laughed and we dutifully joined in.

"Well, seriously, this can be one bad-ass city. I seen some stuff down below that scared me white. Ah, no offence. So I do fear for my wife and boys. My dream would be to earn enough scratch to give up the city and head out to the country where it's safer and I don't have to go underground no more. Thanks."

He sat down.

The young scrawny heavily tattooed guy, who'd been bouncing around in his chair since Clark had started, then jumped to his feet even before the applause had died away.

"This is too weird. You're Clark Kent? Wild! Well, get this. I'm Peter Parker. Yes, that's my real name, Peter Parker. It's crazy that Peter Parker is sitting right next to Clark Kent. That is some crazy shit right there. Who's next? Bruce Wayne! Wow. Too weird.

"So I'm a window washer on high-rise buildings. You know, one of the guys who dangles from the swing seat down the outside of skyscrapers. I know that's hard to believe that Peter Parker likes to hang off of tall buildings, but it's a cold hard fact. It's not because I'm trying to be like, you know, Spider-Man. It's more that I kind of like to be by myself, so window washing is a good job if you like working alone."

The group laughed.

"I don't have too many fears. I don't mind snakes. I don't even mind those ugly-ass lizards. But if we're telling truth here, now don't anyone laugh, I really got a hate-on for spiders. They just totally creep me out. Always have. I think my own name fucked with my head. Oops, sorry. But there must be bad karma going down when Spider-Man is scared of spiders.

"So, my dream is to, well, I don't talk about it much. But, see, I really like to cook. You should see the dinners I whip up in my little bachelor. One day, I'd like to work in a restaurant."

He sat down and we, of course, clapped.

The middle-aged corduroy jacket man rose.

"Good evening, all. I'm Professor James Moriarty. Now in case you're wondering why that name is significant, because not everyone in this country is quite as familiar with it, let me point out that Professor James Moriarty is the name of the most diabolical criminal mind in the history of literature. He is the arch nemesis of Sherlock Holmes, the greatest consulting detective in the history of literature. So in the proper circles, my name is utterly infamous. I'm sixty-nine years old, widowed, and a professor emeritus of mathematics right here at Columbia. As you can probably tell from my accent, I was born and raised in England, but grew so tired of the baggage my name still carries in the country of Sherlock Holmes, that we came to America some forty years ago, first to UCLA, and for the last twenty years here to Columbia.

"Due to my name, you might think that I would eschew the Sherlock Holmes canon, but you'd be wrong. Despite my appellation, or perhaps because of it, I fell under Conan Doyle's spell as a boy, and my love of his Holmes stories continues unabated. In my spare time, of which I have much, now that my academic responsibilities are on the wane, I research and write scholarly essays on Sherlock Holmes esoterica. A few have been published in Sherlockian journals.

"I'm sure a few of you might wonder why I don't use my middle name to mitigate this infamy. Well, I'll tell you why. No one in their right mind, particularly a mathematics professor, would ever wish to be called 'Euclid.' Like Mrs. Kennedy, I too lost my spouse prematurely. She died nearly a decade ago and life without her has at times been a formidable challenge. But, like Mrs. Kennedy, here I am.

"I would venture to say that I have two fears. One, deep water. I don't swim. I can't swim. And two, I fear that my cursed name might thwart my admission to the Baker Street Irregulars, the leading society for Sherlock Holmes aficionados, based here in New York, and to which I have tried in vain to be admitted for years. In fact, being accepted into that illustrious society would be my dream."

"You know, Professor, they have swimming lessons here at the Y, just in the basement," offered Jackie Kennedy. "I'm thinking about signing up. They run them on Tuesday afternoons."

"Very kind of you, Mrs. Kennedy, but I think I'll have to work up to that gradually," he replied. "Thank you all for having me here this evening."

I did a mental count while clapping. Six down, three to go. This was taking some time to get through, but everyone seemed interested and fully engaged. I certainly was. It was very cool to meet eight other people who carry famous names. Kindred spirits.

Next up, the youngish Italian/Spanish-looking shy guy.

"Hi. I'm, um, a student at NYU. I'm studying botany, you know, plants and such. I live at home with my parents. Oh yeah, sorry, my name is Mario Andretti. Does everyone know who he is?" he asked.

Hat answered. "We most certainly do! He's one of the greatest American racing drivers in history. I think he was the Indy 500 champion as well as the Formula 1 world champion. Not many have done that. Not many, indeed."

"Right. Well, Andretti is not an uncommon Italian name, especially in Italy, where my parents were born. And, of course, Mario is a very popular first name, even more so in Italy. Anyway, I think Mr. Hemmingway may be on to something when he says we're connected to our famous names in strange ways. You see, the funny thing is, well, it's not that funny to me, but I've failed my driver's test four times and still don't have my licence. I'm a very nervous driver, a very bad driver, I guess."

"Who needs a driver's licence in this city? The subway takes you everywhere, man," said Clark Kent.

"Well, I really want my licence. I really want to drive. When my grandfather died, he left me his bright red 1980 AMC Pacer. You know, the amazing car that Mike Myers drove in the *Wayne's World* movie. I've spent five years restoring it, and, man, it is beautiful. I just can't drive it and that really bugs me. Anyway, my major fear is, obviously, driving. My dream of course is to pass my driver's test so I can pull the tarp off the Pacer and, like, hit the road."

"You really think the Pacer is an amazing car?" asked Peter Parker, clearly perplexed by the idea.

"I guess it's a matter of taste. But I know it's the car for me," replied Mario.

Applause. Then the tall big-boned black woman stood. Her dark hair was closely cropped, and she wore dangly gold hoop earrings.

"Hi, I'm Diana Ross, and yes, I can sing, but only when in the shower or under the influence of alcohol. I work in human resources at the NYPD. I get along well with everyone, but I think I pay for being so good-natured. A lot of my colleagues at the office like to have fun with my name. Kind of like Clark's experience. It never seems to get old for them but it's been old for me since I was about thirteen. And because I don't appear to mind, it just keeps on happening. I have heard them all. And I'm telling you, it is getting tired, and I am getting tired!

"The current thing is for them to hurl lyrics from Diana Ross songs in my face, just for the hell of it. This morning I was walking by the accounting department and an older guy who works there just up and said, 'Stop, in the name of love.' You know, holding up his hand and all. Then he laughed himself into a coughing fit so bad, I almost called the paramedics. The other day on my way to the bathroom, someone else popped up with 'Do you know where you're going to?' So I just pointed to the bathroom and kept walking. Anyway, that kind of thing happens a lot.

"Singing on stage is probably my greatest fear, unless of course Johnnie Walker is supporting me. I just get paralyzed. But my dream is to be able to sing in public one day, when I'm still sober enough to drive. This is fun being here. Thanks for listening."

Clap, clap. The last member of our little group, the well-dressed youngish black woman, stood up.

"Good evening. This has been fascinating so far. I had no idea there were so many people with famous names living in New

York. I'm Jesse Owens, and I'm a dentist. I run a clinic in the part of Harlem that's still kind of rough. I grew up as an only child in a nice, reasonably affluent urban neighbourhood here in New York. My father was a doctor. His much older cousin was the great Olympian Jesse Owens himself. When my dad was old enough to read about it all, he was just so proud of his cousin for sticking it to Hitler at the Berlin Games. Whether I'd been born a boy or a girl, I was going to be named Jesse. I lettered in three different sports at university and was an All-American soft-ball player. I've always loved sports.

"I've been close to a couple of other famous people and have seen how it changes their lives, and not usually in a good way. My second cousins are the hip-hop brother-and-sister stars J Flash and Cara Tune. Some of you may know them. They can't even go out on their own any more. It's sad. That's why I'm happy it's only my name that's famous. None of us here has real fame. We just have what I call 'namefame.'"

"Your cousins are J Flash and Cara Tune?" asked Mario. "That's incredible. I love their stuff."

"Second cousins. Yeah, they are good, aren't they?"

I'd never heard of them. But then again, James Taylor and Neil Young were more my speed.

"Anyway, my dream is to expand my dental clinic into a full-blown community health centre. The families who live in the area are having a tough time making ends meet, and it would make their lives a lot easier if they could come to one building to deal with anything and everything related to their health. It's going to take a lot of work and a lot of money, but that's the dream."

She paused for a moment and then continued.

"My fear is a simple one, that I'll die alone with my dream unfulfilled."

She sat down to more polite clapping.

"Am I too late?" asked a breathless voice by the door. "I hope not. I got here as soon as I could."

I had seen this woman somewhere before. She was very familiar. Lovely southern accent, too.

"Hello, you're just in time to introduce yourself," I said as I waved her into the one remaining empty chair. "And tell us one fear and one dream. We're just getting to know one another."

I could see that she recognized me as well.

"Oh, hi again! Fancy meeting you here."

I still hadn't quite placed her but I knew I'd recently met her.

"Yes, nice to see you again," I bluffed. "Come and join us. The floor is yours."

"Okay, then. Hello. I'm sorry I'm late. I'm from the south and have recently moved to Manhattan and opened a café-bakery."

"Marie! You're Marie!" I nearly shouted when her name finally dropped into my brain box.

"Yes, that's right. You've got a good memory. My name is Marie . . ."

"Antoinette! You must be named Marie Antoinette," I interrupted. "It all makes sense now."

I put on a self-satisfied look, feeling pretty good about my powers of deduction.

"That's right. I am Marie Antoinette, and I own Let Them Eat Cake!, over on Bleecker. And making a go of that, well, that's my dream. I don't actually mind my rather ridiculous name any more. I've always tried to embrace it. For instance, look at the name I chose for my café-bakery. Yeah. Embrace the name. That's my philosophy."

She noticed Peter Parker looking perplexed.

"Okay, here's the quick hit. Marie Antoinette was the Queen of France around the time of the French Revolution. When told that the peasants had no bread, she apparently replied, 'Let them eat cake!' After the revolution, the people remembered and she was sent to the guillotine. I know it probably seems harsh to y'all, but those were the times."

Man, I could listen to her melodic southern voice for a very long time.

"Anyway, I just moved up from my home in Baton Rouge. So I'm new to the city and I don't know too many people. I stumbled across the ad and thought I might as well meet some fellow New Yorkers with famous names. And here I am.

"As for fears, well, I don't really think I have a burning one, other than the failure of my business, of course. I try to keep my eyes, my mind, and my heart open, but I sometimes worry that I might miss something while I'm so focused on other things, like baking cakes. My dream is quite simply to live long, and do lots."

"I thought you were about to go all Vulcan on us there," I joked.

"Well, I do hope to prosper, too."

I stood up again.

"Well, it sure went fast, but it looks like our hour is just about up. Can I just say that this has been wonderful for me. I never dreamed that nine other people with famous names would show up. I'm amazed. Jesse said something that really struck me a few minutes ago. She said we don't have fame, we just have 'namefame.' What a perfect word to describe our, um, affliction. I move we call our little group NameFame. All in favour?"

Ten hands shot up.

"Motion carries. We've just made our first decision. Another housekeeping matter before we break up. I was asked by the staff here at the Y if we'd like to register a team in the Y softball league that plays across the road in Central Park on Thursday nights. I don't know if there are any baseball fans in the room, other than Jackie, here, and of course our varsity star, Jesse, but if you like, with the number of people we have, we could actually put in a team and tonight is the deadline. It's all co-ed and just recreational. Just for fun. We could meet here a bit earlier on Thursdays, have our meeting, and then head to the park to play some ball. And the games only run for the summer."

"I'm in!" said Jesse Owens nearly before I'd finished.

"Me too," chimed in Hat and a few others.

We kicked it around for a few more minutes and in the end, much to my surprise, everyone agreed. In fact, Diana, Peter, and Clark were arguing over infield positions. I had just asked because I was instructed to by the Y community liaison co-ordinator. I certainly wasn't expecting the group to say yes, other than Jesse. Even Jackie said that while she didn't feel she could play, she'd be there to cheer us on and heckle the other team. As required by the Y, I then collected mailing addresses from everyone for the team list to go along with the email addresses they'd already provided.

"Okay then. A second decision made. I'll register the NameFame softball team tonight. I'll send around the team list to everyone so we can stay in touch. We can meet here next Thursday, same time. Believe it or not, the games start next week, too. In our second meeting, I thought we could talk about a model I've been kicking around that might make it easier for us to identify the different kinds of people who have famous names. I think you'll find it interesting and it might help us all think about how we're affected. We can categorize ourselves and see if it works."

"Intriguing," said Professor Moriarty.

"I'll certainly be here. No doubt," Hat chimed in.

It was time to sum up and bring our first meeting to a close.

"Look, I want to thank you all for taking a chance on this. I had no expectations of anyone showing up, yet here you all are. We all have something in common. And it's hard in this city to meet ten people in one place who all have something in common. I hope this is the start of something fun and interesting for us all."

"Thanks for bringing us together. I gotta say, this is kind of cool," replied Jesse Owens.

"Just before we go, I baked cookies," said Jackie Kennedy as she pulled a tin from her bag and passed it around.

"And, please do not forget, I still have butterscotch!" Hat added.

Something happened in the twenty minutes that followed before everyone went their separate ways. The somewhat formal structure of the meeting gave way to clumps of casual conversations, and the real bonding began. We seemed to have taken a few fledgling steps toward "one big happy family" by the time I restacked the chairs, turned off the lights, and locked the door. That's the power of common ground and shared experiences.

Mahatma Gandhi, Clark Kent, Peter Parker, Jesse Owens, Diana Ross, Professor James Moriarty, Jackie Kennedy, Marie Antoinette, Mario Andretti, and, of course, Earnest Hemmingway, all in the same room. Who knew?

Before leaving the Y, I met again with the community liaison coordinator to submit our baseball registration and find out about our jerseys, the schedule, game rules, and the team registration fee. The fee wasn't a lot of money, so I just paid it. I didn't really like the sample jersey she showed me so I cooked up a plan that would save the Y the expense of producing our jerseys. She was happy and so was I. I called one of the designers from Macdonald-Clark on my way home and she agreed to help. It would be simple, but would still have to be a rush job.

As agreed, the next morning, Friday, I boarded a flight bound for Chicago. I wasn't looking forward to the trip. I never looked forward to Chicago.

CHAPTER 5

When I left home for college, I didn't stray far. I studied business at DePaul University, right in downtown Chicago. I lived in residence my first year, but then moved into an apartment with a couple of friends after that. The business program was not my first choice, or my second, third, or fourth. But my father was paying the freight and held quite strong views on the matter. I had learned to pick my battles. Students enrolled at DePaul's Driehaus College of Business were permitted to take several electives over the four-year program. I didn't clear these non-business courses with my father. Had I sought his approval on them, there probably would have been a battle. Since I didn't, there wasn't. I guess I won that one. Over the years, every elective I took was either in English literature or creative writing. My father would not have approved. His idea of literature was board minutes and annual reports.

It was a hassle to race from my business classes in the Chicago Loop, where Driehaus was situated, up to my English lit and writing courses at the Lincoln Park campus. But I would not have survived an undergraduate business education any other way. I had what you might call a *binary* college experience. There was no middle ground. I hated my business courses. I loved my artsy electives. My emerging passion for the latter ensured my survival in the former, but just barely. Writing had always lurked in the back of my mind. But my English lit and writing courses shoved it front and centre, where it has remained. I also played intramural softball. Modesty aside, I was a reasonably solid player. I roamed the outfield for three of my four years at DePaul. I could swing the bat, too. It was a welcome distraction from my heavy business course load.

After I graduated, my father was interested in having me join Hemmingwear to kick-start the business apprenticeship that would ultimately see the reins of power passed from EH3 to EH4, a.k.a. me. Did I say my father was *interested*? More like *obsessed* and *possessed*. But I had other plans. When I told him I wanted to pursue graduate studies, he was initially quite happy.

"Well, if you don't want to join me in the business right now, an MBA will serve you well when you eventually take over here. Yes, I think it's a fine idea," he said.

Given that I'd just graduated with an undergraduate degree from a respected business school, I understood why he'd naturally assumed I'd meant an MBA. When I explained that I wanted to do an MFA instead of an MBA, still, he was tentatively pleased. Ignorance sustained this pleasant misunderstanding for a few more minutes.

"So it's a master's in finance and administration?"

I shook my head. When I finally clarified that I intended to pursue an MFA in creative writing, he was no longer "tentatively pleased." And his displeasure certainly wasn't at all tentative. In fact, he started vibrating just a little and had to sit down.

"Tell me it doesn't stand for a master of fairy arts," he grumbled, maintaining remarkable enunciation through grinding teeth.

Fairy arts. Good one, Dad. My father has never been celebrated for his enlightened thinking or his sparkling wit.

"Master of fine arts, actually," I explained.

"Well, it's not *fine* with me!"

But somehow I'd been resolute throughout the great MFA debate, now more than seventeen years behind us. My desire to write helped me endure that difficult waltz with my father. It made it easier that Dad was still in his prime as a business leader. He hadn't been anywhere near ready to give up his position at the top of Hemmingwear. So what did it matter if I carried on studying while he carried on running the company? Seemed like a win-win to me. So in the end, my father picked his battles, too.

When we'd finally agreed that I'd move to New York as a creative writing graduate student at Columbia, he'd poked my sternum with a stiff index finger and simply said, *"Paramount and sacrosanct."* It had been difficult to keep my head from nodding in agreement when he'd said it. Nodding, or worse, repeating the phrase to him, seemed a natural reaction at the time. But with all my strength, I'd kept my head fixed in space, like it was stuck fast in an invisible vise, and just let the silence hang between us.

I loved my time at Columbia, each and every minute. Two whole years to concentrate completely on literature and writing without ever even giving passing thought to the fortunes of The Hemmingwear Company. It was a gift. Okay, a gift from my father, I guess. When I started, I wasn't convinced I could actually learn to be a better writer. I feared that crafting timeless words, sentences, and stories might only come through pure alchemy. While dashes of alchemy certainly help, by the end, I really did feel I'd become a better writer. Those around me even agreed. I had learned from, and been inspired by, wonderful faculty and classmates alike. I truly wished the program had been five years.

Though we never spoke openly about it, I'm convinced that my mother had a hand in getting me to Columbia. She was always there for me, without betraying her husband, of course. She was the buffer, the mediator, the great ameliorator. She seemed to have a sixth sense about when and how to intervene to stop my relationship with my father from careening off the rails. I don't think I really understood the quiet but pivotal role she played throughout those years until she was no longer there, no longer alive, to play it. More than anyone else, she understood our family's complex chemistry, and how to render the explosive inert. I missed her. I'm sure my father missed her. He must have. It's just hard to tell. Without her, his edges hardened. There was no need for pretense any more. After she passed away, for my father, it became all about the family business. Who am I kidding? It was always all about the family business. Paramount and sacrosanct.

———————

My flight landed on time at O'Hare around eleven. I picked up my rental and drove. The Hemmingwear Company was located where it had always been, since 1916, out on the industrial lands adjacent to the rail yards. It took me only about forty minutes to drive there. I parked in a designated visitor's space, hyperventilated briefly, and walked in to reception.

"Welcome, EH4. Good to see you. You're expected upstairs. Your father is waiting," said Abby, the long-time Hemmingwear receptionist and an old friend.

"Do I really have to go right up, Abby?" I implored. "Couldn't I visit with you for a while, or with my sister, or with that person I've never seen before watering the plants over there?"

"That's Kyle. He's an outside contractor. He talks to the plants, but he doesn't talk to anyone else around here."

"Well, there you go. I'll take that challenge!"

"Hem, the big man is waiting for you. Better go on up. Besides, his office overlooks the parking lot. He probably saw you drive in and is wondering what's keeping you."

I heard a faint buzz as a light flashed on the complicated-looking telephone console that could have passed for the space shuttle's instrument panel. She pushed the lit button and swung the headset microphone closer to her mouth.

"Yes, sir," she answered while frowning at me. "Yes, sir, he has indeed arrived. He's just tying his shoe and he'll be right up."

She smiled but pointed up the stairs to the executive suite.

"Dead man walking," I said as I shuffled down the corridor toward the staircase. Abby smiled.

Just at the top of the stairs, Sarah was peeking around a door jamb.

"Sarah, just the person I wanted to see," I said.

She grabbed my arm and dragged me into a rather small and spartan office as far from the action as one could be while staying in the same zip code.

"This is your office?"

"Yeah, what about it? It's fine," she replied. "Have you seen Dad yet?"

"Nope, just on my way up. But give me two minutes on MaxWorldCorp. Dad had someone email me our financials and some other noise about the competition, but I didn't have a chance to read it. Rather, I forgot to read it. Rather, I didn't want to read it. What's up on the competitive front?"

"You've got no time, so just listen. You already know that MaxWorldCorp has been trying for years to acquire Hemming-wear to consolidate their global leadership. Their mercurial CEO, Phillip Gainsford, is obsessed with us. He wants Hemmingwear and he wants it bad. MaxWorldCorp has grown significantly in recent years through aggressive acquisitions. They're big on most other continents, particularly Europe, but they're having a tough time gaining much of a foothold in the North American space, largely because we're in the way. So they'd love to make a play for us. They actually have a pretty good underwear line here in the U.S. now, but with nowhere near the market penetration we have. So they're hungry to swallow us, whole."

"Let me guess. Dad won't even let the conversation get out the gate. Right?"

"Right. He shuts it down every time."

"And?"

"So lately MaxWorldCorp has taken a different path. They've started a price war but only on those products that we manufacture. They're trying to weaken us, drive our margins and profits into the ground, separate us from the herd, run us down, and then pounce on their struggling prey."

"Wow, quite the graphic metaphor. Do you watch the National Geographic Channel a lot?"

"Focus, Hem. He's waiting," she said, guiding me back out into the hall. "MaxWorldCorp has us locked in a war of attrition. But because their product line is so much broader than ours, they can afford to suck up price cuts on those few products that compete against our line, but it really hits us hard. Now, go. And don't forget why you're really here."

I knew why I was there. I may not have read the stuff my father had sent me, but I had spent a few sleepless nights figuring out what I was going to say. I just didn't know how he was going to react.

As I approached, I could see him standing in the doorway of his large corner office, no doubt in search of his AWOL son. His long-time secretary, Irene, an older, heavy-set woman, waved at me as I passed by.

"Dad."

"Ah, EH4 has finally arrived." He stepped forward and shook my hand as if we were meeting for the first time.

"Dad, when you call me that, it sounds like you're referring to a fighter jet or a sports car. 'The EH4's rack and pinion steering and sport-tuned suspension make it a driver's dream.'"

Not even the hint of a smile. So much for breaking the ice. He just waved me into his office and closed the door behind me. He pointed to the two ugly mismatched chairs in front of his desk. I sat in the one that looked marginally more comfortable and instantly, for the first time in days, was reminded of my badly bruised tailbone. But the empty chair beside me was worse. Like a machine gunner in a concrete pillbox, my father took his power position in an elevated chair behind a massive oak desk.

I looked around the office. Sarah was right. The wood panelling. The wooden desk. The small board table. The green blotter. The thin-cushioned couch and spindly end tables. The coffee table. The ashtrays, yes ashtrays! The artwork. The carpet. The complete absence of any electronic device more advanced than an early Touch-Tone telephone. Yes, she was right. I seemed to have slipped through a slit in the space-time continuum and emerged in 1962.

"Welcome home. I'm heartened you're here," he began.

Who says "heartened" in everyday conversation?

"Well, it's been a while since I've visited. How are you, Dad?"

"The business is plodding along. Phil Gainsford is a thorn in my bloody side, but we have corporate longevity and customer loyalty going for us – "

"Not the business, Dad. Not just yet," I interrupted. "I meant, how are *you*? You know, as a member in good standing of the human race."

"I don't really understand the question. My legs work. My hands work. A bowl of Bran Buds keeps me regular. Everything is working just fine, if that's what you mean," he replied. "We just have to keep those bastards from eating our lunch. They seem to be able to respond very quickly to whatever moves we make. They are sharp. So we need to be sharper. Faster and sharper."

The silence that followed was one part uncomfortable, two parts awkward.

"Okay, then. We might as well get to the point. Dad, I have an idea that I think just might end the impasse you and I reached about fifteen years ago. You may have been ignoring or avoiding our little stalemate, just as I have been, but we're not getting any younger, and the elephant in the room is just growing bigger."

Dad said nothing and was staring at his green blotter as if salvation might materialize right there on his desk.

"The fluke of my birth and the burden of my name means that I'm supposed to succeed you in the company. You remind me of that, well, often. I get that. I understand how important 'family tradition' is to you. For me, I try to separate those two words. Family is important. That goes without saying. But I'm less convinced about the tradition part of the equation. Honouring a tradition founded on the serendipity of birth order seems almost, um, arbitrary."

"You think three generations of family leadership in an iconic American success story is *'arbitrary*,'" he almost whispered. He always spoke this way when he was livid. It was a measure of his self-control that he could lower the volume while approaching detonation.

"Okay, okay, I can see that's not quite the right word. Hold on. Let me reframe the question," I skated. "Is family tradition important enough to ruin someone's life? To make someone miserable? To prevent them from pursuing what they truly believe is their path to happiness and fulfillment? And just to clarify any confusion, I am that someone. Is the family tradition really worth all of that?"

"You, son, were a post-war baby. Is that why the concept of duty seems so foreign to you?"

"Dad, you were also a post-war baby," I countered. "I have a sense of duty to my family. That's actually why I'm here. But I have to balance it with duty to myself, and to my own dreams." I laughed when I heard my own words. "Wow. I sound like a Hallmark greeting card."

I stood up not because I wanted to add some drama to my next point but because the pain in my ass really gave me no other choice.

"Dad, let's be practical for a moment. I think there's a way to let this cup pass me by while preserving the family tradition you hold so dear. And I say that with great respect."

"Impossible. That makes no sense, unless you've discovered a long-lost twin brother I knew nothing about."

"No, Dad, but there is a first-born daughter."

In one swift motion, he swivelled in his chair to put his back to me, folded his arms across his chest, and shook his head. His alacrity was impressive. He shut me down in half a breath without even saying a word.

"Hear me out, Dad, please," I said in plaintive mode. "Just listen. Sarah finished first in her business undergrad. She finished first in her MBA class at Northwestern. I repeat, in case that didn't register, she placed first at Northwestern! You may not have noticed, but she turned down the world so she could come back to work here. This is where she wants to be. This company is as important to her as it is to you, if you'd just take a moment to notice. She's twice as smart and three times as tough as I am. She is driven to succeed, to make Hemmingwear succeed. She just needs you to give her a chance. Why not give her a shot in finance, let her spread her wings a bit. I think you'd be impressed with what she can do."

"Hem, she's got all she can handle in, in . . ."

"Marketing, Dad. She's in marketing."

"I know where she is. I put her there! And she's being pushed to the edge of her capabilities already. She needs more time before she can tackle anything more challenging."

"Come on, Dad. She's a marketing expert. You know that. And she's already developed a detailed analysis of the competitive landscape and mapped out a vision for the future of company."

"How presumptuous. How precocious," he said while gargling sarcasm. "I can only imagine what she's come up with."

"You shouldn't have to imagine it. She gave you a copy. Have you not read it? It's quite an impressive document."

"Look, son, I've got a lot on my plate right now, as you should know. I gave it to Henderson to review. That's the more appropriate reporting line and a more effective allocation of resources."

"You didn't even read it?"

"Well, what did *you* think of it?" He hurled the question at me like it was a lawn dart.

Great. Pinioned by my own lawn dart. Of course I'd never seen the document. I do have my limits. But since he clearly hadn't read it either, escape seemed possible.

"Well, I found it to be thoughtful, enlightening, informed, and very creative. It effectively balances respect for how we've always operated with the innovation these competitive times demand."

Not bad, I thought.

Dad just sighed.

"She's just so young!" he snapped, swivelling back to face me.

"She's twenty-seven! You were already a VP by her age, according to family lore," I said, getting a little heated. "Dad, is it the 'young' part or the 'she' part that sticks in your craw?"

I was getting close to the line, or perhaps had already crossed it.

"You have not presented a viable option. Sarah as a future CEO is not in the cards. That is not the plan. That has never been the plan!"

"Dad, please. Think about what I've said. Think about Sarah and what this means to her. Besides, testicles are overrated."

Dad winced at the genital reference, but I just barrelled ahead.

"Not having them isn't a good enough reason to pass over Sarah's skills, brains, knowledge, and drive. Not nearly a good enough reason. I implore you to think this through. Not only is this a viable course, it's a much better plan than yours," I insisted. "I'm not CEO material, family tradition or not. So, Dad, if *your* plan includes me coming back here, then I'm sorry, you really don't have a plan at all."

My heart was pounding. With all the resolve I could muster, I kept my eyes fixed on his. He looked like he was about to say something. He opened his mouth a couple of times, but closed it again before any words escaped. He finally turned away. I stood up. My work there was done, for now.

"Um, I gotta go. I'll see you at home later, Dad," I said as I left the room. I wanted to discourage him from coming after me, so I closed his door on my way out.

A good-looking youngish guy, dressed in a dark blue suit with an open-neck light blue Oxford button-down, was heading into the office next to my father's. I pegged him at mid-thirties. He stuck out his hand.

"EH4, I presume," he said as he clenched my hand in a grip more suitable for dangling me from a helicopter.

"You must be the famous Henderson Watt," I grunted, trying to bluff my way past the pain coursing through my right hand. "Does everybody around here use the annoying EH short form?"

He just chuckled. I'm not sure why, but that's what he did. When I eventually repatriated my hand, it felt a half-size larger and throbbed like I'd hit it with a hammer in a cartoon.

"So, COO at such a young age. Congratulations," I offered.

"Thanks. I've learned so much from your father. We seem to make a great team, and I really think we're on the right track."

"Good. I hear that MaxWorldCorp is giving us a run for our money these days," I said.

"Not to worry. We've got them right where we want them," he replied with a smile.

"That's funny, Sarah tells me we've got them right where *they* want *us*."

"Funny line. Don't worry. Trust me, we're in good shape. EH3 and I have been working on some big initiatives that we'll be able to share with you when they're a little closer to fruition. You understand, of course."

"Of course, but I've already got a copy of Sarah's strategy document. Is that what you mean?" I asked, knowing pretty well how he'd respond.

"No, I'm afraid not. Hers was a reasonable if rudimentary first effort, but it's a long way from being much of a guide for actual corporate decision-making. She's coming along very well in marketing. You know, getting her feet wet, testing out the training wheels, learning the ropes and all, but it's a long road, right?"

"Seems even longer with mixed metaphors."

He looked puzzled.

"Sorry, you lost me," he said.

"Yes, I know."

———

I popped into the huge Hemmingwear manufacturing facility on my way back to the car. I climbed up to the mezzanine that gave me a great view of both lines spitting out men's underwear at the far end of the building and packaging it at an amazing rate. It was quite loud, so he didn't hear me approaching. He looked lost in very unhappy thoughts, propping his head up with his left hand while holding on to the mezzanine railing with the other. I put my hand on his shoulder. He jerked away, startled, before lifting his eyes to mine.

Carlos Mendez broke into a grin and spread his arms wide open. I gave him a hug.

"Geez, you scared the crap out of me," he said. "So you've come back to us, oh great EH4."

"Good to see you, Carlos. I didn't mean to scare you," I replied. "Do you not age like the rest of us? You look good."

Carlos pretty well grew up at Hemmingwear. His mother worked for most of her life in the plant. His father had died in a car accident not long after the family moved up to Chicago from Mexico. Hemmingwear became Carlos's second home. His mother worked very hard, learned English, and insisted Carlos study hard so he wouldn't have to work in a garment operation his whole life. There's an irony. Carlos not only went to school, he excelled. Yet he's never worked anywhere else. He did his MBA at Harvard, on a full scholarship. He didn't top his class, as Sarah had. He placed third. Through it all, he worked at Hemmingwear, long after his mother retired and passed away. At fifty-eight, he'd been director of manufacturing operations for the last decade, with no signs of slowing down.

Carlos knew this place inside out. Hemmingwear was still a non-union shop, due largely to Carlos Mendez. He was the voice of the workers, and he had my father's ear, at least he used to. The company's history of success had been partly built on the premise that if you treated your employees fairly, and occasionally generously, they would reciprocate with hard work and loyalty. It was a simple formula. But following it was seldom simple at all. Somehow, Carlos had made it work for a very long time.

"I'm too damn busy to age," he replied. "The competition

has got us hopping. We're always trying to stay one step ahead. But every time I look over my shoulder, they're right behind us and closing fast."

"Can we stay ahead?"

"Well, your sister and I have been down on the lines searching from stem to stern for efficiencies that can help get our production time and costs down a bit. As well, we're looking into 'just-in-time' delivery of some of our input materials so we don't have to warehouse so much. It costs money to carry a big warehousing operation. If we could close Warehouse 2 and get along with Warehouse 1 alone, that would save some dough, too. There's also a bunch of other smaller changes we could make. All of this will translate into better margins, or give us the room to lower prices, without affecting profit."

"So, what's EH3 saying about your changes?"

"That's the thing. I don't know. Ever since the whiz kid showed up as COO, I rarely get to see your father. Everything has to go through Watt."

"Okay, so what's he saying about your ideas?"

"Not too much. I get a lot of 'leave it with me' but very few green lights."

"Hmmm."

"If we can't get approval on these small changes, we're never going to be able to do some of the bigger stuff Sarah has been cooking up," Carlos said, shaking his head. "You know, you've got one smart sister, Hem."

"I know that. You know that. Why doesn't anyone else around here know that?"

Carlos just shrugged.

"So what do you really think of this Henderson Watt dude?" I asked.

Carlos looked off into space for a few beats. His face clouded and he looked older all of sudden.

"All I can say is that I've been doing a lot of soul-searching lately, thinking through my options, you know?" Carlos said. Then he seemed to catch himself. "My mother always taught me to keep my yap shut if I had nothing good to say about somebody."

Carlos mimed zipping his lips. Then he squeezed my shoulder and headed slowly down the metal stairs onto the floor of Line 1. That was odd. I'd never really seen him like that. He looked so . . . tired and sad.

———————

Saturday morning, I awoke in the bedroom and in the bed of my childhood. Nothing had changed. The Chicago Blackhawks poster was a little more curled at the edges, but still it clung to the wall. My Hardy Boys books were still there lined up on the bookshelves above my desk. I knew if I opened the desk drawers, all the stuff I'd stashed growing up would still be there. I left them closed. It felt very strange to be in my old room. I had good memories of my childhood. I got three squares a day, and never wanted for anything. Dad wasn't exactly Ward Cleaver in the father department, but I just thought it was normal for him to be at the office all day every day, and exhausted when he finally made it home for dinner, usually after we'd eaten. In my mind, early to bed, early to rise makes a man healthy, wealthy, and largely absent from his son's life. But I knew nothing else. And my mother was always there, always.

As an only child, at least until I was a teenager, my room was a sanctuary for me. I would listen to the Blackhawks games on the radio, read, make forts, build things, and assemble plane models until the glue made me dizzy. One afternoon, just for something to do, I took the back off my clock radio, detached the speaker, then ran wire under the carpet so I could put the speaker on the other side of the room, high up on top of the window frame. There was no good reason for this. I did it because I could. I just liked the idea of turning on the radio next to me on the nightstand, but hearing the sound coming from a completely different location. Okay, that does sound a little weird in retrospect. Back then, I thought it was cool.

I leaned down and turned on the radio, for old times' sake. It took a minute for the tubes to warm up, but soon the faint strains of music drifted down from the speaker still stationed atop the window frame.

My father had left me a brand-new Hemmingwear two-pack on the desk in my size. I wasn't sure if he were just showing me the new packaging design or giving me two free pairs of underwear. I assumed he was killing two birds with one stone, so I pulled on a new pair. Very comfortable, and I'm not just boosting the brand. One of the reasons Hemmingwear has hung around for so long in a competitive market, where longevity is quite rare, is that the underwear just feels so good when you pull it on. What a surprise! A timeless and simple formula that still works. Product quality and comfort sell underwear.

Sarah had left for a dinner by the time I'd emerged from my little encounter with my father the day before, so we'd arranged to meet at a Starbucks not far away on Saturday morning. She lived in a very nice condo about a ten-minute drive from the family homestead. True to form, my father had risen and left for the office before I had even stirred. Just another Saturday morning for EH3, which was just about the same as any other morning of the week. I confess I was a little relieved to find myself all alone in the family kitchen when I finally made it downstairs.

When I met Sarah an hour later, she was peeking through the front window of the Starbucks. She saw my approach reflected in the glass and turned.

"We'll just stand here and wait for a minute. Trust me," she said.

"Why don't we just go insi – "

She held up a Stop-sign hand.

"Bear with me and just stay where you are. It won't be long."

Two seconds later the front door opened and a rather large, older woman dressed in what Sarah told me later was a Lululemon outfit of some kind intended for someone with much less . . . dimension. Following her out the door were her two tiny long-haired dachshunds. They weren't much bigger than large hamsters. I actually like hamsters. But these were dogs, small dogs, and that made all the difference in the world. I took two quick steps away from the door, giving them a wide berth.

"Okay, the coast is clear," Sarah said as she held the door for me.

"That was very considerate of you," I replied. "Thank you."

"No worries," she replied. "Haven't you and Dr. What's-her-name figured out your small-dog phobia yet?"

"Well, so far, we've determined that I have an irrational fear of small dogs, and should avoid them at all costs. We haven't exactly cracked the 'why' yet."

"Such penetrating analysis. She obviously can see right inside your mind. I now totally get why you see her twice a week."

"Nice."

"I really think you should ask Dad. He might have some insight. I can ask him if you like," offered Sarah.

"No, don't do that. He already thinks I'm a bit twisted. I really would rather he not know that I'm also still terrified of tiny, harmless dogs," I said. "I just don't think that would help strengthen our relationship right now."

"Okay, fine," she said, holding her hands up in surrender. "So enough about you. How was your little chat with Dad? Can I pack up my office and move down the hall? I thought he might call me last night, but the radio silence continued."

"Well, I'm not sure you should be picking out paint chips just yet," I said. "No matter how clearly I stated my case, he hasn't yet abandoned the idea of me taking over. I used direct sentences that I thought left virtually no room for misunderstanding or misinterpretation. For instance, at one point I believe I said something like:

"'Dad, I have no desire and no plan to return to Chicago to take over your position, notwithstanding family tradition. I'm not equipped for the role. I have no interest in the role. It wouldn't be good for the company if I were to take on the role. I have other plans. Sarah is the much better choice, and she's just as much a Hemmingway as I am.' Or words to that effect.

"I don't think I could have been any clearer. I was quite purposely using English as a blunt instrument. Yet, somehow, he came back with:

"'So you're still thinking it over.'

"I'm not making this up," I assured her.

"I know. I've seen it, too. It's a blind spot, all right."

"Oh, I think you're shortchanging it to call it a blind spot," I commented. "It's much bigger than a 'spot.'"

"Okay, okay. But what did he say when you suggested I might be the answer?"

"Well, here's the thing. I made a very strong case to move you into a leadership role with the ultimate goal of you taking over. I talked about how brilliant and tough and dedicated you are. I told him you're so much better prepared to do this than I ever will be. And that this is your dream."

"But . . ." she prodded.

"But he's not convinced you're ready."

"Yeah, well, he'd say I was ready if I had a penis," she blurted.

"Uh boy, here we go," I said in mid-wince. "Sarah, why don't you stand up and shout that a little louder. The woman who just headed into the bathroom may not have caught that."

Sarah was not happy after I briefed her fully on my session with Dad. Not happy at all. We sat in silence for a few minutes.

"Okay, so tell me in a nutshell, what is your grand vision to ensure Hemmingwear's prosperity and stave off the very aggressive folks from MaxWorldCorp?"

Sarah sighed.

"You really want to hear this?"

"I really want to hear this," I replied, not wanting in the least to hear this. "Actually, it's the last thing I want to hear, but if we're going to crack this nut together, I'd better be in the loop on your vision."

"Okay, in a nutshell, for this plan to work, we need to violate one of the sacred operating principles Dad has clung to for far too long," Sarah said. "For the first time in Hemmingwear's history, we spice up the waistbands with better branding and a little colour, and then we add a new product line. Hemmingwear for women."

I turned her statement over in my mind, and each time I came to the same conclusion. Yes, she really had just proposed that Hemmingwear start manufacturing women's underwear. Breathtaking.

"Are you deranged? You know exactly how Dad would react. He'd sooner approve a coffee table book on the history of the wedgie in America than give the go-ahead to make women's underwear. You know that!"

"Well, if we can't pull his head from his ass, we'll miss the boat and Hemmingwear will limp along until MaxWorldCorp swoops down and makes Dad an offer he'll no longer be in a position to refuse."

"But what about the efficiency argument? Can we get the economies of scale we need if we double our product line?"

"Look, Hem, think it through. We've got two big, but separate and parallel, manufacturing lines. Both lines operate independently of the other and are at full capacity for two shifts each day. So we add a third shift on Line 2 and run the women's product there overnight, reverting to men's for the two daytime shifts. There should be no loss in efficiency or productivity. We'll be creating another shift's worth of new jobs. We're paying the overhead on the manufacturing lines anyway, so why not spread them out over an additional shift? It actually lowers our per-unit costs. If the women's product takes off as I think it will, we still have the potential to run a third overnight shift on the other line without affecting the dayshift production of the men's product. And we'll be introducing a comfortable, trusted product to what is essentially an untapped market for us. Women want comfortable underwear, too. That's the path to prosperity and sustained market leadership."

There was silence between us for a time as I considered her bold initiative.

"Well, that's some ambitious plan you've got. But before we can get there, we need to cook up an even more ambitious plan for removing our father's head from his ass."

———————

When I finally stepped back into my apartment Saturday night, I was eager to put Chicago behind me and get back to work on the novel. I pulled on my favourite sweats and my L.L. Bean flannel shirt. It's what I always wore when working on the novel. I had to be comfortable. Then I fired up my laptop and opened my manuscript to where I'd last left off. You know, Chapter 12. Then, despite my desire and best intentions, I simply stared at the screen. Finally, I managed to bang out a few sentences, but they were terrible, really quite bad. So I deleted them. I wish the delete key worked on Hemingway's ghost. Alas, no. On a whim, I grabbed every Hemingway book I owned from my bookshelves, stuffed them in an empty box I found in the closet, and took them down to my storage locker in the basement. Perhaps his ghost lives in his books. I felt better when I sat back down at my laptop. But still, no words. I left a message for Madelaine Scott.

CHAPTER 6

"What makes you think Hemingway's ghost is to blame?" Dr. Scott asked as I sat across from her.

"He just seems the most likely suspect," I replied. "I mean, I have no personal connection to the ghosts of F. Scott Fitzgerald or Ezra Pound, now do I?"

"Let me try again. What I'm asking is, don't you think that all on your own, you might be capable of failing to write, of being blocked, without any spectral assistance?"

"I suppose it's possible, but I much prefer the scenario where I'm haunted by Hemingway. That's just what it feels like. He hovers around me, trying to turn my long, flowing, ornate sentences into his simple, barren, boring, First Grade reader prose."

"So resist him. Ignore him. Focus on your story, block out everything else, and write."

"What a revelation! What an innovation! What an epiphany! If only I'd thought of that," I mocked. "Sorry, Doc, I'm kidding.

It's just that, I've been trying to use my powers of concentration for six weeks now, to no avail. That's why I'm here. The mind-over-matter gambit isn't doing it for me."

"Mind over matter? Are you saying there's a physical presence with you in the room?"

"If I say yes, are you forced to send me to Bellevue?"

"Of course not. I'm just trying to understand what you're experiencing," she assured me.

"It's not a physical presence. It's just a feeling that Hemingway is not a fan of my writing and is trying to disrupt it by messing with my head. Does that make sense?"

"I'm really not the one who has to make sense of it, but I think I understand what you're saying," she said and then paused before continuing. "However, beyond the fact that I tend not to believe in ghosts as a general rule, I'm not convinced that there isn't a more earthly explanation. We just have to find the right questions that will draw it out from between your ears."

We kicked it around for another twenty minutes or so before the session was over. I didn't feel any closer to an answer. I just wanted to be able to write.

––––––––

Most of them were there already when I arrived. Some even had ball gloves with them and most wore running shoes. I put the cardboard box I'd carried in with me on the floor next to my chair.

"Hi, Hem. Have a cookie." Jackie Kennedy passed the tin my way.

"Jackie, you've outdone yourself. Oatmeal raisin, my favourite."

She beamed. Everyone else in the room was busy chewing on what really were outstanding cookies.

"I have butterscotch too, Mr. Hemmingway with two Ms, if you like."

"Thank you, Hat. I don't mind if I do," I said as I took the candy he proffered. "Now remember, we have a game in an hour, so let's not eat ourselves into a coma just before we're supposed to take the field."

Five minutes later, everyone had arrived. We had perfect attendance. Marie gave me a little wave and a big smile when she hustled in.

"Okay, we probably only have about forty minutes before we should head to the park. So let's get started. I thought what we might do this evening, if you'll indulge me, is to talk about the various categories there might be of people who live with famous names. I've been thinking about this for a while now and maybe it's helped me come to grips with all of this. So bear with me as I go down my list. Then we can talk about them and add some others if we can think of any more. Okay, see what you think of these."

I stepped up to the whiteboard, uncapped a black marker, and started writing down words as I defined what I meant by each.

"Now, I don't attach values, good or bad, to any of these. These are just categories for us to consider. First, we have the 'Befores.' They are people who had their names *before* someone else made it famous. So, for instance, there were probably plenty of John Glenns back in the early sixties before the astronaut helped that very plain and ordinary name rocket to fame. Pun intended."

I saw a few nods around the room.

"Good one. 'Rocket to fame,'" said Hat, chuckling. "Yes, a very good one."

A few other people were actually taking notes.

"Then we have the 'Afters.' As you can probably guess, these are people either by design, accident, or through ignorance who were named after someone famous. Like our butterscotch-loving friend Hat here. He told us last time that he was named in honour of Mahatma Gandhi. Then we have Clark over here, whose mother, if I recall the story, may not really have known about Clark Kent, the comic book hero, when she named him. Both Hat and Clark would be considered Afters in this little taxonomy. Their name-sakes were already famous."

"When you put it that way, I am very happy being an After," noted Hat.

"Okay, carrying on. 'Projectors' are those who start to emulate their namesakes in appearance, in behaviour, in beliefs, or in some other way, sometimes in ways that are beyond their con-trol or their notice. So, with the greatest respect, Jesse, we might consider that you could be a Projector. You certainly have the athleticism of your famous distant relative, given your collegiate career. And in some ways, you resemble him physically. Um, that didn't come out quite right. I just mean that you have the, um, lean and athletic build of a track star."

"Yes, I can surely see that," Hat agreed, nodding with vigour. Jesse took me off the hook with a smile.

"Well, boys, if you could have seen me at twenty-five, you would definitely have called me a Projector," Jackie Kennedy piped up.

"Madame, I certainly have no difficulty envisioning that," agreed Professor Moriarty.

Jackie Kennedy looked very pleased.

"And I bet you bake better cookies, too," said Peter Parker.

"Thank you, gentlemen. Aren't you kind," she replied. "Well in my books, there's no shame in being a Projector. Okay, what's next?"

"Well, then we have the converse, the 'Rejector.' Those who knowingly or unknowingly seem to reject aspects of their name-sake's character and/or life."

"Why is everyone looking at me?" Hat snapped, leaping to his feet, wild-eyed. Just as suddenly, he sat back down, rocking just a little. "Sorry, sorry. That was not good on my part. I apologize."

I jumped back in before anyone started explaining to Hat why a muscle-bound, temper-prone East Indian man named Mahatma Gandhi just might qualify as a Rejector.

"If Mario doesn't mind me using him as an example, I think he might be considered a Rejector although I think it's unintentional. Mario Andretti has, unfortunately, and not for lack of trying, failed his driver's test four times. The famous Mario Andretti is known as an, um, excellent driver. See what I mean? No offence, Mario."

He smiled and shrugged.

"Okay, I'm watching the clock here, so let me fly through a few more. You're a 'Mask' if you have a famous name but use a non-famous name in everyday life. You're in hiding. And you're 'Out and Open' or 'O&O' if you're living like most of us seem to be, out and open with our famous name. We're living openly."

"Right on!" said Clark Kent, with several others nodding in agreement.

"Here's one I just came up with a week or so ago. A 'Coat-tailer' is someone who actually changes their name to cash in on the profile of someone famous. I think we'd all agree that they would not be welcome here."

"You got that right!" Peter Parker said.

"Yes, I could never in good conscience countenance a Coat-tailer, as you refer to them, joining us here. The subterfuge seems underhanded, unbecoming, and certainly would make one unwelcome among our small society here," observed Professor James Moriarty.

"The bastards!" shouted Mahatma Gandhi as he once again leapt to his feet.

Jesse Owens put her hand on his wrist and gently eased him back into his chair.

"It's okay, Hat. We have no Coat-tailers here. We're all legit," she soothed.

Hat nodded, and smiled at Jesse.

"Okay, just a couple more before we throw open the floor for discussion," I said, trying to get through my list before things got out of hand. "A 'Partial' is someone who only has part of a famous name, like a Brenda Sinatra or a Norman Hitler."

"Man, they have it easy," said a usually quiet Mario Andretti. "How I'd love to be Mark Andretti. My life would be completely different."

"Two more. A 'Carbon Copy,' also known as a 'CC,' is a person whose name is exactly the same, as in carbon copy, of the famous person's name. There are lots of CCs in this room. In fact, I think I'm the only one who isn't a CC. So what am I? Well, I'm a 'Sounder.' My name sounds exactly like the famous writer's name, but I have an extra 'a' in my first name, and an extra 'm' in my last name. I don't think there are any other Sounders in the room, are there?"

We all looked at each other and quickly confirmed that I was alone in this category. I stood back from the whiteboard to admire my handiwork.

"So there you have my first stab at a taxonomy, or classification system, for people who live with famous names," I concluded. "Thoughts?"

Jesse Owens raised her hand to claim the floor.

"All of that makes sense, but I think there's at least one category missing. What about those who have simply given up and changed their name, moved away, and restarted their lives somewhere else? It's not something I'd consider, but I bet it happens quite often."

"Kind of like the witness protection program," added Diana Ross. "Down at the NYPD, we put a bunch of people into that each year, but I guess their names are usually well known for all the wrong reasons."

"I think Jesse has raised an awfully good point," commented Professor Moriarty.

"Agreed. Why don't we call them 'White Flaggers,'" suggested Marie Antoinette with a smile. She seemed to be smiling most of the time. I loved listening to her voice.

"White Flaggers. Not bad," I said. "All in favour?"

"Aye!" came the unanimous response.

I stepped back to the whiteboard and added the new category and definition.

We spent the next half-hour kicking around the various categories and citing examples we knew to help explain them. We then went around the room and tried to categorize each other. For instance, we decided that I was an "After 'O&O' Sounder." The discussion ranged far and wide with pretty well everyone participating. At one point, I just sat back and watched as the group batted around ideas. I looked up to see Marie looking at me and gesturing to the animated discussion with a kind of "look what you've done" smile. I smiled back and shrugged.

It did feel good to hear that others had experienced exactly what I had. The stories shared were always greeted with empathy, because we'd all experienced them. I guess that's why support groups form. It actually seems to work. It makes you feel like you're not alone.

Okay, I know what you're thinking. We're not exactly a group that has suffered at the hands of some malevolent force. We're not the victims of injustice. Nobody has been lined up and shot because they have a famous name. No one has earned less than a colleague doing the same job because of a famous name. No one has been detained by the police or imprisoned without trial because of a famous name. In other words, I don't think we'll be organizing a TV telethon or a star-studded NameFameAid benefit concert to raise money for our so-called cause. After surveying the group, I seem to have had the experience that outraged the group most when I was briefly denied a driver's licence. No, a telethon was not in the cards.

"Okay, folks, we've got to get over to the park for our ball game. We can continue our discussions next week, same time, same place. But right now, the moment you've all been waiting for." I flipped open the cardboard box beside me, pulled out a jersey, and held it out to the group.

The applause was long and loud. Jackie Kennedy slipped two fingers in her mouth and whistled, nearly perforating every eardrum in the room.

The jerseys looked great. Green with yellow trim, like the Oakland Athletics uniforms, with NameFame in the lovely Lucida Calligraphy script font across the front. My friend at Macdonald-Clark had done a great job. The material was soft and comfortable cotton, not the ugly plastic polymer mesh that they usually were. It was worth the effort and expense to upgrade.

I walked the box around the circle doing my best to give each person their choice of size and number.

"Hem, what do we have to pay for these?" asked Peter Parker, the window washer, looking uneasy.

"Peter, this is just one of the benefits that comes with being in this select group," I replied. "Now, you'll notice that we did not go with our own names stencilled on our jerseys. I hope everyone is okay with that."

We walked over as a group to our designated diamond in the North Meadow of Central Park. We gathered along the first base line and I filled out the game sheet with the positions and jersey numbers we'd hastily determined before leaving the Y. Like most rec leagues, you pitched easy under-handers to your own batters and were allowed a fourth outfielder called a rover.

NameFame Starting Lineup

1st Base: Jesse Owens #5

2nd Base: Peter Parker #8

Shortstop: Mario Andretti #2

3rd Base: Diana Ross #4

Left Field: Marie Antoinette #9

Centre Field: Earnest Hemmingway #10

Right Field: Mahatma Gandhi #6

Rover (4th outfielder): Clark Kent #7

Catcher: James Moriarty #11

Umpire Liaison and Senior Cheerleader: Jackie Kennedy #3

I just made up Jackie's position. Even though she wasn't offi-cially a player, I wanted her to feel included in the team. After all, she had her own jersey. I was feeling pretty good about our squad, on paper. Unfortunately, we were playing on a field. Only Jesse, Clark, Peter, Mario, Diana, and I had any real experience playing the game. Jesse was the real standout of our team, hav-ing been a star in college. As a kid, I'd played Little League for five years, so I'd also played my fair share of games. And of course, I played intramural softball at DePaul, though it was clear from the very beginning that the major leagues were not in my future. Marie was game to play but had assured me she would not be an asset and could very well lose us the game if the ball ever came her way. But she was still smiling as she said it. Professor Moriarty and Mahatma Gandhi were the wild cards. They'd both played cricket growing up, but since coming to the U.S. had really only appreciated baseball from the grandstands and on TV. Plus, the professor was sixty-nine and probably wouldn't be tearing up the base paths if his bat ever managed to make contact with the ball.

We agreed that I would serve as our outfield coach, talking incessantly to rookies Marie and Hat on either side of me. As our rover, Clark, who'd played in the subway league a few years back, would float over to whichever field the batter seemed pre-disposed to hit toward. In the infield, Jesse would be our, er, quarterback, making the fielding decisions and shouting the appropriate instructions to whomever had the ball headed their way. Yes, we were very well organized. If only we'd been able to practise our system for, say, three years, we might have been able to make it work on the field. Thankfully, it was only a rec league, where participation and fun were the main goals. At least, that's what the brochure had said.

I walked over to the scorekeeper, who sat behind the home plate screen at a card table, a megaphone resting next to his paperwork. I handed him our game sheet, and waited. Three, two, one . . .

"Is this some kind of a joke?" he asked, waving the game sheet my way.

"No joke. These are all our real names, I can assure you," I explained. "We're a group that meets at the Y to discuss coping strategies for living with famous names. And no, I'm really not kidding. We can all produce ID if you like, but save yourself the trouble. Look at the name of our team. We're legit."

"Okay. Strangest thing I've ever seen. You guys are up first. Seven innings. In this league, we play a ten-run mercy rule in each inning. Everyone on the team has to bat. Got it?"

"Got it."

"Good luck against the Meteors. They're all landscapers here at the park, so they practise a lot on their lunch breaks. They were league champs last year."

"That's just awesome. Thanks."

I headed back to our dugout along the first base line. Communal gloves, helmets, and bats provided by the league were in a bag at my feet.

"Okay, team, gather round. The Meteors are apparently quite good at this game. So keep your head up out there."

I handed out gloves to those who needed them. Hat, our right fielder, refused a glove.

"Hat, I think you're going to want to use one of these. It makes catching the ball much easier," I suggested.

"Mr. Hemmingway with two Ms, I assure you, as an experienced cricket player, I'm much more accustomed to bare-handing the ball. Just make sure you tell me where to throw it when I get it."

With that, he pulled off his pants to reveal bright red Adidas running shorts from the 1970s. I can report that these "shorts" really lived up to their name. They were tight, too. To add to the eye-catching ensemble, he also wore black dress socks and white canvas sneakers probably purchased when he bought the shorts, yes, in the 1970s. I figured he might actually prove to be an effective distraction to the other team's batters.

Everyone else looked good out there on the field, with perhaps the exception of Professor Moriarty, our catcher. He was still in his dress pants and black brogues, a lovely formal contrast to his green and yellow jersey. He also eschewed the glove, citing Hat's cricket rationale. I tried to persuade him that he'd be just like a wicket-keeper in his position behind the plate, so wearing a glove would be okay. No luck.

I pitched for our team. Jesse approached me as the Meteors, in their rather bland black shirts with white trim, took the field.

"I like them low and outside."

The umpire threw me the softball, which was really not soft at all.

"Batting leadoff for NameFame, number five, Jesse Owens," announced the scorekeeper on his megaphone, with all the audio fidelity of a first-generation tin-can telephone.

There were a few titters among the small band of spectators upon hearing our leadoff hitter's name. Jesse stepped into the batter's box. The Meteor catcher held his glove at the ready. I delivered my first pitch. It was definitely low and outside.

"It's not bowling," shouted the Meteor catcher as the ball rolled along the ground on the wrong side of Jesse. There was laughter in the infield.

"Leave him alone, smart guy! It's his first pitch of the season!" hollered a voice from our dugout that could only belong to Jackie Kennedy.

With one pitch behind me, I figured I now had my range. Jesse, a right-handed batter, kept eyeing left field as if she were going to drive the ball right over third base. She even pointed her bat there once or twice during her warm-up swings. The Meteor outfield dutifully shifted toward left field. This time, my pitch headed just where Jesse wanted it, low and outside. She actually shifted her feet, turning slightly to her right, and blasted a line drive out over the first baseman's head into right field. Because he'd already shifted over toward centre field, the right fielder was a long way from the ball when it landed. Jesse was on third when the ball came back in.

Our bench erupted as if we'd won the World Series.

"Now at the plate, number ten, um, Peter Parker."

"Ooooh, my spidey senses are tingling," yelled someone from the Meteors dugout.

"Yeah, like I've never heard that one before," snapped Peter as he took a few practice swings in the box.

He pounded the first pitch right back from whence it came. I had time to turn ninety degrees so the ball struck the fleshy part of my right buttock, side-on. A direct hit. It felt just excellent. I seemed to be having my share of ass injuries in the previous week or so. As I lay there, writhing on the pitcher's mound, the umpire added insult to my injury by calling Peter out because I'd interfered with the hit. I stayed in the game, my right buttock visibly larger than my left. On the bright side, it took my mind off the persistent pain in my tailbone.

"Batting third in the lineup for NameFame, number two, I'm not kidding here, folks, Mario Andretti. You might call him a speed merchant on the base paths."

Pitching to your own team is intended to ensure that each batter actually hits. At least, that's the theory. I'm not sure Mario understood this. I struck him out on four perfect pitches, each of them right in his wheelhouse. Well, it's clear now that Mario doesn't actually have a wheelhouse where baseball is concerned. He would have been out on three pitches, but the umpire generously offered him a fourth strike with no complaint from the Meteors.

"Batting cleanup for NameFame, number four, the supreme Diana Ross."

The scorekeeper was starting to enjoy himself. Diana shot him a look as she walked up to the plate. She took a few tentative practice swings. I pitched. The ball sailed right across the plate as the bat remained resting on her right shoulder. Strike one. The same thing happened on the second pitch. Strike two. This happened three more times, although my pitches were outside of the strike zone, leaving Diana with a full count. She was frozen. I'd seen it before. I waved Diana out to see me and met her halfway to the pitcher's mound.

"Diana, if you can't swing, can you just hold your bat out over the plate?"

She nodded and walked back to the batter's box. She lifted the bat off her shoulder and held it over the plate. I took a couple of small steps closer to the home plate without arousing any reaction from the Meteors. I took careful aim and then bounced the ball off the bat. I was quite pleased with my aim. The ball trickled up the first base line. The catcher had sprinted to the ball, picked it up, and tossed it to first before Diana was even out of the batter's box. In fact, I'm not convinced Diana was intending to leave the batter's box anyway. In the meantime, Jesse was sprinting for home on the full count, two out, pitch. But it was a wasted trip. Diana was out.

"Okay, good first ups, everyone," I chirped. "We've got six more innings to score some runs. There's lots of time."

Actually, there wasn't. But I didn't yet know that as we took our places in the field and the Meteors came up to bat. They were very intense. The mercy rule was invoked after they scored ten runs on ten hits. We failed to get a single out, though Hat almost caught a fly ball. He was backing up to make the catch, his bare hands in perfect cricket position, cupped in front of his nose, when he tripped on a rough piece of turf and fell, landing on his back. As he lay there, the ball struck him in the stomach and bounced harmlessly to the grass next to him. He was not happy. Let's just say a lot of butterscotch was handed out before his equilibrium was restored.

With the score 10–0 for the Meteors, it was our turn to bat again. Marie was up first. She actually hit the first pitch I served up to her. It was a solid hit. I watched the infield roller go by me on the first base side of the mound. The second baseman snatched the ball off the grass with his bare hand and threw Marie out in the nick of time, just before she crossed the half-way point in her dash to first base. It was just that close.

Jesse came in to pitch when we reached my name in the batting order.

"Now batting for NameFame, number eight, he likes hunting, fishing, and bullfighting, the centre fielder, Earnest Hemmingway."

Hilarious. The fans were getting a real kick out of it all.

I glared at the scorekeeper as I made my way to the plate, but he was chortling away at his own comedic brilliance and never noticed.

Jesse threw me a perfect pitch and I swung for the fences. It was a thunderous crack. The ball sailed up and up, and just kept going. I was nearly at second base when the left fielder caught the fly after backing up nearly to the fence. Solid contact, but easily caught. I trotted back to the dugout, leaving Jesse to pitch to Hat.

"Now at the plate, looking overdressed and without his spinning wheel, the right fielder, number six, Mahatma Gandhi."

When I looked up, Hat was screaming and sprinting to the backstop. He smashed his bat against the chain-link fence separating him from the shocked scorekeeper cum comedian. Hat's hollering ceased just as Jesse and I reached him. As we'd come to expect, he'd already caught himself.

"I'm so sorry. I should not have reacted that way. Although, sir, it's a little bit offside to poke fun at someone's name. You don't hear us commenting on your gargantuan and misshapen nose that looks something like an overcooked yam, because that would be rude. Please accept this butterscotch as a token of my shame. It's very sweet and tasty, the candy I mean."

Hat pushed his index finger, his thumb, and the candy through the screen, and then flicked it toward the scorekeeper. It fell short, but Jackie Kennedy had materialized on the scene. She picked it up and placed it on the table in front of him. Then she leaned down, placed her hands palms down on the card table, and lit into the scorekeeper for the next several minutes. Jesse and I left Jackie to her lecture and led Hat back to the batter's box. The umpire and the Meteor's catcher were unsettled.

Hat swung like a cricketer, with the end of his bat pointing down to the ground. It was certainly unorthodox, but he actually made it work, knocking a sharp line drive right into the second baseman's glove to end the inning. He apologized to the score-keeper again before trotting, still gloveless, out to right field.

In the next two hours, Team NameFame set a New York City Y softball league record that I doubt will ever be broken. They called the game after five innings, prompting what has come to be called "the NameFame mercy rule amendment." The additional clause states that if the margin in the score reaches fifty runs, the game is forfeited. Each inning the Meteors batted, they scored their full allotment of ten runs without us once, not even once, getting a single out. We never got a chance to see how Professor Moriarty's bare-handed spell as a wicket-keeper was going to work. He crouched in position very formally, as if he were wearing tweeds, and the batters hit every single pitch. Even the throws to home plate tended to end up rolling around the pitcher's mound, so Professor Moriarty was largely unemployed.

We knocked out a smattering of hits but managed to strand every one of our baserunners. So the game ended after five innings in a 50–0 victory for the Meteors. On the bright side, we were drinking earlier than we would have been had the game gone the full seven innings.

"Well, that was quite a game," I said to my assembled teammates.

We'd gathered in a bar on Central Park West to celebrate our groundbreaking performance. Only Clark had left to get home to his wife and children. The rest of us were drinking draught from the three pitchers on our table.

"Holy shit, those guys were good," Peter said. "Even their girls were good."

"Hey, what's that supposed to mean?" snapped Jesse.

"Oops. That didn't come out right," replied Peter. "I meant that everyone on their team was a star. And on our team, we only have you."

"Nice recovery," Jesse conceded. "Hem's okay, too."

"However, they did seem to take the game a little more seriously than did we," offered James Moriarty. "I was just looking for bit of fun. For our friends, the Meteors, winning the game seemed like their singular mission in life."

"They were jerks," said Diana, who'd already downed three glasses of draught. "Especially the man with the megaphone. I think we should have let Hat go a few rounds with him. Anyway, we got pounded out there."

"We'll turn it around. We'll start to feel more comfortable out there, and our game will get better," I said.

"Hem is right," said Hat. "I'm quite convinced that it would be impossible for our game to do anything else but get better."

"Well, I suppose it could stay the same," suggested Mario.

It was kind of nice just hanging out. The conversations splintered into smaller groups as we got to know one another. Jesse was chatting with Jackie and Mario. Diana was deep in discussion with Hat, Peter, and James, though the professor was casting glances Jackie's way. Marie slid into the seat next to me.

"I think I'm starting to figure you out," she said.

"Hmmm. That sounds ominous."

"You upgraded our uniforms out of your own pocket, didn't you?" She had tilted her head and was smiling, as she usually was.

"What do you mean?"

"I spoke to a few players on the Meteors. They noticed right away that our jerseys were not the standard Y-issue shirts that they were wearing. They said ours must have been custom-ordered."

"Yeah, well, I hate the feel of those scratchy, plasticy, meshy shirts. It's like I'm wearing a garbage bag."

She just nodded.

"You could have just worn a T-shirt underneath. You didn't have to go to the trouble and the expense of ordering us all better jerseys. That was very nice of you."

"No need for the others to hear about . . ."

"Your secret is safe with me. You're a nice man, Hem. But now I've got something on you," she said, grinning.

"So who's running the café-bakery when you're patrolling left field on a Thursday evening?" I asked.

"I have a second-in-command, Tina, who can close up. She's very good. We're not that busy yet in the evenings anyway. We're more of a lunchtime operation, at least for now."

"Is it going well?"

"I knew it would be tough. Running a restaurant in Manhattan is always hard, but we're on track. We're right where we should be at this stage, so I'm encouraged, feeling good."

"That's great. Well, now I have another reason to come by, I mean, beyond the great food, ambience, and service."

She patted my forearm.

"Thanks, Hem. Come by anytime."

During our brief conversation, for the first and only time since the game, I was oblivious to the painful welt on the side of my right butt cheek.

The karaoke had started and Diana Ross was feeling no pain. With a little encouragement from us, and a final shot of tequila, she wobbled her way up to the microphone. She chose her song and waited for the music, and for the lyrics to start scrolling on the monitor. I recognized the intro to Diana Ross's hit from the movie *Mahogany*, "Do You Know Where You're Going To." I kind of thought she might choose a more up-tempo number from any other singer in the world. Then she opened her mouth and the raucous bar fell silent. The rest of us at our table just looked at one another in astonishment. What a voice. It was beautiful, stunning. She never looked at the audience. Not once. She was looking above our heads, focused on the back wall.

We started it, but in the end, the whole bar gave her a standing ovation when the last notes died away. After her performance, no one else went near the microphone for the rest of the night. Diana Ross of the NYPD was a born karaoke killer.

"Well, I guess Diana is what you would call a Projector," commented Marie.

"Yes, I guess she is."

CHAPTER 7

The next week was frustrating and dispiriting. It left me a little unnerved, even a little afraid. It honestly felt like I might not ever be able to write again. Not a good state for the wannabe writer blessed, for once, with time and money simultaneously. I found that I'd actually forgotten how it felt to craft sentences, to find the perfect word, the perfect tense, the perfect construction. The sensation of rearranging the words in a sentence to heighten its impact, its interest, had all but deserted me. No literary laxative could unblock my writing, and I tried many. The Internet was a bottomless well of never-fail cures that in my hands were never-cure fails. I could sense Hemingway's ghost hovering, an oppressive, smirking, sneering presence. I waited for it to speak. But it never did.

I tried a few writing exercises where you're prompted by a phrase. I tried, I did. I even completed a few, but my words, my sentences, sounded like someone else's. I wanted them to sound like mine again. I liked my sentences. I wanted them back. I resaved my manuscript and shut down my laptop, again, as I had the previous six days. The only words I seemed to save on a daily basis were "Chapter 12."

Thursday dawned rainy, although "rainy" seems wholly inadequate to describe what was going on outside. It was the kind of precipitation that made boat-builders feel superior. The rain came down in sheets, switched to buckets for a while, then back to sheets. It was not a good day to be driving. It was an even worse day to be teaching someone to drive. But why stop there? If you were teaching someone who had already failed his driver's test four times, it was the absolute worst of days to be driving. So why not postpone it? Well, even driving underwater was preferable to staring at my blank laptop screen. You see, in a moment of weakness, when my faculties were dulled by beer and the kumbaya camaraderie of the NameFame baseball and karaoke night, I'd offered to help Mario practise for a record fifth attempt at his driver's test. The look of gratitude on his face was worth it. At least until he slipped behind the wheel of my Infiniti G35. I loved that car.

"Okay, Mario. You've got your seat belt buckled, you've set your mirrors, and you're no longer hyperventilating. So let's turn the wipers up to full speed so we can actually see," I suggested. "Um, no, that's the cruise control. Nope, that's the radio. Sorry, Mario, you just turned on the rear window defroster."

I stopped him when he reached for the sunroof control.

"I give up." Mario sighed.

"It's right there on the end of the turn signal arm," I pointed as I said it. "Good. Now we can see. Sort of."

I'd driven us out of town a ways to the burbs. We were in a large, freshly paved parking lot that would be packed with cars just as soon as the several big box stores still under construction opened their doors. But on this particular Thursday afternoon, in the midst of a monsoon, there were no other cars in the lot. Given the deluge, a canoe would not have looked out of place.

"You seem to be stretching a bit for the steering wheel," I observed. "Are your feet anywhere near the pedals?"

"Well . . ." Mario started.

I reached over top of him and nudged the control button on the side of his seat. Mario smiled while the electric motor inched him forward.

"Cool," he said. "Nothing on my Pacer is automatic."

"Okay, say 'when,'" I said and waited while Mario and his seat continued their slide toward the dashboard.

"Okay, I can feel the pedals now!"

"Excellent. That should make it easier for you to control the car. Always a good thing."

Mario nodded, gripping the wheel.

"Okay, let's give it a little gas and drive down to the end of the lot, then you can turn and loop back around to here."

"All right. Here goes," he replied.

Mario pressed down on the accelerator and the engine responded. The rain was coming down hard and loud, so it was tough to see very much. He gripped the steering wheel, making minute adjustments supposedly to keep the car rolling in a straight line.

"Um, Mario?"

"Gee, it's a big parking lot," he noted, looking intently through the windshield.

"Mario, you're still in Park. We're not actually moving yet."

Over the course of the next hour, Mario drove laps of the parking lot, and "drove" is a very generous characterization, while I strained my right quadriceps pushing the imaginary brake pedal on the passenger-side floorboards. If the G35 had a handbrake and not the driver's side foot-activated type, I'd have pulled it at least four times. Mario seemed to have a problem with his perception of speed. And when he realized he was going just a little too fast, usually when my voice moved into a different register, his reaction was to step on the gas rather than lift his foot from it. Eventually, after nearly jumping the parking barriers a few times, he became more comfortable with the concept of moving his foot from the accelerator to the brake, you know, the pedal that makes the car stop.

I'm exaggerating. Okay, no, I'm really not. At one point, I was ready to suggest we practise a bit on one of Mario's Xbox racing games before returning to the parking lot. Collisions don't cost as much on the Xbox. After Mario had been driving for nearly forty minutes, I had him park in an isolated corner of the parking lot so we could go through some of the rules of the road, like no right turns on red lights in New York City, how to position your wheels when parking on a hill, and the importance of driving on the right side of the road. I didn't see the police car approach through the sheets of rain until it pulled up next to us and lowered his window a crack. I lowered mine an inch or two.

"Lower your window so I can see the both of you, please," the older, somewhat puffy, officer asked with a slight edge.

I hit the button and the window sank farther while the rain swept in.

"You boys unable to find a quiet and private place indoors somewhere?" he asked. "You feel the need to cruise empty parking lots? I guess it's cheaper than a room, huh?"

"Officer, I can assure you I was just helping my friend practise for his road test. That's all."

"Well, you been stopped over here in the far corner for the last twenty minutes with your windows fogging up. So I just assumed that your friend was, you know, pulling on your handbrake. Whaddam I s'posed to think?"

"Officer, with great respect, you're supposed to consider other options that are far more likely than two guys making out in broad daylight in a parking lot during a typhoon. Not that there's anything wrong with that," I said.

"And anyway, there is no handbrake in this car," added Mario helpfully.

Officer No More Mr. Nice Guy was not impressed.

"I need the driver's learner's permit."

"Uh boy, here we go." Mario sighed as he passed it to me so I could hand it over to the officer.

The cop burst out laughing as he looked at it, which I think was better than some of the other reactions he might have had.

"No, this cannot be true. You have got to be shittin' me," the officer said, laughing.

"Believe me, I wish I were," Mario replied.

"Yes, I know it seems unlikely and, um, to some, hilarious that a guy with my young friend's name here needs driving lessons, but however far-fetched it sounds, that's really what's going on here," I said. "It's the truth."

"Unbelievable. You can't make this stuff up," the officer said between snorts. "Okay, now I need to see some ID from you as well."

"Is that really necessary?" I asked.

"You got somethin' to hide, smartass? Hand it over."

Fan-friggin-tastic. I took a deep breath and dug for my wallet.

"Officer, I really think giving you my ID is just going to, um, make matters worse." I passed my driver's licence over to him. He studied it for a moment. I watched closely and waited for the expression on his face to change, for the penny to drop, for that particular synapse to spark, for his mind to blow. When all four happened simultaneously, I delivered my standard pre-emptive strike. "No relation."

At first, he accused both Mario and me of, as he so delicately put it, "fuckin' with me." It took three more pieces of ID from each of us and long exchanges on his radio before he was satisfied that we might actually be who we claimed to be. Luckily, I'd managed to reacquire enough of my ID following the lost wallet fiasco to survive the situation. Twenty minutes later, having squeezed all the fun he could out of our entertaining encounter, the police officer finally drove away, bearing his precious cargo, a great story he could hardly wait to tell his colleagues at their post-shift beer-guzzling. We waited until he was out of sight around a bend in the road before switching seats. I drove Mario home.

"I really think I learned something today," Mario said when I pulled into his driveway. "About driving, I mean. Thanks a lot, Hem. I've got no one to help me get better, so that was awesome. Thanks."

"No worries. I could really see improvement by the end," I lied, wanting to be encouraging. "Next time, we'll do it on a sunny day when it'll feel more like driving a car and less like helming a submarine."

As I pulled away, Mario waved from his front porch, so I waved back. Thinking more clearly on the drive home, I wasn't sure there'd actually be a next time. Reviewing our little driving lesson, I realized I'd feared for my life the entire time. Yes, I guess a generous observer might conclude that Mario had improved over the course of our session. But successfully adjusting your mirrors and remembering only once to bring the car to a full stop before ramming the gearshift into Park was setting the improvement bar rather low.

—————

"So how goes the exciting and interesting life of Earnest Hemmingway the fourth?"

Dr. Madelaine Scott was seated where she always was for our sessions, and I was in my regular chair.

"Oh, you know, same old, same old," I started. "I've managed to persuade nine other New Yorkers with famous names to show up for our little weekly pity party at the Y. We lost our first ball game so spectacularly that the *Times* may consider assigning a sports reporter to document our season. For weeks now I haven't been able to put two words together on the novel that make any sense thanks to an arrogant literary spectre who's trying to flatten my prose so much it would bore an entire English-as-a-second-language class. And, wait, there's something else I'm forgetting. Oh yes, I was almost arrested this morning for teaching Mario Andretti how to drive. Otherwise, it's been an uneventful couple of weeks."

"All right, then. I think our work here is done. Thanks for stopping by," Dr. Scott replied.

I just looked at her.

"Hem, I'm kidding. Contrary to popular belief, psychiatrists quite often have a sense of humour."

"Sorry, I just hadn't picked up . . ." I fumbled. "Um, your deadpan delivery was outstanding."

I took the next fifteen minutes or so to bring Dr. Scott up to speed on the NameFame group. I tried to be nonchalant about it all, but I think she noticed the pride I'd gained in the process.

"Congratulations. I confess I was uncertain you'd find anyone to join," she replied. "So what have you learned and how has it made you feel?"

"Well, there was this almost instantaneous comfort knowing there were others in the same position. I could see they felt it, too. There was a sort of kinship among us that surfaced as the meeting continued. It's hard to explain."

"Actually, it's not hard to explain at all," Dr. Scott observed. "Even disparate groups with diverse demography that share an unusual life experience quite often come together very quickly. I'm not surprised at all. It's elemental group dynamics."

"Okay, so maybe it's not that hard to explain. All I can say is, I wasn't really expecting it to unfold that way. It was, you know, nice."

"All right, we have about twenty minutes left, so let's move on to the third party in the room," Dr. Scott proposed.

On instinct I looked around her office.

"Hem, I'm referring to the ghostly presence you believe is thwarting your efforts to write the great American novel. What makes you think the ghost of Ernest Hemingway is haunting you?"

"Okay, I admit it's a little weird. But I can feel him when I sit down to write. He, um, feels big, bold, brash, cocky, manly, and it's like he's taunting me."

"Do you see him or hear him at all?" she asked.

"Of course not. I don't believe in ghosts. I accept that it's all in my head, but his presence feels real enough to stop my brain from assembling words the way I used to."

"You still speak in rather nice flowing sentences," she noted.

"Well, the words may be flowing, unimpaired, from my mouth, but they're certainly not flying from my fingers."

"And what steps have you taken to manage this . . . situation?" she asked.

"Well, I've tried to rid myself of any traces of Ernest Hemingway. All of my books by him or about him, my fisherman knit sweater, my *History of the Spanish Civil War* DVD boxed set, even the Paris etchings that hung in my hallway, are now all in my storage locker," I said. "I've also imposed a personal moratorium on big game hunting on the African savannah, and I've cancelled my subscription to *Bullfighter Quarterly*."

"I see you've been very thorough. But do you think that's a rational response? And even if we accept your premise, are you certain it's Ernest Hemingway and not someone else?"

"Who else would it be?" I replied.

"Who else, indeed?"

"Now that's another one of your cryptic comments designed to turn everything back to me, right?"

"Remember our roles here, Hem," she replied. "My job is to pose questions. Your job is to remember, reflect, and respond. Just because you don't yet know the answers doesn't mean you don't have them."

"That sounds great on paper, Dr. Scott, but I've been scouring my own brainpan for quite some time now and I'm not finding much."

"We're not there yet. But take heart, we're not where we started, either."

———

The torrential downpour rained out our second ball game. I suspect our opponents were more upset about it than we were. Still, all ten of us met at the Y for our third meeting, a few of us wearing our NameFame jerseys. I took it as a good sign that everyone thought it important enough to brave the monsoon to get there. Then, just as we were about to start, two new people arrived. Just like that we were an even dozen.

"Hey, new recruits!" said Jackie Kennedy.

The good-looking couple, a man and a woman in their mid-thirties I figured, looked at us and then at each other. The slim woman with long blond hair had a deer-in-the-headlights look as she scanned the room. The guy with the highlighted layered hair and chiselled jaw looked as if he'd just finished starring in the sequel to *Top Gun*, for which he had been ridiculously highly compensated. He just had that way about him. Though I tried, I could not deny his movie-star good looks, and I could see that all the women in the room were paying close attention. Including Marie.

"Welcome to our humble little group," I said as I stood. "This is the weekly meeting of the group we call NameFame. Are you in the right place?"

"Yes. I just saw the notice in the Y newsletter. Sorry I missed the first two meetings," the blond woman replied. "Should I just take a seat?"

I waved her into the final vacant chair next to Marie and turned to engage the matinee idol. He was running his eyes over the group, lingering on Marie and the new blond woman beside her.

"Um, are you two not together?" I asked him.

"Not yet we're not," he replied, flashing her a Hollywood grin.

"Whatever do you mean by that comment!" Hat snapped as he bounced to his feet and then immediately threw himself back into his seat. "Sorry, so sorry. That was clearly an overreaction on my part. Pray, continue."

Hat reached into his pocket, where I assume his butterscotch candies resided.

"I was just kidding. No harm, no foul," the man said, his hands up as if at gunpoint.

Hat leaned over and put a candy on the arm of the new guy's chair.

"Please, recommence your introduction but don't eat that butterscotch until you're finished. It makes it hard to speak, but it's very, very tasty."

We all smiled at him and nodded. Hat did, too.

"Um, right then, well, I'll start again. Hi everyone. I'm John Dillinger, you know, the famous bank robber."

"Ahhh, America's first official Public Enemy Number One back in the thirties," piped up Hat. "Am I not right? Tell me I am not right."

"Bingo," said John Dillinger, aiming and firing his finger gun at Hat, who looked very pleased with himself. "Anyway, I'm an actor, born in Georgia, but now living here. I was in the Y working out – gotta keep my physique in shape, you know – when I heard two trainers talking about this group. I sure enough know what it's like to be named after an outlaw and a folk hero. Thought I'd check you out."

"What have you been in?" asked Peter Parker. "Would we have seen you in any movies or TV shows?"

"Well, ah, no, not yet, but it's only a matter of time," he explained. "I've done a TV commercial to tide me over until I get my break."

"Oh yeah, which one? Maybe we've seen that," asked Clark Kent.

"Nah, I doubt you've seen it."

"Come on, don't be shy. What was it for?" Clark persisted.

"Depends," John Dillinger replied.

"Depends on what?" Jackie Kennedy said.

"No, I mean the commercial was for Depends. You know, those adult diaper thingies."

We just looked at him, trying to picture the ad. At least no one snickered.

"You know, it paid well, and it got me in front of the camera. And I wasn't that busy, so I took it."

"I think I know that ad," Hat jumped in. "Were you that handsome lad dancing in a disco, then skiing, and then bouncing on a pogo stick to prove the product's superior efficacy?"

"Well, I guess at least one of you has seen it." John Dillinger puffed out his chest just a bit.

"You were very convincing in it, I must say," Hat commended. "And you kept dry through all of that? Impressive."

"Actually, I was just the actor. I wasn't really wearing the product at the time. Um, as I said, I was just the actor."

"Well, I certainly thought that pogo stick looked like fun." John Dillinger nodded.

"Ah, thank you, Hat," I intervened, lest our new member be scared off. "You're welcome here, John. Grab a seat," I suggested, pointing to the stack of chairs in the corner.

He picked a chair off the stack and, despite several spots with more room, sidled up right behind Marie and the new blond woman, forcing them to separate their chairs so he could squeeze between them, beaming the whole time. They didn't seem to mind.

"Why don't we hear from our other new member," I proposed, gesturing with an open hand toward the very attractive blond woman.

"Oh, okay," she said as she stood, smoothing out her dress. "I'm afraid my name is Julia Roberts, a perfectly normal and serviceable name until 1990 when a little movie called *Pretty Woman* changed my life. I'm a tax lawyer in Manhattan and I take fitness classes here at the Y. You have no idea how often I have to endure funny looks and comments because I happen to have the same name as a Hollywood superstar. It's been very difficult, especially when I'm in court."

"A cracking movie," noted Professor James Moriarty.

"Yes, and her boots were certainly memorable," Hat said.

"Um, nice to have you here, Julia," I said. "And to your point, I would just say that the people in this room may be among the only ones who actually do understand what you've been going through, because we're going through it, too, every day. Let's just go around the room quickly so that Julia Roberts and John Dillinger know who we all are. By the way, we tend to use complete names here. It's a reminder that our names are totally acceptable and should be freely used."

It took another ten minutes or so to circle the room. Julia and John looked a little shell-shocked by the end. Their eyes opened a little bit wider as each NameFame member stood to announce themselves.

"All right, so now that we've all been formally introduced, let's get started," I said. "At our last meeting we arrived at a consensus of sorts on our little NameFame taxonomy, a basic classification system to help us understand our own, and each other's, situations. So tonight, I thought one of you could tell us more about the personal challenges your name has created, and then as a group we could brainstorm some strategies for making life a little easier. Next week, someone else would step up and be the focus. Make sense?"

There was much nodding around the circle.

"Sounds like a plan," said Diana Ross.

"Okay, so who'd like to volunteer tonight?"

For the first time since the meeting started, silence reigned. No hands and no voices were raised to claim the floor. Finally, I saw Jesse Owens start to lift her hand. I jumped on it fast in case she was reaching up to scratch her nose or adjust her bangs.

"Excellent, Jesse. Thank you," I said.

"Well, actually, I was going to suggest that as our fearless leader, you could tell us what's going on with you, just as a way to kick-start us a bit. I'm sure by next week we can find someone else to step up."

"Yes, I think that is a very wise proposal," chimed in Hat. "Very wise, indeed."

"Capital idea," echoed Professor James Moriarty.

This was not what I had planned. But I felt my hands were tied, not to mention suddenly sweaty. I decided if I set a good example, we'd have clear sailing at future meetings.

"It sort of feels like I've done a lot of talking during our first two meetings. Are you sure no one feels ready to jump in with their story tonight?"

A second bout of silence descended.

"I guess it's decided," I conceded. "Rather than give you my entire life's story, let me focus on one recent problem that is directly related to my name, Earnest Hemmingway."

I stood up and moved a little toward the middle of the circle. I always think better when I'm on my feet and moving.

"The legendary writer Ernest Hemingway and I do not get along. Despite his undisputed status as a literary god, I have never understood the adulation and the idolatry he inspires. I'm convinced his fame is driven by the no-holds-barred life he led rather than by his writing. And to be clear, I have nothing against the way he lived. I just don't like his writing. In fact, I hate it. So flat, so spare, so barren, so devoid of the richness and glory of the English language. When I open one of his novels, I feel like I'm reading from a Second Grade reader. Now some think his writing is pure and pristine, the ideal for which all writers should strive. I say no. Emphatically, no.

"Anyway, I've been trying to write a novel for several years now. It was all going quite well until a few weeks ago. I've come down with a severe case of writer's block. I seem to be able to speak fine but the only writing I've been able to do is a weekly shopping list. Writer's block is nothing new for many writers, but it's never happened to me. I'm stuck.

"But the good news is, I actually think I've figured out what's happening. I just don't know how to fix it."

"So what's your diagnosis, doctor?" asked Jackie Kennedy.

"I hope I can count on you all for understanding and empathy, because this is going to sound a little strange. I'll try to be brief. The bottom line is I believe the spirit of Ernest Hemingway has infiltrated my mind, staked his squatter's claim, and stayed."

Despite my promise of brevity, I talked for the next twenty minutes or so about how I could sense not only Hemingway's presence, but his rejection of my prose. It all came pouring out of me in one long torrent. I told them everything. It was close to cathartic. I explained how I'd excised all vestiges of Hemingway from my apartment and my life, yet nothing had changed. I conceded that I didn't believe in ghosts but accepted that my name had somehow brought all of this on. Finally, I admitted that my psychiatrist was not persuaded by my Hemingway's ghost thesis, though she declined to offer any viable alternatives. The more I spoke, the more depressed I became. The looks on their faces told me that few if any creative solutions would be forthcoming. Well, it had been a good try.

"I believe in ghosts," Hat said in solidarity. "My great-grandmother appears now and again in a little snow globe that I keep on top of my dresser."

"I sometimes hear noises at night when I'm closing up the café-bakery. I've been meaning to research the history of the building. Maybe it's haunted," offered Marie.

The debate over the existence of spirits and ghosts raged for another ten minutes or so. Occasionally, the discussion even veered within spitting distance of my particular problem. In the end, there was no shortage of suggestions, prescriptions, home remedies, and incantations, but neither were there any epiphanies that evening. A few suggested medication ("SSRIs are all the rage these days"). Others were interested in employing some kind of shaman or ghost-buster to send Ernest packing ("Who you gonna call?"). In one of the more thoughtful suggestions, Jesse proposed that I write about the presence of Ernest Hemingway in my apartment, or perhaps even write to him. Marie thought I should try writing elsewhere, perhaps in the café-bakery. (Not a bad idea.) Hat even suggested I consider electroshock therapy ("Yes, it sounds scary, but I assure you, it really isn't that bad"). Jackie Kennedy urged that I pray ("When I have a problem, I drop to my knees next to my bed").

"What about yoga?" asked John Dillinger, who'd spent most of the meeting in what appeared to be intimate private conversations with Marie Antoinette and Julia Roberts on either side of him. "I do it sometimes to cleanse my mind before auditions so I can assume any role I'm assigned."

I bet cleansing his mind didn't take very long, I thought.

"Interesting idea, John Dillinger, but I think it's going to take more than pulling a hamstring in a Downward Dog to clear Mr. Hemingway out of my mind. But thank you."

I felt a little bad being so dismissive, but I didn't really like the vibe I was getting from America's first Public Enemy Number One. He had slipped into our midst a little too easily, a little too quickly, a little too smoothly. I wondered if anyone else in the room shared my reservations.

The discussion sort of petered out after Julia suggested filing a restraining order against Ernest Hemingway. I knew she'd said it in jest, but not everyone around the circle picked up on the joke. The meeting broke up shortly thereafter.

"Thanks, everyone, for the helpful suggestions. I'll give it all some thought and keep you posted," I said, drawing the meeting to a close. "Think about who might like to share their situation next week. Sorry about the rainout, but the long-term forecast suggests that we'll be back playing next week. Julia and John, you're welcome to play on our softball team now that you've passed the initiation to join the group. We could use the support."

I don't know what I was expecting from the meeting, but I left feeling very down and discouraged. Perhaps I'd put too much faith in the power of the group to help one another. I had already considered and rejected the suggestions that had emerged in the meeting. Okay, I confess I hadn't really considered electroshock therapy or yoga. But I wouldn't be going down those paths.

Marie had invited the group to come back to Let Them Eat Cake! for dessert and coffee after the meeting. Very nice of her, and most of the group was going, except for Clark Kent, who really felt he had to get back home to see his kids. I just couldn't bring myself to go. I was just too bummed out. So I begged off. Marie looked sad when I told her, which made me feel even worse. She touched my arm and urged me to come, saying that I'd feel better. But I said no. I jumped on the subway and went home as the group piled into cabs. My last image of the scene, before I headed down the stairs to the platform, was of John Dillinger escorting Marie to a cab, his hand resting on her shoulder as they walked. He climbed in beside her.

When I walked back into my apartment, I immediately noticed Hemingway's *The Old Man and the Sea* under the back leg of the couch. I'd stuck the paperback there the day I moved in to compensate for the minor slant in the hardwood floor that left my couch exactly 128 pages shy of level. I'd missed it when removing Hemingway's works from my living space. I replaced it with Wodehouse's *The Code of the Woosters* and instantly wondered what it would be like to have my own valet, like the inimitable Jeeves. Then I took *The Old Man and the Sea* down to my storage locker to join the rest of my incarcerated Hemingway cache. On my way back up to the apartment, I had a faint hope that this final act of eradicating, erasing, expunging, extinguishing, and eliminating Ernest Hemingway just might liberate the words trapped between my head and my fingers. But no. After an hour in front of the laptop with a menacingly flashing cursor and a blank screen, I slammed it closed and lay back on the couch, approaching what seemed like rock bottom. I think I'd known even before I turned on my computer. You can feel it when the words are there, ready to flow. And you know when they just aren't. What I didn't yet know was whether my current barren state was permanent. But it was beginning to feel like it might be.

I snapped awake at the urgent knock on my door. I swung my legs off the couch, my heart pounding a bit. I could see through to the kitchen that the clock on the stove said 10:45. It felt like I'd been asleep for days, not minutes. The peephole distorted Marie's face, leaving her wall-eyed and hydrocephalic, yet still strangely attractive. Barely conscious, I opened the door.

"Hem, we know it's late, but can we come in?" Marie drawled. "It's important."

Mahatma Gandhi and Professor James Moriarty were very close behind her.

"Um, of course, please come in."

I opened the door and waved them across the threshold. Fortunately, my apartment was still in pretty good shape to welcome visitors.

"What a splendid flat you have, Hem," Professor Moriarty said.

"Yes, it must be wonderful to live on a street with trees." Marie looked out the window to the swaying branches illuminated by the streetlights.

It took ten minutes to give them the tour and get them seated. They had all declined my offer of beer, wine, orange juice, or water.

Marie was the one to explain this visit.

"At the café-bakery, we were all thinking more about your, um, situation, and James here had an idea that got us really excited," she began. "So we batted it around for a while and we just felt we couldn't wait until tomorrow to share it with you. You'll understand in a minute why the three of us were nominated to present it to you."

"Yes, she's absolutely right," Hat confirmed. "A most excellent introduction, Miss Marie."

"Why thank you, Hat," she replied. "James, will you present the idea to Hem now?"

A warm feeling of gratitude washed over me, even though I'd not yet heard their plan. How nice of them to do this, and to be so excited about it. All three of them were leaning forward, their eyes alight. At that point, I felt that whatever harebrained scheme they had in mind didn't really matter. My spirits were lifted just by their presence, their energy, and their thoughtfulness. I was touched.

"Well, Hem, it occurred to me that your approach to dealing with Mr. Hemingway's hegemonic occupation of your subconscious may well be entirely and precisely opposite to what is required. When one is trying to rid oneself of a fear of spiders, or of public speaking, or of driving, or I dare say, of deep water, the remedy most often prescribed by psychiatrists and psychologists alike is to confront the fear, to challenge it directly, to overcome it by co-existing with it. With support, you learn about spiders. You hold them. You see that most are harmless. Through knowledge of them, and, more importantly, proximity to them, your fear subsides. Thoughts of them no longer distract. You may remain uncomfortable in their presence, but the raw fear is blunted, and perhaps even banished. Your mental space is liberated from arachnophobia to pursue more important endeavours. Am I being clear?" James asked.

"I'm with you, Professor. Carry on," I replied.

I wasn't quite sure where he was going, but there was a certain logic to his words.

"You've told us that to try to deal with Mr. Hemingway, you've removed anything connected to the great writer from your immediate surroundings – his novels, books about him, artwork from Paris, the DVD of *Midnight in Paris*, a jolly fine film, and so on. We contend that in so doing, you are running from Mr. Hemingway rather than confronting him or his spirit. We fear you may be inadvertently fuelling the fire rather than quenching it. So we have developed a proposal that my good friend Mahatma Gandhi will now share."

Professor Moriarty formally bowed in Hat's direction.

"I thank you for your kind words, Professor James Moriarty," Hat started. "It is late and I will try to be short, though I am not fatigued in the least, no, I'm not."

Marie was just sitting there smiling at each one of us in turn. She really looked lovely.

"Okay, Hem, here we go," Hat continued, leaning so close to me he invaded what any reasonable observer would consider my personal space. "What we are proposing this night is built upon Professor Moriarty's premise that you must confront your demon, not hide it away. Hem, we know that you have some free time right now and we have a sense that you are financially sound. I pray that our assumptions are valid."

All three of them leaned in even closer to me. I worried they might soon fall onto the coffee table in unison.

"Well, I guess that's a reasonably accurate description of my current situation."

"That news is excellent, just excellent," Hat gushed. "Okay, Hem, this is it. We are strongly encouraging you to embark on what we have decided to call the Ernest Hemingway Exorcism

World Tour. What do you think? Is it not a fabulous thought?"

I was at a loss for words, largely because I had no idea what Hat was talking about.

"Um, Hat, I think you need to share the details of the EHEWT," Marie suggested.

She pronounced it "ee-ute."

"There's already an acronym?" I said. "Wow, you guys work fast."

"Oh, I'm so stupid," Hat said, slapping both his thighs and shaking his head. "Yes, of course, Marie, thank you for setting me back on the path we agreed to take. Please bear with me, Hem. We're all quite excited about this and it's caused me to forget my place. The plan would be for you, Hem, to visit those places where Mr. Ernest Hemingway spent time. To go where he went, sit where he sat, write where he wrote, immerse yourself, body and mind, in the world of Ernest Hemingway. This is how you confront the spirit of the famous author who has you so blocked up that you cannot write."

Hat nodded at Marie, and she tagged in.

"You wouldn't have to spend long in each place, and you wouldn't have to do it alone. In fact, we think you shouldn't tackle it alone. So thanks to an hour or so on the Internet, here's the plan. We think starting in Toronto makes sense. Hemingway worked for the *Toronto Star* and lived there in the twenties when his wife Hadley gave birth to their son, Jack, inexplicably nicknamed Bumby. James here is happy to go with you there. Next stop, Paris. By coincidence, I'm already booked to be there for a pastry course, ten days from now. I could be there at least on the weekend and in the evenings to help you explore Hemingway's Paris. I'm afraid you'll have to handle stop number three, Pamplona, Spain, on your own, but it's a manageable side trip by train and bus from Paris. Hemingway loved Spain, as you probably know. Then you'll fly back to Miami, where Hat will meet you to catch a connecting flight to Key West, where of course Hemingway lived and wrote for quite a few years. Finally, you're on your own again for the last stop, as Hat needs to get back for the start of the Jets spring training camp. Your trip closes out in Ketchum, Idaho, to confront Ernest Hemingway where he died by his own hand. You land in Boise and then rent a car for the drive to Ketchum, near Sun Valley. Then it's home to New York. And there you have it, the Ernest Hemingway Exorcism World Tour!"

Hat reached out and clasped my shoulder.

"It will be so much fun, Hem. And you'll see. It will work. I know it will. We know it will," he said, rubbing his hands together. "Oh, and I'm sorry to say, Hem, that the cost is not inconsiderable, if I may put it gently like that. But we know it will be worth every one of the hard-earned dollars you'll be required to spend."

CHAPTER 8

"And they're calling it the Ernest Hemingway Exorcism World Tour?"

I nodded. Dr. Scott jotted down a note, her face impassive, blank. She did noncommittal very well.

As soon as Marie, Hat, and Professor Moriarty had left my apartment shortly after midnight, I'd called Dr. Scott's office and left a message. Her return phone call arrived at 8:30. She managed to squeeze me in at 10:00.

"And what did you think when this little delegation arrived and presented their grand plan?" she asked.

I'd anticipated this question.

"After they left, my mind and my body disagreed on what should happen next," I explained. "My body was ready for sleep, but my mind was spinning and flatly refused to shut down. So I just lay in bed thinking long and hard for a good chunk of what was left of the night. Two ideas were still swirling in my head when you called me this morning. Number one, I was filled with gratitude for the time, care, and thought my new friends had devoted to my little writer's block problem. They seemed so excited about it, and that made me feel great. I was touched, and told them so."

"And number two?" she prompted.

"Number two, the more I thought about their crazy idea of flying around to Hemingway's haunts, no pun intended, the less crazy it all seemed," I replied. "In the light of day, sitting here right now, it still strikes me as a well-conceived plan, rooted in something approaching reason. I think that's what scares me. It all seems to make sense to me."

"Do you think your first point is unduly influencing your second point?" she asked. "Is your gratitude for your friends' thoughtfulness colouring your conclusion about the value of the trip itself?"

"I thought you might ask me that," I noted. "No. I tried, I think successfully, to isolate the warm and fuzzy feelings and consider the idea on its merits, with some distance and objectivity. Each time I think it through, I still reach the conclusion that it just might help me with my writing. It feels like it should work. I actually think it will work. And I've tried everything else, so what have I got to lose other than the cost of the trip and a week of my life?"

She stared off into space for a moment, I assume thinking about what I'd said, but who knows?

"Hem, if you believe this to be true, if you really are thinking and reflecting, and not just reacting and yearning, then you should take the trip," she said. "I don't know whether this will work. Nobody knows. So if you really feel this will help, but then decide not to go because I counselled against it, the 'what ifs' will get in the way of everything else we might try in the future."

"So you think by confronting Hemingway on his own turf, I can make this all go away?" I knew what her response would be.

"Nice try. What's important is that you believe it. And if it turns out that it's not Hemingway's ghost haunting you, and this doesn't work, there are far worse ways to spend a week than visiting Paris, Pamplona, and Key West."

————

The first person I saw when I walked into Let Them Eat Cake! was John Dillinger. The second was Marie. They were sitting at a table for two, and they were laughing.

"Hem, you're here!" exclaimed Marie, standing up. "I tried to call you earlier but I got your machine."

"Yeah, I had a meeting this morning and I was just on my way back home."

"Hey, Hem, how's it hanging?" John Dillinger said, wearing a loopy grin.

"Excellent alliteration, John," I replied. "I'm fine, thanks. I didn't know you were much of a café-bakery type."

"I'm not, really. I came for the scenery," he said, snatching a glance at Marie while he straddled the line between smiling and leering.

She giggled. Yep, she giggled. Not good. I turned to her.

"I just wanted to thank you again for last night. That was really quite special."

Out of the corner of my eye, I saw John flinch just a little.

"You dog, you!" John said. "I think I've misjudged you, Hem."

"And Hat and James were also amazing. It was quite a session," I added.

"I've definitely misjudged you!"

Marie rolled her eyes, slapped John on the shoulder, grabbed my arm, and led me to a quieter part of the room. We sat down at the same table Sarah and I had taken a few weeks before.

"I'm so glad you weren't mad at us for barging in like that so late. We couldn't stop ourselves," she said. "You could probably tell we were a little excited about it all. So, um, what do you think now that you've had some time to mull it over?"

Marie leaned in with her elbows on the table. Her fresh scent reached me and almost threw me off.

"Well, I've decided that since you put so much thought into this, it would be downright insulting and ungrateful of me to pass up such a trip. So I'm going. I really am."

Marie shrieked, grabbed both my hands, and squeezed until my fingernails turned pink.

Everyone else in the restaurant was looking our way, including John Dillinger.

"I actually think it's an idea that might work," I explained. "I wanted to tell you first and confirm your Paris dates. Then I'm going home to start planning the trip and booking flights."

"Woo-hooo! The Ernest Hemingway Exorcism World Tour is a *go!*" Marie released my hands and thrust both her arms above her head. I recognized the gesture. Apparently, I'd just scored a touchdown.

Ten minutes later, I rose to leave. Marie wrote down the Paris dates along with the details of where she was staying during her course and handed the slip of paper to me.

"So what's with Johnny D over there? Does he come here often?"

"He was here last night with the rest of the group and seems to have taken a shine to our great food," Marie said.

"It looks to me, and to everyone else in the room, that he's taken a shine to more than the great food."

"Underneath his act, he's actually pretty nice. He made some good suggestions as we refined the exorcism tour idea. It's just tough to get him to step off the stage for any length of time," Marie observed.

"Do you want me to try to get him out the door for you?"

"No, he's fine, but thanks. He's taking me out later on anyway. Besides, he may actually order something soon and I don't want to miss the sale."

"Wow, he moves fast," I said as I headed to the door. "Thanks again for bringing this crazy tour idea forward. I'm grateful. It actually means a lot to me that you and the others would go to that trouble."

"Well, we NameFamers have to stick together," she said before going back over to John Dillinger's table.

Just before I opened the door, I looked over at him.

"Thanks for your help on the trip idea, John. Very kind of you." I waved to him.

"No worries, bro. Happy to help. I hope it quiets the voices in your head. If not, well, I've got a special jacket you can wear when you get back. But you'll need help putting it on."

"Thanks anyway, but you keep it. You may need it again sometime. You never know," I replied. "Oh, by the way, we could use whatever baseball skills you may have for our Thursday game this week. Are you in?"

"Well, it's true, quite a bit of my youth was spent tearing up the diamond. So let me just check the old schedule to make sure I don't have an audition that night. You know, I'm juggling quite a few of them right now."

As he checked his BlackBerry, he sighed heavily, nearly overcome with the trauma of managing so many audition requests.

"Oh well, will you look at that, I'm clear that night, so I guess I can play."

"Just our luck. I'll bring your jersey to the game."

By this time, Marie was standing next to him. I saw him put his hand on the small of her back as he spoke to her, presumably to place his long-awaited order. Then I was out the door.

———————

When I revved up my laptop, there were separate emails waiting for me from Professor James Moriarty and Hat with more information about dates and flight times. They were very well organized and seemed quite committed to this journey. I'd already sent separate emails to James, Marie, and Hat offering to cover the costs of their respective portions of the tour. I thought that was only fair. Marie and James turned me down flat. Marie had already booked her Paris trip for the pastry course and would be staying with a friend who had an apartment in Saint-Germain. James said that he'd always wanted to visit Toronto anyway as they have an extensive collection of Sherlockiana and Arthur Conan Doyle artifacts at the main branch of the Toronto Public Library. Besides, he had plenty of frequent flyer miles he could cash in for his flight. Mahatma Gandhi, on the other hand, was not quite so quick to decline the offer though he was clearly uncomfortable with the idea of "freeloading," as he put it in his return email. I hit Reply and told him that I appreciated his support, and just to leave it to me. I think he was relieved.

Two hours later, the entire trip, you know, the EHEWT, was planned and booked. It's amazing what one can do on the Internet with a Visa card. Here was the basic itinerary:

Thursday, July 4:   I fly to Toronto with Professor James Moriarty.

Friday, July 5:   I fly from Toronto to Paris to join Marie Antoinette, who will have arrived for her pastry course a few days before.

Tuesday, July 9:	I take an overnight train on my own from Paris to Vitoria, Spain, and then a bus to Pamplona, arriving early Wednesday morning.
Wednesday, July 10:	I retrace the same overnight journey from Pamplona back to Paris, arriving Thursday morning.
Thursday, July 11:	I fly from Paris to Miami, arriving midafternoon, local time, where I meet Hat. Then we catch a connecting flight to Key West, Florida.
Saturday, July 13:	Hat and I fly back to Miami, where we separate. He heads back to New York while I catch a flight to Boise, Idaho.
Sunday, July 14:	I drive my rental car from Boise to Ketchum, then back again to Boise in the evening.
Monday, July 15:	Fly from Boise back to New York, having shed the judgmental and conceited spirit of Ernest Hemingway somewhere along the way.

Here endeth the Ernest Hemingway Exorcism World Tour.

It wasn't exactly shaping up to be a leisurely vacation. Then again, it wasn't intended to be relaxing. I considered it to be more akin to rehab without security and the shakes. I was trying to rid myself of a toxin that was preventing me from reaching a goal I'd set for myself a very long time ago. I was angry. I was motivated. I was ready. It's quite possible, even likely, that I was deluded. But I was going to give it a shot.

I wasn't certain about the idea of sharing this adventure with Marie, James, and Hat. But I never would have thought of this without them. This was their idea. I actually felt a little misty-eyed whenever I replayed their late-night visit to my apartment to "present" the solution they'd devised. It was thoughtful, generous, and kind. More accurately, *they* were thoughtful, generous, and kind. So there was no way I was going to question their notion that I be accompanied for as much of the journey as possible. That was part of the deal.

There was perfect attendance again for our NameFame meeting on Thursday. It all seemed to go very well. Jackie Kennedy told us more about her life and the challenges of carrying such a famous moniker. As I listened to her, I was reminded of how much easier it is to handle the baggage that comes with a famous name when you're a confident and strong person to begin with. As well, unlike some of the other members, take me for instance, Jackie had lived until she was a young adult before her name was suddenly thrust into the national spotlight when JFK ran for president in 1960. I decided that if you can make it through childhood before someone else with your name becomes famous, it's often easier to handle what follows.

We walked en masse to Central Park for our second ball game. We were facing the Spin Masters, a team composed of public relations professionals. They were all young and good-looking, even in their uncomfortable, plastic mesh jerseys. Having John Dillinger and Julia Roberts join the team meant that Professor James Moriarty could join Jackie Kennedy in our cheering section, still leaving us with one player in reserve on the bench in case we ever wanted to put in a pinch hitter or runner with the game on the line. Yes, with our roster up to an even dozen, we could now add those kinds of sophisticated baseball stratagems to our arsenal. And considering our rather pathetic hitting, fielding, and baserunning, we needed all the sophisticated baseball stratagems we could get.

John Dillinger was actually not a bad player, but he "acted," in the truest sense of the word, like a major league all-star, or major-league ass, depending on your perspective. He'd gone out and purchased brand-new genuine baseball pants, spikes, and batting gloves. He had a tough time breaking the little plastic tie that kept the two batting gloves together, but he got it eventually. Then he wore them as he sprinted up and down shallow left field, lifting his knees so high on each step he was in danger of knocking himself out. Then he lay on the ground and stretched as he'd probably seen Derek Jeter do it in the Yankees pre-game warm-up.

"I hope the new kid plays as well as he stretches," Jackie said, shaking her head.

I handed in our roster to the announcer behind the screen. It was the same man with a megaphone who'd had such fun with our names in our first game. Great.

NameFame Starting Lineup

Centre Field: Earnest Hemmingway #10

1st base: Jesse Owens #5

Shortstop: John Dillinger #1

2nd base: Peter Parker #8

3rd base: Diana Ross #4

Left Field: Marie Antoinette #9

Right Field: Mahatma Gandhi #6

Rover (4th outfielder): Clark Kent #7

Catcher: Mario Andretti #2

Substitute: Julia Roberts #12

Umpire Liaison and Senior Cheerleader: Jackie Kennedy #3

Assistant Umpire Liaison and Cheerleader: James
Moriarty #11

———————

Yes, it's true. I had reluctantly agreed to John Dillinger's request and given him the jersey with number one on the back.

Then Jesse Owens called us all in to the dugout for a pep talk as the Spin Masters took the field.

"Nothing fancy out there tonight, guys," she started. "When you're at the plate, we're just looking for a little bat-on-ball contact. When you see the ball come off the bat, your eyes should be focused on one thing and one thing only . . ."

"The ball, right?" Hat interjected. "We always must watch the ball. Am I not right, Ms. Owens?"

"Actually, Hat, you watch the ball *before* you hit. But after you've connected with the ball, you should be looking only at first base. Concentrate and run for the bag as fast you can."

"Oh, I'm so stupid!" Hat shouted, slapping both his thighs hard enough that mine stung in sympathy. "Listen, Mahatma, listen!"

He looked ready to break something, and I hoped it wouldn't be his legs.

"Hat, it's okay. You're okay. Have a butterscotch and breathe. That's it, breathe," soothed Jesse, her hands holding his hands to prevent a self-inflicted bilateral charley horse. "You're right, Hat, watching the ball is very important when you're at the plate and the pitch is coming toward you. By all means, watch the ball then. But after you hit it, run for your life."

Then Jesse looked back to all of us.

"Remember, when you hear the bat hit the ball, think about nothing else but reaching first base."

"That's easy for me," said a smirking John Dillinger. "I've spent a good part of my life getting to first base."

Only John Dillinger chuckled.

Jesse had decided that we should front-load our batting order to try to get some runs on the board early. It actually worked, at least for a while. With Clark Kent pitching us easy ones from the mound, I led off with a double down the third base line. Jesse then pounded one out to right, as she had in our first game, bringing me home and earning herself a second triple in two games. Then John Dillinger spent a bit too long swinging in the on-deck circle and doing squats with his bat behind his head.

"Okay, superstar, get in the batter's box," instructed the umpire.

"Now at the plate, Public Enemy Number One, wearing number one, the very tough-to-catch John Dillinger," intoned the announcer.

I was sitting next to Hat and grabbed the waistband of his red short-shorts to stop him from storming out of the dugout. I'm glad the shorts held together. Hat really did not like announcer-guy.

John settled in the box, took far too many practice swings, then signalled to Clark that he was finally ready. On the first pitch, he belted a triple into the gap between centre and right, bringing home Jesse. We led 2–0, with no outs. This was great. The team was thrilled to be leading. Jackie and James were hooting from the stands behind the plate. Well, Jackie was hooting. James stuck with "Bravo" and "Good show" and "Well played."

As announcer-guy reached for the trigger of his megaphone, I put my arm around Hat, more in restraint than in affection.

"Now batting, wearing number eight, the absolutely perfect number for him, the shortstop, Peter Parker."

I hugged Hat a little tighter, and he stayed put. I felt like a jerk for having given Peter number eight. The connection never occurred to me until the comedian at the scorer's table gave voice to it. I'm not sure Peter had yet figured it out as he stepped up to the plate. I made a mental note to switch jerseys with him for our next game.

Peter smashed a grounder directly into the glove of the short-stop. Damn. But wait, the throw to first was high and sailed into the fence. Peter sauntered to second on the error as John came home, waving to the crowd, to make it 3–0.

Then, in quick succession, Diana Ross and Marie Antoinette both grounded out to the second baseman, bringing Hat to the plate for his swing at the ball. I looked over at the announcer and saw that Jackie Kennedy was standing next to his little table, holding his megaphone. I'm not sure how she'd relieved him of his precious PA system, but she had. Hat was not formally introduced before he cricket-hit a dribbler to the first baseman for our third out. Don't mess with Jackie.

The triumphant first half of the first inning is what I choose to remember of our game against the Spin Masters. We were lead-ing 3–0. We were winning. Really! Regrettably, no thunderstorms arrived to rain out the game. There was no power outage to throw the field into darkness. There was no brush fire in Central Park to send us fleeing for the subway. No, the game just continued. It ended after the fifth inning with the Spin Masters winning 50–3. The ten runs per inning mercy rule got another workout that night. There was no need for the PR pros who whipped our ass to "spin" their victory in any way. They didn't have to search for a tiny sliver of positive news and then embroider it into a colossal victory. No, the 50–3 truth was quite convincing all on its own.

Our Achilles heel as a team, although our weak spot covered a lot more than our heel, was our defence. In the entire game, we caught two fly balls, threw out two at first base, and managed a single force-out at second. We could have had another out when their cleanup hitter tried to stretch her single into a double. Hat made quite a good pickup of the looper into shallow right, catching the ball in his bare hand on the second bounce. But instead of throwing it to second for an easy out, he promptly threw the ball to me deep in centre field. I'm still not sure why, and neither is he. When I managed to return the ball to the infield, the batter had stretched her single into a triple, bringing in two more runs. Over the course of five innings, we'd only managed to get five outs against the Spin Masters. Without the aptly named mercy rule, we might still be playing the game.

"We'll drive you home," I said to Marie. "My car is here."

Mario, Marie, and I had just walked back to the Y, where I'd parked. The others were headed for the bar.

"Very kind of y'all. I'll take the lift. My legs are sore from running after all those balls," Marie replied as I held the car door open for her. "Why can't they just hit them closer to us?"

I considered it to be a rhetorical question and wasn't sure how I'd respond anyway. I handed her the seat belt and closed the door.

"Do you think it'll be safe?" Mario whispered. He was somewhat agitated.

"Of course it's safe. You'll be fine," I assured him.

I got in the front passenger side as Mario slipped into the driver's seat.

"Okay, Mario, you know the drill," I said and waited.

Mario reached for the power seat control. A motorized hum accompanied the forward slide of his seat.

"Okay, that's far enough!" Mario said, alarmed.

His seat just kept sliding forward, his knees pushing up against the steering column.

"Make it stop! That's far enough. It's squishing me!"

"Let go of the button," I said. "Just let go!"

He did. He stopped.

"Sorry, lost my head," Mario said. "I'm a little claustrophobic and it makes me forget what I'm doing."

He worked the button again to move the seat back to where he wanted it.

"Bring it up a little closer, Mario. Remember where your feet need to be. Okay, stop," I said. "How's that feel?"

"Good, I guess."

"Okay. What's next?"

"Three Hail Marys?" he asked. I hoped he was just kidding, but he didn't look like it.

"Mirrors," I said.

"Right."

He adjusted them.

"Okay, we're set to go as soon as we're all belted."

"I'll be having a belt as soon as I get home," Mario replied. "Marie, are you sure you don't want to catch a cab, or jump on the subway, or crawl on your hands and knees back to your place?"

"You're doing just fine, Mario. I'm just where I want to be right now," said Marie.

The traffic was reasonably clear. It was as if everyone had been warned that Mario would be on the streets that night. Ten minutes later we pulled up to Let Them Eat Cake! Well, to be a bit more precise, we pulled up on the sidewalk in front of the café-bakery. But it was a good try. He'd actually done quite well, staying in his lane for most of the trip, and twice remembering to use his turn signal before he'd completed the corner. And fortunately, when he ran that red, there was no cross-traffic in the intersection. Believe it or not, I could see improvement. And there still was not a scratch on my G35.

I hopped out, relieved to be on the sidewalk, albeit along with my car, and opened Marie's door.

"Why thank you, sir," she said, taking the hand I offered. I liked the feel of her hand.

"Keep her running, Mario, I'll be right back."

I walked Marie to the door that led to her second-floor apartment.

"It's awfully nice of you to put your life and car on the line helping Mario get his licence," she said.

"He just needs more practice. He'll get there."

"I know he will, but that wasn't my point. You're a good guy to do it."

I didn't really know what to say to that.

"So, um, how was your date the other night with Public Enemy Number One?"

She laughed.

"Oh, it was fine. It was nice."

"What role was he playing?"

"It was a little hard to tell. I think it was changing over the course of the night. But eventually, I think he was actually playing himself. It takes a while to get there but it was worth the wait. He's really quite nice – much more than just a very pretty face attached to a well-toned body."

Awesome. Glad to hear it. Shit.

"So, um, you leave for Paris next Wednesday and then I'll see you there Saturday. My flight lands in the morning," I said.

"Yes, Hem. The plan hasn't changed since we last discussed it at the game about an hour ago," she said, but smiled just the same.

"Do you arrive back here in time to make it to our ballgame?" I asked. "Hat and I will still be in Florida, so we'll need the bodies at the park."

"Yep, my body will be there, jet-lagged and all."

"Great. Jesse may need a hand. I hate to miss it, but I'll probably be judging an Ernest Hemingway lookalike contest in some Key West bar right about then."

"I'll talk to Jesse before I go. And I guess I'll see you at the front entrance of Notre Dame next Saturday at noon."

"*Absolument, mademoiselle,*" I said with a bow. But she was looking past me down the block.

"Um, Hem, there's a cop on the beat coming down the street."

"See you in Paris," I said as I hustled back to the car, still sitting on the sidewalk, and jumped in.

Mario managed to avoid hitting anything as he pulled back onto the street, and we were off.

––––––––––

When I got home that night, the car still in one piece, I went directly to my storage locker in the basement and repatriated all of my Hemingway-related books and objects, and spread them around the apartment in prominent places. I stacked his books right next to my laptop on the table. I wanted to get a head start on confronting my spectral nemesis. I then stiffened my resolve further and pulled out *A Moveable Feast*, Hemingway's posthumously published memoir of his time in Paris. The book was still very sparely written, but the writing seemed less affected than in his novels. And I confess it was cool to read about all those literary and artistic luminaries hanging out together in the Paris of the 1920s. I was starting to get excited about the trip.

––––––––––

In the days leading up to my departure, I still wasn't able to coax any meaningful words onto the laptop screen, despite following Professor Moriarty's direction and immersing myself in Hemingway. Perhaps it was going to take some time to complete the exorcism.

My phone rang the morning I was scheduled to depart for Toronto. My caller ID did its job.

"Hey, Sarah."

"Hi, Hem. Are you all packed?"

"I'm pretty well set to go," I replied. "Is everything cool in Chi-Town?"

"Well, Dad's acting weirder and weirder. He's keeping his office door closed all the time, now, and Henderson is with him constantly. Something is up. And Dad just looks so sad and worried all the time."

"Well, have you asked him?"

"I can't get close to him. I ambushed him in the parking lot the other day but he brushed off my questions and just claimed to have a lot going on right then."

"Well, that sounds like a reasonable explanation," I suggested.

"Hem, it's not the same. Something is happening."

"Then this is a great time for me to be spending a week or so on the road and away from the phone."

"Sorry, Hem, I shouldn't be dumping this on you just as you head to the airport. But it's freaking me out a bit. Carlos is acting kind of strange, too, and he's always been my rock."

"What do you mean?"

"I don't know. He just seems preoccupied and distant. Like he's not quite there, you know?"

"Sarah, I'll be back in ten days. I'll come to Chicago and we'll corner Dad and get to the bottom of it all. Okay?"

"You're on," said Sarah. "In the meantime, try not to think about all of this when you're gone. I really hope you find what you're looking for and that the words start pouring out of you when you're back."

"Thanks. Me, too."

———————

An hour later, I looked out the window and saw the cab pull up in front of the building. I grabbed my suitcase, made sure my passport was in my pocket, and headed out the door. My mind was a blank slate as we drove to LaGuardia. I always feel a little out of sorts when travelling and the feeling usually begins as soon as I get out of my own building. We were almost at the terminal when my cellphone chirped.

"E Hemmingway" appeared on the screen. Great. Under normal circumstances I'd just hit the button and send the call to my voice mail. But my conversation with Sarah made me hesitate, sigh, and then answer.

"Hi, Dad."

"Yes, son," he opened. "Look, I don't have time to lollygag on this right now so I need an answer from you."

"Dad, despite the fact that I now self-identify as a writer, I still am not clear on what the word 'lollygag' actually means. Besides, I don't have much time either. My cab is just pulling up to LaGuardia and – "

"This won't take long," he interrupted. "I know you're leaving for a couple of weeks and I just feel this can't wait until your return. So here it is. Is your mind absolutely and terminally made up on not, I repeat, not joining the company? I must have your answer."

"Dad, what's going on? What's happening?"

"Son, it's not polite to answer a question with one of your own. I'm giving you one final opportunity to fulfill your family destiny and come back to Chicago where you belong. I won't be asking again."

Part of me was relieved that this might just be the final time I'd ever have to deal with this. But another part of me was alarmed at the apparent urgency of it all.

"Dad, why the rush? Why the full-court press right now when I have a flight to catch?"

"I just need to know, once and for all, where you stand on this," he replied in a voice that sounded older, thinner, and fainter than my father's.

"Well, Dad, I've been trying for years to get you to understand and accept where I stand. I'm afraid I'm standing where I've always stood. I'm truly sorry but I cannot in good conscience accept a position that I know would make me miserable for as long as I held it. And it's not just a job I'd be accepting. It's a life. A life I'm afraid I don't want. I'm sorry. It's not a decision that I came to lightly. In fact it's weighed on me for the last twenty-five years or so. So, I'm very sorry, Dad, but I have to decline. I know that's not what you wanted to hear, or what you've *ever* wanted to hear. But to me, it's a decision that's clear and considered."

There was silence for a time, though I could hear him breathing.

"Okay, I get it. You don't want it. You never have. Have a good trip."

"Dad . . ."

He'd hung up. If I had to sum up his demeanour in one word, I'd go with "defeated."

"Hey buddy, we're here and the meter's still running," the cabbie said from the front seat while eyeing me in the rear-view mirror. "They won't let me sit here much longer, you know, so you planning to get out anytime soon?"

CHAPTER 9

As soon as I got into the terminal, I sat down on my suitcase and banged out an email to Sarah to brief her on my strange call with Dad. I hit Send and looked up to see Professor James Moriarty staring down at me. He looked very professorial in a light blue Oxford button-down shirt, a brown, elbow-patched tweed jacket, and brown corduroy pants. A pair of dark brown well-worn brogues completed the ensemble. He looked like he was primed to pose for the centrefold of *Cambridge Professor Emeritus Quarterly*. He travelled light with only a small shoulder bag to sustain him for the next two days. I wore a pair of Levi's and a blue golf shirt. It was hot out.

"Greetings, Earnest. You know there are chairs available just adjacent to us."

"Hello, Professor. Yes, I did see the seats, but I've sat in those before and I can assure you, my suitcase is more comfortable," I replied. "But I'm all set now. Shall we?"

I stood up, grabbed my suitcase, and rolled it toward the check-in counter with James alongside me. I always try to use the automated check-in kiosks to save yet another conversation with an incredulous Delta Airlines employee about my name. But as luck would have it, there was only one kiosk working, and it was besieged by what looked like a Little League baseball team and its harried coach.

The professor and I approached the check-in counter together.

"Passports, please," came the expected request from the young man staffing the counter.

We both slid our passports across the counter. He picked up mine first and opened it. Three, two, one . . .

"I'll need to see some additional ID from you, sir, if you please."

"Of course," I replied, handing him the birth certificate, driver's licence, and Visa card that I'd already pulled from my wallet in anticipation of this.

"May I inquire why additional documentation is required of my friend when you already hold his passport?" asked Professor Moriarty.

"It's just a secondary check we employ when names seem like they might be falsified or fabricated."

"It's okay, Professor. I don't mind. I'm quite used to it, in fact," I said.

"Thank you, Mr. Hemmingway," he said as he passed back my ID along with my boarding pass. "Gate A6, boarding at 11:20."

The Delta check-in staffer then flipped open the second

passport, scanned the flight manifest on his computer screen, printed out the boarding pass, and handed everything back to the professor.

"Pardon me, if you don't mind," the Professor said. "Why did you not seek additional identification from me? Do you not recognize my name as potentially falsified or fabricated?"

"No, you're good to go. Gate A6, boarding at about 11:20," he replied.

"Well, thank you. But I should explain that in some circles, my name is even more famous than my friend's. Good day to you."

"Next, please," the Delta guy said.

Our flight was uneventful and we arrived at Toronto's Pearson International Airport six minutes ahead of schedule. After we safely navigated Customs with only a minor furor over my name, we piled into an airport limo for the drive into downtown Toronto.

I'd never been to Toronto but I felt like I knew it from all the research I'd done in preparation for the trip. I felt I owed it to Marie, Hat, and James to immerse myself in this odyssey. Eventually, we turned south off Bloor Street onto Sherbourne Steet, pulling up in front of the Clarion Hotel. It was a lovely, somewhat ornate, old, and well-proportioned red brick building. The sign out front had a sort of down-market motel vibe, but a beautiful lobby told a different story.

"Welcome to the Clarion, gentlemen, the home of Ernest Hemingway when he lived in Toronto in the 1920s," the clerk said in greeting.

"Is that right? Did Hemingway really live here?" I asked.

"He did indeed. Hemingway and his wife Hadley lived here while he was employed by the *Toronto Star*. It was called the Selby Hotel then. Some say, and who am I to disagree, that he wrote parts of his first great novel, A *Farewell to Arms*, right here in the Clarion."

"You don't say," I replied. "Well then, this is certainly the hotel for us."

"Could I have your name please, sir, and we'll get you checked in."

He was kind of staring at me, as if trying to place me.

"Certainly. Well, I guess we should get this over with," I said. "My name is Earnest Hemmingway. No relation."

He looked startled. I handed him my passport, Visa card, and driver's licence to try to move things along. He scanned the documents, looked back at me, and then his eyes widened as if he were witnessing a UFO landing. Then they opened even wider as if the alien probing had begun.

"Right! I know you!" he exclaimed. "This is very cool! And I'm glad you finally got your new driver's licence."

I just nodded. There is no fame like YouTube fame. It's the gift that keeps on giving.

"What an awesome coincidence that you should be staying with us here at the Clarion, Mr. Hemmingway," the clerk gushed as he pulled my reservation up on his screen.

"Awesome, perhaps. Coincidence, no," James observed.

The clerk was still looking at his computer screen.

"Well, then I guess it's no coincidence that you'll be staying in the Hemingway Room while you're with us."

It made no sense to come all the way to Toronto and then stay in the room down the hall from the Hemingway Room. So I'd splurged when I made the online reservation and had booked the full-meal deal. I was to stay in the very room Ernest Hemingway and his wife occupied. According to a leaflet on the dresser, some of the furnishings, including the beautiful writing table, were actually used by Hemingway during his time there. It was nearly impossible for me to get any closer to the man, his memory, his ghost.

James was in an equally glorious room just across the corridor, though his was not freighted with the same literary significance.

"Okay, what's first on the itinerary?" I asked when I met James in the lobby a little while later, though I knew exactly what we had planned. We'd worked on the schedule together.

"I think the subway is the easiest way to get to our first destination."

Twenty minutes later we emerged at the intersection of King and Yonge streets. I checked Google Maps on my cellphone and headed west along the north side of King Street for about seventy-five yards. We stopped and stood in front of 20 King Street West. From the rather pedestrian architecture, I suspect the building was erected in the fifties or early sixties. The words "Royal Bank of Canada" were etched into the stone façade along the front.

"Is this is it?" asked James.

"This is the address, but it's not the original building," I explained. "In the 1920s, a brick building stood on this site and served as the headquarters of the *Toronto Star*, where Hemingway worked as a reporter."

"Do you feel anything peculiar standing right here nearly a century later?"

"I'm not sure I'm supposed to feel anything."

"We'd better go inside. The therapeutic impact may be diluted standing out here," James suggested.

Therapeutic impact? I shrugged, and up the stairs we went into the Royal Bank of Canada building. It was a bustling bank branch with a lineup awaiting the next available teller. I had a DMV flashback, but pushed it aside.

"Are you aware of any unfamiliar sensations, now that we're inside?"

"Come to think of it, I do feel a little uncomfortable, but I think it's because we're blocking the path here and people are glaring," I replied.

"What about over here?" James asked as he moved over to a quiet corner.

I moved over beside him feeling vaguely uneasy.

"Hem, I suggest you close your eyes, empty your mind, and try to picture Ernest Hemingway coming through the door and what you would say to him."

"You're a man of science, Professor. I didn't think you'd go in for this occult stuff."

"I don't really. But as a career academic in the endless search for truth, I make considerable efforts to keep my mind open to new possibilities. There is so much we don't yet understand about the inner life of the human mind. The lion's share of our cerebellum and cerebrum remains shrouded in mystery."

So, feeling a little uncomfortable, I stood there in the one relatively quiet corner of 20 King Street West in downtown Toronto, with dozens of customers milling around, tilted my head back a bit, and closed my eyes. I snatched a quick peek and saw that James was doing the same thing beside me. Presumably, we were both attempting to empty our minds.

"It is quite an interesting feeling, I must confess," said James in a louder voice than was necessary given my proximity to him. "I don't really know how to describe the sensation, but it is quite markedly different from ambulating with your eyes open sustaining multiple lines of thought simultaneously. Markedly different."

A moment or two later, I lifted my lids and stared into the smiling face of a rather large security guard. I knew he was large because my head was still tilted back yet I was making direct eye contact with him. Of course, James was just settling into his meditative trance and carried on a kind of psychoanalytical play-by-play just so he could keep me informed of his evolving mental state.

As compelling as it was, I interrupted his colour commentary.

"Um, Professor, I'm quite sure that it's time for us to leave now," I said.

The nice security guard said nothing, but nodded his agreement and then swept his hand toward the door, showing us the way out.

"Really, Hem, I'm just starting to feel something. Let's give it a few more minutes, shall we."

Of course, his eyes were still closed, and he rocked gently, his hands now raised above him, perhaps to catch more spiritual transmissions, but I really don't know. My DMV flashback returned with a vengeance, skipping directly to the security guard–assisted climax.

"Um, James, I really do think it's time we took our leave."

I hoped Professor Moriarty had not yet emptied his mind to the point where rational thought was compromised. I took his arm and we moved toward the door.

"Thanks so much," I said to the guard.

"My pleasure, sir," he replied, bringing to life the cliché of the polite Canadian.

By this time, James, roused from his reverie, had instantly caught up with the more concrete developments outside of his mind.

"Yes, many thanks, indeed, sir," James said and bowed slightly to the guard.

"Well, were you receiving any Hemingway vibes while you were inside?" James asked when we'd made it safely out to the sidewalk again.

"No, not that I'm aware of, but my hunger pangs may have been impairing my spectral sensors."

"Perhaps because the original building was demolished to make way for this less than spectacular architectural offering, contact with Mr. Hemingway is no longer possible at this site. You may well have better luck in your own hotel room."

"I think our work here is done," I said. "How about we head to our second stop?"

"Capital idea. And I think we can buy a copy of today's *Toronto Star* in the subway. You should at least read the newspaper that employed Hemingway."

Just before we left, I asked a young woman walking along King Street if she would mind taking our photo standing together in front the Royal Bank of Canada building. True to its billing as a friendly city, she gladly agreed. In fact, she invited us out to dinner, though we politely declined, given our tight schedule. As she lined us up for the shot, I noticed the security guard eyeing us through the glass, still smiling.

Five subway stops north left us at the major Toronto intersection of Bloor and Yonge streets. We walked a couple more blocks north and then a few to the west and found ourselves in the middle of Yorkville, a very tony shopping district. Eventually we made our way to, yes, Hemingway's Restaurant and Bar, on Cumberland Street. When James and I were planning the trip, we'd decided we couldn't pass up visiting this establishment. Perhaps we should have done a bit more investigation.

Don't misunderstand me. Housed in a modern building with a lovely outdoor patio, it was a very nice place with friendly staff, great food, and a seemingly endless selection of alcoholic beverages, many of which we tried. But to call the restaurant's link with Hemingway tenuous was to endow the word with far more substance than it really deserved. In fact, the positioning statement for the restaurant, emblazoned on coasters, napkins, and the sign out front, was "Little New Zealand in Yorkville." I'm not sure Ernest Hemingway ever made it to New Zealand. It seemed that the restaurant's only tie to Hemingway was that the writer once roamed the streets of Yorkville in the twenties. We stayed anyway.

"I have concluded that you and I have had different experiences living with famous names," said James. "I concede that the burden you have borne has been greater than mine. I'm convinced of it."

"What makes you say that?" I asked, the vodka and orange juice starting to close the fuzzy curtains in my brain.

James raised his single malt scotch, Balvenie it was, and looked through the amber liquid.

"You see, young Hem, your famous name is universally famous. Very few sentient beings, at least in the Western world, are unfamiliar with Ernest Hemingway. He is recognized perhaps as much as any other human being in history, with the possible exception of the Pope, the Queen of England, Adolf Hitler, and Elvis Presley. While a considerably smaller number will have actually read any of Hemingway's words, virtually everyone can identify him as one of the great writers of this, or any other, century. Are you with me thus far?"

"Yes, very few fair-minded observers could disagree," I replied. "Carry on."

"My own name is famous, too. In fact, as I observed to our friendly Delta check-in chap, among a very select and much smaller population, its fame would rival that of Hemingway's. But the point is, the share of the world's population that has ever heard of Professor James Moriarty, let alone knows who he is and his particular place in the history of letters, is minuscule compared with those who instantly place Hemingway in the pantheon of literature. Our respective levels of *namefame*, as our friend Jesse Owens might put it, are on completely different planes."

"I'm not certain how planes suddenly came into the discussion, but through what singular series of events did you come by your name, anyway?" I asked. "I've been seriously curious about that ever since you showed up at the Y that night."

I tend to pronounce the phonetic sound *s* as *sh* when I've had a few drinks, or when I'm doing my very bad Sean Connery impression. "Certain" becomes "shertain." "Suddenly" become "shuddenly." In this instance, I was not doing Sean Connery. James didn't seem to notice.

"My parents were not well educated. My father was a miner in the north of England and my mother did what women of that era did. She kept the house, raised the children, and left the light on so my father didn't break his neck on the stairs after returning from the pub, almost every night. Neither were avid readers. In fact, I'm not clear on whether my father actually could read. I know my mother could, but it didn't occupy much of her spare time. Frankly, she had very little time to herself."

James paused for a moment to take a draw on his single malt.

"Moriarty is not that uncommon a name in the part of England from which I hail. Neither is James uncommon. In fact, had Conan Doyle never created Sherlock Holmes, the name James Moriarty would strike the mind and the ear as wholly natural, commonplace, and ordinary.

"My poor parents simply had no knowledge of literature's most infamous and diabolical villain. It was well beyond their ken. It was eventually brought to their attention when I was about four years old. They were amused, and not at all concerned. By then, it was too late anyway."

"So who is the fictional Professor Moriarty? I really haven't read many of the Sherlock stories."

"Shame on you, Hem," he chided. "It is some of the very best writing you'll ever read. As for Professor James Moriarty, well, simply put, he is evil incarnate. There are many famous villains in literature, but none as bereft of mercy yet blessed with intelligence as he. The sophistication, reach, and complexity of his demonic vision have no equal in life or literature. Mercifully, he exists only in Conan Doyle's writing, and not nearly as often as his malevolent presence might suggest. Moriarty and his criminal hegemony appear in only two of the sixty Holmes stories and are fleetingly referenced in only five others. Yet he casts a pall over the entire Holmes canon."

"He sounds like a lovely guy," I said. "But there is also a similarity in our plights. We have some common ground that most of the others in our little group don't share, except perhaps Marie Antoinette."

"I await enlightenment," James replied.

"Well, I carry the name of a famous writer, yet I want nothing else than to be a writer myself, as masochistic as that sounds. You bear the name of a notorious character from the pages of the most famous detective stories in history. Yet you have immersed yourself in the world of Sherlock Holmes and dream of being invited to join the ranks of . . . what are they called again?"

"The Baker Street Irregulars."

"Right, the most respected organization dedicated to understanding and honouring the world of Sherlock Holmes. So, whereas many people living with famous names run from the world of their namesake to escape their burden, you and I, on the other hand, have run directly into the big bright light."

The silence that greeted my comment eventually caused me to look over at James. He was staring at me, faintly nodding his head. I couldn't see any smoke issuing from his ears, but he was clearly deep in thought. The silence endured a little longer.

"That, dear boy, is an utterly fascinating insight sprung from a very thoughtful and fertile mind."

"Ah, but it's a fine line that separates a fertile from a febrile mind, don't you think?" I asked rhetorically.

I downed the last of my screwdrivers in one chug. I knew it was my last, because I no longer had feeling in my lips. What I didn't know was how many had come before it. It was time to go.

"One final question," I said. "Do you think James Bond could defeat Professor Moriarty?" I asked.

"I'm afraid, dear boy, that you have just crossed over to the febrile side of the line."

Yes, it was definitely time to go.

———————

Despite the previous night, I was awake at 6:45 the following morning. I'd forgotten to close the curtains so the morning light was doing what morning light does in such circumstances. My head was a little heavy, but not nearly as foggy as I expected it would be. It was very quiet. The room was wonderful. I had just passed an entire night in the very room Ernest Hemingway occupied so many years ago. He not only occupied this room, he wrote here, made love to Hadley here, read here, ached for Paris here. He *lived* here. And now I had lived here, for one night. And I'd done it in the fashion Hemingway was said to have spent far too many of his nights. I drank too much, stumbled home, and flopped. And now, the morning after, as it was so often for him, it was time to write.

I grabbed my laptop and placed it very gently on the writing table, as if the famous furniture might be offended supporting anything other than a Moleskine notebook and a sharpened pencil, or perhaps an ancient Underwood. A freestanding, framed photo of Hemingway eyed me from the corner of the table. I sat down in the chair, as he had nearly a century before, and slid myself into position, as he surely had. I turned on the vintage reading lamp, as he had. I placed my fingers on the keyboard, as he had on his typewriter. Then, awash in the history of the moment, I sat there for forty-five minutes straight, my best intentions and desires falling away, and wrote not a single word. Not one. It was not that the exorcism was failing, I told myself. It was just too soon. It was not yet time.

I surrendered and signed onto the Clarion's Wi-Fi network, not something Hemingway ever would have done. I grazed the Internet and researched a revised schedule for the day ahead before I was to cab it back out to the airport for my overnighter to Charles de Gaulle Airport.

"I have a plan for today that departs somewhat from what we originally mapped out," I said as we finished breakfast.

"What have you got in mind?" said James. "I want to make sure we get to the Connable house, where the man initially lived when he arrived in Toronto."

"Professor, let's be logical about this. I've just spent an entire night and early morning in Hemingway's room. I sat at the very table at which he wrote. I've been closer to him here than I could be almost anywhere. I really think there's little to be gained by standing on the sidewalk staring at a house that

Hemingway lived in for a very short time and didn't even like. I spent the night in Hemingway's room. Everything else pales."

I told him my idea, and after a gentle debate, James acquiesced. I made a couple of quick calls while James went to check out. Then we were off. As luck would have it, the walk from the Clarion to the Toronto Reference Library consumed all of eleven minutes. A member of the library's staff met us at the front counter and gave us directions to a gallery in another part of the building.

It was obvious to anyone who might have been looking our way that Professor James Moriarty was excited. His arms were snapping as he walked. We turned a corner and down the hall could see a sign on the wall proclaiming "Adventures with Sherlock Holmes." As soon as he saw it, he quickened his pace and left me in his dust. He was already poring over the showcases when I entered the room. Apparently, the Toronto Reference Library held one of the most extensive collections of Arthur Conan Doyle artifacts anywhere in the world. Only a small portion of the collection was on display, yet James was spellbound. There were some original manuscript pages in Conan Doyle's own hand, along with letters he'd written. There were also first editions of the Holmes collections and several copies of *The Strand* magazine in which the Holmes stories initially appeared in the late 1800s. It would take several pages to enumerate all the Conan Doyle treasures offered in what seemed to me to be an all-you-can eat Sherlockian buffet. It took an hour and a half before James was sated. I suspected that if I hadn't been with him, he would have stayed all day.

"What a magnificent collection," he bubbled. "I was hoping to get a chance to visit. Very kind of you to propose this in the middle of a trip that was to be all about you and Hemingway."

"James, I slept in Hemingway's room. Short of meeting him, I think we've achieved our goals for the Toronto stop."

James swept his arm to take in the whole room.

"I imagine all of this does not have the same hold over you as it does over me."

"On the contrary, I think it's all quite fascinating. In fact, you've inspired me to read the Holmes stories."

"Excellent. We're always looking for new and younger recruits!" he replied. "You know, you can download all the stories and the four novels on your newfangled tablet device for free, as they are now all in the public domain."

"Good to know," I said. "James, if you think you're nearly done exploring this Holmesian cornucopia, there's one more stop we should make, and there'll be food."

"Splendid. I'm ready to venture forth," he said. "What's on our itinerary now?"

"Lunch at the Duke of Kent. It's a handful of subway stops north of here."

"Lead on."

We thanked the librarian on the way out and were back on the subway a few minutes later. The Duke of Kent is on the southeast corner, one block north of Yonge and Eglinton. As you might infer, it's a pub, serving, yes, pub fare. I didn't really know if it was well known for its food. The man I'd spoken to on the phone this morning had proposed it. He was waiting at a table for two wearing the paisley cardigan he'd warned me about.

"Mr. Hemmingway?" he said as he rose. I reached out my hand and we shook. "I'm Barclay Grant."

"You're Barclay Grant? The Bootmakers of Toronto?" James piped up.

"None other."

"You wrote that brilliant piece about *The Five Orange Pips* in the *BSJ*, what, two years ago now?"

"Very impressive, Professor. You're right," Barclay replied. "And though I never thought I'd ever say this, you must be Professor James Moriarty?"

James's jaw dropped as they shook hands. He kept looking from Barclay to me and then back to Barclay. It was nice to watch his dawning understanding.

I'd discovered a reference to The Bootmakers of Toronto when I'd been surfing the Internet that morning in search of the Sherlock Holmes exhibition at the library. Barclay Grant led what was, apparently, one of the leading societies devoted to literature's great detective. I had no idea that James would also know of the organization, but I guess I shouldn't have been surprised.

After a demolishing a plate of what the Duke of Kent pub claims is its "famous bangers and mash," I left James and Barclay deep in debate while I walked back down the street to the Starbucks we'd passed earlier. When two deeply steeped Sherlock Holmes experts get together, it's probably best just to leave them to it. So I did.

I ordered a double tall latte and sat down in the leather armchair that had just been vacated. It was still warm. I pulled out my iPad mini and confirmed that my flight to Paris that evening was still scheduled to leave on time at 8:15. I also checked my Gmail account and amid the spam was a response to my airport email to Sarah. It was short.

> *Thanks for the update. I'm not surprised he called. Have a great trip, but don't dawdle coming home. Dad is acting mega-weird right now and is still holed up in his office with a few suits coming and going. Not sure what's happening. Do not, under any circumstances, change your travel plans. This will keep for a week, but head for Chi-Town when you're back. Sarah*

I called her but only got her voice mail.

I wanted to give James and Barclay some more time, so I called up Hemingway's A *Moveable Feast* on my iPad mini and turned my thoughts to Paris.

––––––––

On the way to the airport, the cab driver stopped for a moment on Bathurst Street, south of Eglinton Avenue, so I could see the apartment house Hemingway and Hadley had lived in for most of their time in Toronto. Gold script on a green awning out front now announced the building as The Hemingway. I got out of the taxi and pressed my hands against the brick wall just adjacent to the entrance. Hemingway would have touched these same bricks in 1923, perhaps after a night of drinking, bracing himself as he pulled open the front door. I felt nothing. I slipped back into the cab and we were off again.

At the airport, Professor James Moriarty and I shook hands. Our respective gates were at different ends of the terminal.

"Hem, I must say I'm overwhelmed with the day. Taking it upon yourself to track down Barclay Grant and arranging lunch for us was an act of kindness and generosity I'll not soon forget," said James as he gripped my hand for much longer than your garden-variety shake.

"It was nothing. We did the Hemingway thing, and it was great, but we had extra time. Don't give it a thought."

He reached into his bag and pulled out a paper stapled in one corner.

"I gave Barclay a copy of this new paper I've just written about "The Adventure of the Blue Carbuncle," one of my favourite stories in the canon. I've just submitted it to *The Baker Street Journal* and am hanging on tenterhooks awaiting their response. I'd like you to read it, if you feel so inclined."

"Thanks, James. I have a long flight ahead of me so I'm glad to have it," I answered. "And I'm glad your lunch with Barclay was enjoyable."

"Enjoyable? It was dazzling. He has a fine mind for Sherlock. I'm thrilled to have met him. And it is you I have to thank."

Then James put both his hands on my shoulders as if he might be about to bestow upon me a heartfelt head butt. He smiled and fixed me with a rather intense gaze.

"Sincerely, I thank you for a wonderful visit to a lovely city," he said.

I felt a rush of warmth for this thoughtful, kind man.

"James, I'm supposed to be thanking you," I replied. "It meant a lot to me that you came up with this idea in the first place, and that you wanted to come along for the ride. It's been a great couple of days, and I won't forget it."

"Now steel yourself for what lies ahead," James said with considerable gravity. "Hemingway was never more formidable than he was in the Paris years. He hated Toronto. But he loved Paris. Confronting him on his home turf, in the City of Lights, may not be so easy. Godspeed."

A final squeeze of my shoulder and he was off.

CHAPTER 10

I realize I'm not the first to make this observation, but, um, there really is something about Paris. For many visitors, certainly for me, there's a vibe in the city that transcends the history, the architecture, the people, the pure and unalloyed significance of this special place. I can't describe it, but if you were in Paris with me, I think you'd know exactly what I mean. You would.

I took a cab from Charles de Gaulle airport directly to Hôtel de Buci, located, appropriately, on rue de Buci in the heart of Saint-Germain-des-Prés. What a lovely little hotel. I've stayed there before and have never had call to try anywhere else. The location is perfect. The staff is wonderful. The rooms are charming. And the price is at least reasonable and, I think, worth every euro. You see, I've been to Paris several times over the years. It took a few exploratory visits before I knew that Saint-Germain was my favourite part of the city and where I would always choose to stay. It's also where Hemingway spent much of his time, living, loving, writing, fighting, and drinking, in the Paris of the 1920s. I'm sure it was just a coincidence that we both preferred Saint-Germain. Yeah, that's it, a coincidence.

The dull ache in my buttocks confirmed that I had just endured a very long flight, despite the prevailing west wind. The plane actually arrived on schedule, but the thinly padded seats made it a long haul. In Toronto's Pearson International Airport, I'd downloaded *The Adventures of Sherlock Holmes*, which included "The Blue Carbuncle," the story James had examined in his paper. He was right. The story itself was wonderful, and the writing was downright glorious. I suspect I fell so hard for the prose because it tends toward my own. I'm not suggesting for an instant that I'm anywhere near Conan Doyle's league. It's just that he writes the way I aspire to write. Unlike Hemingway, Conan Doyle doesn't just plod along from point A to point B in minimalist prose, but crafts complex and ornate sentences that make you feel good about the trip. If Hemingway's writing is a competent skater crossing a frozen river, Conan Doyle's is an elite figure skater, elaborately costumed, tossing off triple Salchows and quad toe loops along the way. Yes, both writers get you across the river, but Conan Doyle makes the journey as entertaining, significant, and rewarding as the destination.

Don't get me wrong. I certainly understand those critics who hail Hemingway as the master, believing his simple, straightforward writing gives the reader free and immediate access to the story. Those same critics often contend that Conan Doyle's florid prose distracts and detracts from the tale it's telling. I understand what they mean. I get it. I just don't agree. I doubt I ever will. And the warm tinges I felt reading "The Blue Carbuncle" lent physical affirmation to the judgment my mind made a long time ago.

Then I read James's paper. Intentionally or not, it was written in a style similar to Conan Doyle's, which seemed fitting. In part, James examined the extraordinary deductive conclusions Holmes draws early in the story about a mystery man, based solely on the careful scrutiny of a dusty, creased, and cracked hat. It's a wonderful scene that leaves Watson reeling from the detailed descriptions and predictions Holmes provides about the man's life and habits. It is as if Holmes had known the man for years rather than simply "knowing" the man's hat for minutes. That section of the story alone is worth the price of admission.

I thought the paper was outstanding. It was thoughtful, substantive, enlightening, and very well written. There was even a dollop of humour thrown in to leaven the academic rigour. Even though I know very little about the Sherlockian world, I could not imagine a respected periodical like *The Baker Street Journal* rejecting this submission. But James was filled with doubt. He really did believe that sharing the infamous name of Sherlock's nemesis compromised, perhaps even crippled, his chances at publication.

When I'd finished with "The Blue Carbuncle" and the Moriarty paper, I read a few more Holmes stories and was entranced all over again by the writing. It was as if I were reading on two levels. I was enjoying the stories themselves with their intricate plots and fully formed characters, while marvelling at the wonderful words assembled to tell them. My brain was fatigued after all that, so I killed the rest of the flight watching the aptly named film *Dumb and Dumber*. It was dreadful, but it took my mind off the pain in my inadequately cushioned hindquarters. I slept not a wink and arrived in Paris early Saturday morning feeling a little dazed but thrilled to be back in the City of Lights.

I was a little early for my rendezvous with Marie Antoinette so I decided to walk from my hotel to Notre Dame. If you have the time and the right shoes, I would always recommend walking in Paris. It's the best way to lose yourself in this spectacular city, figuratively, and often for me quite literally. I've learned never to wander the streets of Paris without the aid of my smartphone map app. When you're walking, you're in the streets with the crowds. You're seeing the architecture up close. You're hearing the city, and smelling it, too. You're jostling with citizens and tourists alike, navigating market stalls, and passing more little cafés than you ever thought one city could ever support. Full immersion is the best way to get inside and underneath Paris. It's really the only way to be a part of Paris.

As well, walking in Paris is recommended simply because it's infinitely safer than driving in Paris. Then again, professional knife-catching is safer than driving in Paris.

I left my hotel and walked east along rue Saint-André des Arts, past the local Starbucks. I veered north when I hit rue Danton and headed toward the Seine. I took a right at the river and continued east along the bank until I crossed over the bridge to Île de la Cité with Notre Dame beckoning on my right. All of the tourists around me, and there were many, were slack-jawed at the beauty of the famous cathedral, one of the finest examples of Gothic architecture anywhere in the world. But I was staring slack-jawed at Marie Antoinette.

She hadn't yet picked me out of the crowd so I just stood there on the periphery and watched her for a few moments. We had surfed Google Images together for photos of Notre Dame and picked out a bench in front as our meeting place. She was sitting there smiling at passersby. She looked, well, radiant, content, perhaps even expectant. Warm tinges, not unlike those triggered on the plane by Conan Doyle's writing, returned, but I recognized their origins had nothing to do with words on a page.

Like a tap on the shoulder when you think you're alone, feelings can sneak up on you, and catch you off guard. I didn't need Dr. Madelaine Scott to explain that my ambivalence toward John Dillinger was linked to his obvious interest in Marie. But still, I had not really understood that my heart was involved until that moment when I saw Marie, bathed in sunlight, in front of Notre Dame. It seems that Paris in July can clarify and crystallize.

She was wearing what I think would be called a yellow sundress, though the nomenclature of women's fashion was definitely not my forte. Even under the tutelage of a trusted high school classmate, it had still taken me an unduly long time before I could correctly distinguish among skirts, dresses, shifts, pinafores, culottes, and gauchos. Enlightenment eventually came only through the heavy use of flash cards.

Marie looked lovely. After a sleepless transatlantic flight, I was quite sure I did not. But when she saw me, she waved and stood up. She'd already been smiling before she'd laid eyes on me. But she seemed to turn up the wattage for me. Did I mention she looked lovely? When I reached her, there was no hesitation. She hugged me. I hugged back, trying to figure out if this were anything more than a "Nice to see you, Uncle Bill" interaction.

"Hey, stranger, you made it," she said, beaming.

"Jet-lagged, hungry, and sleep-deprived, but in one piece, and on time," I replied.

"Yes, but the consolation is we're in Paris. We're really in Paris." She sighed and did a little pirouette with her arms outstretched.

The German backpacker, heavy-metal guitar spilling from his earbuds, was not expecting the back of Marie's hand smashing into the side of his head. Neither was she. Fuelled by her plaintive apologies and impromptu temple massage, Heinz soon calmed down and before long was back on his way.

"I thought you handled that very well, under the circumstances," I said.

"That's it. I'm imposing a moratorium on celebratory spinning in all touristy hot spots," she replied.

Then she took my arm, perhaps to help enforce her own edict, and led me back across the bridge to Left Bank. It really felt nice walking through the winding, narrow streets of the Latin Quarter, with Marie Antoinette on my arm. We had a leisurely lunch at a tiny café not far from the Seine. I felt much better after putting away a bowl of spaghetti bolognaise and a half-litre of shiraz. Marie drank the other half and devoured the classic French dish croque-monsieur.

Beyond "Oui," "Non," "Merci," and "Ou est la toilette," I spoke very little French. But Marie's training in Paris over the years had left her very nearly fluent, as you might expect someone carrying her name to be. It was very impressive to watch her switch from one language to the other, and back again.

"So how has the pastry course been so far?"

"Oh, it's been wonderful, but quite demanding. The chef is a bit of a prima donna, but you know how pastry chefs can be."

"Oh yes, of course," I replied with a wave of my hand. I paused. "Actually, I have absolutely no idea how pastry chefs can be. How can they be?"

It wasn't intended to be a funny line, but she giggled. Not a laugh, not a chortle. It was definitely a giggle. I could tell by the way she put her hand up to her mouth as she kept her eyes fixed on mine. I went somewhere else for a brief moment.

"Well, let's just say he's very, very uptight and has little patience for sloppiness and carelessness," she explained. "When you're making the dough, the slightest slip-up in measuring and mixing can turn a perfect, flaky croissant into just another bun with the relative shape and texture of a horseshoe."

"And I always thought horseshoes were good things."

We talked, ate, drank, talked, drank, and talked for quite a while. We learned more about each other in those three hours than we had in all of our previous time together. I gave her my entire convoluted family history, including the expectation that I would take over Hemmingwear, and the recent developments with my sister and father. I told her everything. She made it easy. She told me about growing up in Baton Rouge, watching Julia Child on television, and deciding after her undergrad that baking was her true calling. I told her about Dr. Scott. Back and forth we went, spilling our selves before each other. It felt not unlike confession but without the priest, cramped venue, and absolution. We both just seemed to feel comfortable with each other. There was a natural feel and flow to the conversation, as if we'd known each other for a very long time. Even when there was silence, there was no pressure to fill it. As my mother might have put it, had she ever known Marie, "She has a very nice way about her." And yes, yes, she did.

"If you can still walk after that wine, we should really make our first stop on the tour," Marie suggested, checking her watch.

She took my arm again and we walked back toward the great cathedral where we'd met and onto rue de la Bûcherie. I knew where we were headed. It was one of my favourite stops in Paris. I'd visited there on every one of my Paris trips.

Since 1951, Shakespeare and Company, a cramped and

jam-packed English-language bookstore, had been located at 37 rue de la Bûcherie, overlooking the Seine and Notre Dame beyond. Its distinctive yellow and green storefront signalled a welcome refuge for literary types with limited French-language skills. If you were eager to hear English spoken or to find a book in English, you came to Shakespeare and Co.

It was just as I'd remembered it, locked in time, destined to be the messy, overstuffed, two-storey literary labyrinth that it had been for more than sixty years. I wandered around from room to room soaking in the ambience and trying to inhale the history of the place. As I walked up the staircase, I read the inscription on the archway above me: "Be not inhospitable to strangers lest they be angels in disguise." I loved that. There are worse credos by which to live one's life.

The original Shakespeare and Company was established by Sylvia Beach in 1919 over in the 6th arrondissement, where it quickly became a hangout for artists and writers, including one Ernest Hemingway. He even used Shakespeare and Co. as his mailing address in Paris. In the 1920s, it was a fixture in the city's literary firmament. It was not unusual to bump into Ford Maddox Ford, Ezra Pound, James Joyce, Hemingway, and many others in the store. With Sylvia Beach's blessing, George Whitman opened the current Shakespeare and Co. back in 1951 and, thankfully, it's still hanging on in the 5th arrondissement.

I went straight to the shelves with Hemingway's writing. They had many books by him, and about him. Marie stood well back and let me commune with anything Hemingwayesque I could find. Standing near a photograph of him, I read passages from his novels. I leafed through coffee table books about him. I read the little notations about Hemingway in the store. I closed my eyes a few times and concentrated, trying to summon up his spirit, daring him to make himself known. Armed with flowing, intricate, gossamer sentences of my own, I was ready to do battle with Hemingway's blunt, spare, flat, anvil-pounded prose.

"Are you all right, sir?"

I opened my eyes to face one of the many young, somewhat bedraggled, lit-loving travellers who lived and worked in the store. He was Irish, I think.

"Oh, yes, I'm fine, thank you. Just, um, trying to immerse myself in the history of this place." I was skating. "You know, get a sense of what it must have been like here in the early days."

"Well, we have a first edition of *The Time Machine* by H.G. Wells in very good condition, if you think that would help."

Marie and I left soon thereafter. I was pretty well wiped after the flight and time change. We walked back toward my hotel through the meandering streets that had completely escaped the hand of an urban planner with a straight edge. But that's part of the Paris charm. I was reminded on the way back just how popular small dogs are for Parisians. I'd somehow managed to blot that out of my memory from earlier visits. Three times I stopped and stiffened in my tracks with Marie still on my arm as a leashed poodle or a Pekinese pranced by.

"Right! I remember now," she said with a sympathetic look. "You're petrified of dogs, aren't you?"

"Well, it's true I'm scared of dogs in general, but to be precise, for some reason, I'm only petrified of small dogs."

"You mean you're more frightened of a poodle than you are of Bernese Mountain Dog?"

"I have no idea what a Bernese Mountain Dog is, but if it's larger than a breadbox, your assertion is correct," I replied. "I'm well aware that my canine condition is utterly bereft of logic and reason, but it still has a powerful hold over me. I'm working on it."

"It's actually quite fascinating," she replied, always looking on the bright side.

"Well, rest assured, if we are ever attacked by a mountain lion, or a silverback gorilla, or a thirty-foot anaconda, I will gladly hold them off while you escape. But if we happen to run into a Pomeranian, I'm afraid you're on your own."

"Got it," she said. "Have you spoken to Dr. Madelaine about it?"

"It's been a frequent topic of discussion between us but we haven't yet unearthed any reason for my Chihuahua aversion."

"What about hypnosis?"

"Been there, done that."

"And?"

"Well, it wasn't a complete washout. I have a short video of me waddling around her office quacking like a duck, of which I have absolutely no memory."

"That could be fun to watch," she said with a straight face. She squeezed my arm.

In my addled brain, that Marie was comfortable poking fun at me felt like another frontier crossed.

Conveniently, the apartment where Marie was staying was quite close to my hotel. Despite my objections, she insisted on getting me safely back to Hôtel de Buci. By this time it was nearly 6:00 p.m., but eating was the last thing on my mind. I managed to take off my shoes before collapsing on the bed.

The next day, Sunday, was a full-on, no-holds-barred Hemingway jamboree. After breakfast in a café simply known as Paul just down the street from the hotel, Marie and I made the long walk over to the Cardinal Lemoine Metro Station in the 5th arrondissement and met up with a clutch of tourists for our walking tour of Hemingway's Paris. Tom, our guide, was an ambulating encyclopedia of Parisian literary history. It was a great way to see at least one important section of the Latin Quarter, including fragments of the ancient city wall, the building wherein Joyce penned part of *Ulysses*, and, of course, several sites where Hemingway and his wife Hadley spent time. When we arrived at the apartment they shared, I actually sidled up and pressed myself flat against the building. It sounds irrational, I know, but according to Marie, that was nothing compared to how it looked. I'd come all this way, so I wanted to get right up into Hemingway's face, figuratively speaking.

We spent the afternoon drinking red wine and eating baguette and cheese in the Luxembourg Gardens. Hemingway was said to have spent a lot of time in the Luxembourg Gardens, occasionally bumping into Gertrude Stein as she walked her dog. We were reclining on the blanket Marie had brought and watching the people move through the gardens while we ate and drank.

"Did you know that when times were tough in Paris, Hemingway even caught pigeons in the gardens?" I said. "He'd take them home, pluck them, and Hadley and he would cook them for dinner."

"How do you think he caught them?" Marie asked.

"Who knows? Perhaps he just glared at them and they'd keel over dead in a cloud of his fatal manliness."

"Yes, that's probably how he did it," Marie agreed.

Something else happened in the gardens that I'd not been expecting. As we lay back watching the clouds and soaking up the sun, I felt Marie's hand slip into mine. I barely noticed it. That's how natural it seemed, as if we'd held hands a thousand times before.

At about 4:30 we walked over to put another check mark on our list of Hemingway landmarks. We had coffee in Les Deux Magots, Hemingway's favourite café. It was on the corner of boulevard Saint-Germain and rue Bonaparte, with seating outside and in. Its illustrious clientele, including Jean-Paul Sartre, Simone de Beauvoir, Picasso, and of course Hemingway, has made Les Deux Magots one of the most famous cafés in all of

Paris. Hemingway's favourite table was in the northwest corner of the room, marked by a photograph of the man himself on the wall behind. Our timing was good. The table was open and I sat where Hemingway sat whenever he was in the café, which was often. As had become my practice, I closed my eyes for a moment to try to feel the significance of this place. Nothing. I opened my eyes and Marie was staring at me and, yes, still smiling.

A square pillar rose from floor to ceiling just in front of our table. Mounted high up on two adjacent sides of the pillar were the famous statues of two sitting figures, les deux magots to be precise, who perched and presided over the café.

"What exactly is a magot?" I asked after we were seated in the coveted Hemingway table for four.

"I looked it up this morning and bookmarked it," Marie replied, pulling her iPhone from her backpack. "Okay, here we go. Apparently, a magot is a 'fanciful, often grotesque figurine in the Japanese or Chinese style rendered in a crouching position.'"

I looked up and noticed that the figure on our side of the pillar did appear to be Asian but was far from grotesque. I thought he looked a little like Curly from the Three Stooges but born somewhere in the Far East.

Just then, an older man, perhaps in his mid-sixties, appeared, dressed in walking shorts and a dress shirt, with a leather satchel slung over his shoulder. He stood below the statue, gazing up at it. His eyes glistened and his lower lip seemed to tremble. He lowered his head and turned to us.

"Excuse me, but do you speak English, by chance?"

By his accent, I assumed he was from somewhere in North America.

"Not just by chance, by birth. It's our native tongue, and I like to think we speak it well," I replied.

Marie had her back to him and hadn't seen his approach. She turned and smiled at him but then noticed the melancholy in his face.

"Are you all right?" she asked. "You look, um, upset."

"I'm sorry to bother you, but would you mind terribly if I sat down with you for just a moment? It really has to be this table. I hoped it might be free. Would you mind?"

While I would have preferred to have just spent more one-on-one time with Marie, she made the call without consulting me. She stood up and touched the man's elbow.

"You're welcome to. We have two empty places here. Please, join us. You look as if you could use a rest."

"I know there are other tables open, but it has to be this one," he said. "Thank you very much. It's so nice to be able to speak English."

He sat down next to me on the bench seat against the wall with Marie facing us on a chair. She waved to a waiter, who came over, took the man's hot chocolate order, and slipped away again. Our tablemate was looking over Marie's shoulder at the *magot* statue up on the pillar.

"It's so high. I don't know how I'll ever get up there. This is never going to work," he sighed before burying his head in his hands.

Marie and I exchanged perplexed looks.

"Um, is everything all right? Can we help you with something?" I asked.

Marie leaned in with a very concerned and sympathetic expression. The man paused, looking at the satchel he held in his lap. He nodded once and lifted his eyes to us.

"I'm Hugh Rowland. I'm Canadian, from Vancouver."

"Nice to meet you. This is Marie, and you can call me, um, Hem. We're from New York."

He looked at Marie.

"New York? You sound like you're from the south," he said.

Marie nodded.

"I grew up in Louisiana, but I live in New York now."

Hugh still looked uncertain about us. But as I'd experienced the day before, Marie has the kind of open and welcoming face that makes you feel like you've known her for years and can trust her with your life. My face probably says "Move along, pal," but Hugh was getting a very different message by looking directly at Marie.

"I'm on a mission, but I don't think I can do it all on my own," Hugh said, looking up at the magot again.

"Can we be of assistance? You look like you could use some help." Marie turned to me. "We could help, right?"

"We're not robbing a bank are we, Hugh?" I joked. Marie shot me a look. "I mean, sure. Um, yes, ah, of course we can help," I replied, deciding not to say out loud that I hoped it wouldn't take too long because I was on a mission myself.

Hugh paused again.

"That's very kind. Okay, here we go, I guess. It's hard to know where to start, or how to start. But you see, my life partner, Robert, died twenty-nine days ago. We were together for forty-three of my sixty-seven years."

Hugh had to stop for a moment to gather himself. Marie patted his wrist and nodded.

"Robert idolized Ernest Hemingway for most of his life, which is funny in a way, because Robert was nothing like Hemingway. Not at all. My Robert is . . . Robert was a small man, not very confident, hated guns and hunting, didn't drink, certainly didn't womanize, though that would have been a sight to behold, and was surely one of the least manly men I've ever met. The last three years of his illness showed me he was brave. He faced it with great courage and stoicism. Even so, he was definitely not manly. But I loved him, and he loved me. And he loved Hemingway.

"For the last thirty years, we've come to Paris every second year, without fail. Even in these last years, when he was deteriorating, we still came. We would spend hours just sitting here at this very spot, at Hemingway's table. He would hold my hand underneath the table and read me his favourite passages from Hemingway's novels. He knew most of them by heart. We were here six months ago, and he was too weak to read for very long. So he marked his books for me, and I read the passages to him. It happened right here. But no longer, I guess."

He looked away again and I thought he was going to lose it. I thought Marie was going to lose it. I thought I might lose it. Marie kept her hand on his wrist. That seemed to help. With his other hand, Hugh reached into his leather bag and pulled out a small white cardboard box and placed it on the table.

"What have you got there?" I asked.

"Robert," Hugh replied.

"It belonged to Robert?"

"No, it is Robert," Hugh said. "He was cremated. These are his ashes."

I recoiled, slightly. I don't think it was noticeable, although my elbow knocked my fork off the table onto the bench beside me. Even so, Hugh's focus was elsewhere. He didn't seem to notice.

"So what's the mission, Hugh? How can we help?" said Marie.

Hugh looked up at the magot.

"You know that both statues are wearing hats. You can't see the guy on the far side of the pillar from here, but he has a kind of a droopy hat that just won't serve our purposes. But you can see that this guy, on our side, has a hat that's shaped kind of like a cereal bowl. That one will work."

Marie and I looked up at the statue in unison.

"Don't both look at once, they'll know something's up," Hugh whispered.

I jerked my head around and made a big show of looking out the window.

"I'm not following you, Hugh," I said. "What do the statues' hats have to do with it?"

Hugh seemed fragile. He looked around the café as if uncertain how to proceed.

"Okay, here goes. I've told no one else this. You see, Robert's dying wish, which I promised him I would fulfill, is to have at least some of his ashes scattered here at Les Deux Magots. He wanted to be high up. The last time we were here, we agreed that somehow I'd put them in that magot's cereal bowl hat. He was insistent. So I agreed. What else could I do?"

I looked up at the statue cantilevered from the pillar about fifteen feet off the ground.

"This could be interesting, Hugh," I said. "It's really quite high. How tall are you?"

"I'm about five-ten, but I'm skinny and light. I think you'll have to boost me, I mean if you would. I hate to ask, but I really must complete this, somehow."

"I'd be happy to boost you, but I don't think the management here will be too thrilled if we start scaling their statue like it's a YMCA climbing wall," I countered.

"We need a distraction," Marie said.

That doesn't sound good, I thought to myself before saying, "That doesn't sound good."

"Come on, Hem, we don't need long. A little distraction and then you can boost Hugh up and he can do the deed and be back on the ground in no time," Marie urged.

"But even if I boost him, I'm not sure I can get him high enough to reach the hat."

"Ah, but I can help with that," Hugh said as he pulled something else from his bag. It was one of those telescoping devices they use in the hardware store when they need to reach a box of wood screws high up on the top shelf. It had a little squeeze handle at one end, and a claw at the other that opened and closed.

"I can reach another four feet or so with this thing when it's fully extended."

"There, problem solved," concluded Marie. "But we still need a distraction."

"I've already got the distraction ready to go," said Hugh. "Are you prepared to execute this plan?"

Marie looked at me square on. This seemed like a test. I wondered if she'd laid all this on. No, that's crazy. But it sure felt like a test.

"Okay, Hem. You're ready, right?" Marie asked.

"Well, to the extent that one is ever ready to lift a stranger onto his shoulders so he can scatter a loved one's ashes into the cereal bowl hat of a statue fifteen feet off the ground in a famous Paris café, then yes, I guess I'm ready," I replied. "But what's the distraction?"

Hugh suddenly gripped Marie's hand and mine in what felt like some kind of Three Musketeers' gesture of solidarity.

"I'll be forever in your debt if we can pull this off. Wait here and be ready when I come back, if you please," Hugh said before darting out the front door of the café.

"I'm worried that the only thing to be 'pulled off' will be the statue from the pillar," I said.

Hugh was back a moment later. He took a penknife from his pocket and cut a clean hole in the corner of the box. I could see the greyish ash inside. Hugh kept looking back toward the entrance. He then put the box in the claws of the hand-held telescoping thingy and secured it with some duct tape he pulled from his satchel.

"You're very good to do this. I don't think I could do it solo," he said, looking very serious. "It won't be long now, but when it's time, we'll need to move quickly."

Keeping the extendable claw shielded from view as best as he could, Hugh handed it to Marie beneath the table.

"I'll try to get up there first with your strong friend's help, then you hand me the ExtendaReach."

"That's what it's called? The ExtendaReach?"

"Brilliant name, don't you think? It actually says what it does," Hugh replied.

I could smell something, something burning. Black smoke was issuing from the concrete cylindrical garbage can on the corner just in front of the main entrance.

"I guess they haven't yet elected a new Pope," I quipped.

I thought a bit of humour might lighten the mood, though from their reaction, neither Marie nor Hugh seemed to consider it humour.

"Just a second or two more," said Hugh.

By this time, orange flames were leaping at least a foot or so out of the top of the garbage can. A few customers shouted and stood. Then all eight waiters on the floor rushed for the door, followed by several customers. The people enjoying their café and pastries in the seating area outside had all risen and moved out of range of the billowing smoke.

"Now!" Hugh snapped.

We all stood and took two steps so that we were up against the pillar. I interlocked my fingers and Hugh slipped his foot in while holding both of my shoulders. I lifted and up he went. As promised, Hugh was very thin and light. For a time on his way up, his crotch was pressed against my face. I tried not to think about it and kept lifting. First his knees, and then his feet were on my shoulders as if we'd practised this dozens of times. He had plenty of handholds on the pillar and the base of the statue to help hoist him up.

I had a belated moment of reflection as Hugh stood up on my shoulders. *How the hell had this happened? What the hell was I doing?* But then the moment passed.

Marie was standing behind the pillar, nearly out of sight. The fire was doing its job, and most of the customers were now blocking the main entrance so they could get a better view of the miniature, self-contained inferno. Had we been on the shore of a lake in Upstate New York, we'd have been breaking out the sharpened sticks and marshmallows.

At Hugh's signal, Marie handed him the, yes, you know, the

ExtendaReach, and he set about fulfilling Robert's last wish. While this was happening, I was actually leaning nonchalantly against the pillar to brace myself with my arms crossed over my chest, just as I might were I casually waiting for a table, but without another human being standing on my shoulders. I even closed my eyes briefly. When I opened them I was staring into the face of our waiter. It was hard to identify the look on his face. Surprise? Anger? Outrage? Perhaps a mélange of all three. Before I could say a word, Marie leapt into action. She engaged the waiter in an animated discussion, *en français*, pointing first to the fire and then up at Hugh, who was still, you know, scattering Robert's ashes in the cereal bowl hat of the magot, fifteen feet off the ground.

The waiter was now gesticulating wildly, but Marie was keeping up. In among the French I thought I caught the word "Harvard." Then I decided it must have been "havarti." Eventually, the waiter was nodding, and then even smiling. Then, as I felt Hugh start his descent, the waiter actually reached up to steady him. A small cloud of ash preceded Hugh's return to terra firma, which caught the waiter somewhat off guard. I knew what *"Mon dieu"* meant. The waiter looked at me.

"It's dusty up there," I offered sheepishly.

Marie took the ExtendaReach from Hugh. Then for a brief moment, though not brief enough, Hugh was sitting directly on my head. He had a remarkably bony butt. I instantly wondered how he'd survived the flight across the Atlantic in those hard airplane seats. As soon as Hugh was back on the ground,

Marie leaned in ostensibly to brush, um, Robert, from his shoulders, and to brief him as discreetly as she could. The fire seemed to be under control by then. The waiter was standing there looking expectantly at Hugh.

"So, Professor, were you able to determine whether it is indeed a Yamamoto?" Marie asked him, in English.

Hugh seemed to be weeping but tried to compose himself. Through his tears, there was just the slightest suggestion of a smile. I could tell the waiter was puzzled by Hugh's streaming eyes.

"It's dusty up there," I repeated. It was all I could come up with in the drama of the moment.

"Alas, no, it is not a Yamamoto, but a very, very convincing imitation," Hugh replied.

"I'm so sorry, Professor," she replied before turning to the waiter, who clearly was not fluent in English.

She babbled on to the waiter for a few minutes, brushing the ashes from his shoulders, and shaking her head slowly with the kind of sombre expression normally reserved for a funeral visitation. But I suppose that was appropriate under the circumstances. The waiter sighed and nodded. All I caught of the exchange was when the waiter said, "C'est dommage" and "Merci." He shook Hugh's hand and turned back to his duties.

We actually sat back down at our table as if nothing had happened, but we didn't dawdle. Hugh collapsed the ExtendaReach, taped over the hole in the box, and repacked his bag. He was trembling and held a handkerchief to his eyes for a moment before rising.

"I don't know how to express my thanks," he started, holding both Marie's hand and mine. "I could never have done it alone. I was foolish to think I could. But it is done. Robert is where he wants to be. Thank you. Thank you."

Marie hugged him. He handed me a card with his name and address on it.

"If you are ever in Vancouver, you'll always have a bed in our home. In the meantime, you'll always have a place in my heart. You have restored my faltering faith in humanity."

With that, he walked out the door, his now lighter leather satchel hanging from his shoulder. As he passed, he glanced at the still-smouldering and smoking garbage can and nodded at the four firefighting waiters surrounding it. Then he sauntered up Saint-Germain and disappeared from view.

"Okay, spill," I said to Marie after we'd made good our escape a few minutes later. "What were you spinning with the waiter?"

"I just told him that Hugh was a Harvard professor and a leading authority on magots. I said that we suspected that the one Hugh was 'examining' might well have been made by the greatest Japanese magot artist of them all, Yamamoto, and that it could be worth millions of euros if we were right."

"I see. And 'the professor' discovered it wasn't the real McCoy."

"Regrettably, yes. I guess the artistic discovery of the century was not to be."

"Very impressive. While my head was supporting Hugh's butt, your quick thinking was actually saving it."

———————

After an amazing three-hour dinner that passed in the blink of an eye in a tiny restaurant on rue de Seine, we wandered back to Hotel de Buci. Marie wanted to see it for future reference, for those times when her friend's apartment might not be available. She loved my room. In fact, she didn't leave until morning.

CHAPTER 11

The sun was streaming into my room. Marie had left early to make it to her course. She had two days remaining, which meant that I had two days to complete the Paris leg of my little Hemingway tour and sort through just what the hell had unfolded the previous night. After lying in bed for another hour, I decided that there really wasn't much to figure out. It had all happened. I felt better than I'd ever felt before. There was a comfort and a calm that seemed to cradle me. I liked the feeling. Then I wondered how I was going to make it through the entire day until I could see Marie again that evening. I also wondered what was going through her head and heart. I tend to overanalyze.

After showering, I pulled out my laptop and stared at the screen for a while. Chapter 12. Nope. Not today. Was it too much to ask that I might just write a few words on the novel? Yes, I guess it was. Despite communing with Hemingway's past for the last few days on two continents, I still seemed no closer to breaking my psychological logjam and constructing sentences again. I gave up and checked my email.

There was an email from Susan at the University of Chicago Library and Archives. She wanted to let me know that they'd purchased a packet of letters from an estate sale following the passing of the daughter of the woman who had been the housekeeper for Earnest Hemmingway I. They were actually carbons of letters EH1 had sent to various people over a fifteen-year span. The archivists had not yet read the letters, but Susan just wanted to let me know about this addition to the family archive. In accordance with my father's instructions, she had informed only him and me, even though it was Sarah who was the family history buff. I wasn't particularly interested in a stray set of letters written by the family patriarch, but I thought Sarah might be. I flipped her the email. There were no other emails of any consequence other than the standard spam promises of a Nigerian prince's fortune, and enhanced sexual performance, which immediately made me think of Marie again. Although, almost everything made me think of Marie.

I spent Monday walking all around Montparnasse. Hemingway spent a lot of time in this artistically diverse and rich part of Paris, hanging around in cafés with other writers and artists. He and his friend, the Canadian writer Morley Callaghan, apparently met F. Scott Fitzgerald in the Dingo Bar in the heart of Montparnasse. It's no longer there, but many of the cafés Hemingway frequented and wrote in for hours on end were still in operation. So I spent time in each one of them, including Le Dôme, La Closerie des Lilas, La Rotonde, Le Select, and La Coupole. I tried. I really tried. I sat there just as he would have nearly a hundred years earlier, my Moleskine notebook open, my pen poised, willing and wanting to write. But I couldn't even scrawl a few primitive phrases. There was still nothing there. Was this working? Would it ever work? I reserved judgment. I decided, based on no evidence whatsoever, that it would take time. Courtesy of my day of café-hopping, by late afternoon, I was so wired on caffeine I didn't think I'd ever sleep again. Then I thought of Marie, again, and stopped worrying about sleep.

———————

On Tuesday evening, standing on the platform of Gare d'Austerlitz, I said goodbye to Marie. Monday night had been even better than Sunday night, and we hadn't had to scatter anyone's ashes anywhere. We just ate, drank some more wine, and headed back to the hotel. It was lovely. She was lovely. There were feelings and emotions I don't ever recall having when I'd been with Jenn. I hoped Marie felt the same way, but couldn't quite bring myself to ask. The evidence was positive, however. Like that she was still there beside me in the morning and was not in a hurry to leave. All good signs. Marie was heading home on Wednesday, so I was on my own for Spain.

I boarded a southbound overnight train for Vitoria, just over the border. Marie waved as the train pulled out. I waved back, and she was gone. I suddenly had second thoughts about Pamplona.

What was to be achieved by hanging out in more of Hemingway's haunts? Hadn't I done enough of that already? And what had it reaped so far? Nothing on the writing front. I was still blocked. The best part of the trip so far was walking out of the Gare d'Austerlitz alone, while I steamed in the opposite direction toward Spain.

As the sun sank and the train rattled south, I opened a file I'd brought and read about Hemingway's time in Spain. When I awoke, we were already in the station in Vitoria. I'd been out cold for nearly the entire journey. By the time I'd grabbed my bag and walked out of the station, it was just after 5:00 a.m. It was still dark but the first blush of dawn was rising in the east. My bus for Pamplona left at 6:15.

I'd timed this leg of the tour to coincide with Pamplona's annual Fiesta de San Fermin, best known around the world for the famous running of the bulls, a tradition dating back to the fourteenth century. And I was arriving in Pamplona in the middle of it all. In fact, my bus was packed with young men already dressed in the white pants and shirts and red sashes and neckerchiefs that were standard fare. Oh yes, not surprisingly, they all wore expensive-looking running shoes. No wonder.

I'd seen enough YouTube clips of the running of the bulls to know that I would steer well clear of the route. Every morning at eight, half a dozen bulls are chased out of a corral and through the streets of the old part of the town up to the bullring a mere nine hundred yards away. But what a chaotic, frenetic, terrifying, and dangerous nine hundred yards they can be. As soon as the bulls hit the streets, they are met by hundreds of runners who, as the word suggests, run in front of, behind, even beside the terrified bulls. It is absolutely insane, yet tradition dictates that the bulls and runners make the same mad dash each morning for the duration of the festival. Runners being killed in action are not uncommon. Bulls being killed in action are guaranteed, if not on the route, without fail in the bullring.

I would love to have been a fly on the wall centuries ago when some bright light cooked up the idea of the running of the bulls. I picture a group of town elders seated around a table at a local Pamplona cantina. The mayor takes control of the meeting.

"Okay, guys, we need to get the bulls from the corral in the centre of the village up to the bullring for the festival. I suggest we lead them up there early in the morning, around eight, when it's quiet. The streets would be pretty well deserted at that hour. Are we all agreed?"

"Wait a second," says another guy at the table. "Wait just one second! I've got a great idea. This could be big! This could be really big!"

"Enough with the hype," someone says. "Just spill the idea, already!"

"Okay, okay. Here it is. Instead of just leading the bulls through the streets, why don't we rile them up, taunt them, tease them? We'll get them angry. We'll agitate and aggravate the bulls. Hey, we could even hit them with sticks and make loud noises so they start to stampede in terror and rage. Okay but wait, there's more. Here's the kicker. Then, instead of the bulls running alone, we add several hundred men to run behind them, beside them, and in front of them, slapping them, and generally enraging the bulls for the entire sprint to the bullring."

"Gee, that sounds kind of dangerous," notes another elder.

"Nonsense. Sure, there could be some injuries, I guess – tourists trampled, heads cracked, blood spilled, bones broken. But think how exciting it would be for the bulls, for the runners, and for the townsfolk. And people would flock here for the festival. Well? What do you think?"

"I like it," concludes the mayor. "All in favour?"

———————

Hemingway loved festival time in Pamplona. The action, the danger, the blood, all called out to his macho sensibilities. Pamplona has always been a place where young men test their mettle. There's a famous old photo of Hemingway, clad in the classic white and red garb of the runner, taunting a bull in the middle of the bullring. As much as I wanted to walk in Hemingway's footsteps, my feet would not be taking me anywhere near the centre of the bullring. The stands, maybe, but not in the ring itself. I would do a lot to rid myself of this writer's block, but I do have my limits.

I was famished after my long train and bus journey. Even at this early hour, there were dozens of food stands already open for business, catering to the bull-run participants and spectators.

I ordered what seemed to be called a San Jacoba, a very popular snack, or tapa, in Spain, particularly in Pamplona. It's quite basic, really. You put a slice of salty cheese between two pieces of meat (I'm not sure what kind of meat) and then deep-fry the whole concoction to guarantee every last ounce of myocardial malevolence. It tastes amazing but it ought to come with a health warning and a defibrillator.

I had just taken my first heavenly bite when I heard the famous eight o'clock rocket go off in the distance, signalling that the corral gates had been opened and the bulls were on the move.

I had purposely retreated to a less crowded street running parallel to the bull-running course. I could feel the tension in the air and hear the runners' chants. I was walking up this little lane gnawing away at my glorious sandwich when they appeared. Bulls? Nope. Three, yes three, brown Chihuahuas on leashes, being walked by a small, round, older woman with white hair. The dogs were barking up a storm and doing their best to drag their owner toward me. I looked at the very aromatic sandwich in my hand. They were now about forty feet away from me, still straining at their leashes. Then, in slow motion, a five-year-old boy trying to escape his mother darted out of a side alley and smashed headlong into the dog woman. They both went down. I didn't actually see the old woman hit the ground because in the midst of her fall, she let go of her three leashes and released her hounds, er, Chihuahuas. Thoughtless tiny dogs that they were, they had no interest in ensuring that their owner was all right. No. All three of them had my San Jacoba in their cross-hairs. I took off, just ahead of the Chihuahuas.

"Out of the way!" I shouted. "Coming through!"

I tore through the streets of Pamplona just a few steps ahead of my ferocious pursuers. How could dogs with such tiny legs run so fast? I bobbed and weaved, faked one way, went another, just to gain a few feet of breathing room. But still they stuck to my trail. I was impressed with their stamina and worried about mine. A block later I was still sprinting, and so were the three Chihuahuas. In fact they were closing. They had spread out behind me to dilute the impact of my cuts and dekes. Still they ran. As I looked to my right down the cross-streets at each inter-section I ran through, I could see the crowds of bull-runners and even caught the occasional glimpse of the bulls themselves. My heart was pounding in fear and near exhaustion. The mutts must have been on something to enhance their performance. They just wouldn't quit.

I had to change something up here. I wasn't going to last in a straight-line dash. The dogs were still with me and clearly com-mitted to running me down. So at the next cross street, with noth-ing left to lose, I feigned left and darted right. Bad idea. I should have feigned right and darted left. I tend to make bad decisions when stressed. It turned out I was running directly toward the major thoroughfare occupied by a thousand runners and six very angry bulls. As I approached the crowds who were cheering on the brave runners and enraging the bulls, I suddenly had a thought. It was not an earth-shattering idea. In fact, it was really quite basic and should not have consumed five blocks of thinking time. My hunger and fear had combined to cloud my normally quite sound judgment.

These vicious dogs were not interested in me. They were after my half-eaten San Jacoba. Yep, that was my epiphany. Impressive, I know. Instantly, I dropped the cursed sandwich and kept running. And just as instantly, the dogs broke off the chase and fought one another for what was left of my San Jacoba. But I was still in full flight, and I reached the mass of spectators just as six or seven frightened and exhausted bull-runners broke through the crowd into the cross-street. We all crashed together and fell in a frightened and exhausted heap on the cobblestones. They'd barely escaped the wrath of the final angry charging bull, and I had outwitted all three of the Chihuahuas. We all just lay there, a tangle of arms and legs, breathing hard, trying to regain our wind and our senses. Our mutual brushes with death turned the air around us electric. When we all realized that we'd beaten the odds and survived, we helped each other to our feet and engaged in much hugging and backslapping on our death-defying achievement. We had looked mortality in the face and outrun it. We had survived, together. We stood there, our chests still heaving as we sucked in air, our arms interlocked, the bonds between us forged in a common crucible where danger was denied and defied.

Clearly my brothers-in-arms were not aware that while they were braving that final angry bull, I was dodging dogs not much larger than guinea pigs – although there was not one but three of the tiny terrors chasing me down. So I just kept my mouth shut and went with the backslapping.

I slipped away from my compatriots in the crowd outside the bullring where bulls and runners alike had ended the sprint. I saw a little cantina on another side street. After ensuring that the premises were canine-free, I ordered wine and another San Jacoba. I'd burned so many calories in the chase, I was ready to eat again.

I wasn't looking forward to my afternoon, but felt I had no choice. As 2:00 p.m. approached, I walked back to the Pamplona bullring. Apparently it's the third largest in the world and seats nearly 20,000. The tickets had gone on sale the evening before so there was nothing available in what we would call in the U.S. the box office. So I just bought a scalped ticket on the street and filed in. Thanks to some old photos and some research I'd done online before the trip, I knew approximately where Hemingway liked to sit for the bullfights. My seat was actually quite close. I looked over to where he'd sat and tried to picture him there, excited and moved by the matadors' feats of bravery.

Then the first bull galloped into the ring as the spectators hooted and hollered. After his grand and glorious entrance, it was all downhill for the bull. It was painful, physically painful, to watch. I doubt the bull enjoyed it much either.

Here's how it generally goes down. To open the proceedings, the bull is mercilessly taunted by picadors and matadors. When the bull charges, the garishly costumed men simply duck behind a secure wooden wall where they are perfectly safe. Predictably, the bull grows more and more frustrated and angry.

Then to add injury to insult, the picadors start sticking sharp multicoloured skewers into the bull's back. The blood flows. The crowd cheers. The bull weakens. When there are five or six skewers sticking into the animal, a matador then moves into the ring and forces the bull to charge through his cape over and over again until he's nearly overcome with exhaustion (the bull, not the matador). The bull seldom makes satisfying contact with anything more substantial than the air. Then the matador stabs the bull with a few barbed wooden sticks with little flags attached. The bull slows more, the blood loss and fatigue taking their toll. Then, when the bull is barely able to stand in one place, we reach the climax of the sordid proceedings, the *coup de grâce*. The matador stands before the half-dead beast, raises a sword above his head in a move that almost looks balletic, and thrusts the blade deep between the bull's shoulders to sever the aorta or pierce the heart. If it is done properly, the bull drops to the ground, stone dead. But often, it's not done properly and the bull suffers terribly before being dragged from the ring and killed offstage. It's a great dishonour for the matador to fail to kill the bull cleanly and quickly. Oh, the poor matador.

I'd researched all of this before the trip. I'd forced myself to watch bullfights on YouTube so I knew what to expect. But I didn't see much of my first live bullfight. The sun was beating down and the temperature in the stands must have been close to 100° Fahrenheit. Naturally, I was not in the shade. As well, I was tired from my overnight journey not to mention my terrifying Chihuahua chase earlier in the morning. The heat and my fatigue, together with the gruesome spectacle playing out before me, proved a potent combination.

I had no idea I'd passed out until I came to outside of the stadium. As far as I could figure out, two security staff had been alerted by the person sitting in front of me, the fat man I'd just fainted on. They carried me out, sat me in the shade, and tossed a little cold water on my gills until I revived. How embarrassing. I took the next bus back to Vitoria and boarded the overnight train for the return trip to Paris. Madrid was closer, but it was still cheaper to fly back to the States from Paris.

Shortly after take-off, with Hemingway's Paris and Pamplona receding behind me, I turned on my laptop. I launched Microsoft Word and opened the file holding my manuscript. Chapter 12. Twenty minutes later, I was playing solitaire. Shit.

———————

Hat was waiting for me in the Miami airport Arrivals area shouldering a red and blue Adidas sports bag, circa 1974. He was a little excited.

"Hem, you're here! You made it! You are really and truly here," he spouted. "I'm in Miami and you're here, too."

I was exhausted and wasn't exactly sure how to respond.

"Hey, Hat. Good to see you. Um, Key West, here we come,"

I said in a voice that was better suited for announcing the death of a cherished pet budgie.

"I can tell you that I've been exploring this very impressive airport since my flight arrived just two short hours ago and our gate is just down this way," he said, grabbing my elbow and leading me along the corridor as if we would surely lose each other without his hand gripping my arm. "I am also very pleased to report that our flight is on time. I even had the nice airline people put me in the seat next to you. It is all working out so well, is it not?"

"It couldn't be better, Hat. But don't take it personally if I fall asleep on the flight. I'm completely spent."

"Well then you really must use this on the plane. It is just so comfortable. It is the only way to sleep on a plane."

Hat unzipped his bag, reached in, and pulled out one of those inflatable neck collars passengers use to make in-flight dozing a little easier. Except this one was gigantic, pink, and sparkly. Judging by its size, there could not have been much room left in Hat's sports bag for clothes, toothbrush, and whatever else he may have packed. The sparkles and splinters of reflected light would surely make it impossible to sleep while wearing this gaudy tractor-tire inner tube around my neck. It was more likely to induce a migraine. Hat pushed the collar into position, hyper-extending my neck. With it installed, I could only see directly in front and above me. It was that big.

"Um, Hat, this is huge. Are you sure this isn't a pool chair or perhaps a life raft?"

"Oh, Hem, you are always so hilarious," Hat replied, shaking his head and laughing. "Life raft. Ha! So very amusing."

I hadn't really been trying to be funny at all.

———

I'd never been to Key West. Coming in for a landing, you get a clear sense of how lopsided and overpowering the ocean-to-land ratio is. I found it somewhat disquieting. It really doesn't matter where you are in Key West, the ocean isn't far away. The sea is always just outside your window, down the street, across the road, sometimes beneath you. It lent the city a vague sense of fragility that settled over me as well.

I checked us into the Westin Key West Resort and Marina at the confluence of Front and Whitehead streets. Though Hat fought it, I insisted on paying for the taxi, the rooms, and our quick dinner in the hotel restaurant. As far as I could tell, Hat's only income came from his part-time gig as an audio-dish aimer at the New York Jets games. It hardly seemed fair that he should pay so I could try to evict a long-dead writer from my psyche. Although it was only about 7:30 p.m. in Key West, my body was still in Paris, in the middle of the night. Hat reluctantly allowed me to go to bed so I might be reasonable company the following day. We agreed to meet in the restaurant at eight the next morning for breakfast.

Just as I was about to crawl under the covers, something slid under my door. I picked it up, turned it over, and looked at the itinerary Hat had developed, printed, and laminated. All that was missing was a magnet so I could hang it on the fridge. Okay, the fridge was missing, too. Here was Hat's plan for the next day:

9:00–10:30 *a.m.*	Visit the Ernest Hemingway Home and Museum on Whitehead Street.
11:00–4:00 *p.m.*	Walk to the docks for our afternoon of marlin fishing. (I hope they will be biting!)
4:30–6:00 *p.m.*	Free time for naps and/or shopping.
6:00–6:15 *p.m.*	Walk from hotel to Sloppy Joe's Bar on Duval Street.
6:15–*Closing time*	Dinner and related festivities at Sloppy Joe's Bar.

I felt a rush of warmth for Hat flow through me as I pictured him crouching outside in the corridor, trying to slip the schedule under my door without making a sound. The itinerary actually was laminated. I could take it home and use it as a placemat. He would have had to go to a Staples or a print shop to have it plasticized. Now that's commitment. I was touched.

As expected, I awoke early, still on Paris time, but did not even reach for my laptop. I just lay there and watched the sunrise through the picture window. Hat was waiting in the restaurant. We both did the breakfast buffet to save time. We were walking along Whitehead Street by 8:30 or so. It was only a few blocks to the Hemingway House. Hat went straight to the ticket booth. We could see the young woman inside but she was busy working on her computer. Hat knocked on the glass partition.

"Good morning. We are very eager to tour Mr. Hemingway's home. Might we have two tickets, please?"

"I'm sorry but we're not open . . ." Hat, who was instantly livid, interrupted her.

"Not open? This is an outrage! Your website says you are open 365 days a year, yet you are closed today? I will not stand for it!"

"Hat?" I said.

"We must get inside the home. My friend's very sanity hangs by a thread and depends on it."

"Hat!"

"He is a writer and that wily son-of-a-gun, Ernest Hemingway, is preventing my friend from finding the words to tell his important story."

"Hat, please!" I finally got his attention by gently touching his shoulder. Believe me, in his current state, anything more aggressive than a shoulder tap might result in a full-on fistfight.

"What is it, Hem? I'm trying to get us into the house."

"Hat, I don't think she was done. Ask her again and let her finish her answer."

Hat looked back at the irate ticket seller.

"Sir, if you'd just let me continue, I think you'll be satisfied. As I was saying, we aren't open until 9:00 a.m., which is in approximately four minutes. I'll give you your tickets now, but you'll have to wait until the doors open at 9:00 before you can come in."

"I am so sorry. I am so stupid. I completely thought you were saying that the museum was not open today. Please accept my apologies for my most offensive behaviour. I'm well aware that my fuse is very short indeed, and I'm working diligently to lengthen it. Here, please enjoy this butterscotch as a symbol of my regret."

She took the candy.

"Thanks," she said before sliding two tickets our way.

Five minutes later, we were safely in the home where Hemingway lived and wrote for nine years of his life. We had the place to ourselves at that hour. We took our time exploring each room, leaving Hemingway's writing studio on the second floor until the end. Even though I was far from a Hemingway fan, it felt quite special to be within the very walls where he penned nearly three-quarters of his literary output. I was only slightly uncomfortable with the many cats roaming freely about the house and property. Many of them were an anomalous breed of six-toed felines, directly descended from Hemingway's own cat. Because cats aren't dogs, I could tolerate them, though I didn't rub their bellies or engage them in conversation.

I stood alone in Hemingway's writing studio while Hat stood guard at the door. A velvet cordon roped off the writing table Hemingway is said to have used. There were bookcases, a mint green lounge chair, and trophies from his African safaris and Caribbean fishing trips hanging on the walls. It's hard to describe the feeling of being in the room where he had written. He was nearby. I was sure I could feel him. Then, though it was not allowed,

I sat down in his chair and placed my fingers on the very typewriter keys he had depressed and released to record his simple, austere prose. I pushed the keys of his Royal portable typewriter and watched the metal arms bearing their letters swing into the centre to meet the page. Whatever you might think of Hemingway's works, for the serious writer, visiting his home can be a powerful, even a pseudo-religious experience. I suppose there are many Meccas for aspiring writers. Surely Hemingway's home is one of them.

I sat in his chair and thought for about half an hour as Hat respectfully patrolled the hallway outside. Eventually, I heard footsteps on the staircase as a few other early-bird tourists arrived. I rose and stepped back over onto the right side of the cordon. We departed a few minutes later. Hat left me in silence as we walked down toward the marina a short distance away.

———

I'm not a big fishing fan. But you can't trail around in Hemingway's wake without taking a shot at deep-sea fishing. Hemingway was close to obsessed with fishing. For days on end, he and his Key West cronies would ply the Caribbean waters in search of tuna and marlin. They often found both.

The boat Hat had chartered and that I gladly paid for was known simply as *Papa*, one of Hemingway's more enduring nicknames. I hadn't spent much time on the water, beyond a few excursions on the Finger Lakes of Upstate New York. I had only a literary understanding of seasickness gleaned from countless novels of the sea I'd read over the years. Regrettably, I can now claim first-hand experience and contend that the writers I read grossly understated the mariner's malady.

A steady six-foot swell kept the boat and my breakfast in constant motion. I'm pleased to report that I did not throw up, though I spent the last two hours of our voyage wishing I would. Hat was utterly unaffected by the incessant rocking and hooked three fish, though he was only able to land one of them, a mid-sized marlin. When it was hoisted aboard, it flapped about the boat for a time before it was stowed on ice below. Our captain fed me Dramamine like they were M&Ms, but my nausea was not to be quelled. Finally, I saw the marina in the distance. Hat reeled in his line for the last time and stowed the rod. The captain hit the throttle and we made a beeline for the dock. When we landed, I made a beeline for the bathroom.

———————

"I'm so sorry you were not feeling yourself during the fishing," Hat said. "You missed a wonderful lunch. If Hemingway himself had been with us, he would have taken one look at you and written *The Green Man and the Sea.*"

"Were you working on that line all afternoon?" I asked.

"Yes. As a matter of fact, I was. I'm quite pleased with it, though I hope you have not taken it personally."

We were sitting in the famous Sloppy Joe's Bar, where Hemingway spent parts of almost every day he lived in Key West.

It had taken me a few blocks of walking and weaving before I eventually found my land legs again. We decided to dispense with the scheduled naptime and move directly to the drinking. By the time we'd reached the bar, I was starting to feel a little more like myself. I began by drinking straight Coke, but then switched to Papa Dobles, a potent concoction of rum, lime juice, grapefruit juice, and grenadine. I can't really tell you what they tasted like. I think my taste buds were anaesthetized after downing my first mouthful. Hat was at the bar, talking to some locals and passing out candies. Other patrons in the joint were just passing out.

"So tell me the tale of the butterscotch candies," I said when Hat rejoined me at our table. "Surely there's a story there somewhere."

"Well, it doesn't yet have a happy ending, but I'm convinced it someday will," Hat began. "Shortly after I joined Con Ed and was responsible for the electrical side of the steam-driven co-generation project, I was harassed and bullied because of my skin colour and my faint accent. You know it's very easy for stupid people to parody the Indian accent. They can't do Australian, or South African, or Dutch very well, but for some linguistic quirk, Americans find it reasonably easy to imitate an Indian accent. Well, this fellow, who worked in maintenance, was always on my case. He just never let up. He would offer all his co-workers these butterscotch candies, right in front of me, but would never give me one. The whole situation might have been avoided had he just offered me a butterscotch. As time passed, he then started imitating my accent, badly. He somehow learned that I was Hindu, perhaps because I had mentioned it, and that seemed to push him over the edge. He was relentless in his verbal attacks."

"It sounds like this was going on a long time," I said.

"Oh yes, he started up in the morning and then carried on right through the day until I lost my temper, as you know I can do, and put an end to it, once and for all."

"Wait a sec. How long did this abuse continue? Weeks? Months? Years?" I asked.

"Hem, I already told you. He started in on me in the morning and continued right through lunch and late into the shift. It was my first day on the job. At about 3:30 in the afternoon I gave him a little bop to the nose."

"Well, a 'little bop' doesn't seem so bad," I replied.

"In truth, it was quite a significant bop, I have to say."

"I see. Was he hurt?" I asked.

"Oh no. Not badly. Though for a while his nose did consume far more facial real estate than it had originally. And he did have to breathe through his mouth for about six or perhaps seven months until the surgeries were completed."

"You're not serious. Surgeries? Plural?"

"Well, yes, four would definitely fall into the 'plural' category."

"No shit. You're kidding," I said. "Were you fired?"

"Oh, yes, directly, on the spot. Charged, too. But they dropped the case after a while. I don't think they wanted it to look like it was racism."

"I see. But it was racism, wasn't it?"

"Oh, I think most assuredly it was racism in the mind and heart of my tormentor. They just didn't want it to *look* like it was racism. I have long since forgiven the gentleman, and I send him a bag of those butterscotch candies he likes, every month."

"Has he forgiven you for breaking his nose?"

"As I say, I have forgiven him. And he is back breathing through his nostrils as if nothing had happened, even though his nose still looks very much like something happened. Maybe even something significant."

"Well, it sounds like he had it coming."

"Perhaps. He was quite a mean man, but even he did not deserve to have his nose rearranged, moved to a slightly different location, and then reassembled approximately in its original position. No, he did not earn that. I pray for him every day. I have forgiven him. I do not yet know whether I can ever forgive myself."

Hat paused to eat a pretzel or two from the bowl on our table and take a swig of his fruit punch. Hat did not drink alcohol.

"The company also promoted him as part of the agreement to drop the case against me. He has definitely risen higher than his intellect, capabilities, and acute xenophobia might normally permit. But I'm happy for him."

"But you've never been able to get another engineering job since, right?"

"Technically, that is true," Hat replied. "My microscopically short temper has branded me as what is known in the HR world as a 'troublemaker.' My reputation seems to precede me. I am an honest man. So I tend to have some difficulty when the prospective employer asks why I left my previous job. But I work hard, do my best, and persevere. That is how this country has been built. I now think of it as my country, too. So on weekends I put my engineering degree to good use by aiming an audio dish at the line of scrimmage. I love the Jets. I may sound bitter, though I hope I don't. For I am not unhappy. There is really no place I would rather be."

"Your equanimity about it all is inspiring," I said and meant it.

"Why, thank you. Now can you please remind me of the meaning of this word, equa . . . minity?"

"Equanimity. It kind of means you never seem to lose heart when things aren't going as well as you'd like them to."

"I try to focus my efforts on those things over which I have some power, if you understand my point. Things I can actually change by my own actions. I try very hard to remember that it is not useful, in any way, to lament what I cannot control or influence. And most important of all is to have and show a positive spirit. Without that, I think I would be lost."

It may have been the multiple Papa Dobles I'd somehow downed, but Hat's words were making sense to me with crystal clarity. While we'd been talking, the place had filled to the gunwhales with tourists and all manner of Key West partiers. Alcohol seemed to be the glue that bound us all together, except Hat. The bartenders and waiters were slinging drinks as if the return of Prohibition were imminent. I knew my head would be pounding on the plane the next day. But at that moment, I could no longer feel my head, or any other part of my body, so I dismissed the thought.

At the table next to ours, a big man who bore a striking resemblance to Hemingway himself swayed to his feet and hoisted his nearly empty glass above his head. It looked as if keeping his balance for too long might be a challenge. So he barrelled ahead, his friend steadying him with a grip on his belt. He started by burping as many of Hemingway's titles as he could in one foul breath. And then he turned serious, quieting the group with an open palm.

"Friends and fans of Papa. Here at the famous Shloppy Joe's, Hemingway's favourite watering hole, I raishe my glassh in honour of the greatesht proshe stylisht in the hishtory of literal . . . literatch . . . littrach . . . books!"

All six men at the table lurched to their feet, or in one case toppled to the floor, drank what was left in their very large glasses, and then crashed their asses back down. Most of them even landed in their chairs.

"Bullshit, hogwash, and hyperbole!" someone shouted nearby. "Hemingway's writing sucks! It's like he only knows about twenty-five different words but refuses to use all of them. It's more basic than my First Grade reader. His writing is so boring, I can barely read it. Nobel Shmobel."

Hat looked at me with a very strange expression on his face. I leaned in to confer with him. I was quite surprised to learn that the thoughts running through my head had in fact run straight out of my mouth at taxi-hailing volume. The big guy at the next table struggled back to his feet and had his hands on my lapels before I could bolt from the room. And don't think I didn't try to bolt from the room.

"Now just a minute, sir, violence cannot solve this dilemma. This will not end well," implored Hat. "Let us discuss this like civilized gentlemen."

The big guy let go with one hand so he could rear back and launch a right cross in the general vicinity of my face. In a spasm of bravery, I closed my eyes. I heard the punch land, but didn't feel it. I opened one eye in time to see Hat's fist connect with the big guy's mouth a second time.

It occurred to me at that moment that I'd never actually been in a barroom brawl. There were six of them against the two of us. Well, I guess there were really only five left after a crazed Hat dropped the first guy. Hat bobbed and weaved, trying to slip the punches that flew his way while delivering a few of his own in between. He was quite good at it. I, on the other hand, opted for the berserker-windmill-flailing technique, which I may very well have invented that night. I now understand why no one had ever employed it before. I quickly learned that it's a very short trip from flailing to failing. Not recommended.

I took one roundhouse punch directly to my left ear. I'm not sure my ear was the target, but I turned my face away at the last second and apparently offered up my ear. I felt another hard shot strike my ribs. That really hurt and knocked the wind out of me. Finally, for good measure, I stopped a blow with my forehead that I think was intended for my nose. I somehow dipped my head a bit at the just right moment and saved my schnoz. It didn't hurt that much, at least not until I regained consciousness a few moments later. My assailant was on his knees, moaning and pressing his injured hand against his soft, overhanging belly. I think it was broken, his hand, I mean. He was not happy about it.

When the far too tardy bouncers finally waded into the melee, three of the six Hemingway acolytes were on the floor holding various parts of their anatomy. One other had passed out, and the final two were pummelling me, though I was getting in a few shots myself. In no time the police were there. Hat and I, and at least three of our adversaries, were cuffed and led to cruisers. I was bleeding from my nose and a small cut in my eyebrow. Hat looked unscathed.

You know how on TV, when the cop is helping someone into the back of the police car, they always put one hand on top of their prisoner's head so they don't bump it getting into the back seat. Well, the cop escorting me clearly had never watched police shows on television. My head hurt all the way to the station.

The desk sergeant sat across the table from Hat and me in a little interview room. I looked for the two-way mirror, but there wasn't one. He started with Hat.

"Okay, let's try to make this quick so we can all get the hell out of here. Name?"

"Yes, sir. My name is Mahatma Gandhi."

The cop rolled his eyes and smacked his pen onto the table.

"Yeah, sure it is, smart ass, and I'm Ernest Hemingway."

"On the contrary, sir. In fact, that would be my friend here," Hat said, proudly placing his arm around my shoulder.

"No relation," I added.

The situation deteriorated from there.

Eventually, after we'd presented multiple pieces of identification and told the sergeant that we were getting out of Dodge on a morning flight, he relented. Twenty minutes later, Hat and I were both in our hotel rooms. It was 2:30 in the morning.

I don't really have words to describe how I felt four hours later when Hat and I settled into another back seat, this time of a taxi. A police cruiser was parked across from the hotel's entrance, as we'd been told. They were really quite eager to see us off the island. I gave a friendly wave and the police officer nodded. When our cab pulled out and headed toward the airport, the cruiser fell in behind us. When we took the airport exit, the police officer stayed on the highway and gave us a tip of his hat. Apparently we'd convinced him that we were in fact leaving town, a condition of our release with no charges pending.

Thanks to his temper, Hat was no stranger to fisticuffs and the odd barroom brawl. And this barroom brawl had certainly been odd. But this was really my first experience as a ruffian, a hoodlum, an undesirable. As I thought about it in the back seat of the cab, inexplicably, I felt a certain pride, mixed in with the humiliation of being run out of a city for the first time. I looked over at Hat. Unperturbed, he was humming a happy tune as we pulled up to the terminal.

CHAPTER 12

In the Miami airport, Hat hugged me before his connecting flight for New York started boarding.

"I truly hope this trip will liberate you," he said. "But it may take some time. Do not hang unrealistic expectations around your neck. Give it time to work, and it will."

"Thank you for everything you've done, Hat. This was very, um, special for me. I'm grateful."

He beamed.

"I cannot remember when I've enjoyed a weekend more," Hat said. "I even liked our time at the police station. It makes a big difference when you're there with a friend."

I waved and turned to go.

"Oh, Hem, you know if you keep that itinerary I made, you can use it as a placemat back in Manhattan," he said as he joined the line for boarding, smiling and waving.

I had an hour before my flight to Boise. I found her in my contacts and hit the Call button.

"Dr. Madelaine Scott," she answered.

"Oh, I'm sorry, Dr. Scott, I was just hoping to leave you a message," I stammered. "It's Hem. I didn't expect to find you at your office on a Saturday."

"Hello, Hem. I was just getting through some paperwork that had been piling up. Where are you now?"

"Miami. I've been in Key West for the last couple of days and I'm just catching a flight to Boise for the final stop in this strange little tour."

"And has this strange little tour of yours had any effect on your ability to write?"

"No, and I'm bummed out about it," I replied. "I was convinced it would work. It just made so much sense to me. I really thought I'd be burning out my laptop keyboard by now."

"Hem, you've been blocked for many weeks. You can't expect it all to be resolved within hours of touring the man's house," she cautioned. "Even if you've made the right diagnosis in the first place, it will take some time."

"That's just what Hat told me five minutes ago."

"I'm heartened that your friend with anger management issues and a butterscotch fixation has drawn the same clinical conclusion as I have."

"I don't think I've ever heard you employ sarcasm, Dr. Scott."

"It's Saturday. I'm allowed just a pinch on weekends."

"And what do you mean 'even if you made the right diagnosis in the first place'?" I asked.

"Hem, when we last met you were clearly convinced that Ernest Hemingway was causing you the difficulty with your novel. While I want to be supportive, you'll recall that I've said from the beginning that you should be open to other possible causes."

"So you still don't buy the 'exorcise Ernest' theory."

"What I buy isn't nearly as important as what you buy."

"I'd better go, they're calling my flight," I said.

"Let's pick this up when you're back. I suspect your travels may in fact help us get to where we need to be, but perhaps not in the way you had hoped."

The drive from Boise to Ketchum was not too onerous, though neither was it particularly picturesque. I rejected the five-hour route along scenic mountain roads in favour of the two-and-a-half-hour highway drive. Ketchum is not far from Sun Valley, the famous ski resort. In Hemingway's day, the skiing was underdeveloped. It was the fishing and hunting in Idaho's Silver Creek Valley that was the real draw for the famous writer. Hemingway moved from Cuba to Ketchum with his fourth wife, Mary, in 1959 after the revolution led by Fidel Castro. Two years later, Ernest Hemingway was dead.

After Toronto, Paris, Pamplona, and Key West, the last leg of my tour was depressing in almost every respect. It was a cloudy, dreary, and rainy day. The sky closed in on me as I drove. The weather was enough to dampen the spirits of even the most jubilant of optimists. But I was laid low by more than meteorology. Upon touchdown in Boise and throughout the drive to Ketchum, I simply could not stop thinking about Hemingway's final days, not to mention his final act. By the time he moved to Ketchum, he was no longer the writer he once was, and he knew it. He had concluded that his writing had irretrievably declined to well below the standards he'd always set for himself. This realization was a devastating blow he just couldn't sustain. He even tried electroshock therapy in the hopes of restoring his gift. But it was futile. In his final months, he acted strangely, pushing away friends and descending into depression and paranoia. He claimed "the feds" were out to get him, tailing him everywhere, and even bugging his phones. He'd always been a drinker. But in his final decline, he drank even more, with predictable effect. Then, in the early morning of July 1, 1961, he arose before Mary, pulled his favourite shotgun from the rack, shoved in two shells, and ended his life.

My mind tried not to recreate the scene that Mary, alerted by what she described as a muffled thump, must have confronted when she stepped into the front vestibule of their home and found him. While he was clearly not in his right mind, it was an unspeakable act to leave for his wife to discover. He had been self-centred his entire life and remained so even in death.

It was evening when I rolled in to Ketchum. I pulled into a Best Western, spent fifteen minutes corroborating my identity at the front desk, and finally escaped to my room. I ordered a cheese omelette from room service and tried to shed the abject melancholy that weighed me down like a dentist's lead X-ray blanket. I grabbed my cellphone.

"Hem, is that you?" Marie asked.

"You're there! I so needed to hear your voice."

"What's wrong? Are you all right?"

"Oh, I'm fine. I'm just discouraged and a little lonely, I guess," I said. "I mean, I'm in the town where Hemingway ended his life. It's just so depressing. I almost expected the highway sign to read 'Welcome to Ketchum, the beautiful hamlet where Ernest Hemingway shot himself.'"

"Maybe we should have bumped it from the tour," Marie said.

"No, I think it's an important stop. I visited Paris, where he was in his prime. It makes sense that I also see Ketchum, where he was in decline, at his most vulnerable, even pathetic."

"It does sound sad," she replied. "How was Key West?"

"It was fun, well, parts of it. I had a great time, other than being seasick for four hours, getting my ass kicked in my first bar fight, and earning a police escort to the airport, and not in a good way."

"Ouch! Sounds like a novel in the making," she said. "Why don't you try to write something now that you're on your own? It might make you feel a bit better."

"I didn't even bring my laptop in from the car. The words just aren't there. It's not working. It still feels like I'll never write another sentence ever again."

"Don't write off the trip yet," she said. "Oops, sorry, poor choice of words. It still might work if you give it some time."

"I hope you're right, but it doesn't really feel like the floodgates are going to open up any time soon."

"Hem, we never knew for certain that this would work. It's always been a crapshoot. We were all just hoping it would."

"And I'm truly grateful. I had such a wonderful time in Paris. Spending a day or so with Hat and getting to know him a bit more was kind of fun. He's a good guy. But Paris was, um, special. It was just so nice, so comfortable. It felt so natural, like we've known each other for years, not weeks."

"For me, too," she replied.

Silence reigned for a few seconds.

"Anyway, I assume you passed your pastry course at the top of your class?"

"I did fine. It was quite gruelling, particularly with so little sleep, thank you very much. But I picked up a few great tips and my croissants are better now than they've ever been. So I'm happy, for a lot of reasons."

"Despite being in Ketchum, Idaho, site of one of the world's most famous suicides, and being eager to get home, I'm happy, too, even if I'll never write again."

"Hem, you'll be writing again soon. I know it. I can feel it."

I often order a cheese omelette when I'm staying in hotels. I've never been a big fan of room service, but I figure it's tough to mess up a cheese omelette. It's a safe bet. After my Idaho stay, I've revised my room service standard operating procedure by adding what I call the Ketchum Corollary. It's tough to mess up a cheese omelette, *but not impossible*. I've since switched to the club sandwich as my room service standby.

———

Sarah texted me around 10:00 p.m. All it said was: "When do you land tomorrow?"

I texted back the flight time but heard nothing more from her.

———

The next morning, I drove out to the Hemingway home. The rain had only just stopped coming down but the low dark cloud cover hung heavy and close and claustrophobic. When she died in 1986, Mary Hemingway had bequeathed their home to the Nature Conservancy in Idaho. The endowment she left was not sufficient to pay for the upkeep, so the house is not open to the public, even though it remains the top tourist destination in Ketchum. I have no idea what other attractions might round out the top five, but the Hemingway home has always been number one.

It was not much to look at. Homes built from concrete blocks with a faux wood exterior are certainly durable, but seldom do they grace the cover of *Architectural Digest*. It looked in reasonably good condition, but was clearly empty. It had initially served as the offices of the Nature Conservancy before the organization outgrew the premises. Since then, the home has been maintained, but never occupied.

I got out of the car. The place was deserted. I just stood there for a time taking in the front entrance. The vestibule, where he spent his final minutes alive, was just beyond the door. I had no desire to move closer. The Hemingway who had lived and died there was a pale reflection of his earlier self – depleted, deluded, and suddenly older than his years. It all seemed so sad. Although it was a warm morning in July, a chill passed through me. I walked around to the back of the house. While the views of the surrounding landscape were quite scenic, the house was no more attractive from the other side. In the sun, in shadows, summer or winter, concrete is concrete. I sat down on the ground in the lee of the home and tried to take stock. There had been no exorcism. I'd lived in Hemingway's world for the past ten days in four different countries yet my writer's block seemed no closer to being cured. I began to question my initial diagnosis.

Sitting behind the house, I hadn't heard the state trooper's car approach. I must have been very deep in thought, as I don't recall hearing the trooper's door slam either.

"You are not supposed to be here, sir," she said. "This is private property."

I jumped when I heard her voice, which caused her to put one hand on her holster.

I put my hands up in anticipation.

"Um, sorry, Officer, you just startled me," I stammered. "I didn't know this was not allowed. I was about to leave anyway."

I pulled myself to my feet and faced her.

"What are you doing here?" she asked.

"Well, um, I just wanted to visit his home. I'm on a kind of Hemingway pilgrimage, and this was my last stop. Fitting, I guess, as this was, um, his last stop."

"Have you touched anything or taken anything from the grounds?" she asked.

"Of course not. Why would I do that?"

"We have a lot of trouble with Hemingway fanatics trying to chip off chunks of concrete from the house or peeling off weather stripping as souvenirs. You'd be surprised what they do."

"Well, I can assure you, I've just been sitting and thinking. I have no interest in taking any part of this place with me. It all seems so depressing, what happened here. In fact, I'm eager to leave."

"Well, now that I've found you here, I'm sorry to say that there are procedures to follow, information to gather, and a report to file. Had you stayed in the car out in the driveway, I could probably have cut you some slack. But your fate was sealed when you opened your door, stepped out, and walked onto the property. It's what we call around here *trespassing.*"

"Trespassing? You're kidding. Really?" I said, my voice rising to a higher register. "You know I meant no harm. I've touched nothing. Couldn't we just both forget that this ever happened and I'll be on my way?"

"Sir, I take my job very seriously. You did not really just advocate dereliction of duty, did you? Is that what I just heard?" she asked with an edge, and taking one step closer.

Uh oh. I backpedalled, literally and figuratively.

"Absolutely not. I'm all in favour of paperwork. When can we start?"

We both walked back around to the front of the house where her cruiser was parked just behind my rental car. She reached into her front seat and pulled out a steel clipboard and then leaned against the police car's front fender. I stood next to my car and knew exactly what was coming next.

"Okay, sir, let's begin with your name, and I'm going to need to see some identification."

And we were off.

———

I made it back to the hotel just in time to check out. After she'd accepted who I was and why I was in Ketchum, the officer turned out to be very nice about the whole thing.

My flight landed at LaGuardia at 9:10 that night. The Arrivals area was not too busy for a summer Sunday night. But Departures would surely have been swamped with tourists heading home after a Manhattan weekend. I grabbed my bag and headed out of the sliding glass doors.

They were both standing there together gabbing away like best friends at a sleepover. Sarah and Marie. My plan had been just to grab a cab and head home. I was not expecting a welcoming party. Marie saw me first, beamed, and thrust her hands in the air in a gesture that seemed to say, "Ladies and gentlemen, Earnest Hemmingway is in the house!" though I'm not skilled at simultaneous translation.

She threw her arms around me and squeezed tight, rubbing my back as if comforting a whimpering child. I gave Sarah a surprised and somewhat awkward look, but she just gave a conspiratorial wink.

"It's okay, Hem, Marie filled me in on your Paris hookup," Sarah said. "I'm not surprised."

Sarah had a rental car and drove us downtown. Knowing that Sarah wanted to talk family dysfunctions, Marie thought it better if we dropped her off at her place. She had early baking to do anyway. When she got out of the car, she kissed me in a way that told me what happened in Paris might also happen in Manhattan. I was feeling better already.

I dumped my bag in the bedroom while Sarah fetched a couple of beers from the fridge.

"I need your couch tonight but I'll be gone when you get up," Sarah shouted from the kitchen. "I'm on the first flight back to O'Hare tomorrow morning."

I joined her on the couch in the living room and took a long pull on my beer.

"Ready?" she asked.

I nodded.

"Okay. I do want to hear all about your trip, particularly how you and the cake queen came to be an item. By the way, I really like her. But first we gotta talk about Dad."

"The floor is yours and I'm all aquiver in anticipation." I sighed.

"Things have gone from bad to worse. Something is going down, and I can't figure out what it is. Dad and Henderson are spending almost every waking hour together behind closed doors. A few other suits come and go throughout the day. Dad won't return my calls. Then Henderson will disappear for a day. It happened a couple of weeks ago. About ten days before we were going to introduce a new four-pack, the first of its kind in the marketplace, I see Henderson coming out of the Starbucks and getting into an airport limo. When I got into the office, I asked his admin assistant where Henderson was. She told me he'd called in sick that day. Then, the day before our four-pack was to be launched, MaxWorldCorp brings out a five-pack, just like that. So we look like we're following, not leading the market. We snatched defeat from the jaws of victory. We looked stupid. It's all very strange."

"That could be just a coincidence," I said. "I mean packaging multiple pairs of underwear is hardly a groundbreaking idea."

"But hang on, I'm not finished," she cut back in. "A couple of days ago, I found this waiting for me on my desk."

She passed over a plain brown envelope. I opened it and pulled out three photographs. They were taken from above at a very large meeting. In two of the shots, lots of people were milling about. In the other, the meeting was clearly in session.

"What is this?" I asked.

"It's the annual general meeting of MaxWorldCorp."

"Yeah, so?"

She leaned over and pointed to a figure sitting and listening during the meeting.

"*Carlos!* What's he doing at our prime competitor's AGM?" I asked.

"Good question," Sarah replied.

Then she pointed to the two other photos.

I could now see Carlos standing there in conversation with three men. He seemed to be smiling in one of the shots. In fact, everyone seemed to be happy-happy.

"Thanks to Google Images, I've confirmed that those are two senior MaxWorldCorp execs he's talking to. Not sure about the third suit."

"Surely you're not suggesting Carlos is feeding company secrets to the bad guys, are you?" I asked.

"I can't believe that's possible, but neither can I explain photos of Carlos at the MaxWorldCorp AGM. It makes no sense."

———

Sarah left early the next morning. I didn't even hear her, despite my best intentions of making her coffee and seeing her off properly. My body clock was still a bit messed up. I agreed to fly to Chicago on Friday. I spent the next four days confirming that Marie and I were, for all intents and purposes, a couple. I feared that it might just have been the escapism of Paris at work, but it felt the same in Manhattan, just with bigger cars and better drivers. Of course, Marie only had limited time as she had a business to run. I had lots of time as I had no job and was no closer to writing the sentences that would start Chapter 12 of my novel than I'd been before embarking on the Ernest Hemingway Exorcism World Tour. So I just kind of hung out at Let Them Eat Cake! and helped out where I could. I was particularly good on cleanup duty. I'm actually quite adept with a scrub brush when dirty pots and pans are in the sink. Fortunately, business had been picking up as word spread. The catering side of the operation was also growing. I credited the chocolate cake with the uptick in customers, but really, everything on the menu was great. This all made Marie even happier than she usually was, which made me happy, too.

———————

Most of them were there by the time I arrived. I'd taken my car into the shop for a long-scheduled brake job and the subway had been a little slower than usual. As I stepped through the door, the room burst into applause.

The makeshift banner taped to the wall read "Welcome home, Hem!" Everyone was there except for John Dillinger and Julia Roberts. A trestle table off to the side was bowing slightly with all the food it supported. Marie had brought two cakes. Jackie Kennedy had filled two large plates with four kinds of cookies. Mario Andretti had cooked a vat of meatballs and tomato sauce. Professor James Moriarty had brought wine, which we were certainly not supposed to be serving in an unlicensed room in the Manhattan Y. Everyone else seemed to have come loaded with culinary contributions. Jesse Owens brought salad. Clark Kent made a very good batch of nachos. Peter Parker actually made some outstanding butter tarts. Hat and Diana Ross seemed to have joined forces to make butter chicken.

A few minutes later, John Dillinger and Julia Roberts arrived together, both looking a little giddy.

"Sorry we're late," John said with a kind of smug look on his face. "We were, well, you know, 'busy.'"

He put the word "busy" in finger quotes. Julia giggled and slapped his arm. They may have been a little tipsy.

"Well, we're very pleased for you, um, both," I said. "I'm particularly happy for you."

I couldn't help but glance over at Marie as I said it. I didn't really mean to, it just happened.

We all stuffed ourselves. It was wonderful to be back in their midst.

I gave a full, day-by-day account of the trip and all the adventures we'd had, although I did not provide quite as detailed a night-by-night summary. James, Marie, and Hat all added their own colour commentary. In fact, Hat kept cutting in to correct or augment my version of the Key West stint. We spent nearly the entire hour laughing.

"But did it work?" asked Professor Moriarty. "Have the words and the ink started to flow again?"

"Alas, not yet," I admitted. "And if I'm being honest with myself and with you, I fear it may not even work in time. I'm beginning to question whether it's really Hemingway haunting me at all, or someone or something else. If it were Hemingway, I'm quite sure the trip would have resolved it. But I'll get to the bottom of it all, eventually."

There was an awkward silence for a moment or two as if I'd just cast a pall over the proceedings – probably because I'd just cast a pall over the proceedings.

"But let me say again how grateful I am for the thought that went into the exorcism tour idea. I think there are many good things that have come from the trip," I said, unable to stop myself from looking at Marie again. "I've gotten to know some of you much better. And I'm no longer intimidated by the man whose name sounds exactly like mine. In fact, by the time I reached Ketchum, Idaho, I'd come to feel sorry for him. He lived hard and burned out early. I hope to be writing well past the age Hemingway was when he died by his own hand. So the value or success of the trip should not be measured on whether my writer's block is cured. I will be writing again, perhaps even soon. In my mind, the trip was a rousing success from so many other standpoints. So thank you all, particularly James, Marie, and Hat, my fellow travellers."

Everyone applauded again. This was a group that liked to clap.

The good feelings carried over into our baseball game. We actually got on the board first. Jesse Owens homered at her first at-bat and then so did I. Then three quick singles by John Dillinger, Clark Kent, and Hat loaded up the bases with nobody out. Mario popped out to the catcher. Julia Roberts then bunted up the third base line. Well, she didn't mean for it to be a bunt, but that's what we're calling it. The third baseman eyed John back to the bag and then easily threw out Julia. Peter Parker then stepped to the plate and cranked a triple that cleared the bases. Diana Ross managed to make contact with the ball, although it was with her shoulder as she whiffed on her swing. The ball rolled up the first base line. Fearing she might never get near the ball again, the umpire accepted her shoulder hit but the catcher threw her out at first. So after our half of the first inning, we were up 5–0. I considered calling off the game convinced that we'd hit our zenith, but there was no real way of doing it within the league rules.

Of course, I was right. While we scattered a few hits in the rest of the game, nothing came close to the offensive tsunami of our first inning. We lost 31–5. Julia and John were inseparable at the bar afterward and left together long before the rest of the team headed their separate ways. They were holding hands when they left. That made my day. For the third night in a row, I stayed at Marie's apartment above Let Them Eat Cake!

The veil finally lifted the next morning as I walked to my appointment. There was no flash of epiphany, but more of a slow but steady dawning of realization over the course of ten or fifteen minutes. I remained calm. I had no regrets about the exorcism world tour, even though I now knew it had been nothing more than a wild goose chase. The revelation was almost anticlimactic.

"So what conclusions have you drawn from your trip?" Dr. Scott asked.

It was 8:00 Friday morning, the only opening she had. I'd just spent about twenty minutes describing, in considerable detail, my Hemingway junket.

"Well, either confronting the spirit of Hemingway on his own turf is ineffective against writer's block," I started.

"Or . . ." she prompted.

"Or the tour failed because it's not Hemingway causing my writer's block at all, but something else."

She nodded with a look that said "Finally."

"Let's stay with that for a moment. If Hemingway isn't your problem, then who or what is? Actually, let's stick with who."

"I'd been thinking about it nonstop since Key West and had come up empty. But then I finally checked my voice mail after my trip and noticed several calls from my father. No messages were ever left, but he made the calls. Then it all fell into place quite easily after that. I didn't really accept it until I was nearly here this morning. So it's very fresh in my mind. Now that I know, I cannot understand why it took me this long to see it. It's been right there in front of me for a very long time."

Dr. Scott was smiling now.

"So, just to be clear, are you suggesting that it was not Ernest Hemingway the writer haunting you and your novel, but Earnest Hemmingway your father?"

"You've known for a long time, haven't you," I said.

"I haven't 'known,' but I tagged it months ago as a strong possibility," she admitted.

"Why let me twist in the wind and gallivant around two continents if you knew the answer resided in the family home in Chicago?"

"You don't really want me to answer that, do you?"

"Yes, I really do, but let me try first," I replied. "You believe that had you suggested my troubled relationship with my father was the root of all of these issues, it might have taken me much longer to reach enlightenment. That leading me to my father before I understood what it meant, and accepted it, might well be worse than not ever finding the answer."

"In a manner of speaking," she replied. "Knowing the answer is not always enough. Ideally, you come to the answer in your own way, in your own time, and then can confront it, embrace it, and actually deal with it. That's far superior to just knowing the answer."

"You're very smart."

"Not smart enough to get you there any faster than this. But I'm glad you feel you've arrived now."

"It's no wonder I'm still blocked. I just spent ten days chasing the wrong guy."

"Yes, but you got the girl, did you not?"

"So far, it seems I did. So I owe Hemingway that, I guess."

"Seems like a good time to wrap, for our thirty minutes are gone."

I was just back out onto the sidewalk when my cell chirped. "Sarah?"

"Hem, I need you to do something for me. I just have a hunch it's important."

"I'm yours. What do you need?"

"I've just learned that Henderson Watt is flying into LaGuardia this morning. I have no idea why he's going, nobody knows. I just got his flight info from his admin assistant. I told her I needed to speak with him today."

"Okay, so what can I do?"

"I want you to go to LaGuardia and tail him. Find out where he's going. I think it could give us the answers we need. I'm convinced he's not what he seems. Putting it another way, he's an asshole and he's up to something."

"So let me get this straight. You want me to go to the airport, hide behind a post because he knows who I am, and then shadow him until he gets back on the plane?" I asked, sounding as incredulous as I could.

"Yes, that's exactly what I'm asking you to do. It's all connected somehow with Dad and the future of the company. I can feel it. Hem, it's important."

I said nothing while I thought it over. When she put it that way. I didn't really feel I could say no.

"Hem, are you there?"

"Okay. I'm just trying to figure out how I can go all gumshoe on this guy without him knowing."

"You'll figure it out. He's on Delta 253 from O'Hare, arriving at LaGuardia at 11:15 this morning."

"Whoa, I gotta get moving."

"Don't let him see you, whatever you do."

I hung up and headed home. Halfway there I realized I had a problem. My car was in the shop and wouldn't be ready until late in the day. I couldn't very well jump in a cab and say "Follow that car," could I?

Think.

I did not call a taxi. Instead, I phoned Hat.

CHAPTER 13

Hat pulled over to the curb to pick me up. He was driving a bright green, beat-up van with a New York Jets logo on the side with the words "Stadium Audio" stencilled on the door – very discreet for shadowing purposes. Mario Andretti was with him. Bless Hat. In my absence, he had taken over helping Mario prepare for his driving test. I'd interrupted one of their sessions.

"Thanks, guys. You're life-savers," I said as I climbed in. "This could be kind of fun."

"Where to, Hem?" Hat asked. He looked deadly serious.

"LaGuardia, and we're a little behind schedule."

I didn't think you could stomp on the accelerator of a beat-up nine-year-old van filled to the rafters with audio equipment and still squeal the tires. Well, you can, and Hat did. I banged my head on the side window as he flipped a U-turn and headed for the airport. Mario flew into the back of the van, but eventually reappeared a few blocks later, when Hat actually decided to respect a red light at a busy intersection. Mario gripped my seat in a submission hold and hung on until we made it to LaGuardia. I briefed them on the drive. They were quite excited about it all.

Hat drove us to the Arrivals level and pulled up to the very end of the pickup lane. We were just going to make it. Mario and I leapt out and dashed inside. Hat kept the engine idling, which doesn't sound as if it would be a challenge, but trust me, with that van, it was. I scanned the Arrivals screen and saw that Henderson Watt's flight had already landed. We stood behind a concrete pillar and peeked around to the sliding doors spewing passengers from the baggage area. I'd found a ratty old New York Jets ball cap in the van and grabbed it before coming inside. I pulled it down low until the brim was pretty well resting on my nose. I could still see if I tilted my head back.

"Stand right in front of me," I said to Mario. "I've met the guy we're waiting for, and it will make it tough to follow him if he recognizes me. He'll be suspicious immediately."

Mario leaned against the pillar, trying to look casual, while I hovered behind. We hadn't been there more than five minutes when the sliding glass doors parted and released Henderson Watt wearing a light olive green suit, a blue button-down Oxford cloth shirt, and a yellowish striped tie. He sauntered right toward us. He carried nothing with him.

I inched around to the other side of the pillar as he passed to keep it between us. So far, so good.

"There's our guy," I said, nudging Mario.

We fell in about twenty yards behind Watt and tried not to look as if we were following him. We achieved this, or at least attempted this, by chatting amiably with each other and looking around at all the sights a modern airport has to offer. But through it all, I tried to keep one eye fixed on Henderson Watt. The operative word being "tried." I'd just sent Hat a quick text citing our code phrase, "The eagle has landed," but when I lifted my eyes again, Henderson Watt was nowhere to be seen. At that same instant, I walked straight into Mario, who had stopped in his tracks.

"I lost him, Mario. I lost him," I hissed. "Where'd he go, and what's with the sudden stop?"

"Bathroom," Mario whispered, turning his head and elongating his mouth to aim the words back at me.

"Why didn't you go before? There's no time right now. You can go when we get back."

"No, Hem, I mean our guy's in the bathroom. That's why I stopped."

"Oh."

We found a second pillar close by and the stakeout continued. Two minutes later, Henderson walked back out and headed for the door. We watched him join the taxi lineup before we slipped out the door and rejoined Hat in the very inconspicuous big battered green New York Jets van. We had a perfect view of the taxi stand. When Henderson slipped into a cab three minutes later and pulled out, we followed. I just hoped he had not heard the screeching brakes and angry honking of the airport bus Hat cut off in the process.

I memorized the number of Henderson's taxi just as two other cabs snuck in between us. It took some concentration to keep the right cab in sight, particularly as we entered Manhattan. Henderson's cab eventually slowed and pulled over in front of a sidewalk café in SoHo. I think it was on Prince Street.

"Okay, he's stopping," I said, then pointed. "Hat, drive right on by and then, if you can, pull a U-turn and park across the street there. That's how they do it in the cop shows."

He actually pulled it off without attracting too much attention, although Mario took another unexpected trip into the depths of the van when Hat yanked on the wheel to make his sudden turn. By the time Henderson stepped from the cab, we were already parked a little way down the street from the café. I only hoped he was actually going to the restaurant. We were in luck. A nattily dressed man already seated on the patio stood, called out to Henderson, and waved. The guy looked vaguely familiar, but I couldn't place him. Henderson approached, shook hands with the other suit, and sat down. It was only a table for two, so, using my well-honed powers of deduction, I assumed no more guests were expected. Unfortunately, we weren't parked as closely as I would have liked, but there were no open parking spots any nearer. Besides, we couldn't hear what they were saying anyway, so it really didn't matter, I guess.

The two of them looked very comfortable together. They obviously knew each other reasonably well, judging by what looked like the easy back-and-forth of the conversation. It's amazing how much you can discern from a café conversation, even without the benefit of sound.

I didn't really know what more we could do, other than observe and take note of anything that seemed noteworthy. They both ordered drinks and food. Mystery man had a pizza while Henderson had what looked like a Caesar salad, but it could have been the Niçoise salad. We just weren't close enough to be sure. They were having quite an animated conversation. In a flash of brilliance, or it might just have been the glare of the obvious, I pulled out my cellphone and snapped a couple of photos, assisted by its built-in digital zoom. I confirmed the Caesar salad. We just sat there and watched until dessert and coffee were delivered to Henderson and his lunch partner.

"I must say I'm getting a little peckish watching the two of them enjoy what looks to be a very nice meal indeed," Hat said.

"Me too. I just wish we could hear what they're saying to each other." I sighed.

"What? You want to hear their conversation?" Hat asked. "Why have you waited until now to make that point clear?"

Without waiting for a response from me, he squeezed between the two front seats and into the back of the van. I continued to watch the lunch meeting while Hat created quite the ruckus behind me digging through the equipment.

"Hem, would you please be so kind as to start the van up?" Hat asked from the back. "I'll be needing to plug in back here."

I did as I was told and then turned around. Hat was holding a parabolic dish in his hands.

"Mario, would you mind terribly plugging that cord into the outlet you'll find at the base of the door jamb, there. Right there."

Mario did as he was told.

"Now, Hem, is your smartphone equipped with an audio recording app?"

"As a matter of fact, it is. I use it for dictating story ideas that occur to me when I'm not near my laptop. At least I used to do that when I used to have ideas for my novel."

"Excellent. Will this input jack fit into your phone?"

He handed me a small-gauge wire that originated in the black box on the backside of the parabolic dish. The jack fit perfectly when I inserted it into the port in my phone.

"Now, open the recording app and hit the big red button to start recording, if you kindly would."

"Okay, I've done that, and – look – it's picking up our conversation! I can see the sound waves jumping on the screen in time with our voices."

"That is just splendid news, Hem, splendid news," Hat said in a tone tinged with triumph. "Then we are definitely ready. Mario, slide open the door if you would."

Mario did as he was told.

"Actually, Mario, could I suggest you open the other door, you know, the one facing the restaurant," Hat proposed.

Mario closed the door on the sidewalk side and then opened the one on the other side of the van, giving Hat a clear line of sight across the street and up the block a ways, directly to Henderson Watt's outdoor table. Hat sat on the floor, scooched over toward the gaping rectangular opening in the side of the van, and aimed the dish toward our quarry. Cars were whizzing by beside the van's open door.

"Mario, you'll need to lie here and hold the door open so it doesn't slide shut."

I was a little concerned that aiming a rather conspicuous parabolic dish toward unsuspecting patrons enjoying lunch on an outdoor patio might seem just a tad suspicious. But I kept that thought to myself.

Hat was wearing headphones and kept shifting the dish, trying to get a line on Henderson's conversation. At one point he slid a little too far out the door and a car honked and nearly took out the dish and Hat, too. He pulled back inside the van.

"Damnation! I'm starting to feel steamed!" Hat snapped.

"Whoaaa, Hat, it's okay, calm down," I soothed as I patted his leg from my perch up front.

"Thank you, Hem, but I will need your services back here, if you please."

I crawled back so that all three of us were crammed into what little space there was behind the two seats.

"I believe I can get a better angle if I'm kneeling rather than sitting, but I'll need you to steady me and keep me from falling over. The dish gets heavier the longer you hold it. Could you do that for me, Hem?"

"I'm your man."

I straddled him from behind. Hmm, that didn't come out quite as I had intended. I sat behind Hat with a leg on either side of him as if we were riding a toboggan together or perhaps a motorcycle. Yes, that's a little better.

"Okay, Hem, you must push me up now so I can get to my knees."

I did my best to hoist him up. Then when he was on his knees, I grabbed his belt to keep him steady while he aimed the dish again.

"I can only get little snippets from this distance. We must get closer. The cars are interfering and we're just a bit out of range," Hat said. "And that delivery truck parked in front is in no way helping, either."

At that precise moment, I noticed through the front windshield that one of the cars parked up ahead, nearly directly across from Henderson's table, was pulling out into traffic. No, check that, two cars were pulling out, one in front of the other. Hat saw the double parking spot opening up and looked at me. We were both stuck where we were and had only limited range of motion. I sighed.

"We have no choice," I whispered to Hat. He nodded.

"Okay, Mario, your moment is now," I said.

"What?" he replied. "What do you mean?"

"This is important and you need to move fast. Get in the driver's seat and move the van up to the parking spot that is just opening up ahead. You can drive right into it. It's a double spot. No parallel parking required. But you have to do it now," I said with some urgency. "Or we'll lose it."

"I don't know, guys," Mario stammered.

"Right now!" Hat shouted. *"You must do it right now!"*

Mario was startled, or perhaps terrified, by Hat's outburst, and leapt into the driver's seat. He turned the key in the ignition, making the most hideous metal-on-metal shriek imaginable.

"Mario, the van is already started, just put it into Drive and get into that spot before someone else does."

As Mario sat there adjusting his seat and mirrors, Hat lost it.

"Forget the blasted mirrors! We're only driving seventy-five feet! Go! Go! Go!"

Mario threw it into Drive and pulled into the lane. A miracle blessed us with an opening in the traffic and we moved up the street. A red Porsche had pulled up ahead of the double parking spot and was about to back into it when Mario darted in frontward, jumping the curb and screeching to a halt with two wheels on the sidewalk and two wheels on the road. Oh yes, he also knocked over a green wire garbage can, spilling its contents all over the ground. As Mario hit the brakes – and believe me, I'm grateful he did – the open door slid shut with a bang, nearly decapitating Hat. We were thrown around the back of the van and landed in a heap on the floor.

The driver of the Porsche was not happy and had gotten out of his car. Mario was paralyzed in the front seat. Hat saw the guy coming, so he threw open the door and bounded out to intercept him. Hat must have put on his most menacing look, to which I've grown accustomed, because without saying a word, Mr. Porsche turned on his heel, zipped back to his little red sports car, and squealed away.

The eyes of everyone on the restaurant's patio were fixed on our van, including those of Henderson Watt and his co-conspirator. Fortunately, I was buried in the back in a mess of wires, cables, and electronic equipment, far from prying eyes. We reassembled in the van and stayed quiet for a few minutes until Mario reported that life and lunch had returned to normal across the street. Then Hat slid the door open again and, as discreetly as possible, once again aimed a three-foot-diameter parabolic dish at the patio patrons across the street. I hid behind Hat, though my legs and shoes would have been clearly visible from the restaurant.

I snuck a peek around Hat's hip and saw that Henderson and the other guy were both standing and shaking hands. It was all but over. They walked out onto the sidewalk and got into separate cabs, both going the same way, which was exactly the opposite direction the van was facing. They were gone.

Hat sat back down, on top of me.

"Sorry, Hem."

I pressed the button on my phone to stop the recording.

"Hem, I think I got just the tail end of their conversation. Did you get it?"

"Well, it was recording the whole time, so we got whatever you heard."

Mario was still sitting in the driver's seat with his white knuckles gripping the steering wheel. Or it's possible he was trying to pull the steering wheel right out of the dashboard. It took us another ten minutes to calm him down.

I called Sarah when I made it back to my apartment.

"Okay, mission accomplished, with mixed results," I started my report.

"Well, which is it? Was the mission accomplished or were there mixed results? You can't really do both."

"It's always nice to start a conversation with hairsplitting. When I say mission accomplished, I meant that we actually managed to intercept Henderson, follow him to a restaurant, photograph the guy he met with, and even record an all-too-brief snippet of their conversation."

"That sounds pretty good to me. Sounds like Q set you up with a bug for the table," she replied. "So why do you call those impressive results mixed?"

"Well, it turned out we probably could have recorded their entire conversation had I thought to raise it sooner. My friend Hat is a whiz with a parabolic receiver."

"Okay, cut to the chase."

"Henderson met with a sharp-dressed man in his forties who looked a little familiar to me but I don't know where or even if I've seen him before. I've just emailed you his photo and the short MP3 recording of their parting words."

"What were those parting words?" she asked.

"It starts with Henderson in mid-sentence. He says: '. . . almost taste it.' Then the other guy responds with 'Me, too. Hang in there. We're just about home. Just keep doing what you're doing.'"

"Interesting and very suspicious," Sarah said.

"I assume Henderson went directly back to the airport, but I'm not certain. We just couldn't get our act together to tail his cab after the meeting."

"He must be on his way back. I'm told he's due back in some big meeting with Dad at 5:30."

———————

I didn't even try to write that afternoon, even though I had the time. If nothing had changed with my father, nothing would change with my novel. As Madelaine had said, finally knowing the root cause of my travails usually doesn't resolve them. It just makes it easier to chart a course toward resolution.

So instead of not writing, I met with my mechanic and picked up the G35. The new brakes were a bit touchy, as he had warned, turning the Stop signs into STOP signs. I made it home safely.

———————

Sarah called again at 11:30 the next morning. "Come today, now," she said in a very tight voice. "Come as soon as you can."

———————

One of the benefits of living in New York is that if you ever need to fly to Chicago on very short notice, there's a flight bound for O'Hare every twenty minutes or so. An hour and twenty-five minutes after her call, my seat belt was fastened for takeoff.

———————

"Good, you're here," Sarah said when I stuck my head in her office.

She stood up, grabbed my arm, and propelled me down the corridor.

"Okay, so I was thinking we could strategize a bit on our approach," I said as we walked, fast. "Then we could pull Dad aside tonight at the house when it's quiet and really get to the bottom of this."

Sarah said nothing, until she, or rather we, barrelled right past my father's secretary, Irene, and headed directly for his closed office door.

"Ms. Hemmingway, I'm afraid he's in the middle of a big meeting right now," Irene said from her desk, standing up as she spoke.

Sarah seemed not to have heard her.

"Um, Sarah," I said.

"Ms. Hemmingway, now is not a good time . . ."

Sarah, or rather we, didn't even slow down. She, we, threw

open the door and barged into our father's office and slammed the door behind her, er, us.

"Okay, just what the hell is going on?" Sarah snapped. "And don't tell me 'nothing,' because it's all too obvious that something big is happening."

Our father was seated at the head of the small board table without his suit jacket on. That was not good news. I'd very rarely seen him without his jacket. He looked pale and not himself. Henderson Watt, his shirt-sleeves rolled up, sat to Dad's left, with the company lawyer, Michael Kingsley, next to him. The man across the table turned in his chair to face us. I didn't recognize him.

"Sarah, please, calm down," said our father.

Not a line I would have recommended.

"*I will not calm down when my own father will not return my calls*," she shouted. "*I will not calm down. What is going on? I'm not leaving until you tell me!*"

Then she turned on Henderson Watt.

"And why were you in New York yesterday? What were you doing?"

Henderson put his pen down on the table very slowly before meeting Sarah's eyes.

"Not that it's any of your business, but I was meeting with an old friend. We sit together on the board of a national charity based in New York and we're dealing with a very messy HR fiasco involving our executive director. It's not a pleasant situation and it requires sensitive and discreet management. The phone simply would not suffice. Face to face was required. That's why I was in NYC."

"Oh," Sarah said.

Surely we hadn't misread the whole play.

"And who are you?" Sarah said to the one stranger in the room.

"Sarah, please. Show some manners," our father said.

"It's okay," the stranger said. "I'm Stephen Jacobs, from Paragon Counsel. Nice to meet you."

"The M&A firm?"

Stephen Jacobs just nodded.

"Dad, what's going on?"

"Gentlemen, could I call a brief recess. I clearly need to speak with my family."

"I've got to get something from my car anyway. Let's take a break," Henderson said, pushing his chair back and gathering his papers. "But we don't have a lot of time, EH3."

"Just give us fifteen minutes, and then come back in," my father said.

Kingsley and Jacobs stood, closed their notebooks, reloaded their file folders, and piled documents into gigantic briefcases. A moment later, the top of the board table was bare. Then they all left the room, closing the door behind them without making a sound.

No one said anything for a few seconds. We just stood there looking at Dad. He was looking at his hands clasped in front of him.

"Sit down, please," he said.

Sarah and I sat next to each other on the near side of the board table.

"I'm sorry you're hearing about this in this manner. I intended to talk to you both this evening. But your rather dramatic entrance has overtaken my plans."

He paused for a moment before continuing. He was looking at me when he spoke.

"I have signed a letter of intent to sell the company to – "

"Not to MaxWorldCorp!" Sarah interrupted.

"Don't be ridiculous, we're not that desperate. You know I'd never sell to Buccaneer Gainsford. That will never happen. Preston Holdings is, as the name suggests, a holding company. They seem to know what they're doing in the clothing trade. They've made us a very generous offer that's well above Hemmingwear's current market valuation. In the end, it was an easy call, after Earnest, here, refused to assume his rightful place at the helm and ended nearly a century of family ownership and management of this place. This keeps the company out of Gainsford's megalomaniacal hands and gives it a fighting chance. It was the responsible decision to make under the circumstances."

Ouch. That stung a bit. But even then, I did not question my decision. In fact, I was feeling something almost akin to relief at Dad's news. Sarah started to say something, but Dad held up his hand to silence her.

"Preston is largely based in Europe, and they were looking for a beachhead in the North American market. Hemmingwear is it. This is the right time. This is the right buyer. And this is the right price. The deal is done."

He lowered his hand.

"No, you can't do that," Sarah said. "We have the ability to lead the market if we just make a few changes around here. We can do it. I know we can."

"Sarah, MaxWorldCorp is slowly crushing us. We're the frog sitting happily in water that's about to boil. Open your eyes. Every time we make a move, they anticipate it and undercut us. They're heavily capitalized and can simply starve us out of business unless we act. They are going to take us out, one way or another, unless we make this deal."

"Dad, no, you're wrong. I'm sorry, you're just wrong," Sarah persisted. "We have a viable plan to use our own strengths to compete with them, to defeat them. You just have to push the button on the plan."

"If you're referring to your plan, it won't work. It won't help us," Dad replied. "In fact, Henderson has been over it in some detail and believes that it will substantially weaken us at a time when that would simply guarantee our demise. This deal will keep the Hemmingwear brand strong in the marketplace."

"Exactly how will the plan weaken us? Tell me how, precisely!" Sarah snapped.

Our father, well, he hesitated a little too long.

"You haven't even read it, have you?" she said. "I guess I'm not surprised. Don't listen to Henderson Watt. He's a jackass who's not nearly as smart as you think, and nowhere near as smart as he thinks."

"There was a time when you thought quite highly of Henderson Watt," he said. "You brought him to the company, wanted me to hire him."

"And I regret it profoundly."

"Henderson Watt has given me outstanding counsel from the day he arrived here. We are a better company for his intelligence and dedication. We'd be in deep trouble without his support. I'm thankful you introduced him to me. I think, perhaps, that personal feelings you may have for him are clouding your judgment."

Sarah stiffened and seemed to grow an inch or two. She clenched her fists and emitted a noise from somewhere deep within her that sounded a lot like a collision of rage, exasperation, and frustration. Then she bolted from the room. I turned to follow her out, having made absolutely no contribution to the meeting thus far. But my father said:

"Hem, wait. There's something else I need you to know. I'll tell Sarah when she's cooled down."

I sat back down as Dad closed the door that Sarah had almost pulled off its hinges.

"I'm not well. I'm going into hospital in four weeks for what's called a prostatectomy. I have prostate cancer."

"Dad . . ."

"We've caught it early, and the odds of a full recovery are good. But it's not a sure thing. I'm not yet out of the woods.

My desire for you to come back to Chicago was driven as much by my illness as by my respect for family tradition."

"Dad, I'm so sorry. You should have told us."

"I didn't want your decision about joining the company to be complicated by my medical situation. When you gave me your final answer a week or so ago, I felt I had to act. Do not say anything to Sarah about this. I think I have the right to share this news with her. I want her to hear it from me."

"Yes, of course."

"Hem, this deal is all but done. The final paperwork will be signed tomorrow and we're making the formal announcement in the afternoon, here. I'm sorry you found out this way."

I shook hands with Dad and left him there. I wasn't sure what else to do. I found Sarah in a little alcove down the hall a ways. She was leaning against the window with her head in her hands. I put my hand on her shoulder. A movement caught my eye. I looked past her through the glass and saw Henderson Watt closing the trunk of a sparkling brand-new Mercedes.

"Wow, that is one nice and expensive car," I said.

Sarah followed my gaze.

"That's a new car. He drove a Nissan before. He must have just picked it up."

"I can see that it's a new car. That model was just introduced last month. I love that car," I replied, snapping a photo of it with my cellphone.

We stood there for a moment saying nothing to each other.

I heard a stairwell door open down the hall and then footsteps headed our way. A second or two later, Henderson Watt appeared. Sarah took two steps forward and placed her index finger on his sternum. Henderson didn't back away an inch and just smirked.

"I'm going to find out what's behind all of this, and when I do, I know it's all going to come down on you. You will be held to account for all of this."

"You've got the wrong guy. If I were you, I'd keep an eye on Mendez," he said. "It's always the last place you look."

Then he turned and walked back toward Dad's office.

"He's just trying to throw us off the scent," I said, but deep down, I guess I wasn't sure. I looked out the window again at the sleek silver Mercedes. "Well, whatever his game is, he must be doing pretty well to score those wheels."

"I don't think he's on a Mercedes salary," she said and then sighed. "Man, I need a drink."

———

We spent the next few hours in a bar, doing what one usually does in a bar.

"What the fuck are we gonna do?" Sarah asked.

"It sounds to me like the deal is done. I'm not sure there's much we can do. I'm not even sure there's much we should do."

"Hem, there's no reason that this three-generation family business can't be a four-generation family business. I don't want it to end like this. There's something else going on."

Yeah, our father has prostate cancer. I wanted to say that, but didn't.

Beer was our poison of choice that afternoon, Miller Genuine Draft, to be precise. And we had many. By early evening, we were pretty well talked out. After a plate of chicken wings that served badly as dinner, I opened up the photo of Henderson's new car to make it my new cover shot on my cellphone. I loved that car.

"Messy HR issue, my ass," Sarah said to no one in particular before biting into another wing.

That triggered a thought. I mean her comment, not her chicken wing. It sparked just a sliver of an idea, really more of a hunch. On a flyer, I shot off a quick email, but said nothing to Sarah.

She leaned back in her chair in the general direction of the bartender.

"Two more MGDs here, please."

CHAPTER 14

I drank Coke for the rest of the night so I could drive us home. We arrived at Sarah's condo shortly after midnight. We'd just flopped on the couch when my cellphone chimed with an email. It was from Diana Ross.

> *Hi, Hem,*
> *Sorry it took me so long to respond but I was at my daughter's music night at the school and had to shut down my BB until we'd suffered through all 34 acts. I love my daughter, but I've now accepted that she is not destined for Broadway. Anyway, I forwarded your email to a friend who was pulling the night shift and she was able to run the plate. Here's the scoop. The car is leased from Harper Mercedes in Chicago. It's a fleet car registered in the name of MaxWorldCorp. Hope that helps. Cheers!*
> *Diana*

"Um, Sarah, we've got something here," I said, sitting up and leaning forward to reread the email.

"Yeah, I've got a headache already and I didn't even have the benefit of being fully drunk. Seems unfair, somehow."

"No, I'm serious. Listen. Henderson's fancy new car is registered under MaxWorldCorp's fleet lease," I said. "Why would our principal competitor be paying for Henderson Watt's car? Even if I didn't watch too many cop shows on TV, this would strike me as suspicious."

"No way! You're shittin' me," Sarah replied, joining me in the bolt-upright position. "Let me see that."

I gave her my cell.

"Who the hell is Diana Ross? Do you actually know someone named Diana Ross?"

"It's a long story, but yes I do. She's a great singer, after a few drinks, and she works at the NYPD. This is definitely legit. Or as they might say on TV, 'This intel is solid.'"

"Holy shit! Holy shit! We've got him."

We sat in silence for few minutes, letting the news swirl around in our heads.

"Okay, how did you meet Henderson, in the very beginning, I mean," I asked.

Sarah looked up at the ceiling for a few seconds before responding.

"Our first meeting was in a bar."

"Do you go there often?"

"Every Thursday night a bunch of us go from the office. It's kind of a weekly girls' night out."

"Do you always go to the same bar?"

"Almost always."

"What about the second time you met him?"

"Hmmm. It was a few days later at my Starbucks."

"Do you go there regularly?"

"Every friggin' morning," she replied. "Wait. No. No way. You think this whole Henderson thing was set up? You think Henderson planned all this, meeting me, getting me to introduce him to Dad?"

"I don't know. I'm just trying to follow the steps laid out in the Hardy Boys Detective Handbook. But it's plausible, isn't it?"

"So you're saying Henderson was following me for a while, learning my habits, where I regularly went and when?"

"I don't know. But there's a pattern there. He shows up at the bar on a Thursday night, knowing you'd be there. He starts up a conversation, turns on the charm, flashes those very white and very straight teeth, and cocks that nicely coiffed head of his. And you like him."

"Well, it wasn't quite like that," Sarah replied, then paused. "Actually, it was quite a bit like that."

"He doesn't push his luck that night. There's too much at stake," I continued, pacing the room now as my conspiracy-addled synapses kept firing. "So he shows up at Starbucks a few days later and just happens to bump into you. You renew the conversation, and the first date is made. Right?"

"Well, um, yeah," she said. "I'm starting to feel stupid now. I'm starting to feel played."

"Do you remember how he introduced the idea of him working at Hemmingwear?"

"It was my idea. But he did kind of lead me right to that conclusion. He kept saying he was keen to land a gig back in the rag trade."

"Did he say that early on, before you told him where you worked?"

"Hmmm. Yes, he did. I remember thinking it was kind of an odd thing to say so soon after meeting."

"He wanted to get that on the table before you told him where you worked. Of course he already knew where you worked, but he didn't want you to know that he knew."

"That circular thinking is doing nothing for my headache." Sarah sighed.

"It all fits. You just happen to meet this apparently nice guy who just happens to work in our business and just happens to be looking for a new job. He turns on the charm, you collapse into a quivering heap of 'I think I like this guy,' you take him to meet Dad, he cranks up the charm again, blows sunshine up Dad's back door, and the deal is done."

"Well . . ."

"Wait, I'm on a roll. Let's just play this out," I said, reclaiming the floor. "As he sucks up to Dad, finds his hot buttons, pushes them all, slides in closer and closer, he starts to drift away from you. He doesn't need you any more. He's achieved his goal, accomplished his mission. A plant from MaxWorldCorp is now inside

Hemmingwear, right where the decisions are made. What's worse, Henderson Watt is actually on the Hemmingwear payroll."

Sarah sat and looked out the window for a good three minutes. That's a long time when silence hangs. I let her think it all through. By then, I was certain of my theory. It seemed far-fetched and very high risk, yet all the pieces seemed to fit. Still, I waited and said nothing. She stood up and walked around a bit. Then she went out on the back deck and sat down in the dark. It had been fifteen minutes since either of us had spoken when she came back in.

"Okay, let's assume I've been completely duped by that conniving, duplicitous asshole, and I'm not certain that's what's happening here, but let's assume it is. Why would he do all this and then work on the sale of Hemmingwear to . . ." she paused and narrowed her eyes. She looked as if she were staring through me and all the way to the horizon.

"What's the name of the holding company making the play for us?" she asked.

"Preston."

She pulled her MacBook Air out of her bag and sat down at the kitchen table. Her fingers flew over the keyboard as she surfed the Internet, opening and bookmarking multiple pages. She was very focused. I could catch glimpses of websites as they flitted across her screen. I saw plenty of Google search pages, the New York Stock Exchange, some major business databases, the Securities Commission, and several government websites.

I wasn't sure what she was doing but neither was I about to ask. She was in a different zone. She might as well have hung a Do Not Disturb sign around her neck. So I grabbed my iPad and did a bit of work myself.

I called up the photo I'd snapped of Henderson's lunch partner. Then I scoured the MaxWorldCorp website for bios and images of their senior leadership team. No matches. Then I checked out the MaxWorldCorp board of directors. Nothing. I knew I'd seen the guy before somewhere. I looked over at Sarah. She was head down and deep into her research. She'd grabbed a roll of shelf paper from under the sink and pulled off a three-foot-long strip. Now she was drawing boxes and connecting lines in a massive network that looked like a web spun by a spider on crack.

I saw a brown envelope next to her bag on the table.

"Are those the Carlos shots?" I asked.

Sarah didn't even acknowledge that I was in the building let alone that I'd just asked her a perfectly simple question. She had shut everything and everyone else out as she burned up the Internet. I grabbed the envelope and pulled out the photos taken at the MaxWorldCorp AGM. And there it was. In one of the shots, I could see our mystery man standing behind Carlos, not quite in the fray. Only half of his face was visible and even then his hand was covering part of his chin. But it was definitely the guy Henderson had met for lunch. There was no doubt in my mind. He was well in the background of the photo but his eyes were clearly focused on Carlos. I was about to interrupt Sarah with this news, but realized that nothing short of a cruise missile could distract her from her task.

So I waited. I even dozed for a bit. Still seated on the couch, I was awakened at 2:45 a.m. by what can best be described as a cry of anguish.

"I am such a fucking idiot!" Sarah shouted. "I am a tool!"

"I like you," I said, slowly emerging from my nap.

"Small consolation, because we are screwed. We are so royally screwed."

She closed her laptop, grabbed the sheet of shelf paper, now covered by intersecting lines and squares, and overlaid with a thick red line she'd traced with a Sharpie. The red line meandered from the bottom left corner of the sheet to the top right, with umpteen stops in between.

"Let's go."

I grabbed the Carlos photos and followed her out the door.

At that hour, it took only about six minutes to drive to the family homestead. Sarah mapped out the plan on the way over. I listened and said "Okay" four times. Before we got out of the car, I turned on the dome light and showed Sarah the Carlos photo with the partially obscured but still clear shot of Henderson's lunch date in the background. She just shook her head. When we reached the front door, Sarah grabbed the heavy iron door knocker.

"Whoa, it's three o'clock in the morning," I said.

She banged the door knocker not twice, not three times, but seven heavy blows. Had there been neighbours' homes anywhere near Chateau Hemmingway, they'd all be awake now and about to dial the police.

After waiting only long enough for Dad to have awakened and pulled back the covers on his bed, Sarah swung the knocker another six times. Eventually, the light in the hall turned on and the angry eyes of our father shot daggers through the small leaded panes in the door window. He slid back the bolt and opened the door. He stood there in paisley pyjamas and a burgundy silk robe. He looked positively patrician. Then he shouted.

"What in heaven's name are you doing here at this ungodly hour! This is my home!"

"Dad, there was a time when this was our home, too," I said.

"What do you want? I said everything I'm going to say on the topic this afternoon. The deal is as good as done. It's too late."

Sarah pushed past him before he could finish.

"Important!" she said. "You're going to want to see this. It cannot wait."

She was out of sight in an instant, heading for his study just off the hallway. I shrugged when Dad looked my way. I said nothing, just motioned with my open hand to suggest he follow her in. He did. I closed the door behind me and caught up as Sarah was leading Dad by the hand to his chair behind the desk. She'd already turned on a floor lamp and his desk lamp, casting a warm and inviting glow over the room.

"What is going . . ."

"Shhh! No talking," Sarah commanded. "Give us thirty minutes to lay something out, and if you're not convinced at the end, go ahead and sell off the family company just as you planned. So for half an hour, just sit and listen, please, Dad."

I thought he was going to lose it then, but he pulled back and closed his mouth. Sarah stood in the middle of the lamplight spilling onto the floor in front of Dad's chair. He interlocked his fingers and rested his hands in his lap.

"Dad, if you believe what we're about to say, you cannot sign the acquisition agreement tomorrow. It's not what you think," she started. "Just hear me out on this and, please, do not interrupt me until I'm finished. We've got three important and related points to make. Until we've made them, please, just listen, except when Hem poses a few questions. You can answer them, but nothing more till we're done. Understood?"

Dad was beginning to get the sense that she was serious, that this was serious. He nodded.

"First of all, we have gathered indisputable evidence that Henderson Watt is in the employ of MaxWorldCorp. Hem confirmed with an inside contact at the New York Police Department that the new Mercedes he's now driving is actually registered to MaxWorldCorp. It's part of their fleet lease."

Dad opened his mouth, first in shock, and then to say something.

"Shhh, not yet!" Sarah cut him off. "With that revelation as our starting point, and putting the pieces together, Henderson Watt almost certainly had me under surveillance before he engineered our first meeting at a bar way back when. He then arranged to bump into me a day or so later at a Starbucks. Building a relationship with me was how he planned to land a job at Hemmingwear and get close to you and could start to work on his real agenda. And that's exactly what he did. I fell for it. I'm sorry. When his rapport with you became strong enough, he sacrificed me. He used me only to get to you."

Dad raised his hand.

"Not yet, Dad."

He lowered his hand.

"Okay, secondly . . ."

She nodded at me. I stood up, pulled out my BlackBerry, fiddled with the photo on the screen, and handed it to Dad.

"Do you know this guy?" I asked.

"Of course. That's Tim Withrow, CEO of Preston Holdings."

I hadn't been expecting this, but clearly Sarah had.

"No shit!" I exclaimed.

"Shhh! We're not done yet!" Sarah snapped and then gestured for me to continue.

"Dad, have you authorized anyone else to speak to Preston Holdings during the negotiations, or have you been doing all the talking yourself?"

"Of course I've been doing it all myself. It's my company," he said. "I'm the only one allowed to speak to Preston."

Then I leaned down to pinch the image on the screen as Dad still held my cellphone. The photo grew smaller and a second figure now appeared across a café table from Tim Withrow.

"This is one of the photos I took of Henderson Watt lunching with this Withrow dude in New York, yesterday."

Dad's eyes widened as he just stared at the photo, as if Henderson might disappear from the shot if he just stared long enough. I took the phone back and held it a little higher.

"Listen," I said. "You're about to hear the voice of Henderson Watt speaking first, followed by Withrow. These were the last words they exchanged at this lunch. I wish we had a longer recording, but we don't."

I hit the button.

"*. . . almost taste it.*"

"*Me, too. Hang in there. We're just about home. Just keep doing what you're doing.*"

I replayed it. I sat back down.

"So Henderson had a meeting with the Preston guy. But where's the link to MaxWorldCorp?" he asked.

I slid the Carlos photo from the envelope and pointed out that Tim Withrow had also attended the AGM of MaxWorldCorp.

Dad nodded, but decided against saying anything more. Instead, he looked back at Sarah. She stood up again.

"Okay. Number three. And this is the biggie. You want a Preston-MaxWorldCorp link? Well, here it comes. Preston Holdings, through an incredibly complex set of connections, affiliations, and relationships intended to obscure and even conceal the truth about its ownership, is actually controlled by MaxWorldCorp. Ultimately, Preston is owned by MaxWorldCorp. Preston is owned by Phillip Gainsford. I hope that's a strong enough link for you."

"Impossible . . ."

"Shhh, Dad! Not finished yet. Just listen. I have traced the provenance of Preston through their required online filings with various regulatory authorities here in the U.S. and in Europe. I have saved screen captures of all of it. Trust me, this is all true and accounted for."

Sarah then spread out her big sheet of paper and walked Dad and me through Preston's labyrinthine and quite ingenious corporate structure. She led us along the red Sharpie line through myriad twists and turns, shell corporations, other holding companies, and several offshore entities. It took twenty minutes for her to cite all the official sources to justify each of her conclusions. At each stop along the circuitous path, she'd called up another official website and showed Dad the incontrovertible trail of evidence that culminated in an ironclad conclusion. By the end, Phillip Gainsford's big play was all too obvious. When the ducks were all lined up, it was hard to argue. It was such an impressive and compelling piece of work. The Internet is a wonderful thing.

Dad said nothing for what seemed like a very long time. His wheels were turning, turning.

"Dad, Henderson Watt used me. We had a relationship. We slept together, Dad. He used me to get to you, to get to our company, and ultimately to *get* our company."

Dad winced at the "slept together" line.

Dad was avoiding Sarah's eyes as he said, "He told me you had severe mood swings, that you had a serious temper problem, and that you suffered from depression. He alluded to medication that you were taking. Is any of that true?"

"Dad, I do have a temper, and I pop Advil for my migraines, but the rest is pure fiction. Mood swings? Depression? Why didn't you say something to me? Why didn't you ask me about it?"

"Henderson asked me not to. He said that you were sensitive about it all."

"Christ! What a snake."

Dad just sat there, looking shell-shocked.

"Do you now understand how MaxWorldCorp could so easily anticipate and then pre-empt every corporate move we've made for the last two quarters?"

He said nothing. He just stared into space.

"Dad?" I prompted. We had some decisions to make.

"I can't believe Phillip Gainsford would stoop to this level. It just can't be real. Even he is not capable of this," he said in one last grasp at one last straw.

Sarah then played a card I didn't even know she had. She called up Phillip Gainsford's Wikipedia entry on her MacBook Air, highlighted a section, and handed the laptop to our father.

"Dad, do you know the name of Phillip Gainsford's youngest daughter?"

He looked confused by the request, but his eyes flitted across the highlighted section.

"Oh God," he croaked.

"What's the name, Dad? Tell us," she pushed.

A good ten seconds passed before he finally spoke.

"Preston."

Dad looked ashen. I said nothing. And Sarah just let the silence hang to entrench the revelations, to make them real. I was about to fill the awkward vacuum with some small talk – you can always count on me for small talk – when Dad raised his hand to extend the silence. We sat there for another minute or so before Dad stood up.

"Hem, could you call Kingsley and get him over here? We need to know our options," he said.

"Sure. And I'll give some thought to what we should do about tomorrow's news conference. We should probably cancel it, shouldn't we?"

Both Sarah and Dad answered in unison.

"No."

Dad was about to speak, but with a wave of his hand, he ceded the floor to Sarah for the explanation.

"The media are coming here tomorrow because they expect an announcement. There's already rampant speculation about the sale of the company. We're going to want the media here because there will still be an announcement. Just not the one Henderson Watt and Phillip Gainsford are expecting."

"Now, we've got work to do," Dad said. "Do you have your plan on that fancy computer of yours?"

Sarah smiled and nodded.

"Let's go through it. If Henderson killed it because it threatened his ulterior mission, I want to see your plan," he said. "Actually, it's time I looked at it anyway. Hem, brief Michael Kingsley when he gets here. Sarah and I are going to be tied up for a while."

I left them in the study and went out into the kitchen to call the company lawyer and get him over to the house. I also scanned the U.S. newswire site to see how the Hemmingwear announcement scheduled for that afternoon was being positioned. Fortunately, the media advisory was not particularly detailed and only referred to a "major corporate announcement." That could mean anything.

Michael Kingsley arrived about half an hour later, at 4:15 a.m. He looked worried. I took him through the whole story with as much detail as I could muster. Lawyers like details. Cases are often won on the fine points. He whistled a couple of times during my monologue and shook his head often. He did not look good by the end.

"Henderson? What balls. What unbelievable temerity," he said.

Dad and Sarah emerged from his study at 7:30. Michael Kingsley and I were sprawled out in the living room, dozing.

Okay, I was in a deep coma, but did my best to make it look as if I'd just nodded off.

"You've been thoroughly briefed, Michael?" asked Dad.

"Yes, and I'm still reeling from it all. Who else knows all this?"

"Other than the perpetrators themselves, we are the only ones on the planet who know," replied Dad. "All right, Michael, do we have a clear-cut and actionable case of corporate espionage or not?"

"Well, there's often a fine line between competitive intelligence and industrial espionage, but not in this case. I don't think I've ever seen a more blatant abrogation of the law."

"So we actually have a case against MaxWorldCorp?" I asked.

"Often these kinds of cases are built on hearsay, innuendo, and circumstantial evidence. In this situation, we've got photographs, audio recordings, strangely prescient pre-emptive actions from the competitor, and a pattern of subterfuge that I think would hold up very well in a court of law. Even if we lost the case, the evidence and publicity would sink MaxWorldCorp in the court of public opinion," Michael concluded.

"As a senior exec, Henderson signed all the standard non-compete, non-disclosure clauses in his contract when he joined us, didn't he?." Dad looked to Michael for confirmation.

"Yes, of course he did. I supervised all of that myself," Michael replied.

"Well, then I think we just might have our announcement for later today," Dad said.

"Yes! Let's string them up. Let's humiliate them. Let's make them wish they'd never tangled with The Hemmingwear Company," I said, rubbing my hands together in anticipation.

"No."

She said it quietly, but still, we all heard it. The three of us rubbernecked to look at Sarah. She was shaking her head, with authority.

"No. We should not proceed with any charges – industrial espionage, or breach of fiduciary responsibility, or even a violation of a personal employment contract. We should not even go there, period, full stop, end of discussion," she said.

"Why ever not?" Dad asked. "I want Gainsford to pay for his audacious and diabolical play for our company. I want justice."

"Dad, think it through," Sarah said. "Do we really want a long, drawn-out, and very public court case that describes in minute detail how an employee of our principal competitor waltzed in and landed a big job in the C-suite of Hemmingwear, fed company secrets to MaxWorldCorp for years, and almost engineered the sell-off of our company at a discounted value to a holding entity that is actually controlled by Phillip Gainsford? Is that what you really want? And to what end? So they lose the case and pay a few million dollars in fines? Big deal. They've probably spent much more getting this far in their plan. The whole exercise would make us look like we can't manage our own future. The value of Hemmingwear would plummet on all the ensuing bad press. We just cannot make this decision based on a desire for revenge. We have to do what's truly in the best interests of the company.

"Introducing Henderson Watt to you, Dad, is on my head. I'm not going to compound it by tilting at windmills in a legal case that stands to hurt us more than help us. No. Bad idea."

Sarah had this way of making everyone else in the room feel like complete and utter imbeciles. In this case, it was because we were all actually behaving like complete and utter imbeciles.

"So what is our announcement this afternoon, then?" Michael asked.

"Don't worry, we've got a lot to talk about at the media briefing. We don't often get the chance to hold the media hostage, but we've got them where we want them today," Sarah said.

Just then, the doorknocker sounded from the front. I walked through to the front hall and opened the door. There stood Carlos Mendez.

"Carlos, you're up early," I said.

"Sarah called me and asked me to stop by."

"I think I may know why. Come on in."

When we made it to the living room, Sarah grabbed the manila envelope that was resting on the coffee table and jerked her head toward Dad's study. The others were mapping out the announcement based on Sarah's proposed approach. Carlos and I followed Sarah into the study. I closed the door behind me and sat down next to Carlos in front of Dad's desk. Sarah stood, but leaned against the desk. She pulled out the photos of Carlos taken at the MaxWorldCorp AGM.

"Carlos, what were you doing at the annual meeting of our principal competitor?"

"How did you get these? Are you having me followed?" Carlos asked.

"Of course we're not having you followed. We think Henderson Watt had the photos taken and then passed them along to me in a plain brown wrapper, like it was a porn video," Sarah replied. "Carlos, what were you doing at their AGM?"

"Know thine enemy," replied Carlos.

Then he paused before continuing.

"I was trying to get a sense of them, how they think, how they might have gotten the inside info that allowed them to screw us on the multi-pack launch."

"So you walked right into their AGM?" Sarah asked.

"It's an open meeting. You don't have to be a shareholder to be in the room. You can't vote of course, but you can go. I went."

"What's going on in the photos?" I asked.

"I was recognized and asked to leave. This shot is when I was attempting the charm offensive to avoid being ejected. And this one is when I realized it was failing. I know it looks like we're pretty chummy in that one, but if they'd sent you a shot taken about five seconds later, they had me in an arm lock and were hustling me out to the parking lot."

"Well, that's a relief," Sarah said.

"Wait a second. Did you think that I might be passing stuff to them?" he asked, incredulous. "Give me some credit, guys. I've spent my life here. I could barely stand to be in an auditorium with a MaxWorldCorp logo on the front screen. I felt queasy."

"We've had to be very cautious and make sure we know who our friends are," Sarah explained.

Satisfied that Carlos was an unwitting pawn in Henderson's attempt to throw us off his scent, she then spent the next ten minutes bringing Carlos into the fold. He was livid. Borrowing a phrase from my mother, Carlos was ready to rip Henderson's arm off at the shoulder and beat him over the head with it. I did little to discourage him.

The five of us then huddled for an hour to finalize our plan for the media briefing. The butterflies in my stomach were no longer flying in formation but were locked in an all-out dogfight. By ten that morning, I thought we were ready. Sarah and I decided we'd zip back to her place to change our clothes for the media briefing. Dad walked us to the front door. He was still wearing his pyjamas and silk robe, but he wasn't heading for bed. And there was an extra spring in his step as the three of us walked out onto the front porch.

"For the first time in, well, ever, it feels like a family business again," Dad said. "Thank you for caring enough about it to stop me from making what would have been a catastrophic decision."

It seemed he was making heavier eye contact with Sarah as he said this. I was fine with that. In fact, I was feeling lighter on my feet than I had in a very long time, perhaps ever. As he spoke, Sarah's eyes glistened.

We climbed into the car. Sarah drove.

"So, um, did Dad talk to you about anything other than . . ."

She put up her hand to stop me from finishing my question.

"Yes, he told me. Thanks for the heads-up on that," she said, little bits of sarcasm flying from her words.

"Sarah, I'm sorry, but he gave me explicit instructions not to say a word to you. He insisted on telling you himself. And I guess I decided that was his right. I thought I owed him that."

She had a faraway look in her eyes as tears made a fleeting appearance until she wiped them away.

"Yes, I know." She sighed, taking her right hand off the wheel and holding it out to me. I slipped mine in hers and she squeezed. "We'll worry about that tomorrow. But right now, we have to focus on the media briefing. We at least have some control over the outcome of that."

"Right. I don't know what's more satisfying, stopping Dad from selling off the company or getting to see Henderson Watt take the plunge from his pedestal," I said.

"Yep. Can't wait for that. Then we'll scrape him up off the floor and have security throw him out on his ass," she replied.

"Well, as you may recall, I know a little something about being thrown out on my ass. It's no fun, for the 'throwee,' but if you're lucky enough to see it happen to someone else, I gather it can be quite enjoyable."

"I'm counting on it."

CHAPTER 15

Dad had called Henderson to explain that he was spending some time with his children that morning and wouldn't be in until noon. This would have been extraordinarily unusual behaviour for Dad, particularly when the final sale documents still had to be signed before the 1:30 announcement. But Henderson was apparently unperturbed. Dad confirmed the final signing meeting for 12:30 in his office with Henderson Watt and Preston Holdings' CEO, Tim Withrow.

When Sarah and I returned to the family home, we joined Dad, Carlos, and Michael Kingsley in the study to put the last touches on our plan for the final signing meeting with Henderson and Withrow and the subsequent media briefing. I was fairly quiet during the meeting and tried to stay on the periphery of the decision-making. I made a few comments and helped wordsmith a few lines when it was required, but I let the business grown-ups deal with most of it.

Although I could feel myself getting caught up in the drama of it all, I was never inclined, not for an instant, to rethink my chosen career path. I still had no interest in making a career at Hemmingwear. In fact, I was thrilled that in the last twenty-four hours, Dad's view of his daughter seemed to have changed, and changed completely. I could tell by the way he looked at her when she spoke. I could tell by the way he held his hand up to silence others when she held the floor. I could tell by the way he focused and changed his mind to support her view when divergent ideas were on the table. It also seemed clear that he wasn't siding with her because she was his own flesh and blood, but rather because she consistently advanced thoughtful and compelling positions with which the opposing arguments simply could not compete. She was winning him over with her brain and her toughness. It was just a coincidence that she was his daughter, and my younger sister. I could feel the family noose that I'd worn since birth loosening around my neck. A warm surge of pride in Sarah germinated in my chest and grew.

I took a minute to fire off an email to Marie to bring her up to date and let her know that I expected to be home that evening. I was missing her.

"Look who I found in the parking lot," Henderson said as he walked into Dad's office with Tim Withrow in tow. It was 12:30.

Dad was sitting at the head of the board table. Sarah, Michael Kingsley, Carlos, and I sat along the side to Dad's left.

"Gentlemen, right on time. Sit down, please," Dad said, waving them into the two chairs on the side of the table to his right.

If Henderson was surprised or concerned by the lineup facing him across the table, he didn't let on. Because I was farthest away from him, it was easiest for me to observe him closely without him really noticing. So I did. There were no telltale beads of sweat on Henderson's forehead, no furrows in his brow. He was one cool customer.

Tim Withrow opened his big, rectangular lawyer's briefing case with the pull handle and wheels and lifted out about ten inches of documents, all nicely cerloxed. The multicoloured plastic tabs presumably marked the pages to be signed to turn The Hemmingwear Company over to Preston Holdings and, ultimately, to Phillip Gainsford and MaxWorldCorp.

"All right, here are the docs," he said as he dropped them on the table with a thud. "Earnest, I believe the protocol is for you to sign first, and then I'll sign on behalf of Preston. Michael, you can witness them, and then it's official."

Dad shoved the documents to our side of the table and turned to Henderson Watt and Tim Withrow.

"Thanks for these. They'll become interesting souvenirs of this little adventure. I won't be signing them. We will not be announcing the sale at 1:30 this afternoon, because we do not have a deal."

Henderson looked momentarily shocked, but then chuckled.

"Good one, EH3," he said before turning to Tim Withrow.

"Just a little eleventh-hour humour. He's just kidding. We're all good. Right, EH3? Tell him we're good."

Dad was not joking. Dad was not smiling. But I do think Dad was enjoying himself, perhaps for the first time in a long while.

"Have you ever seen me kid before, Mr. Watt?" Dad asked. "And all is most decidedly not 'good,' as you so colloquially put it."

"What's going on?" Withrow said, alarmed. "You signed an agreement in principle two weeks ago. You shook my hand on it."

"Yes, I did, but the acquisition is not complete until the final documents are signed. And I'm not signing. There is no deal. Further, that handshake was based on a malevolent and Machiavellian premise that has only just come to light."

"EH3, I don't understand, we've been working on this for months." Now Henderson was whining. "It's natural to have some last-minute misgivings, but this is a fair deal, it's a good deal. It will save Hemmingwear."

The next words out of my father's mouth were delivered in a low, even, almost sinister tone.

"Henderson, I would be very grateful if you would just shut your mouth. Do not say another word until you're invited to speak."

Tim Withrow looked as if he'd been shot. The look on Henderson's face suggested he was in the midst of a prostate examination, which, in my father's eyes, would probably have seemed fitting. Dad then leaned back in his chair, laced his fingers, and rested his hands on the table in front of him. When the silence became almost excruciating, he raised his eyes to the two men.

"Henderson, we now know that you have direct financial ties to MaxWorldCorp, starting with the lease for your ostentatious new car that is parked just outside."

"You fucking idiot!" Tim Withrow snapped at Henderson, drawing away from him.

"We now know that your insidious infiltration here at Hemmingwear has been carefully orchestrated to result in the sale of my family's company as outlined in these documents. We also now know that you, Mr. Withrow, also have a connection to MaxWorldCorp."

On cue, Sarah pulled the mysterious MaxWorldCorp AGM photos from their envelope and pushed them across to Tim Withrow, pointing out his partially obscured face in the shots. She then turned to Henderson Watt.

"You should have taken a closer look at these pictures before trying to impugn Carlos's motives," Sarah said. "Not very smart. But thank you very much for getting them to us."

"I have no idea what you're talking about," Henderson replied.

"Yeah, right," Sarah said.

"I'm not listening to any more of this bullshit," Withrow said as he pushed back his chair and stood.

"Oh, I think it is in your own personal legal interests to stay just a little longer before you slink away," Michael Kingsley interjected.

Withrow's eyes narrowed, but he sank back into his chair.

"Thank you, Michael," Dad said before continuing. "Where was I? Oh yes, we now know that Preston Holdings, despite great efforts to obscure the trail, is actually owned and controlled by Phillip Gainsford and MaxWorldCorp."

Sarah then stood and spread out her hand-drawn diagram showing the complex but unmistakable link between Preston and MaxWorldCorp. Both men went white.

"I'm almost done, so bear with me," Dad continued. "We also now know that the two of you just met for lunch in New York, in contravention of my directive that I be involved in all discussions with Preston. Now I know what you're thinking. Having lunch is not against the law. You're right. But the photos and the audio recordings we have secured certainly help to establish the basis, the opportunity, and some compelling evidence for a charge of corporate espionage."

As planned, I slid my cellphone across the table with the photo of them both on the screen.

"EH3, please, this is ridic – " Henderson said.

"Shut up, Henderson. It's still not yet your turn to speak," my father replied, holding his hand up. "The depths to which you stooped to put yourself in this position leave me feeling physically ill."

Henderson followed Dad's eyes as they both glanced at Sarah.

"Clearly you abandoned your moral compass a long time ago, if you ever had one. Mr. Kingsley here will now explain the legal ramifications of your predicament."

Michael Kingsley pulled two documents from a file folder and slid them over to Tim Withrow and Henderson Watt. They both picked them up and started reading. They were obviously worried, though both tried to hide it. It's hard not to look scared when all the colour has drained from your face and there are legal papers in your hands.

"Gentlemen, the briefing notes you are holding outline how you have both systematically and purposefully breached the laws of this state and nation, exactly when you breached them, and what the standard range of penalties normally associated with such offences might be expected to be meted out by a fair-minded judge. You'll note that some of them are in fact criminal offences."

Both men were listening very carefully now.

"Under normal circumstances, federal and state authorities would be called in and you, gentlemen, would be led away right about now. But instead, in a few minutes, we are going to allow you both to get up, walk out that door, and never come back. As corporate counsel to The Hemmingwear Company, I am officially informing you that we have not yet determined if or when we might pursue legal action against MaxWorldCorp and/ or you as individuals. When you, or your lawyers, review the evidence we already have in our possession, notwithstanding the reams of further evidence a formal investigation would certainly uncover, you will conclude, as we already have, that the courts would hand Hemmingwear a landmark and precedent-setting victory. It's hard to predict precisely where you two would end up, but needless to say, it would not be a happy place. You may keep the briefing notes as a reminder of what evidence we already have in hand at this very early stage. You will obviously be informed should we determine that legal action is in our best interests. When and if we decide to pursue this further, it certainly will not be in your best interests. One day, there could be a knock at your door, and papers will be served. Just to note that the statute of limitations on such offences is very, very long indeed, so we have plenty of time to make a decision."

Michael nodded at my father. He was done.

"Sleep well, gentlemen, and please leave right now."

Carlos got up then, as we'd agreed, and opened the door. Two burly security guards were standing on the other side. Henderson Watt and Tim Withrow said nothing, did not look at each other, and did not look back at us as they departed. Carlos closed the door.

"Well, I think that went rather well," said my father.

He then shook his head and started to chuckle. Yes, I'd call it a chuckle well on the way to a full-on laugh. It was a sound I honestly could not remember ever hearing. I know that sounds odd, but it's true. Sarah laughed along with him.

I walked over to the window overlooking the parking lot for a parting view of that beautiful Mercedes. I watched as Henderson Watt and Tim Withrow, both clearly distraught and arguing openly, jumped into the Benz and squealed out the front gate, narrowly missing a satellite truck arriving for the media briefing. What gall. They'd actually driven in for the final signing meeting together. Unbelievable audacity.

When I looked around, my father was giving Sarah a hug. That was almost as rare as hearing him laugh. Sarah looked flabbergasted. He then turned to me. We didn't hug, but he shook my hand while gripping my arm with his other hand. I took it to mean that he intended to convey deeper feelings than those inherent in the garden-variety handshake.

"Thank you," he whispered.

By 1:20, the large corporate boardroom down the hall from Dad's office was packed with local and business media. The huge table had been removed and replaced by theatre-style row seating. There were six cameras mounted on tripods lined up at the back. About fifteen journalists sat patiently awaiting the start of the proceedings. Carlos, Michael Kingsley, and I stood along the wall on the side. At 1:30, my father and sister entered. He went directly to the podium that stood on a riser at the front of the room, while she stood a little off to the side. Showtime.

"Welcome and thank you all for coming this afternoon. I'm Earnest Hemmingway. I hope after nearly a century of manufacturing here in the U.S. I no longer have to say 'no relation' when I say my own name," he said, using an old line that pushed him to the very limits of his sense of humour.

He paused to let the nonexistent laughter fade and then continued.

"This is a very important day in the life of Hemmingwear. In fact, I think it's as important as the day in 1916 when my grandfather founded this company. In a way, today marks the rebirth of Hemmingwear. Some of you have undoubtedly heard rumours of a takeover or a merger. To be fair, there were certainly offers and opportunities but in the end I, um, we simply weren't thrilled with the idea of giving up a family company that's been a leader in the market for nearly a hundred years. It just did not feel like the right path to pursue. We've certainly had a rough few years, and without changing our ways, I think we can all agree that the prospects are not exactly rosy in this competitive climate. But there will be no sale of the company. Hemmingwear will be staying right where it belongs, in the hands of the Hemmingway family. But we do have an important announcement about the future of the company. Well, we are in fact about to change our ways to carry us into a new future. I'll now turn it over to Sarah Hemmingway, my daughter, who will lead us all through the strategy that will strengthen and reposition Hemmingway for continued growth and prosperity in the coming years. Sarah?"

Dad moved off the riser and took a seat in the front row. The stage was hers.

"Thank you, um, thanks," she stumbled, barely avoiding saying "Dad," which, under the circumstances, I don't really think would have been so bad.

"Thank you for coming. I'll be brief. This is actually rather a simple story. From the very beginning, Hemmingwear has manufactured high-quality men's underwear in a very narrow range of styles at a single large and fully integrated facility on this site. Our close proximity to this country's largest rail hub offers very economical continental distribution. In fact, in the beginning, our workers merely pushed wagons filled with product to a rail spur about fifty yards away. All of this has allowed us to maximize economies of scale in the manufacturing process and strike that sometimes elusive balance between product quality and price. All these factors were in place at Hemmingwear by 1920, and they remain at the core of our longevity today. But we are in a new century, with new demands, new challenges, and, yes, new threats. Today, while we honour Hemmingwear's history, we seize the opportunity to secure our future."

Very nice. She had not a note in front of her, and this allowed her to make eye contact with each of the reporters assembled in front of her. I watched Dad as she spoke, and he was clearly impressed, perhaps even moved.

"In the coming months, Hemmingwear will introduce some product changes that, taken together, represent a significant but imperative departure from our past. While keeping the company name, we'll modernize our brand and add some much-needed colour to our products. Most significantly . . ."

Sarah looked down for an instant to take a deep breath, but then lifted her head to barrel ahead.

"Most significantly, at the earliest opportunity, Hemmingwear will introduce a line of products for women and girls so that the other half of the population finally has access to the same quality and comfort that only men have enjoyed since 1916. We've known for years that women have been buying and wearing the products Hemmingwear makes for men. Well, we think it's time women and girls have their own line of underwear, designed just for them. The way our manufacturing lines are configured allows us to add a new shift to handle the women's product line without compromising in any way the manufacture of the men's line. We'll be creating new jobs and preserving the economies of scale that have kept us competitive for so many decades."

She paused again before wrapping up.

"So in summary, we're preserving the very best parts of Hemmingwear's history – a still-narrow product line, efficient manufacturing and distribution, market-leading comfort and quality – and we're adding colour, more contemporary and fashionable branding, and a new line of products for women and girls, effectively doubling our potential customer base. That is the strategy that will sustain Hemmingwear's leadership in an increasingly competitive market.

"I'm happy to respond to your questions."

The plan had been for Dad to rejoin Sarah at the podium for the Q&A period. She glanced over at him, but he just stayed put and waved his hand for her to handle it.

A reporter stood and raised his hand. Sarah nodded his way.

"Peter Mercer, *Chicago Trib*. We heard very strong rumours from some very solid sources that you had done a deal with a group called Preston Holdings for the sale of Hemmingwear. Was that ever true?"

"Peter, as we were mapping out the future of the company, we ended up having many conversations with many different players. I'm comfortable saying that we even got some ways down the road with one potential suitor, but we just never felt completely comfortable with giving up what has been in the family for so long. So we've decided to chart a new course, our own course."

"So there was a deal on the table," he persisted.

"It's not a deal until the paperwork is signed and the parties shake hands. That never happened."

There were several more questions that she skillfully parried or answered, as the situation required. When it was clear that the proceedings were winding down, my father finally stood and stepped up to the podium. Sarah sat down in the chair Dad had just made available.

"Thank you, Sarah," he began. "Just before we close, I have one other announcement to make of a more personal nature, though it does bear on the company. I will taking what I expect will be a six-month sabbatical from the company to deal with a medical issue that we all expect to be successfully resolved. Until my return, Sarah Hemmingway will be acting CEO, with the loyal support of Carlos Mendez. And that's all I'll be saying about this situation. Thank you all for coming."

From my angle, I could watch Sarah's reaction while the reporters really could not. That was a good thing. Clearly, Dad had made the call during the media briefing. I wasn't surprised. Dad's view of his daughter had come a long way in the last twenty-four hours. When he made his announcement, Sarah's eyes widened, but she recovered quickly. She glanced at Carlos. He was grinning at her and nodding his head slowly.

A number of reporters conducted one-on-ones with Dad or Sarah after the formal briefing concluded. When the boardroom door closed on the last journalist, I grabbed Sarah in a bear hug. Carlos made it a threesome. Well, you know what I mean.

"You were amazing! So confident, so articulate, and so thoughtful. You absolutely nailed it!" I said and meant it.

Dad just beamed. And trust me, never before have the words "Dad" and "beamed" lined up in the same sentence.

"I was so nervous, I thought I was going to pass out," she replied.

"You're kidding?" I said, genuinely shocked. "Well, you looked and sounded like you were born to do this."

"Yes, you certainly, did," agreed Dad. "I'm just sorry it's taken me so long to see, as your brother has so appropriately put it, that perhaps you really were born to do this."

"All right, enough reflecting and contemplating, we have a lot of work to do," Sarah said.

_____

Two days later, I picked up Mario out in front of his home.

"Are you ready?" I asked him as he slid into the driver's seat I'd just vacated.

"No, I'm terrified!"

"Why, you've been doing great. You've got this! This is your time," I said. "I can feel it."

He put his seat belt on, adjusted his mirrors, sighed heavily, checked his blind spot, and then turned the wheel to pull out into traffic. We did not pull out into traffic.

"Sorry, Mario, but I turned the car off when I pulled up," I explained. "You'll have to turn the key."

"You see! I can't do this!"

"Of course you can. I always forget to start the car. It's a very common mistake. And it's one of the safer driving errors you can make. Now come on, you've got this. I know you do. Let's go."

I hoped Mario could not see through my misplaced enthusiasm. I was a little nervous letting Mario take his road test in my G35, but it was the logical decision. It made no sense to have the DMV examiner climb into the front seat of Hat's dilapidated equipment-packed van, the only other vehicle Mario had recently driven. We made it to the DMV without incident. I've chosen not to categorize as "incidents" things like cutting off a bus and then nearly running down an elderly pedestrian who saved himself through quite impressive and athletic evasive action for a man his age.

"Good luck," I said to Mario as a clipboard-bearing examiner approached. "Try to stay calm and don't forget to check your mirrors."

Mario nodded. He had his game face on.

I sat in the waiting room and resisted the temptation to watch out the window as Mario and the examiner pulled out of the parking lot and onto a very busy street. I waited for the sounds of squealing tires or crunching metal, but I heard nothing. I texted Hat to make sure all was ready. He confirmed it was.

I thought about Marie while I waited. She'd picked me up at the airport when I'd returned from Chicago. We talked like we'd been best friends for years. She wanted all the gory details on the Henderson Watt flame-out. She was even more interested in Sarah's great success. They'd become quite good friends. I still wasn't writing but I was feeling better about it, well, about everything, than I had in ages.

Twenty-five minutes after Mario and clipboard guy departed, they drove back into the parking lot. Mario was still driving. That was a good sign. My eyes scoured the car's exterior and it still looked unblemished. That was also a good sign. Finally, the examiner was conscious and did not look as if he'd just finished a ride on Space Mountain at Disneyland. In fact, he looked quite calm. I suppose he might have popped a Quaalude halfway into the test to make it through, but I didn't think so. Mario parked the car in the same spot we'd pulled into before and stopped. I watched through the window and could see the examiner bobbing his head as he went through the assessment.

Mario was nodding his head in return. Neither looked agitated, although I certainly was. Come on, let's go. The suspense was killing me. Finally, after what seemed like about half an hour, but was really only about ten minutes, they both got out and walked into the building. The examiner shook Mario's hand, which I thought was kind of formal for a driver's test, and then disappeared through the door that said "DMV Staff Only" stencilled on the glass.

As soon as the door closed, Mario started jumping up and down, and turning pirouettes in the air, in a good way. Then he bopped his way over to me and hugged me, singing a new song he seemed to have written for the occasion. I thought the lyrics were a tad repetitive.

"I passed, I passed, I passed, I passed, I passed, I passed, I passed. Spread the good news, I passed."

I thought he might be singing it to the tune "We're Off to See the Wizard," but I couldn't really be sure. I doubt Mario was sure.

"Wooooo-hooooo, Mario! This is great news. Congratulations!" I said.

"I can't believe it. I passed," Mario said. "Fifth time lucky!"

"See, I knew you'd pass," I said.

Actually, I knew no such thing. Perhaps the examiner was so grateful to make it back to the DMV in one piece that he passed him so he'd never have to ride with Mario ever again.

"So now what?" I asked. "What's the deal?"

"I have to wait in the next room until they call my name and hand over my driver's licence. It won't take long," Mario replied. "Thanks, Hem. I mean it. Without you and Hat, I never would have passed. I owe you big-time."

"No worries. You were ready. And you passed," I said. "You earned it."

As soon as Mario disappeared into the other room, I texted Hat the phrase "Green Light."

In time, Mario strutted back into the waiting room holding his driver's licence out in front of him in both hands as if it were a gold bar. I got up to meet him. He showed me the licence. In the photo, Mario had an almost giddy look on his face.

"Let's go," he said. "I'll drive."

We walked back out to the drop-off zone adjacent to the parking lot. I put my hand on Mario's shoulder.

"Hang on a second, Mario. Just bear with me, but we're going to wait here for just a minute or two. Hat is on his way."

Mario nodded and just kind of hung around the sliding glass door for a bit. Then, right on cue, a bright red, blindingly shiny, 1980 AMC Pacer wheeled into the parking lot and pulled to a stop in front of us. Hat jumped out. Mario was paralyzed. His mouth was open.

"Mario, you did it! I'm just so thrilled that you finally passed," Hat said.

Just then, the driver of the car behind the Pacer leaned on his horn, and not in a happy, celebratory way. He then lowered his window, all the better for us to hear him.

"Move that hunk of junk! You can't park it there!"

Uh oh. This was not good. Hat detonated and moved toward the driver with a look that said "homicide," or at least, "assault causing bodily harm."

"You shut your mouth!" Hat shrieked. "You shut it right now. This car is a classic! You are just so rude!"

As Hat's fiery face approached, the driver thought better of a physical confrontation with an obviously deranged, well-built East Indian fellow, and closed his window. That didn't discourage Hat from leaning down, banging the window, and continuing his tirade so that pedestrians in all neighbouring boroughs could hear him. I darted over, wrapped Hat up in a bear hug, and walked him backward away from the troublemaker's car.

"It's okay, Hat. The guy's an idiot, but we don't want any trouble, do we?" I said, keeping my voice low. "Let's just take a few deep breaths and calm down. This is Mario's moment, remember?"

"Oh no. I've done it again, haven't I? And I've been so good lately, too. I really have. I'm telling you, I've had very few outbursts lately. Very few."

I felt him relax so I unclenched my hands, which were still locked around his midsection. He turned back to the terrorized driver.

"I'm so sorry, sir. You caught me off guard with your rather aggressive and, to be honest, unkind remarks," Hat explained through the still-closed window. "Please, forgive me. I have a temper that still sometimes gets away from me. Someone kind of like you once even called me the Brown Hulk, but I don't think I would ever get violent. No, those days are behind me."

Hat was smiling sweetly, so the driver lowered his window just a crack.

"No problem. Just back away from my car, so I can pull out and get the hell out of your way," he said.

"Of course. I offer you a basket of apologies for my behaviour, and this butterscotch, which I'm quite sure you're going to like."

Before the driver could close his window again, Hat pushed the butterscotch candy through so it landed on the guy's lap. I grabbed Hat's arm and pulled him back over to where Mario was circling his new car. I heard tires squeal as the big-mouth driver pulled around the Pacer and out of the parking lot.

"How did you get the car and how did you get it to look so fantastic?" Mario asked, running his over the front fender.

"It was all Hat's idea," I explained. "We spoke to your parents and they agreed to let Hat pick up the car, have it washed, waxed, and detailed, and then bring it over here. We just made the assumption that you were going to pass."

Hat put on a kind of "aw shucks" look but was clearly very pleased with his stratagem.

"You guys are the best," Mario replied. "I mean it. You're the best. Thanks, guys. This really means a lot. Driving home in this will be the perfect end to a perfect day."

Unless he drives into the side of the building trying to get out of the parking lot, I thought to myself.

Hat and I watched with a mixture of parental pride and terrible foreboding as Mario jumped into his beloved car, buckled up, adjusted his seat and then his mirrors, and finally reached for the key dangling from the ignition.

"Okay, just to be sure, the engine is not running now, right?" Mario asked.

He started the car, gripped the steering wheel for a few seconds, slid the gearshift into Drive, and pulled slowly away. Hat and I waved as if Mario was embarking on a continent-crossing expedition rather than the eight-block drive to his parents' home. He made it out onto the street without any issues, although he came awfully close to a parking meter. Then I drove Hat home.

CHAPTER 16

On Thursday evening, a very big moment in the life of the NameFame baseball team arrived. It was unexpected. Based on our performance in, well, in every single one of our games thus far, actually winning a game seemed in the same probability zone as spinning gold from straw. But what do I know? Mario had passed his driver's test, so perhaps anything was possible.

We were up against the Plumbers and Pipefitters union team that currently led the league. I was not optimistic. Okay, I was downright scared of them. The smallest woman on their team was bigger than Clark Kent, the biggest guy on our team. The ten-run mercy rule was invoked in each of the first three innings. We actually brought home a run in the second inning when Jesse Owens popped a solo shot. So the score at the end of three innings was 30–1.

Let me try to save some time here. By the fourth inning, with the Plumbers and Pipefitters still at the plate, the score was

39–1. A giant of a plumber stepped into the batter's box and took a few warm-up cuts. At least I thought he was a plumber, based on the view every spectator had of his backside partly clad in low-riding shorts. He whacked a base hit right to me in centre field and then foolishly tried to stretch a single into a double. I fielded the hot one-bouncer and managed to throw a strike to Peter Parker at second base with plenty of time to spare. The plumber slid, hard. Peter tagged him, and the umpire, who had trotted halfway to the pitcher's mound for a better view, called him out. It wasn't even close. I don't know how we did it, but it all came together and we actually threw him out at second. My mouth hung open in disbelief. Then the plumber's mouth hung open as he wailed in pain.

He hadn't judged his sliding distance very well, and his lead left outstretched foot slammed into the base, twisting his ankle in a direction it was not designed to go. My own eyes watered at the sight of his joint instantly swelling. I turned my head away. Unfortunately, I could not turn my ears away from his unsettling shrieking as he writhed on the base path. On a positive note, his slide moved his shorts back into the traditional position, improving the view of his now-concealed backside. Eventually, he made the transition to low moans, and finally after a minute or so, silence descended on the field. This ensured that everyone in the general vicinity heard Jackie Kennedy's voice hollering from the stands.

"Come on, big boy, walk it off and play ball!"

It took twenty minutes for the two paramedics to secure the whimpering plumber's ankle. Then with the help of two sturdy teammates, the four of them hoisted the patient onto the stretcher. Judging from their bulging eyes, vein-rippled forearms, and red faces, they could have used a fifth set of biceps. Jesse Owens started clapping respectfully as the stretcher bumped across the infield to the waiting ambulance parked just beyond the fence. The rest of our team and the Plumbers and Pipefitters joined in the applause. The injured player, still in full grimace, raised a limp hand to acknowledge the support of his fellow players.

After the ambulance pulled out, I noticed the umpire talking to the captain of the P&P team. He nodded once and waved me in from centre field.

"This is your lucky day," the umpire said. "They no longer have the minimum number of players required to make this game official."

"Okay, so what does that mean, exactly?" I asked.

"It means that they have been forced to forfeit the game. They have no other choice."

"But they're winning thirty-nine to one!" I said.

"Yeah, they are, and it would probably be fifty or sixty to one by the end. But rules are rules. NameFame wins the game."

"Wait. We win the game?" I asked. "We get the 'W'?"

"You win the game."

In light of the hefty plumber's unfortunate injury that effectively handed us our very first victory in a game we were losing by thirty-eight runs with a couple of innings still left to play, I gathered our team together and asked them not to celebrate openly. I just thought it would be in bad taste to start high-fiving and whooping it up while a key member of the opposing team was on his way to hospital to have his ankle set. Everyone agreed. Unfortunately, Jackie Kennedy was still in the stands and never got the memo.

"Wooooo-hoooooo! We won! We won! Oh yeah, we won!" she shouted at the top of her lungs. "A sweet, sweet win! Oh yeah, oh yeah!"

We all looked over to see Jackie still shouting the glad tidings while standing on her seat doing something with her body that only vaguely resembled a victory dance. To an untrained observer, it could also have passed for a seizure of some kind. James Moriarty made his way around the screen to quell Jackie's enthusiasm.

When we got to the bar and saw that none of the Plumbers and Pipefitters players was there, well, then we did celebrate. We finally had one in the win column. We had a great time that night. There was lots of drinking, lots of carousing, some karaoke, and even some dancing. As for proudly recounting our glorious exploits on the field, well, there wasn't much of that. But as a team, still we were pumped about our win. Years from now, no one will remember *how* we got our first victory, just *that* we got our first victory. Okay, I'll probably remember what happened, but a win is a win.

That night, in Marie's apartment above Let Them Eat Cake!, she took my arm and led me to the bathroom. We stood there in front of the mirror, still a little tipsy, and smiled at each other. Then she opened the top left-hand drawer of the small vanity. It was completely empty.

"If you want it, this can be yours."

I don't know if it was the cumulative impact of the events of the past few weeks or whether I was just feeling a bit emotionally overwhelmed, but for the second time that night, my eyes filled up. I turned and hugged her. After the first few nights I'd stayed with Marie, I'd started carrying a toothbrush in my jacket pocket. I pulled it out and slipped it in the drawer to make it official.

"Thanks. I promise I'll always put the seat down."

She laughed.

In the three weeks that followed, life returned to at least a semblance of normal, whatever that means. I'd pretty well moved in by then. It was nice. Life was good.

One night at about 7:30, while I was cleaning a few cake pans in the kitchen, a text arrived from Sarah.

"You didn't pick up an hour ago. Dad and I just landed and are on our way to your place. Be there."

I checked my phone and sure enough, there was a missed call from two hours earlier. Marie and I had been out running a few café-bakery errands and I'd left my phone on the counter.

I texted back and turned to Marie, who was already drying the cake pans I'd just washed.

"I gotta head home for a while. Dad and Sarah are on their way."

"What's going on?" she asked.

"I have no idea. I'll be back afterwards, so leave this, and I'll finish up then."

"You're very good with a scouring brush."

"Yes, I know," I replied. "I've worked hard at it. It's one of my great assets."

———

They arrived at 8:15. Dad was through the door first, with Sarah trailing, wearing an odd expression on her face. Neither had any bags.

"I've been a damn fool and I'm sorry," Dad said as he collapsed on the couch.

I looked at Sarah. She just shrugged.

"What's going on?" I asked as I settled in the chair facing him. Sarah stood leaning on the bookcase.

Dad said nothing but handed me a clear plastic sleeve enclosing a document. I saw the University of Chicago Library label on the front.

"What is it?"

"Read it, please," was all he said in reply.

I looked again at Sarah. She just moved her hand to second the motion that I read the document.

The official archivist's notation on the label read:

"Letter from EH1 to EH2, June 1945, immediately prior to EH2's return to Chicago from the war in Europe."

I looked yet again at Sarah and then at my father.

"Read!" they said in unison.

The letter was on my great-grandfather's personalized stationery. I read.

June 12, 1945

My dear son,

You're coming back to us. Praise be. It seems a miracle that you should have escaped the deadly maw of this terrible, terrible war. The Japanese front is still open, but we'll close that soon enough.

You asked me often about the grandfather you never knew. Over the years I've employed various subterfuges to avoid responding in any detail. Well, your safe return from Europe and the prospect of working side by side, as the song goes, at long last supplies the impetus to tell you the story. I share it in the sincere hope that your <u>decision</u> to join the company is solely fuelled by your <u>desire</u> to join the company.

My father desperately wanted me to continue the family tradition and become a missionary in China. While I was born stateside, I spent almost my entire childhood in China. I loved it, but I grew restless as I grew older, and

363

far less certain of my future. The pressure he put on me was immense and it drove a great divide between us. The more he pushed me to enter the seminary, the more he pushed me away. Life in China was hard, but I credit my exile there in my youth with guiding me toward the rag trade. The richly coloured and embroidered textiles of the Far East were simply stunning. And I found China's silk operations utterly fascinating. The Hemmingwear seed was sown when I was very young.

When I turned sixteen, we were back in the U.S. for a brief turn. Matters came to a head. I was expected to enter the seminary in Boston while my parents were to return to China to continue the mission. I refused to go to the seminary. I just flatly refused. Then they said I had to come back to China with them. Again, I refused. There was a huge and emotional family conflagration. My parents, I believe out of a sense of abject helplessness in the face of my steadfast opposition, left me in Boston with my uncle, as a last resort. Mother cried when she said goodbye. My father refused even to see me. Such was the depth of my alleged betrayal.

I snuck down to the pier and watched from afar as they climbed the gangway onto the ship, my mother still crying. I was crying a little, too, though my resolve never weakened. Not once. My father appeared grim, stoic, and he disappeared into the ship without so much as a backward glance. When the horn sounded and the ship cast off, I felt a great weight lift from my shoulders. It was an even mix of sadness, regret, determination and freedom.

You know the rest. I bolted for Chicago later the same month. My uncle was not happy, but I stayed in touch with him so he knew I was safe and well, though I was occasionally neither. I loved my father, but after I escaped to Chicago and landed my first position in the rag trade, he never spoke to me again. I never laid eyes on him again. Over the years, I tried to reach out after my company was well established and I was doing well. I sent him letters, and birthday and Christmas gifts, with long rambling recitations of my success, and lamenting what still lay between us, but they were all returned unopened. My mother and I kept up a private correspondence that she kept from my father. She was proud of me, but her first allegiance, of course, was to her husband. I understood, yet the void my father left in me remains even now. Some years later, my father, weak with a fever when he boarded a ship in China to return to New York, died on the crossing. So much left unsaid. When I met the ship, I met only my mother. He had been buried at sea. Having a body on board a ship packed to the gunwales with passengers, whose constitutions were already weak from the voyage, was simply not permitted. The health and hygiene of the living outweighed all else.

I pledged that I would never repeat my father's folly.

You say you want nothing more than to work by my
side manufacturing our quality products for the masses.
I welcome you, but insist that you do it only so long as it
sustains your interest. I would have you do whatever it is
in life that fulfills you, that excites you, that makes you
feel most alive. But you must promise that if the bloom
ever falls off this rose, away you'll go in search of yourself,
in search of your calling, in search of your dream. If you
promise me this, you're welcome to start whenever you
please. You've only just returned, so take some time to
recover from the last three years of Hitler's hell, and
confirm your path.

The choice of where to be and what to do is always in
your hands. To me, this principle is paramount and
sacrosanct. It is inviolate. That freedom is what you've just
fought to preserve. That freedom is what all fathers owe
their sons and their daughters. They deserve nothing less.

Your father

I lowered the letter to my lap. My mind was awash in con-
flicting thoughts, emotions, and questions. But I just couldn't
seem to assemble them in any logical fashion, let alone enun-
ciate anything. I just breathed for a minute and looked through
the wall of my own apartment. Neither Sarah nor my father
said anything, allowing me at least to begin to process what I'd

just read. I picked up the letter and read it again, more slowly this time. The words "paramount and sacrosanct" hit me again with no less force than on the first time through.

"Where did this come from?" I said when I felt I could rejoin the moment.

"You know that EH1's papers and letters, along with those of his sons, were donated to the U of C Library . . ." Sarah began.

"Of course I know that. They call me regularly to donate any letters and papers I might have," I cut in.

"Well, Dad sends a few boxes each year, as did EH2 and EH1. There are thousands of artifacts, loads of business correspondence, even a few speeches. Plus, there are some private letters that are only available for family members to peruse, or in certain circumstances, for certain researchers, provided we give our approval."

"I know all this. But where did this letter come from?" I persisted. "You would have found this in your visits to the archives if it had been there."

"Yes, I would have. But it only just arrived," Sarah explained as Dad just stared at the floor. "For a few years now, I've been reading these old family letters to gain insight into the job of running the company. While I was in there recently, an archivist was working on annotating a new batch of letters that had just been secured from an auction of the estate of EH1's housekeeper, whose daughter has just died. You emailed me about them when you were in Paris. They are the carbons of letters EH1 sent, this one to his first-born son."

"Do we have any of EH2's correspondence?"

"We do, but his letters in the archive are only about the company, not the family. They're actually kind of boring," Sarah said. "It seems EH2 did not want family letters left to the archives."

Dad roused himself.

"Knowing my father, he was certainly not a fan of the philosophy his own father espouses in that letter. He even had the temerity to twist a phrase I now understand was coined by EH1, but intended to convey the opposite meaning. Then my father built decades of momentum behind a tradition that his father clearly rejected. It's an outrage of the first order and it consigned me to a path I felt honour-bound to pursue. As you well know."

My father was looking right at me during this. I held his eye contact throughout. It was a bit uncomfortable, but seemed the only respectful course.

"Your sister gave the letter to me a week ago and I've only now begun to recover from the shock of finding my grandfather's words so deviously twisted by my own father. The letter is so eloquent, so simple, so pure, and yet so true. It has turned my understanding of our family history on its head. If the philosophy the family patriarch presents in this letter had passed through and governed all succeeding generations, my life, our lives, may well have been quite different."

He hung his head and turned it slowly, back and forth, in what could only have been deep regret.

"He's barely slept or eaten these last few days," Sarah said as if the patient were unconscious. "And now we're here."

"I've been a fool, blinded by a tradition that should never have existed," Dad said to no one in particular.

"So what does it mean?" I asked. "What does this change?"

"What does it mean?" Dad parroted. "It means our family is built on a lie, driven by a false belief, all created by my father. In a way, it means that we now have our liberty. It means that the principle of self-determination to which your great-grandfather was obviously so committed can now be restored to its rightful place in our family. It means I will never, ever, ask you to come back to Chicago. Of course you're always welcome, but it is no longer a family edict."

He paused for a moment before continuing.

"I deeply regret the pressure I've put on you for nearly all of your life. It was well intended but, as this letter reveals, clearly built on a false foundation."

"It's okay, Dad. We're both viewing it all in a different light," I said. "Does this also mean that Sarah has as good a shot as any at taking over when you retire?" I asked.

"Ha! If what I've seen of your sister's leadership in the last three weeks is any indication, she's got a better shot than anyone else," he replied. "I've been a fool and I apologize to you both."

"Dad, it's fine. We all bought into the family lore," Sarah said. "Well, Hem didn't exactly buy into it, but we all knew what we were facing."

"So how are you feeling, Dad?" I asked, changing the subject. "And when's the big day, again?"

"I feel fine, but I'll be glad to have this blighted bit out of me. The surgery is next Thursday, hence our little trip tonight. This couldn't wait."

"I don't really know what to say," I mumbled.

"No worries. It took Dad three days before he knew what to say. Take your time."

Over the next hour, we actually had a real conversation that meandered through several different topics. I couldn't ever remember the three of us in the same room, talking so freely, so comfortably. I thought I could feel something shift inside me. It was as if decades of tension just relaxed a little. Yes, it was actually a physical feeling.

"So how go the big changes at the company?" I asked. "Have you got Hemmingwear for women under those jeans?"

"Well," said Sarah, "as it happens, I'm wearing the prototype, not the production model. Next week the new templates and line adjustments will be ready and we can start the inaugural production run."

Dad just sat back and smiled as she spoke.

"And?"

"Do you even have to ask? They feel amazing. I never want to take them off," Sarah said, performing a mini-pirouette. "These are going to fly off the shelves."

"Any word from our friend Henderson Watt?" I asked.

"Not a peep," Sarah replied. "But I think he's gone back to Europe to avoid the shrapnel should we ever decide to go public with his stunt."

"Europe can have him," our father said.

I then spent about twenty minutes recounting the tale of my travels. I decided not to describe my mad run to escape the ferocious Chihuahuas. I did have my dignity, after all. But it did trigger a question.

"Dad, can you think of any reason, perhaps something in my childhood, to explain why I would still have a completely irrational fear of small dogs?"

"Small dogs?" He looked a little troubled by my question.

"Yeah. You remember when I was a kid, whenever we'd be at the park and there was a small dog within a hundred yards of us, I would crawl up your leg until you'd lift me up onto your shoulders? You must remember. It happened pretty well every time we ventured outside the house."

"You're not telling me that you're still terrified of little mutts, after all these years?" he asked, leaning forward. "I thought you'd certainly have outgrown that by now."

"The fear is as strong as it ever was. Why?"

Dad looked around the room and started to wring his hands a bit.

"You've been scared of small dogs your entire life?" he asked. I nodded.

"Did you ever speak to your mother about this?"

"Well, not since I was a teenager. But back then, she said it was just the petless adolescent's standard fear of dogs, and that it was perfectly normal," I replied.

"Well, that was the agreed-upon line in such situations," Dad said, a tad sheepishly.

"Dad, what do you mean? I've been trying to get to the bottom of this for years, and my psychiatrist is taking bushels of my money on this very question."

Dad did not look well. He cast his eyes to the ceiling for a moment or two and then exhaled long and low.

"Dad?"

"Your mother never wanted you to know this. She felt so guilty about it. It haunted her for the rest of her days. But I'm sure if she were here and knew you were still affected by it, she'd tell you herself," Dad said.

He looked over at Sarah.

"Carry on! Inquiring minds want to know," she said, leaning in.

Dad turned back to me.

"Well, I wasn't there when this happened, but when your mother told me about what would forever be known as 'the incident,' she described it in excruciating detail. I'm not sure she ever got over it. But she made me promise never to tell you."

"But you're going to, right?" I asked.

"Well, if she knew you'd been suffering and there would be a therapeutic benefit, I think she'd forgive me," he replied. "Your first summer, when you were about seven months old, Mom had just changed your diaper one morning. You were lying on your blue blanket on the living room floor enjoying yourself, playing with your set of little coloured plastic rings. They made a rattling noise I can still hear in my memory."

"I get it, Dad," I interrupted. "I was having happy plastic ring time on my blanket. Go on."

"Right. Well, a neighbour came to the door to visit. You remember Mrs. Pollard from down the street?"

I nodded. I never liked Mrs. Pollard. She reminded me of the witch in *The Wizard of Oz*.

"Well, she had her little dog in her arms. My goodness, your mother loved that dog, at least until that morning. They went into the kitchen to make coffee or something, and to talk. You were happy as a clam gurgling away in the living room. Well, at one point, Mrs. Pollard put her dog on the floor so she could doctor her coffee or grab a cookie. The dog started sniffing around the kitchen. They paid no attention to it. Then, a moment of two later, you started screaming bloody murder from the living room. Mom rushed out to find you all the way out in the hall. That tiny little vicious dog had sunk his teeth into your right leg and dragged you across the living room and toward the front door. That mutt was absolutely possessed. There was quite a bit of blood. It took the two of them some time to pry open the pup's jaws and liberate your leg. Your mother sent Mrs. Pollard packing and called me at the office. I rushed home and we took you down to the hospital. You needed six stitches to close the four puncture wounds in your calf."

My hand shot to the spot. I pulled up my pant leg and looked at the four little symmetrical scars that I knew so well.

"You told me I'd had four small moles removed when I was baby!"

"Well, we fudged that a bit," Dad explained. "Your mother was distraught. She thought the doctor might call in Child and Family Services because she'd been negligent. It was silly, but she was very scared and racked with guilt. We agreed on the mole story and we stuck to it. In her defence, she didn't want you growing up terrified of little dogs."

"I see. So instead, I've grown up terrified of little dogs," I replied. "That worked out well."

"I'm so sorry, Hem. Your mother would be mortified if she were alive. I honestly had no idea that your fear had persisted for so long."

"It was a Chihuahua, wasn't it?"

Dad just sighed and nodded.

"They called the little critter Chi Chi Rodriguez, as I recall. Sorry, son."

"Well, no wonder the dog was psychotic. They screwed up his name," I noted. "If I know my golfing legends, the real Chi Chi Rodriguez is Puerto Rican, not Mexican."

"What happened to the little guy?" Sarah asked.

"He's still alive and lives in Puerto Rico. I think he's been inducted into the World Golf Hall of Fame, too," I said, taking modest pride in my ability to retain useless information.

"Not the golfer, the Chihuahua." Sarah sighed.

"Oh."

"He bit another small child a few months later, so they returned him to the breeder," Dad replied.

"Bye-bye, Chi Chi," Sarah said.

They left half an hour later to catch the shuttle back to Chicago. Sarah hugged me. Dad shook my hand, but still, it felt like more than a handshake. I was exhausted. It was one thing to have my life returned to me, and my family history rewritten, in a single night. But it was quite another to hear the story that so clearly explained a phobia I've endured for forty years.

I was drained when I arrived back at Marie's. I gave her the highlights of my evening. She held me for a while and then made me show her my scars. I slipped into bed beside her and turned out the light. Despite how tired I was, I just could not fall asleep. At 12:30, I padded out to the little kitchen in Marie's apartment, in our apartment, and sat down at the counter. There was a pad of paper next to the phone and a cup filled with pens beside it. I turned to the first clean, pristine sheet of paper on the pad and started to write. I didn't stop until sunlight angled into the room and I could just hear the faint sounds of the morning traffic below on Bleecker.

CHAPTER 17

ONE YEAR LATER

My apologies for what I think they call in movie parlance the "jump cut" to twelve months later. I guess it is kind of a cheap writerly trick but it seemed to make sense in this case. Change in our lives can seem incremental, modest, inconsequential, when examined continuously. You sometimes don't even notice it. But cut away for a year and then come back, and you'll get a better sense of growth, of progress, of change. The passage of time offers perspective. And in the span of a lifetime, twelve short months flash by.

Marie and I made our way to our seats in the MetLife Stadium in East Rutherford, New Jersey. It was early August, and the New York Jets were about to tangle with the Buffalo Bills in their first pre-season game. They were great seats, midfield, just twenty rows up from the turf. We were right on the aisle. The seat next to us was empty, despite the sellout crowd. I leaned against Marie, just to have contact. It was nice. She pointed down to the group clustered at the end of a red carpet that had been rolled out from the sidelines onto the field.

"There they are! Next to the guy with the clipboard and the bad green jacket."

I followed her finger and found the New York Jets official. Next to him and his clipboard I could see Hat holding hands with Diana Ross, who had donned a New York Jets jersey. She was bobbing from foot to foot.

"She seems a little nervous," Marie said.

"Well, it might have something to do with the 82,000 fans jammed into this place. You never know."

Hat and Diana Ross had been seeing each other for three months by then. She had a remarkably calming effect on him. He still carried butterscotch candies with him at all times, but more often than not he ended up eating most of them himself. Somehow, Diana had lengthened his notoriously short fuse. I don't know how she did it. She claimed not to know, either. All the good in Hat was still there, and even stronger. But the all-too-swift anger had ebbed. Some thought she was brave to take him on, but she needed Hat, too. He was good for her. Relentlessly supportive and kind, he gave her a daily boost of confidence. She had moved directly to the centre of his universe, and she thrived there.

I felt my cellphone vibrate. "James Moriarty" flashed across the screen. I leaned away from Marie and into the aisle to answer.

"Hi, James."

"Hem, I just had to call you. You were the one I wanted to tell first," James said in an excited tone I'd never heard in his voice.

"Tell me what, James? What's happened?"

"You remember that paper I wrote that you kindly read on your trip to Paris, the one about Holmes's deductive powers in 'The Blue Carbuncle'?"

"What do you mean, do I remember it? Of course I do. How could I forget? It was well written and well reasoned. Without it, the flight would have seemed even longer and the seat even harder."

"You're very kind. Well, this morning, I received a telephone call from the editor-in-chief of *The Baker Street Journal*. Did you hear that, Hem, *The Baker Street Journal*?"

"And, and?"

"They're going to publish the paper in the next quarterly edition with very few edits," he nearly shouted. "They're actually going to publish it! I am in a state of shock."

"That's just fantastic news, James. I'm very happy for you."

"But, Hem, that's not the best part, not by a long shot," he continued, almost breathless. "Twenty minutes ago my phone rang again. It was a very senior executive of the Baker Street Irregulars, the society I've been trying to join for twenty years now."

"Right, and?" I had an inkling of what was coming.

"Well, the *BSJ* editor-in-chief is putting my name forward in January at the next major gathering here in New York. It's at the Yale Club. It's lovely there, it really is. Anyway, I'm tickled to my toes. I don't know how it happened. It's totally out of the blue. But it seems I'll stand as what they call an investiture in January. I've been accepted! Oh, I must think of my official investiture name. It's all a little hard to absorb right now, but it seems I'm in, villainous name and all!"

"Yes! James, that is such wonderful news. You've wanted this for a long time. Just savour it. You've earned it. I'm very happy for you. Have you told Jackie yet?"

"She's my next call."

Jackie Kennedy had been circling James since our very first NameFame group meeting. I don't think they were dating per se, but they'd started hanging out with each other and even enrolled in swimming lessons together. It was good for them both. We spoke for a few more minutes. I'd never heard James in such an advanced state of euphoria. When I closed my phone, I was feeling good. The universe was unfolding as it should.

"What was that?" Marie asked.

"Oh, well, um, it seems our James just got some really good news, you know, just some Sherlockian stuff, and he's very happy."

Marie smiled and was about to say something more when the public address announcer drowned out her words.

"Ladies and gentlemen, would you please rise, remove your hats, and join Diana Ross . . . from the New York Police Department in the singing of our national anthem."

The announcer paused after saying her name and before noting her connection to the NYPD. I'm sure he did it on purpose. You could almost see every fan in the stadium snap to attention at the prospect of hearing the Motown legend sing, only to be laid low when they realized they'd been momentarily duped. The sighs of disappointment throughout the stands could not have been more, well, audible, had the home team just missed an easy game-winning chip-shot field goal, wide right.

For the last few years, the New York Jets had invited local fans to audition to sing the national anthem to open pre-season games. Hat had persuaded Diana to apply, but she had done the rest by nailing her audition. Marie and I stood and cheered until the opening bars of "The Star-Spangled Banner" settled over us. Diana stood there alone at the microphone on the fifty-yard line and belted it out. Hat stood a little out of the way but still directly in her line of sight. She had her eyes fixed on his from "Oh say can you see" all the way through to "the home of the brave." He kept smiling and nodding his head in support. Her voice never wavered. Not once. She knocked it out of the park, even though I'm sure there's some NFL edict forbidding the use of baseball metaphors at a football game. Throughout Diana's performance, Marie squeezed my hand tighter and tighter as it became clear that Diana was not just going to get through it, but was delivering the performance of her life. The crowd roared their approval when her last note died away all too soon.

"That was amazing. She was amazing!" Marie said, beaming. "And she had not a drop of alcohol to get ready."

"It's one of the many benefits of dating a man who doesn't drink," I replied.

A few minutes into the game, a very proud Hat escorted Diana up to fill the empty seat next to us. She looked a little wobbly, but that just made her all the more endearing in the moment. I stood to give her a hug as she went by me to sit on the other side of Marie.

"Hey, down in front!" someone yelled from a few rows behind us.

I stiffened and reached out to put my hand on Hat's arm, fearing that his namesake's principle of nonviolence was about to suffer another setback. But Hat had come a long way in a short time.

"Excuse me, my friend, but this is Diana Ross. She just sang our beloved national anthem for you. That is why she is late. So, if you please, just let her take her seat and perhaps show her your appreciation for that very fine performance."

I turned around to catch the fan's reaction. He looked over at the back of Diana Ross's head and nodded.

"Hey, yeah, it's the anthem singer, right here in our section," the fan shouted. "Great job, Diana. You got a nice set of pipes on you."

I grabbed Hat as he started to head toward the fan.

"It's okay, Hat," I said, so only he could hear me. "By pipes, he means her voice, just her voice. It's an expression. He was being nice. Really."

Hat relaxed and waved to the fan. He then made eye contact with Diana, who was now seated next to Marie.

"See you after the game."

She waved to him and he bounded down the stairs to field level to take over his audio dish duties from the intern who had handled the first few plays.

I was proud of Hat. He'd come a long way. Four months earlier, he'd applied for and landed an engineering job at the cogeneration plant at the Brooklyn Navy Yard. It wasn't quite as good a position as the one his temper had cost him over at the station at 14th and FDR, but he was managing, and by all accounts – well, really by his own account – was keeping his employers happy. I believed him. In general, he was an open book, utterly free of pretense. It didn't surprise me that he'd also kept his job slinging the audio dish at the Jets games. That's what any hardcore Jets fan would do. The home team lost the game, badly. But it was just the first pre-season game. According to Hat, it was not yet time to lift the protective shield covering the panic button. He had a good feeling about the coming season.

When the game ended, Let Them Eat Cake! was still open and a little understaffed with Marie taking the afternoon off for Diana's professional singing debut. So she was eager to get back. We said goodbye to Hat and Diana and walked with the crowd back to the car a few blocks away. We held hands.

Two months after I'd been granted my empty drawer in Marie's bathroom vanity, I moved in completely. Two months after that, I sublet my apartment and put most of my stuff in storage. After my ill-fated Jennifer experience, I didn't think I wanted to live with someone else ever again. Wrong.

We entered through the back door directly into the kitchen. Peter Parker stood at the stainless steel counter mixing up batter for the cakes that would be baked very early the following morning.

"How was Diana?" he asked with eyebrows elevated.

"She rocked the house," Marie replied. "She killed it."

"I knew she would. That's friggin' awesome."

"Everything cool here?" Marie asked.

"Busy, busy," Peter said. "It's been a good night."

Peter Parker had given up his high-rise window-washing gig a few months earlier. Marie said she just liked the cut of his culinary jib and took a chance on him. Peter had become good friends with Clark Kent. Without Clark's encouragement, Peter may not have given up his pendulous and perilous window-washing gig. He didn't love cleaning windows but he was good at it. He loved cooking, though he lacked confidence in the kitchen. But a few weeks after the big move, Peter was thrilled. Because he felt a debt to Clark, he started putting a bit of money away each paycheque to help fund Clark's laser surgery so he could finally dispense with his heavy glasses. I made a quiet donation that helped advance matters, on the understanding that Peter would keep our little secret.

Peter worked hard and took advice and direction very well. Marie quite enjoyed taking this rough-cut, tattooed kid and turning his natural but raw culinary talent into a mainstay of her kitchen. She called it her Pygmalion moment.

I walked through into the café-bakery proper and nearly collided with Bob on his way out. Bob. Yes, that Bob. You remember him, the one who had let me go a year or so earlier. Bumping into him was fate, serendipity, or perhaps just plain old sweet justice.

"Bob, what a surprise. Good to see you," I lied.

"Hem? What are you doing here?"

"I actually work here. I handle the marketing and advertising."

"Oh, Hem. I'm sorry. It's not exactly a big-brand account. Could you not land another agency job?" Bob asked.

"Bob, it's fine. I didn't *want* to hook up with another agency. I actually want to be here. I'm having a blast." I changed the subject. "How are things at M-C? I confess I haven't given the old place a second thought since I was escorted out the door."

That felt good.

"Well, you see, I'm not exactly with M-C any more."

"Not exactly?"

"Well, not at all, really. I left a month ago," he said. "I just got tired of the pressures of leadership, you know? So I'm giving freelancing a go. Getting my hand back in the work itself."

"They toasted you, too, didn't they?"

"Well, I wouldn't exactly describe it in that way," he said. "Um, they just decided that we should part ways, and after thinking it through, I agreed."

I said nothing.

"Okay, yes, I was toasted."

"I'm sorry, Bob. I kind of know what that feels like. But it's really worked out well for me. You may really take to it. I have."

"Oh, I'm sure I'll be fine," he replied. "Look, if you ever need some help on taglines or creative for this place, call me?"

"Sure, Bob. I'll keep you in mind. Good to see you."

———

The next morning, I sank into my usual chair in front of Dr. Madelaine Scott.

"Hem, you look well."

"Thanks, Doctor. I feel great. I feel . . . settled. Yeah, 'settled' is a good word for it, I think."

"Have you had many or any encounters with Ernest Hemingway lately, or has he gone off to cover some war or drink wine in Paris?"

"He seems well and truly gone from my head, not that he was ever really there."

"Okay then, more to the point, how are you and your father getting along?"

"In the last few months, he's actually become my father in more than the biological sense. He's about forty years behind schedule, but I'm not complaining."

"Explain what you mean," she directed. "Elaborate, if you could, please."

"Well, we've discussed it before. I barely saw my father growing up. My mother was, for the most part, a single parent. My dad was parenting a big company, and it was often a problem child, whereas I, of course, was always, and for evermore, good as gold. Dad's hands were full with company business pretty well around the clock. But all that has changed, quite dramatically. It was a combination of my sister's intelligence, toughness, and obvious business savvy, and a long-lost letter written in 1945 by my great-grandfather that has transformed my father. Oh, and I'm sure his brush with death was also a factor."

"Ah, the cancer. You told me."

"Right. A prostatectomy is seriously invasive surgery. The recovery was slow, painful, and completely beyond his authority. He's not used to surrendering control over anything, but he had no choice. All he could do was sit back and watch as his daughter completely overhauled Hemmingwear in the process of saving it. It gave him plenty of time to think about his life, the company, family traditions, his children, and his future. As he healed, I think he changed. I think he grew. I think he was able to take a lifetime of family indoctrination and turn it back on itself."

"Is that just your view, or does he see it that way?"

"He hasn't used those words exactly, but the change in his demeanour and in his long-held views on a range of issues is quite startling. I'm getting to know my own father all over again, and I'm learning new things with each encounter."

"When is he due back in the office?"

"As of a conversation Sarah and I had with him last week, he's not coming back. And that's the clearest evidence that his world, that our world, has been altered."

"That's a lot to take in. How are you feeling about it all?"

"It's knocked me back on my heels. But I like it," I replied. "And get this. My father and I are going fishing next week. We're going fishing, in a boat. Neither of us has spent much time with fishing rods. But he wants to try. And strangely enough, so do I."

That afternoon I was seated at my favourite table toward the back of Let Them Eat Cake! in a sun-filled corner. I had a commanding view of the entire seating area. It was a beautiful day. I was working on the marketing plan for the café-bakery. It wasn't very elaborate. We didn't have much of a budget to commit, but even on a shoestring, a little creativity can take you a long way. I had already set up a Facebook page and Twitter stream and was doing my best to sustain a flow of interesting content. For foodies, I took photos of Marie as she created her extraordinary cakes. I then posted the shots in order, including batter mixing, pan pouring, baking, decorating, and finally a close-up of the finished masterpiece. It was quite the process but seemed to fill some deep need among online cake fans. Whether on Facebook or Twitter, or on the Let Them Eat Cake! blog that I started, the audience grew quickly, and thankfully so did the traffic coming through the front doors. After all, an online audience is nice, but to survive, we needed butts in chairs and hands reaching for wallets. It all seemed to be working.

As I noodled through the idea of building a YouTube channel on which we could post baking tutorials and a whole range of other videos, my cellphone chirped.

"Hey, Hem," said Sarah. "Sorry I missed your call earlier. I'm swamped here. What's up?"

"Hey, Sarah. I'm going to send you a photo I took while I was out for a walk this morning. Hang on a sec."

I pulled my phone away from ear and emailed the photo to Sarah.

"Okay, I'm back. Before you open it, let me ask you something. Have you seen any recent changes in sales, I mean in the last few days?"

"Funny you should ask. I'm looking at the daily tracking data right now and there's been this unexplained sales jump over the last two days."

"No kidding! Well, it might not be totally unexplained," I suggested. "Has the spike been in men's or women's or both?"

"It's been a solid uptick for both, but the women's numbers are up slightly more. What's going on? What have you got?"

"Has the photo arrived yet?" I asked, enjoying drawing it out a bit.

"Yeah, it just came in. Hang on."

I could hear her fingering her keyboard to open up the photo on her computer screen. Three, two, one . . .

"Holy shit! Holy shit!" she hollered down the line. "Is that a billboard? In Manhattan?"

"That's exactly what it is. Very cool, eh?"

"Pardon my ignorance, but who the hell are they, and how did you make this happen?"

"I'm disappointed you don't recognize them. You're looking at a cover shot of the brand-new smash album from the hip-hop superstar duo J Flash and Cara Tune. I just checked and it debuted at the top of the Billboard Album charts earlier this week. You've heard their stuff if you've listened to the radio any time in the last three years. They're a brother-and-sister act. Kind of like Donny and Marie, but not really."

I opened the same photo on my iPad in front of me. It was a shot of the two famous rappers, taken from behind them, but with their heads swivelled, looking back into the camera with what I can only describe as benevolent snarls of their faces. True to the strangely and regrettably persistent trend, their jeans were riding low to the mid-curve of their respective buttocks. And there, for the world to see, were their wide and red underwear waistbands emblazoned with the word "Hemmingwear" in a very funky, very hip, kind of jagged white font.

"I've heard of them. They're huge! How did this happen? What did we pay for this? I knew nothing about it! It must have cost a fortune! Where are the billboards?"

"Whoa! Calm yourself, Sarah. Not that we'd ever admit this publicly, but this is pure serendipity, not savvy marketing. I stumbled across the billboard this morning. I saw it, stared at it, and walked right into a parking meter while I dragged my jaw along behind me. One of my NameFamer friends, Jesse Owens, is actually related to them. I was pretty sure she had something to do with it. I called her after I'd recovered enough to construct complete sentences. Under some heavy questioning, she admitted that she'd given them our product and suggested they wear them for the cover shot if they liked them. They both loved the underwear and the rest is marketing history. In addition to the album cover, it's been released in print ads and billboards across the continent, and it all hits Europe next week. But there was a quid pro quo."

"Okay, here we go," Sarah said with a sigh. "What does she want?"

"Well, it's pretty onerous. But as of this morning, I'm now chairing the fundraising committee to help collect the dough we need to transform her dental clinic into a full community health centre in a part of town that could sure use one."

"And? What else?"

"That's it."

"That's it? She arranges for us to get millions and millions of dollars of free advertising and all you have to do is chair a committee."

"Well, it seems like that right now. But her second cousins were always going to wear underwear. Most people do, you know. They just happened to be wearing the family brand. A bit of a nudge from her, and then plenty of blind luck."

"Well, that blind luck is clearly boosting sales, and judging from the retailers seeing the biggest kick, it's right in the younger demo we've had trouble reaching," Sarah replied. "At this rate, we may need to add a second shift on the women's line to keep up."

"The world should have your problems."

"You should talk to Dad, and bring it up at the next foundation meeting. I'd suggest we match whatever funds you're able to raise in the community and maybe make a donation on top of that. Seems the least we can do."

"That, and buy lots of albums."

About three months earlier, Dad and Sarah had asked me to chair the Hemmingwear Foundation and manage the company's charitable and philanthropic investments. Doling out money to worthy causes was a role I thought I could handle.

We talked for a few more minutes, but Sarah was up to her ears and needed to get off the phone and back to work.

"Hem, send me addresses for your Jesse Owens friend and her hip-hop second cousins, too. A skid of underwear is heading their way, on the house."

Soon after Sarah had taken over, Dad appointed Carlos Mendez as the new chief operating officer. I was thrilled for him. His longevity with the company, not to mention his personality, attitude, and understanding of virtually every aspect of production at Hemmingwear made him the logical, if overdue, choice. Sarah reported that he was really stepping up and doing a great job in the face of considerable change in the manufacturing process. I have to say that it was wonderful to hear all of this and, for the first time in my life, not feel any formal obligation to do anything other than wish them well. The curse had lifted.

As I finished my call with Sarah, Marie was sitting on a stool at the counter on what was obviously a catering call. I could only hear Marie's side of the conversation but that's all I needed to hear.

"That sounds fantastic. Thanks so much.

"Yes, January is fine. That gives us heaps of time to plan. How many people are you expecting?

"And how many different kinds of cakes would you like?

"Well, for 175, I'd suggest at least three different kinds, and ideally four or five. You want enough variety for it to be memorable.

"And the venue is . . .

"Hmmmm. The Yale Club. Near Grand Central, right, on Vanderbilt? Very fancy. But do they know about this? Usually, the Yale Club kitchen staff would want to handle this themselves.

"I see. Interesting. Well, if they're all right with it, far be it for me to question it. We'll be there. Can I ask how you heard about us? Just curious.

"Well, thanks so much again. This will be a fun one for us. What's your email and I'll forward some seasonal cake recommendations, a price list, and the contract."

Marie made a few notes as she deftly cradled the phone between her shoulder and ear, something I'd never been able to master.

"Excellent. Thanks again."

I tried not to look at her and kept my eyes on my unfinished marketing plan.

"Well, that was a little strange. Wonderful, but strange," she said.

I lifted my eyes to hers but said nothing.

"An anonymous sponsor for the annual gala of something called" – she checked her notes – "the Baker Street Irregulars at the Yale Club has insisted that we cater desserts for 175 Sherlock Holmes disciples in January."

"Hmmm, that is strange," I said.

"I wonder if James had anything to do with it?" Marie speculated. "Okay, are you ready?"

"Yep, I guess I am."

Marie left Peter in charge and we headed out the door. We walked a well-worn path to the Manhattan SPCA, as we had at least weekly for the last several months. Learning about my encounter with Chi Chi Rodriguez as an infant made it easier for me to follow Professor Moriarty's prescription. He proposed that I start having contact with small dogs, thereby confronting a fear it seemed I'd had for my entire life. It had been going well, and I could feel a difference in my panic level the more time I spent with whatever small dogs they had in the shelter.

We waved to Shelagh, the shelter manager, who ruled the roost with a perfect blend of authority and compassion. She pointed to a big cage in the corner. We walked over. Marie was all doe-eyed at the sight of the smallest brown poodle puppies I had ever seen. She cooed at them as you might to a newborn baby. The pups were tiny and could not have been more than a week or so old. They were very cute. Shelagh explained that they been left in a box on the shelter porch a few days ago.

I pointed to the one off by himself in the corner of the box. Shelagh nodded, and Marie reached in to fish out the brown bundle of fluff. My heart rate elevated, as it always did when we reached this part of the therapy. I sat cross-legged on the floor and cupped my hands in my lap. Marie lowered the pup into my hands. I relaxed as soon as I was holding the little guy. He made a few soft mewling sounds and looked up at me. It didn't even faze me when he chomped down on my thumb. I could barely feel it.

"I think you could take him home this time next week, if you're up for it. I'll get the paperwork together," Shelagh said. "Have you picked out a name yet?"

"Watson," replied Marie. "A good friend of ours suggested it."

In case it wasn't already obvious, I like a nice neat package in the end, with all the loose ends tied up, nothing outstanding. By my count, there's really only one matter of real significance left. The novel. My novel. Well, even though my writer's block lifted after my father and I had our little breakthrough, I never finished the novel I'd been working on for so many years. Chapter 12 and everything thereafter was left unwritten. Why? The short answer is that it just really wasn't very good. I no longer felt connected to the story or to the characters. And I didn't like what I'd written when I went back to the beginning and read it out loud to myself. No, it just wasn't very good. That story had passed me by, or I had moved beyond it. So I wrote a different book instead. It's the one you're holding in your hands. As you can see, I finally decided to go with a pseudonym. I know it's a rather bland and boring name, but believe me, a bland and boring name is just what I was going for. Nothing wrong with that.

We were back at the café-bakery around 5:30. Marie had to head straight into the kitchen to join Peter to get ready for the dinner crowd. I went back to work on the marketing plan until a FedEx guy arrived with a large package. I read the manifest and saw that it was a big stainless steel mixing bowl Marie had ordered online.

"Here you go," Mr. FedEx said as he handed me the electronic slate to sign.

I scribbled a signature and handed it back. He looked at it and frowned.

"I can't read that. Can you give me your name and I'll just note it below? The company needs to be able to identify the person who signed for the item."

I reached for the slate again.

"Sure, but I think it's easier if I just print it below, myself."

I finished and handed it back to him. Again, he looked to make sure it was legible. Again, he frowned.

"Trust me, that's my real name," I assured him with a smile. "No relation."

ACKNOWLEDGEMENTS

Despite appearances, when writing novels, writers are very seldom completely on their own. I, more than many novelists, lean on others. I'm grateful for the guidance and friendship of my editor, Douglas Gibson, who took a chance on me at the very beginning of what still seems to me a miraculous journey. Beverley Slopen has also been there from the start and I thank her for her wise counsel. At McClelland & Stewart, Frances Bedford, Bhavna Chauhan, and the eagle-eyed Wendy Thomas, have been stalwart supporters. Of course, it's wonderful to have Ellen Seligman, Kristin Cochrane, and the rest of the M&S team in my corner. I also thank Scott Monty for his Sherlockian expertise, and Noah Morris for directing me to Hemingway's Toronto apartment.

The seed of this novel was sown at a chance encounter many years ago with a talented lawyer whose name was, and still is, Brian Mulroney — no, not that Brian Mulroney. This particular lawyer had never run for political office and I suspect never will. He may have been the first person I've met afflicted with what I call in this novel, "NameFame." I figure I owe him a debt of gratitude.

Some fine writers read this manuscript and offered encouraging words. In particular, my thanks to two fellow Leacock Medal winners, Will Ferguson, and Trevor Cole. I'm honoured to be anywhere near their company.

Finally, to Nancy, Calder, and Ben, I am only a writer through your patience, encouragement, and love. I hope, over time, I can return at least a share of what you've given me.

TF

November 2013

Also available from
McClelland & Stewart . . .

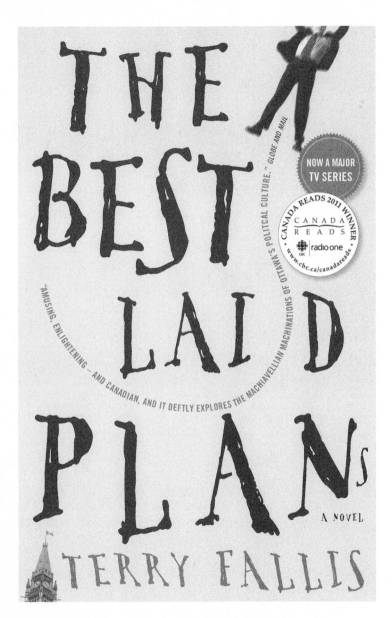

THE BEST LAID PLANs

"AMUSING, ENLIGHTENING — AND CANADIAN, AND IT DEFTLY EXPLORES THE MACHIAVELLIAN MACHINATIONS OF OTTAWA'S POLITCAL CULTURE." GLOBE AND MAIL

NOW A MAJOR
TV SERIES

CANADA READS 2011 WINNER

CANADA
READS
radio one
www.cbc.ca/canadareads

A NOVEL

TERRY FALLIS

ISBN: 978-0-7710-4758-9
ALSO AVAILABLE AS AN EBOOK

THE HIGH ROAD

AUTHOR OF THE BEST LAID PLANS, WINNER OF THE STEPHEN LEACOCK AWARD FOR HUMOUR

ROAD

A NOVEL

TERRY FALLIS

ISBN: 978-0-7710-4787-9
ALSO AVAILABLE AS AN EBOOK

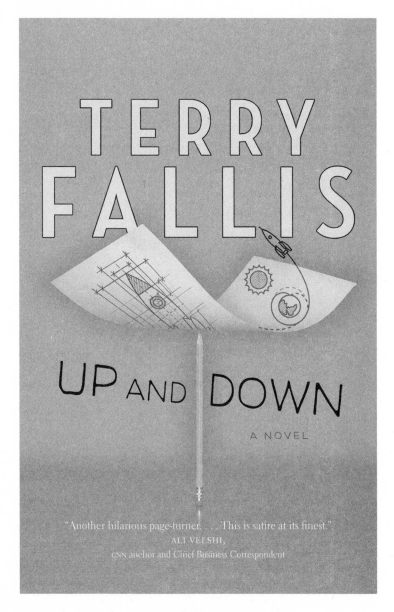

TERRY FALLIS

UP AND DOWN

A NOVEL

"Another hilarious page-turner. . . . This is satire at its finest."
ALI VELSHI,
CNN anchor and Chief Business Correspondent

ISBN: 978-0-7710-4791-6
ALSO AVAILABLE AS AN EBOOK